# GIVE ME LIBERTYCON

## BAEN BOOKS edited by T.K.F. WEISSKOPF

*Tomorrow Sucks* with Greg Cox
*Tomorrow Bites* with Greg Cox
*Cosmic Tales: Adventures in Sol System*
*Cosmic Tales II: Adventures in Far Futures*
*Transhuman* with Mark L. Van Name
*Give Me LibertyCon* with Christopher Woods

## BOOKS by CHRISTOPHER WOODS

### SOULGUARD SERIES
*Soulguard*
*Soullord*
*Bloodlord*
*Rash'Tor'Ri*
*Freedom's Prophet*

### THE FALLEN WORLD SERIES
*This Fallen World*
*Farmer's Creed*

### FOUR HORSEMEN UNIVERSE
*Legend*
*Daskada, the Legend*

### ANTHOLOGIES EDITED BY CHRISTOPHER WOODS
*From the Ashes* (with Chris Kennedy)
*Give Me LibertyCon* (with Toni Weisskopf)

To purchase Baen titles in e-book form,
please go to www.baen.com.

# GIVE ME LIBERTYCON

## EDITED BY
## CHRISTOPHER WOODS
## AND
## T.K.F. WEISSKOPF

A Baen Books Original

Baen Publishing Enterprises
P.O. Box 1403, Riverdale, NY 10471
www.baen.com

ISBN: 978-1-9821-2464-9

Cover art by Melissa Gay

First printing, June 2020

Distributed by Simon & Schuster
1230 Avenue of the Americas, New York, NY 10020

Library of Congress Cataloging-in-Publication Data

Names: Woods, Christopher, 1970– editor. | Weisskopf, T. K. F., editor.
Title: Give me LibertyCon / edited by Christopher Woods and Toni Weisskopf.

Description: Riverdale, NY : Baen ; New York, NY : Distributed by Simon & Schuster, [2020] | "A Baen Books original"—Title page verso.
Identifiers: LCCN 2020014049 | ISBN 9781982124649 (trade paperback)
Subjects: LCSH: Science fiction, American. | Fantasy fiction, American. | Fans (Persons)—Fiction. | American fiction—21st century.
Classification: LCC PS648.S3 G58 2020 | DDC 813/.608—dc23
LC record available at https://lccn.loc.gov/2020014049

Pages by Joy Freeman (www.pagesbyjoy.com)
Printed in the United States of America
10 9 8 7 6 5 4 3 2 1

# CONTENTS

# FOREWORD

## Christopher Woods

If you haven't heard of a literary convention, as a fan, you are missing out on something that can change the way you look at reading books. I spent many years unaware that they even existed. Sure, I had heard of conventions of Star Trek fans, but it never occurred to me to actually go to one. In 2016 I attended the first convention I had ever been to. My wife and I sat and watched people stream by in costumes and saw authors sitting at tables, signing books. I had recently published my first novel and wanted to see what these conventions were like. We enjoyed it so much that we immediately began setting up a schedule where we could attend some of these conventions to sell my novels. We attended several and had a wonderful time. Then, in 2017, we attended a small convention in Chattanooga called LibertyCon.

Most conventions work with you to make sure you have your table and the things you need to sell your books, but LibertyCon treated us like family from the moment we picked up our badges. We spent a great weekend in Chattanooga and decided we really needed to do that again. We returned in 2018 and, having attended quite a few different conventions by then, found that Liberty had once again blown us away. Our trip back home was filled with questions about how to show these people our appreciation. There were thoughts of free books or maybe some sort of gift we could give them. We researched a few items and just couldn't find that perfect thing that would show them how we felt.

Later, I was speaking to our friend Jonny Minion about giving something special to the LibertyCon staff and he suggested drawing names for a Tuckerization. A Tuckerization, for those who do not know, is to have your name immortalized in print. The name would be featured in a story where you can die a glorious death. Or you may become a hero and live happily ever after. My mouth dropped open and I asked Jonny, "What if we used them all?"

From there, I started asking about the likelihood that I could get enough authors to do an anthology where we would Tuckerize the complete staff of LibertyCon. We also decided to give all of the proceeds to Liberty to add to their charitable donations. Then I asked the head of LibertyCon if this would be something she would approve of. Approval was given and we were suitably excited about the prospect.

Then tragedy struck our Liberty family when the creator of the convention passed. Richard T. "Uncle Timmy" Bolgeo created LibertyCon decades ago and his family still runs it today. The project was suddenly a little more than a thank-you to the staff and so it also became an homage to the man who had started it all.

A little later, David Weber, who is an author that has attended Liberty for many years, got wind of the anthology I wanted to build. His interest began a much larger venture than I previously intended and I began speaking to Toni Weisskopf of Baen Books. Baen has been a part of Liberty since the early years and Toni wanted them to be a part of the anthology as well. I was really excited about her wanting to join in the endeavor and quickly agreed. When she presented the list of authors she thought would be interested, I spent several days in a daze. These were the authors I had read for years. The same authors whose books taught me anything I know about the writing craft.

What we have for you is a group of bestselling authors telling original stories, some from very well-known series. Each of these stories includes the names of a number of the LibertyCon staff members. All of the proceeds from this anthology will be split and half will go to LibertyCon to use for their charitable donations. The other will go to a scholarship set up by Baen Books in the name of Tim Bolgeo, administered by the Tennessee Valley Interstellar Workshop. Come join us for a fun trip across galaxies, far and wide. There are Treecat Legends, Fairy Tales, Corporate Agents, Zombies, and an Inter-dimensional Insurance Agent to name a few. Join us as we pay homage to the guy who brought us the coolest group of people I have ever had the honor of joining. Whatever the drink, let's raise a glass to Uncle Timmy, his daughter, Brandy, who continues the legacy, and the wonderful staff of LibertyCon.

Thank you,
Christopher Woods

# "UNCLE TIMMY"

To kick things off, we start with a celebratory song, a "filk" song written by author, editor, and musician Gray Rinehart. He was toastmaster at LibertyCon 29, and a hard act to follow, let me tell you. To quote the Fancyclopedia III (see fancyclopedia.org): "Both a noun and a verb, filk refers to fan-written, fan-sung songs about science fiction or fannish themes and to the events, or filksings, where such music, known as filksongs, are performed by filkers.... [Filk] began as fannish parodies to the tunes of mundane songs...." As is this one, made to memorialize Richard T. "Uncle Timmy" Bolgeo, who founded LibertyCon. When he retired from running the convention, he handed over the reins to She Who Must Be Obeyed, Jr., aka Brandy Spraker, his daughter. *All* he did after that was negotiate with the hotel, advise, lend a hand wherever needed, greet newcomers, and beat David Weber, Gary Shelton, Mark Paulk, Ann Robards, and others at Spades.... He will be remembered.

—TW

"Uncle Timmy" was, of course, a 2019 tribute to the man who started it all. I had written two LibertyCon-specific songs in the previous three years, and I thought of doing this one very soon after I heard that he had died. The prospect of LibertyCon without Uncle Timmy was daunting, even though I hadn't interacted much with him personally because he was usually holding court with a crowd of people around him (or off playing Spades). At my first LibertyCon, for instance, I was the Master of Ceremonies but still he and I didn't have an opportunity to chat beyond friendly introductions.

Writing a traditional filk song—adapting a recognizable tune with new words—can begin with the original song (e.g., "Dust in the Wind" seemed perfectly suited to be turned into "Leaf on the Wind") or with a phrase or line that seems to fit an existing tune. I imagine someone could have done a song using Timmy's real name: perhaps a rousing drinking song in which the chorus would end with a resounding, "Timmy Bol-ge-OH!" But on a walk around a local lake one day I realized that the four syllables of "Uncle Timmy" scanned almost exactly the same as "Sweet Melissa." With that, I was off and digging into Uncle Timmy lore—since my time with him had been so limited—in order to make the song as fitting a tribute as I could. I wasn't sure how the song would be received by his family and the audience, but in the end I was pleased that Brandy, Linda, and Timmy's friends seemed to appreciate it.

—Gray Rinehart

# "Uncle Timmy"

## Lyrics by Gray Rinehart

*To the tune of "Melissa" by Gregg Allman*

Goodbye's one of the hardest words to say
*The Revenge of* more than just *Hump Day*
With love and faith and loyalty
We're here to praise his legacy
So won't you drink a toast with me, to Uncle Timmy

Shuffle well, cut the deck, deal out another game
  (another game)
A round of "Killer Cutthroat Spades"
With Southern Fandom royalty
And all the fannish family
So come on, drink a toast with me, to Uncle Timmy

> *I say the end is not the end*
> *I'm sure he's found some good old friends*
> *They're playing cards and telling tales*
> *Left behind all earthly cares*
> *We'll tarry here before we follow there (follow there)*

Players, gather 'round, let's have another hand
Deal in that Secret Master Fan
We know he's flying high and free
And his spirit lives in Liberty
So won't you drink a toast with me, to Uncle Timmy
So won't you drink a toast with me, to Uncle Timmy

&

## Gray Rinehart

**Gray Rinehart** writes science fiction and fantasy stories, nonfiction, songs...and other things. He is the only person to have commanded an Air Force satellite tracking station, written speeches for Presidential appointees, and had music on *The Dr. Demento Show*. He is currently a contributing editor (the "Slushmaster General") for Baen Books. Gray is the author of the lunar colonization novel *Walking on the Sea of Clouds*, and his short fiction has appeared in *Analog Science Fiction & Fact*, *Asimov's Science Fiction*, Orson Scott Card's *Intergalactic Medicine Show*, and multiple anthologies. As a singer/songwriter, he has two albums of mostly science-fiction-and-fantasy-inspired music. During his unusual USAF career, Gray fought rocket propellant fires, refurbished space launch facilities, "flew" Milstar satellites, drove trucks, encrypted nuclear command and control orders, commanded the largest remote tracking station in the Air Force Satellite Control Network, and did other interesting things. His alter ego is the Gray Man, one of several famed ghosts of South Carolina's Grand Strand, and his website is graymanwrites.com.

# THE BASTION

This entire volume was Chris Woods's idea, and a darn good one it was, too. I was upset I didn't think of it myself, and very glad David Weber roped me in—Chris has been a dream to work with. Of course, Uncle Timmy would have been pleased about that—he was almost always one step ahead of me finding new authors that I would enjoy, and he delighted in uniting readers with authors and artists. I confess that while I was Facebook acquaintances with Chris and his lovely wife, Wendy, I hadn't ever been exposed to his work. I'm very pleased that has been rectified thanks to this project, and pleased in turn to present this excellent story in his post-apocalypse Fallen World universe to you.

—TW

# The Bastion

*A Short Story of The Fallen World*

## Christopher Woods

### Chapter 1

I slipped into the alley and ducked under a small overhang to block the rain that had been falling steadily.

"Good for the garden," I muttered.

*Less worry about Lucy's garden and more on the task at hand,* William Childers chided me from inside my head. *Four ruffians ahead.*

"I see 'em," I muttered to the OSF Operator.

Obsidian Special Forces had been Childers's cover when he was loaded into an Agent. The Agent program was long gone but there were remnants still wandering the city. Remnants like me. Nanite-enhanced men and women, some with psychopathic tendencies. Others who would have been called sociopaths. Then there was me, the schizophrenic. I got the whole enchilada. Now Childers was all mine, along with all the others inside my noggin.

I paused, remembering the lab where I finally managed to come out of the squirrel cage in my head. All of the imprints that had dropped in my head were fighting for control and I, most certainly, would have died without the Agent who kept me alive for the first six months. Then the doctors who showed up kept me alive for the rest of that time. Their way was much more unpleasant as they tried to figure out how to get the database back out of my head intact.

They'd finally given up and were just experimenting to see what reactions they could get with different stimuli. I remembered them all. The shock treatments were the worst. They were trying to bring personalities to the surface. They succeeded, but the one who came to the front was a monster. His name was Luca Stiglioni and it took a long time to get him back under control. The fight to regain control brought me, Mathew Kade, to the surface and I had been the one in charge for the last seventeen years.

In those seventeen years, I had seen the city brought out of that savagery into a better age. It was still a savage place, but it was multitudes better than the city I awoke to. My attention returned to the four guys standing near the door I had been searching for.

"They picked a bad time to park themselves there."

*They may work for the one we came for,* Childers said.

"Could be." I shrugged and stepped out into the rain. Broken glass crunched underfoot as I strode down the narrow alley. Perhaps twenty feet separated the old brick apartment buildings, and the stench of something decomposing was barely discernable. "They'll regret it if they do."

"What do we have here?" the one I had pegged as the leader asked. He stepped forward. "What you doing in my street?"

"I need to go in the door you're blocking. Move aside and this doesn't have to get ugly."

"Boss don't want nobody to come in there."

"You work for the guy inside the building?"

"I do. What's it to ya?"

"Do you know what he does?" I asked.

"Do you?" he returned.

"I'm pretty sure I have it figured out. He won't be doing it anymore after tonight."

"You came for the Boss?" He looked past me. "And you came alone? You not very smart."

I smiled. "Ugly it is, I guess."

"Damn right it's—gak!"

"What was that last bit?" I asked.

He gurgled and toppled over with a knife protruding from his throat.

"What the—" the next closest of the group of four started, before collapsing with another of my throwing knives sticking out of his eye.

The third had seen how quickly his partners had dropped, and tried to turn and head for the door they had been guarding. I threw a final blade to sink into his neck just below the skull. Number four was already in close, swinging an old hardwood baseball bat.

He swung for my head and I caught the bat with my left hand. His eyes bulged in surprise just before I slapped him across the face with the augmented strength of a Corporate Agent. There was an audible crack as his head spun to face the opposite direction.

*That may be the first time I have seen that particular strike,* Childers said.

"Seems like I remember it from somewhere," I said. "But I was a woman when I did it. Which is a little bit weird, because I was still Mathew Kade."

*If you could remember everything, you would have some very interesting stories to tell,* he said.

"I wish I could," I answered as I retrieved my knives.

The one that had severed the spine was a little more difficult to pull out as it was wedged between bones. I pulled a little harder and quickly stepped back to avoid the splash of blood when the skin ripped. It was a short burst of blood, but I didn't want it on my coat.

Before Childers could comment I said, "It's my last one. It already has a bullet hole in it."

I opened the door the four thugs had been guarding. The place used to be an apartment building. This area of the city had fewer scrapers and more of these sort of structures. Eight-to-ten-story brick and stone buildings with numerous small housing units inside.

Somewhere in my cluttered mind I thought of low-income housing. Maybe this had been used for that originally. Now it was something else altogether. The man I had been looking for over the last few days would be inside. I doubted if Lorianne Waldon would still be alive, but I would find her or her body before closing this particular case.

The scuffle outside had made very little noise so I slipped inside and moved away from the door.

My left eye twitched as I took in what I could see. The large atrium of the building was all that was left and it was filled with things that would make a medieval torturer blush. Across the room was a single man with his back to me. I could see a girl strapped to a table in front of him. They seemed to be the only ones in the place. He was holding a serrated tool in his right hand and lowering it toward her.

I was across the room in a flash and I seized the man by the back of the apron-like garment he wore. I threw him across the room to slam into the exterior concrete wall.

He hit hard and dropped limply to the floor.

I looked at the girl, who was gagged and strapped with her limbs pulled painfully tight in a spread-eagle position on the table. My straight razor severed the bonds on her left side and I circled the table to cut the other side.

"You're going to be okay now," I told her.

Then I heard him groan from the spot he had landed on the floor.

I could see her shake when he made a noise.

"He won't be hurting you anymore," I said. "What's your name?"

"L...Lori," she stammered.

"You're Waldon?"

She nodded but her eyes flooded with terror. "C...can't go back there..."

My eyes narrowed. "We'll talk about that in a moment."

I turned to the man, slowly staggering to his feet, rumored to be a former surgeon and a cannibal. "Doctor Gharik, I presume?"

"Who the hell are you?" he asked as he pulled a large knife from the sheath at his side. "I'm going to eat your heart."

He charged at me and I met him halfway, slapping the blade from his hand; he screamed as his wrist broke. He dropped to the floor and grabbed the broken wrist with his other hand.

His scream was high pitched and cut off abruptly as my left hand settled on his neck to lift him from the floor.

"Just...doing...job."

His gasp was barely audible but I could make it out.

"Who pays for something like that?" I growled.

"Father," he gasped.

I dropped him. "Her father?"

"Yes," he groaned, holding the broken wrist.

"Tell me about it," I said.

"You'll let me live?"

"No. I'll let you die quick instead of by inches," I said. "Either way you die today."

He looked at all of the torture devices and shivered. "She ran away and her father paid me to make her suffer for it before she died. He gave me a list of things I was to do and she was to know exactly why it was all happening."

I dragged the doctor to one of his own devices.

He struggled. "You said you would make it quick."

"I lied."

I hit him once to stop his struggling, then strapped him into the device and flipped the switch.

The doctor was screaming as I led the girl from the chamber of horrors she had spent the last day and a half in.

She cringed as we passed the four dead thugs outside of the door and I wished I could bring them back so I could kill them again.

Sometimes I wished the bombs had just taken this city when they took the world. It had once been called Philadelphia, before the Corporate Wars. Before the bombs. All that was left was the skeleton of a huge city and the evil that seems to thrive in it. Warlords ruling city blocks, ruling because they had the most guns or they were strongest. Most ruled with fear but, occasionally, there was someone better. I thought of Teresa Manora and her Society of the Sword. They still give me hope that there is something worth saving in this fallen world.

## Chapter 2

I looked down at the sleeping Warlord. His face was cruel even as he slept. The two naked girls beside the man made my eye twitch. They were several years younger than the girl I had just rescued from the doctor and she had been fourteen.

Lowering the wooden bat I had brought back with me, I tapped lightly on the corner of the bedpost and the man stirred. One of the girls' eyes popped open and she cringed away from me.

I motioned toward the door with my head. She slipped out of the bed and circled around to pull her sister from the bed on the other side. I lowered the bat onto the chest of Gregori Waldon. His eyes opened wide and he tried to sit up. I held pressure on the bat so he couldn't budge.

"What is this?" His eyes landed on me as I smiled down at him. "Kade?"

But it wasn't Mathew Kade standing over the struggling Warlord.

"Hello, Gregori, Mathew is not in today. My name is Stephen Gaunt. There are things we must talk about."

Stephen Gaunt was a Corporate Assassin, one of the most feared of the personalities that reside in my head. He has unmatched fighting skills and a love for his job that is quite terrifying.

"I have fifty men within shouting distance. Give me a reason to—"

"You *had* fifty men. Now you *may* have two children within shouting distance. After what you did to them, I strongly doubt they will be inclined to help you."

"You'll never make it out of this zone alive," he snarled.

"I will certainly get farther than you will with that shattered knee."

His eyes widened. "What?"

The bat lifted from his chest and slammed down as Stephen Gaunt chuckled while the rest of us watched from inside my head.

"I thought I might find you here," a voice said as I rounded the corner.

A very large black man leaned against the wall with a sword resting point down in front of him. He was over six feet tall and three feet wide at the shoulders. The sword was a huge two-hander that was close to four feet long.

"Hey, Poe." I grinned. "How the hell are you?"

"Was doin' just fine until Teresa sent me a message to come get you." He pushed off of the wall and joined me, walking east. "Ran into a girl who looked pretty rough in the Tees. She was being escorted by a couple of Mardins. Once she told me what happened, I figured I better head this way. Is this gonna be one of those zones that'll have a Chapterhouse for the Society in the near future?"

The Mardins were the people who lived in the Tees, the tunnels below the city. They kept the water flowing and the sewer working for a large part of the city.

"Maybe," I said with a short chuckle. "She might think about adding another one. The Warlord seems to have lost his daughter. He's a little broken up about it."

"I'm not sure I want to know."

"Probably not." I grinned. "Wouldn't hurt to send word to Teresa, though. Place needs new leadership."

"No warning this time?"

Several Warlords had been removed over the last year. I typically give them a warning first. The Society of the Sword opened Chapterhouses in each of the zones and they now keep the peace.

"He didn't deserve a warning."

"That bad, huh?" Poe asked.

"Yeah," I said. "Two more girls are on their way to Teresa. I dropped down in the Tees and snagged another Mardin."

"They're gonna get tired of being delivery boys."

"They don't mind, not after that dustup with Derris's savages."
I looked toward the big man. "So what does my lovely lady have
in mind for me next?"

"There was a request from a Zone over east of here. They sent
a message with the Mardins about some cult of savages that were
massing to attack them. You know how she is when something
like this goes down."

"Yeah," I said. "She's not fond of savage cults."

"And this place is supposed to be something pretty special,"
he said. "Not sure what it is but I figure we'll find out when we
get there. Two Squires are already on their way, Rowland and
Green. Several Knights have been notified but they're too far out
to do any good. And then there's us."

"Three Squires are an army in their own right," I said. "And
conflatulations, by the way, on your promotion to Squire."

"I'm pretty sure that's not the right word."

"Sure it is."

"I can't believe I'm doin' this again. But when Teresa says go,
you go. I can't just say no, she might cut me up into little pieces."

"It's not so bad." I patted his huge arm and turned to the
east. "Just think about all the savage cultists."

The big man sighed and strode beside me toward the beleaguered
Zone.

"What's the name of the Zone?" I asked.

"They called it the Bastion."

"Intriguing," Gaunt said aloud.

"Indeed," I answered.

"You know that was disturbing when you only had those
conversations in your head. It's even worse when you do it out
loud. You gonna be doin' that the whole time?"

"Maybe."

He sighed again.

"You gonna be doin' *that* the whole time?"

"Probably," he said.

I chuckled and glanced toward the big man. I had enjoyed his
company on our last venture until that sniper had shot him. He'd
pushed me aside and out of the line of fire. I had been distracted
for a moment and the big man had taken two bullets for me.
Luckily, we had been close enough to the Society headquarters

that he got medical attention in time. He didn't have the healing capability of an Agent and I owed him.

*We all do,* Childers said. *That first would have been a head shot. Even an Agent doesn't walk away from that.*

"True enough," I muttered.

Some debts are more important than others in this fallen world.

## Chapter 3

"That group is eyeballin' us," Poe said.

I pushed my coat back to bring the Sig Sauer in the shoulder holster into view. The two punks in front of the others lost the swagger they had carried when they looked into the cold, dead eyes of a different person from the one they had initially picked out as their mark.

"Why would they even think of attacking someone as big as a house?" I asked as the Bravos turned to retreat into an alley.

"I wonder that all the time. Worse, they take one look at you and crap their pants." Poe sounded puzzled. "Maybe I need to start carrying something to get their attention."

"You could always walk around with a necklace of skulls or something."

"Then everyone runs, not just the Bravos, and I can't stop at the vendors along the streets. I think that might be a little too much."

"Could be." I shrugged. "So, do you know anything about this Bastion?"

"Not much," he answered. "I think Martin discovered them some time back. She's one of the Knights that Teresa would normally have sent over here since she likes to stay in this part of the city. She's doing some work down south, though."

"Lori?" I asked.

"Yeah, that's her."

"I met her once while I was stuck at the Chapterhouse in Stiner," I said.

"Stuck?" he asked. "Weren't you recovering from that thing with the Genofreak?"

"Yep. Teresa wouldn't let me go home."

"You had three broken ribs, a broken leg, and you reopened the bullet wounds from that other case." He shook his head. "You can't blame her for that."

"I guess," I said. "At least I didn't get wounded on the job for Wilderman."

"Fenris said you got shot," he said.

"It was just a scratch," I said. "Can't even call that a wound."

"Probably because you spent the majority of the time watching her cutting that bunch into squishy little pieces."

"What?"

"That's what she said, man." He shrugged. "Sounds about right, though. I remember that time up in Yamato's Zone."

"I distinctly remember killing several of Corso's thugs, along with Corso and his second."

"Yeah, four. I was left with nine. I think I'll take *her* word for it. She is a Knight, after all. They take oaths and shit."

"Have you ever just watched that woman fight?"

"Can't say that I have," he answered.

"It's glorious, it's magnificent, it's—"

"You did just stand there and watch, didn't you?"

"Well, for a while. I'd already killed a bunch of them," I said.

"She said you left another Warlord hanging from a wall with a piece of steel through his shoulder."

"He let close to sixty thugs attack us in his street in broad daylight. He was lucky I didn't just throw him out the window of his scraper."

"Sounds like he might have deserved a warning."

I pulled my coat around and stuck my finger through the hole that had been left in it by the bullet that grazed my side. "Do you see this? This is the last one I have until I get to see the Farmers again."

"You pinned him to a wall with rebar because they put a hole in your coat?"

"Of course not. He was in on the attack. A lot of those guys were his men. I left him pinned to a wall with rebar for sending his men out to kidnap an innocent girl and kill me in the process."

His left eyebrow was raised when I looked toward him.

"I broke his arm for the hole in my coat."

He shook his head.

"What?"

"That damn coat," he said. "One day it's gonna trip you up when you try one of those crazy Agent moves. I just hope I'm there to see it."

"You're just mad because they don't make them in your size."

"Whatever."

"I could see if Marigold will make you one," I said.

"I don't want one of those useless coats."

"She probably wouldn't charge more than double price for the extra material."

"Look how it flops around," he said. "One day you're gonna trip over it and, just like that, you're all dead and shit."

"I can ask when I go order my next batch."

"I don't need one of those damn coats. If I wore somethin' that stupid, I'd be dead in a week."

I shrugged as we continued walking down the street. The smell of humanity permeated the air, and the vendor stalls along both sides of the street reminded me of something that hovered just out of reach of my fractured memories.

*Faire,* one of the voices from deep inside my head said.

I nodded.

He sighed. "Do you think she could do one in black?"

Wonders never cease in this fallen world.

## Chapter 4

The sound of fighting ahead barely reached my ears.

"What is it?" Poe asked. He couldn't hear it, but he could see my pause as I listened.

"How much farther to the Bastion?"

"Next zone."

"Shit," I said. "There's fighting."

He scowled. "Go. I'll be there as quick as I can."

I nodded and launched myself forward. The speed an Agent can attain is much more than Poe would have been able to make. The zone we were in was pretty barren, but you could tell a lot by the upkeep of the streets. Many had clean streets and vendor stalls for the Caravans as they passed through. This one was shabby and dirty. Still, there was no smell of feces in the street as there were in some of them. The Mardins kept the sewers running and I have a great respect for their dedication.

The noise of fighting was closer and my straight razor slipped into my left hand while the right pulled the 9mm from the shoulder holster. It used to have a suppressor but those have a limited lifespan and I had used it enough to make it more of a hindrance than a help.

Rounding the corner, I found the street filled with a lot of armed thugs assaulting a wall of stacked cars. The wall of cars looked to have been there for years and it crossed the entire street between two buildings that had been reinforced with steel plate.

"Bastion," I muttered.

The defenses looked pretty formidable and it would take a lot of people to get through it.

But there were probably fifty or sixty people in the street brandishing weapons. I could see only about ten stationed along the top of the wall. Not enough defenders to stop this mob if they went at it hard.

The fighting was centered, not on the wall of cars, but on a small group of armored forms who had been caught outside of the walls. They were surrounded and the mob would soon overwhelm them.

"That's your cue, Stephen," I muttered and receded into the back of my mind as Stephen Gaunt, the Corporate Assassin, took the lead. He holstered the Sig Sauer and looked at the razor in the right hand.

"Oh, Mathew, I think you've done it again," I said in his voice. "You bring me to the loveliest places. But that is a lot of throats to cut."

He slipped the razor back into its pouch and drew one of the sturdier knives.

"This should do nicely."

I would say that I charged into the group but Stephen doesn't charge. He flowed through the crowd like water and people begin to fall. I severed a femoral artery and flowed past to snake my arm around a neck to pull the chin up and the blade flashed. Then I was gone again. One after another fell before they even realized I was there.

Then there was a roar from behind me as Poe rounded the corner with his four-foot-long blade swinging in a deadly arc. People tumbling backward, several in multiple pieces. The sword swung back in an arc that was just as deadly as the first.

Poe is a very big man and he is all muscle. When he hits something it moves, and he was cutting a swath through the crowd. Another form dropped from one of the buildings to our left. She'd been descending along a fire escape as we hit the crowd.

Peggey Rowland, one of the Society Squires, landed lightly,

drawing the rapier from her side. The sword danced around, and those near her died.

I ducked as a club arced through the spot where my head had been, and I grasped the front of the wielder's shirt. I threw him into several of his cohorts with enough force to send four sprawling on the ground. Then the blade flashed several times and the squirming pile was still.

"Don't worry," Gaunt whispered in an ear as I reached around with the blade. "It will be over soon."

Once again I was moving through the crowded street and screams of rage and hate became screams of fear. There's something terrifying in witnessing a man giggling as he dances through a throng of people leaving only the dying or already dead in his wake.

But Stephen Gaunt is a terrifying sort of guy. Typically, they don't stay terrified long.

I ended up looking into the eyes of Peggey Rowland as both of us reached the same person in our path through the much less crowded street. The majority of what was left were fleeing.

"Hello, luv," Gaunt said.

Peggey looked a bit confused and I stepped forward from the backseat in my head.

"Sorry," I said and smacked the man who was screaming something that I assumed was supposed to be a battle cry. His head tilted at an odd angle and he fell sideways.

"Hi, Peggey." I grinned. "How's it going?'

She was shaking her head. "You should be covered in blood. How did you not get any more than that on your coat?"

"More than what?" I asked and looked down to the right hem she was pointing at. "Damnit!"

There was a red splotch about the size of a closed fist.

Peggey had blood dripping from her armor and I glanced over to our left to see Poe. He was covered with it.

"Last damn coat," I muttered.

I heard the group of defenders that had been cut off from the Bastion approaching and turned around to see the leader take off her helm.

My mouth dropped open, "Brandy?"

There were memories in my head of this woman. There was someone deep inside the pile of people in my head who was doing the mental equivalent of jumping up and down and waving arms. The barrage of memories was fast but they were detailed. I remembered this woman as a baby, a child, a youth, and an adult. The personality that was hailing me was her father.

"Do I know you?" Brandy Bolgeo asked with narrowed eyes.

I scratched my head. "I know you . . . kind of."

"I thank you for your timely appearance," she said. "But *I* don't know *you*. Either way, we need to get inside."

She waved to the men atop the wall and one of them yelled into the interior. "Jonny! Open the gate!"

One of the metal panels that guarded the building on our right pushed outward. A fellow in coveralls with a pair of short swords in scabbards on his back looked out of the door.

"You still with us, Boss?"

"Thanks to these folks," Brandy answered.

*I can't believe she's still alive*, Tim Bolgeo said in my head. He had been pretty far down in the depths of my mind for a long time.

Brandy kept looking at me, trying to place who I was.

"I guess I need to tell you a little story," I said. "It's about your father."

She scowled. "My father is dead. The very same people he spent all those years working for sent him on one of those damned missions and dropped the bombs right on top of him."

I could see the depth of her rage at Obsidian, who more than deserved it. That rage was a common thing to see in this fallen world.


## Chapter 5

We were less than ten feet inside the door when she turned to me. "Now, tell me about my father."

It was an order, not a request. There was an iron in her that filled me with a father's pride. Bolgeo was just under the surface now and I could feel his emotions.

"Okay," I said. "You knew what he did?"

"He was an Agent."

"That makes things easier to explain. Are you familiar with how Agents did their thing? The Imprints?"

"Dad told me how it worked," she said with a shrug. "I know, it was supposed to be classified."

"Nothing's classified now." I pointed a thumb back toward the door we had come in. "Not much point in that anymore."

"That's true."

"If you know of the Imprints, this is easier still. When an Agent goes out needing a specialty personality, they're uploaded to the database. Then they're downloaded back into the body when it returns. There was a copy of your father in the database."

"What's that have to do with this?"

"Everything." I tapped my temple with a forefinger. "When the bombs dropped I was in the Imprinter. Something shorted out and it downloaded the whole database into my noggin."

"And Dad is in there?"

"That's how I recognized you. Some of the Imprints are more accessible than others and your father was pretty deep until I saw you. Now he's right under the surface. I'm going to step back and give you two a couple of minutes."

"This is just a little too much to take. I believe I have heard enough." She turned to walk away.

My head dropped for a moment and someone else was looking out of my eyes when my head raised.

"Brandy Marie Louise Elizabeth Bolgeo," Tim admonished.

Brandy paused in midstride.

She turned back to face me as Tim looked around. "Swimbo? Is she here?"

I could see in his mind the acronym and chuckled inside. SWMBO (She Who Must Be Obeyed).

When Tim said that word, though, Brandy's eyes widened and her mouth dropped open. Up until that very moment, she had not believed.

"D...Dad?" she stammered.

He stepped forward and wrapped his arms around her armored form. "I'm sorry I left you, girl. Wish I had stayed home when they called."

I felt tears running down my cheeks.

"I'm sorry, Mom didn't make it, Dad."

I could feel the well of sorrow as Tim thought of his wife, Linda.

He sighed. "I guess you're Swimbo, now, not Swimbo Jr."

"No one's called me that in twenty years, Dad."

"Well, they should."

"They're coming back for a run at the walls!" one of the guys on the wall yelled.

She grimaced. "Seems like our reunion is going to be short lived. Those bastards mean to kill us all."

"Then what say we kill them first?" Tim Bolgeo said and turned to the two Squires. "Let's join the ranks on the walls."

"One of your Squires is on the front wall," Brandy said to me. "Should we join him?"

Tim glanced around. "They hitting more than one wall?"

"They hit all four," she said. "There are hundreds of them."

"Which one gets hit the hardest?"

"Front."

"How many fighters here?"

"A hundred and twenty people, about half are decent fighters. The others will fight but they're not really fighters."

He scanned the area and made a decision. "One Squire on each of those walls and I'll take the front wall."

He glanced up at the front wall and recognized the Squire. "Joe! Take the right wall!"

"Got it!" he yelled back.

Tim jumped from where he stood to the top of the wall of cars. They had welded a parapet for the defenders to stand on.

He heard Brandy start giving orders. "Jonny! On the right! Hillbilly, join him."

She was motioning to an armored form in the group who had come in with us.

"Got it, Swimbo."

She stared at him and Tim grinned from the wall down at them.

"I got it, Boss." He held his hands up.

He was chuckling as he took off toward the right wall.

Tim turned around to look over the wall of cars at the horde of people coming down the street toward the Bastion.

*That's a lot of damn people*, I said from inside my head.

"It certainly is," Tim answered.

"What?" one of the defenders asked.

"Just talkin' to myselves."

He looked confused but just shook his head and turned back toward the oncoming horde.

"We have contact!" someone yelled from the right wall.

"They're in the back, too!" Poe yelled as he climbed the wall.

The whole defended area was about five hundred feet by five hundred feet and there was very little inside the walls.

"What the hell are we defending?" Tim asked.

"The Bastion is underground, Dad. It's the Bastion of Literacy. We've been collecting every book we can find in the city and preserving them. We're going to need that knowledge in the future."

Tim grinned. "That's my girl."

It explained a great deal about the setup of the defense walls. It was like how the Mardins under the city had walled off the area under Derris's zone to keep the savages in check. This was the same in reverse.

"You affiliated with the Mardins?"

"We know some of them but we aren't part of their society. We have our own setup."

"We can discuss it in a little while," he said. "Let's welcome our guests."

"Ready the pots!" she yelled.

There were about eight big cauldrons steaming along the parapet. They sat on racks with fires burning under them.

"Oil?" Tim asked.

"Boiling water and flour," she answered. "Sticks to them like glue."

The horde reached the wall and started climbing the cars. She waited for a few moments before yelling. "Pots!"

The cauldrons were pushed over and the white liquid was falling into the mass of bodies. Battle cries changed to screams as the boiling concoction clung to their bodies. They began falling backward onto the others where the paste-like substance would also get on them.

There was a vicious smile on her face. "Read that in a book, you assholes!

"Ready weapons!" Brandy ordered.

Tim chuckled and drew the Sig from the shoulder holster. He waited until the flour and water had gotten on as many as it looked like it was going to. Then he raised the pistol.

Rifles and pistols were raised by the others on the wall.

"Target the ones who aren't already injured!"

I felt the great swell of pride that coursed through Tim as he watched his daughter.

"Open fire!"

Tim pulled the trigger and the man he was aiming at toppled with a bullet in his brain. He calmly shifted aim and another head blossomed. This one was a female.

Sometimes a person needs to be an equal opportunity killer in this fallen world.

## Chapter 6

"Here's where it gets nasty," Brandy said as several of her people placed the rifles on the ground at their feet. "We're out of ammo."

She drew the gladius from the sheath at her side. "Now we get bloody."

Tim shot the last round from the Sig and I muttered, "Going to have to get more mags from the Farmers."

The mag released and he started feeding cartridges into it at a rapid rate.

"Damnit, man," Brandy said as she saw the speed the shells were filling the mag.

"Lots of practice," he said as the last one slid into place.

The savages hadn't reached the edge of the wall yet and he leaned over and began firing down into them. Sixteen shots and twelve dead.

*A little sloppy*, Childers said.

"Give me a break," Tim said. "It's been twenty years."

"What?" Brandy asked, looking over toward him.

"Nothing," he said.

As the first head popped over the wall, Brandy took it off with the sword.

*Good execution*, Childers said.

*Quite good*, Gaunt agreed.

Those two agreeing hardly ever happened and it was worthy of notice.

*Use the strength*, I said.

Tim nodded and stepped close to the edge to punch the first savage who topped the wall in our area. The head jerked back at an odd angle.

The savages kept coming and they died as they topped the wall.

Then the wave slacked and we heard a thump as something hit the building between the front wall and the right wall.

"Shit! They crashed a truck into Building A!" someone yelled. "They're inside!"

Tim leapt from the wall into the courtyard just as they poured from the building.

"More of your area, Mathew," he said and let me step forward inside my mind.

My blade was in my hand and I charged toward the screaming savages. I glanced left to see a huge form slam into them as well. Two others dropped from the walls to take up positions on the right and left of Wilson Poe. Peggey's rapier flashed and Joe Green's twin swords blurred. There was a wall of steel when the savages reached them. It channeled them in my direction.

*If you don't mind, Mathew?*

I grinned.

"What have we here?" Stephen Gaunt said as I let him out. "You've brought me playthings."

I glided forward under Stephen's control and slipped under the swinging club of the first attacker. The blade flashed and the man dropped the club to clutch his abdomen where his intestines were trying to spill from the gash I had left. He toppled forward but I was already ten feet away severing an Achilles' tendon. Then a femoral artery was sliced.

I slipped up behind a woman and pulled her chin up with my left hand as the right flashed across her throat.

"This won't hurt...much," I whispered in her ear. Then I was gone again into the crowd.

"Blow the charges!" I heard Brandy order.

I saw someone in the very center of the courtyard throw a lever but nothing happened.

"Something's wrong, ma'am!"

"Son of a..."

I saw two more forms drop from the right wall. One was the guy she had called Hillbilly and the other she had called Jonny.

They slipped into the building.

"What are they...?" I heard from the wall above me.

CRUMPT...CRUMPT.

Debris exploded from the opening the savages were pouring from and I heard screams. Then the whole building shuddered.

"Shit!" Poe yelled. "Back up!"

The Squires all ran away from the building as it collapsed

straight down on top of over a hundred savages and a couple of damned brave men. The debris cloud exploded outward and I went into it after the surviving attackers. All that the rest of them heard were screams and maybe laughter.

Stephen enjoys his job a bit more than is comfortable for most folks. Most think Stephen is crazy, but there's a need for his brand of crazy in this fallen world.

## Chapter 7

As the debris began to settle, we could see what the corner of the Bastion that had formerly been Building A looked like. It was a pile of rubble that would be almost impossible to navigate.

Brandy moved up beside me. "Those magnificent crazy bastards. They set the charges off manually."

I looked toward her and saw the pain on her face.

"Looks like they're coming back for the walls!"

She grimaced and I could feel the fury growing inside Tim Bolgeo.

*Can't go out there while we're needed on the wall*, he said inside my head.

"I know," I muttered and jumped the distance to land on the wall again. "We leave the wall and they get in, everyone dies."

I pulled the Sig and refilled the mag as I watched them come down the street. As soon as the mag slammed back into the pistol I racked it and emptied it into the front of the approaching savages. Fourteen bodies were trampled by the others.

I managed to refill the mag again and unload it with a similar result, then the horde started back up the wall.

I moved back a step and over to the center of the wall where I could go whichever direction I needed.

"You want this?" I asked Tim.

*You're doing better than I was*, he answered. *Been gone for too long.*

I nodded and shot forward as one of the savages topped the wall between two of the defenders. My foot slammed into his chest with a crunch and the body flew backward over his allies' heads. He landed twenty feet away from the wall on top of a screaming woman.

One of the defenders staggered back as a blade sank into his neck where the armor met the helm. I jumped twenty feet to land where he had been, then hit the woman who had just topped the wall with an open hand that sent her sailing backward.

"Karen! Medic!" Brandy yelled and several people scrambled from the center of the defended area. They ran up the stairs to pull the wounded figure down toward the ground.

She stepped into the spot beside me. "I have this position."

I nodded and stepped back to where I could watch for any that got through. One got particularly close to Brandy and one of the twelve blades I wore sank into his right eye.

Almost every one of the defenders had taken damage as the sun began to drop behind the buildings to our west, but the horde had not broken through. Then they fell back.

Everyone stood atop the wall breathing heavily. Swords hung from exhausted hands and the bodies were piled halfway up the wall on the outside.

I watched the savages retreat into the growing darkness with a grim smile as Tim stepped forward again.

"They've sworn for years they would storm our walls," Brandy said. "They would have, without you and the Society."

"They almost had us until those two blew that building."

"Hillbilly always swore he'd go out blowing himself up," she said. "I didn't think he would actually do it. His name was Scott Tackett but we always called him Hillbilly because he came from West Virginia."

She shook her head, "And damn if Jonny Minion didn't do the same. It took two to blow the charges that would take the building down. There wasn't any hesitation in either of them."

"Brave men," Tim said.

"Ma'am," the medic yelled from the center. "We lost Ken."

"Damn," she muttered and turned to the tired men on the walls. "I have to go check on things."

"Ma'am." The closest of the men nodded.

"They're regrouping," Tim said. "Would be a good time to see to the wounded. I'll watch the wall."

"They won't be back 'til morning," Brandy said. "Phobes don't fight at night."

"Phobes?"

"They hate books, they're bibliophobes."

Tim grunted.

"We'll get some rest and see to the wounded," she said. "Then we get ready to do it again tomorrow."

"I don't think there will be any fighting tomorrow," Tim said as he looked out into the darkness. "They've made a fatal error."

"What?" she looked at him in confusion. "What error?"

"I don't have to be on this wall any longer," he said.

My head dropped a fraction and her eyes widened as she saw the transformation. My features became those of someone else. It was the same face but every feature had shifted. As my head raised my mouth curled up in a wide smile.

"Dad?"

"Not at the moment, luv," I said in Gaunt's breathy voice. "Stephen Gaunt at your service. Your father has requested my assistance. He is good at what he does, as is Mathew, and William. But I am the best at what I do. And, oh, the things I am going to do."

She swallowed.

I removed the long coat and held it out to her, "Please be a dear and hold this for me. Mathew would be so upset if I wore it where I am going. Phobes, you say? I wonder if they are afraid of the dark. If they are not, already, they will be. Perhaps it is time for a lesson."

I leapt over the parapet rail and landed on the pile of bodies. Another jump took me out past the pile where I faded into the night.

Stopping, I heard voices from the wall. I recognized Poe's voice. "Did he just give you the coat?"

"Yes. He said Mathew would be upset if he wore it where he was going."

"Looks like someone is going to have a bad night, ma'am. Did he say his name?"

"Stephen Gaunt," she answered.

"Did someone say Stephen Gaunt?" Joe Green asked.

"Yep" Poe said.

"If it was any other day, I would say those poor bastards. But, today? Serves them right."

"He's only one man."

"Not really," Poe said. "I agree with Joe. I'd pity the idiots out there if they hadn't just spent the day trying their best to kill us. As it is, screw 'em."

I grinned and slipped out into the night toward the Phobes as they set up their camps.

There are more dangerous things than savage, book-burning cultists in this fallen world.

## Chapter 8

I sat, patiently, on the edge of the campsite watching the sleeping Phobe. His eyes opened and he sat up.

"Hello, sleepyhead," Gaunt said. "We've been waiting for you."

The man looked to his right and left with growing horror. There had been thirty-two people arrayed around the fire. Now there were thirty-one obvious corpses. Obvious because their heads had been severed and placed atop their prone bodies. All of them were facing him.

He screamed and leapt to his feet to run but I was next to him faster than any human should possibly be.

"No, no, we have things to discuss."

I grabbed the man by his neck and dragged him from the camp. He whimpered as he found himself being placed in the single open position where fifteen living, but unmoving people sat.

I put stiffened fingers into a spot so quickly he didn't even see the hand move and placed him in the open spot in my neat rows of four.

"Now, the lesson begins," Stephen said.

He turned and walked to a spot where all sixteen of them could see him. "Throughout history people have destroyed cultures and left ruin. Some of them even burned all records of the defeated but there is an inherent folly in doing so. You wished to destroy the books that these folks have spent so many years collecting. They wish to preserve what knowledge they can and you want to destroy it. The folly of such a goal is quite obvious if you only look at it. If you destroy all knowledge of the past, you are doomed to repeat it. Herein is the lesson."

He pointed to them. "I chose to keep one of you for each fifty. If I had removed all of you, who would tell the following generations of your folly? As it is, this job falls to you. In about a half of an hour the first of you I brought to this place will regain the use of his—pardon me—her limbs. After the rest of you join her, you will go back to your people and tell them of the horrible fate that awaits them if they ever return. Because if they do, I will also return. And if so, I will not be as forgiving as I have been this night."

I stood up and walked toward the Bastion. Leaving sixteen horrified Phobes behind.

Karen Boyd looked up as I entered the warehouse-sized library in the facility that had been created as an underground bunker before the war. She was the medic from the battle who had spent the last few days patching up the wounded. I could feel the wonder that filled Tim as I gazed at the many shelves of books. I couldn't help but feel some of that wonder as well. Just the monumental task of gathering them was not lost on me. I'd dug and scavenged all through this city.

"Mister Kade," she said. "We can't thank you enough for what you did. If there's anything we can do, please let us know."

*Oh, my,* Stephen said in my head as he saw a stack of books.

"Might I trouble you for a few of those?" he asked. "I know someone who would dearly love to read them."

*Softie,* I said.

"I'm sure we can spare a few."

I nodded and continued toward the person I had come to the library to meet. I stepped back and let Tim take the lead.

"You're leaving again," she said.

"I would love nothing more than to stay here," he said. He tapped the side of his head. "Mathew has started something we've all been needing. He's walking a path of redemption. All of us did some pretty awful things for people who didn't deserve it. He wonders what drives him so hard sometimes. He did things he's not proud of but he isn't the only one in here. That drive comes from the sins of a thousand souls. Or however many of us there are in here. We have a responsibility to the Society and a bunch of Warlords who want to bring civilization back to this broken city. I know Tim Bolgeo died twenty years ago in Los Angeles, but I'm still here. I will always be here. If you don't mind, I would like to stop by and visit from time to time."

There were tears in her eyes as she wrapped her arms around him. "You're welcome here anytime, Dad."

She gave me an extra squeeze. "And all the rest of you."

She stepped back. "There's a big dinner tonight and I expect you to be there. You can't go until everyone gets to thank you."

I nodded.

"I'm going to go get things underway," she said and made her way out of the library.

I picked up the first book Karen had laid on the table and sat down. "It is Tuesday."

*If you don't mind?*

"Of course," I said. He was the last one I would expect to ask. Perhaps the time with us had even changed *him*.

Stephen opened the book. "One fish, two fish, red fish, blue fish...."

There was a sort of movement in the cage inside my mind as Luca happily listened to the words.

I watched as Brandy raised her glass in the air. The room fell into silence.

"Before we take part in this wonderful dinner Connie and Charmalee have prepared for us I would like to raise a glass. To fallen comrades," she said.

"Fallen comrades," I answered along with the others, feeling the pride Tim felt in his daughter. Joe sat on my left and Poe on the right. Peggey was down about halfway on the other side of the huge table where she had been talking to several of the people she had met on her previous encounter with the Bastion.

"Ken Roy," she said.

A tall man down at the far end of the huge table stood. "I met Ken as we fought together to escape a Warlord named the General fourteen years ago. We found our way here after meeting several of the Explorers. He never regretted joining the Bastion and he died protecting her."

"Ken Roy," Brandy nodded.

"To Jonny Minion," she said and another stood.

"Jonny came to us several years ago. We never knew his last name, he just took the name of Minion. He was driving a big truck that surprised us all. There weren't many vehicles still being used in the city. He had a trailer full of canned vegetables that we all enjoyed and stayed after he met us. He was a kind soul and selfless all the way until the end. He loved this place, he loved the people, and he loved arguing with Hillbilly."

"Jonny Minion!"

"Hillbilly...Scott Tackett," she said. "He showed up one day, shot and near death. After he recovered, he started working with Gabe in the forge. Used to be a diesel mechanic before the Fall, which explained why he and Jonny always argued. No truck driver is ever going to get along with a diesel mechanic."

There were chuckles around the room.

"The two of them were arguing on top of the wall," Joe added. "Counting how many of the Phobes they had killed."

I remembered an old movie with an elf and a dwarf and smiled.

The names and stories continued and I listened to each one as the defenders talked about their friends who had fallen.

"Tomorrow, we will have to go out and clean up the bodies and burn them," Brandy said. "But tonight, we celebrate a victory that wouldn't have happened without the aid of our new friends. So eat, drink, and be merry! For tomorrow we all may... work our asses off!"

I watched the people of the Bastion as they cheered and I realized once again that there were things worth saving in this fallen world.

❧

## Christopher Woods

**Christopher Woods**, teller of tales, writer of fiction, and professional liar, is the author of nine novels and a multitude of short stories. He has been writing for six years and with novels in the Soulguard series, The Fallen World series, and the Four Horsemen Universe, he feels he has found his calling. As a carpenter of thirty years, he spends his time building, whether it be homes or worlds. If you wish to see his work, at least the written work, you can find it here: www.theprofessionalliar.com.

# THE FINAL MISSION OF SPECIALIST ASTROGA

Mike Massa was introduced to me at LibertyCon by Chris Kennedy while we sat in the bar. It seems that a lot of the conversations held with the authors I know happened in a bar or a party. You'd think authors might be a bunch of drunks, and you'd be right about a few of them. Mostly we just gather in the bars because they stay open later than the restaurants. I didn't get to talk to Mike very much more than a greeting but he had just coauthored a new book with John Ringo in the Black Tide series. We figured he would be a good fit for this anthology and I'm happy he joined us.

—CW

# The Final Mission of Specialist Astroga

## A Black Tide Rising Story

### Mike Massa

The infected human crossed the infrared beam of the motion detector. Instead of arresting the motion of a descending garage door as it was originally intended to, the detector instead ignited one of the eighty Tesla coils that surrounded the periphery of Watts Bar Dam. The eye-searing bright violet streamers of electricity were muted in the dawn's early light, but the unmistakable snarl that accompanied the discharge, sounding like God's own bug zapper, caught the attention of the watchstander. Located in a cement bunker several hundred yards away, she placed one finger on the book open in front of her, holding her place, and then glanced at the live video feed for confirmation.

*One crispy critter, present and correct.*

Then she tallied the location on the kill board, already well covered in hash marks, before returning her attention to her current read, U.S. Army Field Manual Number 3-21.8, The Infantry Rifle Platoon and Squad. It never hurt to brush up on her professional military education.

*Here sits U.S. Army Specialist Cathe Astroga, Combat Administrator, enjoying a RipIt and killing zombies while maintaining the proper E-4 position of attention; feet up and television on. Hooah.*

Specialist Astroga, or Astro to her friends, was putting exactly the right amount of effort into her job, no more and no less. She'd long aspired to become a member of that august echelon, whose ranks were generally considered too senior for really unpleasant menial work and yet too junior for anything really important. Specialists colluded, Mafia-style, to help each other balance this "sweet spot" of responsibility for as long as they could.

Astro was enjoying the ride. It wasn't bad at all.

Mind you, things weren't perfect. For one thing, the "televisions," plural, were only displaying the security feeds that covered the Tesla coil–protected perimeter, the dam itself and other critical bits of the Watts Bar defense. Monotony, thy name is "Security Feed." Worse, the delicious can of citrus RipIt, though dewy with condensation, was among the very last in the post-Fall world and there wasn't any renewed supply in sight. At least there were no emergencies highlighted on any of the various security monitors that lined her desk and, best of all, the routine chore of decreasing the local population of zombies was proceeding without requiring any effort, apart from a log entry.

As the sole surviving E-4 of the U.S. Army, she was the de facto chairwoman of the Global E-4 Mafia. Sooner or later, though, she knew more E-4s would be promoted, and her power and influence would spread inexorably.

Mwahahaha!

In the meantime, she let the upper-management types worry about the big picture. Except for a looming shortage of RipIts, all was right with the world. Astro took another meditative sip and sighed. The Army's version of an energy drink blended powerful stimulants like taurine, inositol, caffeine and L-glutamine, whatever the hell that was, and paired them quite nicely with high-fructose corn syrup and food coloring. Sucking down just one can produced a pleasant buzz and general alertness.

*Perfection.*

The phone rang, and she answered automatically.

"Powerhouse, Specialist Astroga speaking on a nonsecure line, sir or ma'am."

"Astro, it's Worf," Sergeant James Copley replied. "Call your relief in early, then hustle over to the warehouse. I've got some soldiers for you to meet."

Worf had been her immediate boss ever since the final patrol of New York City had devolved into a nighttime firefight at a goth concert in Washington Square Park. The beleaguered Army team had partnered with an ex-banker, his homicidal nieces and some New Jersey gangsters to fight their way clear of the collapsing city.

Several months and a road trip from hell later, a combination of soldiers and small-town folks had fought a bloody three-way battle to hold the only remaining functional hydroelectric plant in the Tennessee River Valley against a genius sociopath and tens of thousands of infected. Worf, as his inner circle was allowed to call him, had remained a stalwart fighting comrade and a much better than average boss throughout the chaotic saga.

He'd probably been a hell of a specialist, back in the day.

"You got it, Worf," Astro replied, restraining her natural curiosity about "new" soldiers. Unrestrained curiosity led to extra duty of the noncombat sort, as every self-respecting E-4 understood. "See you in thirty."

Astro knew that the best approach to any meeting with her sergeant was cheerful obedience. If the meeting led to a higher zombie body count, then it would be, as her Aussie boss Smith liked to say, all aces. If it was admin malarkey, she'd keep smiling while assessing how rapidly she could delegate new responsibility to others. Plan in place, she put her feet back up and took another sip.

"Worf," Astro whispered emphatically, "those are not soldiers!"

She gestured emphatically at the freshly kitted volunteers, who stood several meters away, forming a neat line outside the warehouse that served as the parts depot for Watts Bar. A couple were watching the exchange curiously, while the remainder stolidly ignored the late January drizzle. They all wore the Army's ACU gray-ish camouflage uniform, bore a rifle at sling arms and stood behind green duffel bags.

"Well, Astro," Worf whispered back conspiratorially, "they're in uniform, they have our basic issue equipment and I personally collected them from the volunteer basic training course at Spring City just an hour ago. I'm pretty sure that they're soldiers."

"Sergeant Copley," Astro said quietly, using his rank in a bid for sympathy, "we both know that the selection criteria for the volunteers was bullshit. Just because they can see well enough to shoot a zombie-sized target at a hundred meters, can stumble a mile in eight minutes and are between fifteen and thirty years old does not make them Army privates! Please don't do this to me!"

She followed her statement with a glare at the line of men and women awaiting her attention. The two that had been ogling immediately looked elsewhere.

*Hell, a couple of them are just a kids.*

She looked again.

*And every single one is taller than me. Sonuva...*

"You are *so* right, Astro," Copley replied, before pushing his camouflage cap back on his forehead and following her look to study the group as if seeing them for the first time. "But all those things plus the first four weeks of basic training and indoctrination *do* make them Recruit Privates in the Provisional Tennessee National Guard. And right now, they need a new squad leader. Where, oh where, can I find one of those?" He subtly mimed looking high and low.

Astro glared at her boss while he continued the show.

"Oh, look!" he said happily, pretending to lay eyes on her in surprise. "A squad leader!"

Astro promised herself that she wouldn't actually curse. It was unseemly for any member of the Global E-4 Mafia to appear other than relaxed and composed, even in the face of this disaster. However, if she couldn't turn this around, she might be forced to break one of the most sacred E-4 proscriptions. She might have to actually *work*. She allowed herself no more than a further narrowing of the eyes.

"Specialist, listen." Copley ordered in a low tone of voice, heading off the predictable objections. "We are forming the nucleus of the military force that will retake and hold the power generation and distribution for the entire Cumberland Valley, not just this place and the Nickajack plant upstream. Smith's out of camp, trying to palaver with the remaining Gleaners. Kaplan's organizing protection for that little jaunt, Risky is running the day-to-day search operations and I've got Gunner actually running the bootcamp for the next set of volunteers. That leaves me to cover our defenses here, the nuke plant next door, and Spring City."

He turned so that his motion shielded their discussion in the direction of the recruits and then lightly tapped the black patch sewn on her left breast. The coveted embroidered flintlock rifle and wreath denoted the wearer as someone who had engaged in ground combat. Since the start of the Fall, Astro had earned hers several times over. "Back in New York, some itty-bitty clerk-typist private argued that I should let her fight, that she was a clerk-typist with the soul of an infantryman. And she was right. I've seen you in firefights against rogue cops, Mafia goons and lots of Gleaners. You've punched the tickets of hundreds of infected."

Astro grinned happily. This trip down memory lane wasn't as good as a warm gun, but it was close.

"So, you've proved that you're a shit-hot fighting soldier." Worf said, carefully keeping his voice low. "But I need more out of you now. That means training up the privates standing over there. So you get to be the squad leader that takes these privates in hand. I was an E-4 once, back before the dawn of time. I get it. But E-4s do perform work, you know."

Astro refrained from gasping at this sacrilege.

"Yeah, it's real work," Worf repeated. "But you're not just the head of some imaginary E-4 Mafia, you're a combat veteran and a survivor. This job means training these kids to survive and win in this shitty world. I need you to get these newbies trained up on our routine. They've got the basics, or as much as they can get in a month. Run them on patrols inside the wire and let them get used to seeing the infected as targets and not monsters. You've got to give them some practical knowledge. Can I count on you to own this and do it right?"

Astro sneaked a look at "her" squad. Worf had a point. While being a squad leader was definitely going to be extra work, the next generation of E-4s had to come from somewhere. This wouldn't be so bad.

"Yes, Sergeant," she said.

"You got this, Astro," Worf said. "Get them inside, feed 'em, and come up with a training schedule. Remember—nothing outside the fence until I say, right?"

"I'm on it, Worf," she said, touching the brim of her cap with the easy familiarity of a combat veteran.

He returned the salute before stepping back.

She turned to face the new soldiers, feeling a palpable weight descend on her shoulders. Without thinking, she cracked her neck and shrugged her shoulders. She sensed, rather than saw, Worf heading back to the battered Suburban he'd used to fetch the recruits.

*Right. Let's do this.*

"Detail, atten-HUT!" she ordered.

The short line of privates raggedly came to attention.

"My name is Specialist Astroga," she said loudly. "I will now demonstrate the superior intelligence of the U.S. Army Specialist. Step one is to get your rag-bag asses out of the rain. When I say 'at-ease,' fall out, grab your shit and we'll get better acquainted."

Astro realized that she'd become accustomed, heck spoiled, by the professional gun- handling of the other New York survivors. Out of an abundance of caution, and long experience with Army privates, Astro decided to run the initial weapons drills with empty M4s. That had been the right call. Despite the basic weapons safety classes in their shortened basic training, "her" privates swept their rifle muzzles across her or their fellows a number of times, creating a friendly fire risk.

*Here lies U.S. Army Specialist Cathe Astroga, Combat Administrator, who accepted command of a bunch of noobs and then got shot by her own boneheaded troops...*

After a brief verbal tussle with Worf, she'd sent the worst offenders back to be recycled. The next step was to let the remaining recruits shoot, one at a time, at real zombies. Results were mixed, much like the overcast sky that alternately dispensed weak sunshine and light rain. The last to shoot, Recruit Private Phil Booker, was having a rough day.

"Well, Books, while I'm enjoying this brilliant range day that the Almighty has seen fit to gift us," Astroga said, carefully staying behind the firing line. "I'm not that impressed. I picked you four because you were the most promising of the lot."

She'd brought her squad out to the fence line overlooking the river bluff and several of the Tesla coils that protected this stretch of perimeter. This little group was performing their seventh morning shooting evolution since she'd been assigned this "important duty" by Worf. Apparently, "important" was synonymous with "aggravating, dangerous and exasperating." Some of the privates were better than others. The one currently in the spotlight was...not.

"There's a little bit of good news, Books. You haven't shot the fracking Teslas. Again. More importantly, you haven't shot me or anyone else in the squad."

"Yes, Specialist!" Private Booker replied nervously, lying prone in the wet grass of the hilltop that overlooked the river. "Thank you, Specialist."

The muzzle of his rifle, tipped with a scratch-built suppressor, wavered a bit. The lanky recruit was really trying, but Astro had learned that Booker had the unfortunate tendency to twitch under stress. It turned out that zombies stressed him. Missing a shot in front of his squad leader stressed him. Being cold and wet stressed him. There was a lot of twitching going on.

"The bad news is that you haven't hit a single infected today," Astro continued. She gestured toward the shoreline two hundred yards away, where the last two ragged-looking infected were pawing weakly at the eight-foot-tall chain-link fence that ran between the Tennessee River and the power plant. Through her binoculars, Astro could make out partially healed wounds and sores, especially on the zombies' feet. Several other naked bodies lay scattered between the fence and the river.

"Remember, keep your red dot on the center of the zombie's chest," she repeated the litany for the umpteenth time. "Take up the slack in your trigger and exhale about halfway. Then just think about squeezing a bit more and let the shot be a surprise."

Booker missed again.

"And we have to get on with the schedule." Astro sighed. "Worms, Hickory, one round each, finish them."

Recruit Privates Kathy Wormsley and Steve Jackson were also prone. Wormsley was a twenty-something transfer from the old Bank of the Americas Site Blue and arguably the most mature of the new soldiers. Jackson had been liberated from a Gleaner's work gang and had yet to come into his full growth, but his gangly teenage frame still left him the tallest of the group, the little shit.

"I've got Mr. Tall, Dark and Handsome," Wormsley announced.

"Bald and Saggy is all mine," Jackson answered flatly.

In near unison, their rifles coughed, the usual sharp reports reduced to tolerable levels. Astroga watched the naked infected drop limply to the rocky shoreline.

"These zombies looked pretty messed up, Specialist," Wormsley said without looking up from her sights. "Don't seem like much of a threat."

"Well, Worms," Astro replied, scanning for more targets through her binoculars, "you have the luxury of looking at a few of them through a fence, not in their thousands, sprinting across open ground to beat each other to a tasty soldier-snack. Besides, the average infected isn't enjoying winter, even in southern Tennessee.

No clothing, no heated buildings, no steady three squares a day. With a little luck, a bunch of them will finish dying between now and spring. Alright everyone, no more infected in view. Clear and make safe, and place your weapons on the folding table, muzzles pointed downrange. The line is cold."

Astro watched carefully as privates dropped their magazines and manually extracted chambered rounds. She watched as they visually inspected each other's empty rifle—*it's your own ass if your buddy shoots you, see?*—and then she checked herself before allowing any of the privates to stand.

"Does that mean clearing all the zombies will be easy later, Specialist Astroga?" asked Wormsley.

"Nope," Astro replied, squinting at the recruit she was supposed to be teaching. She refrained from making a smart-assed reply while she popped a fresh RipIt from the cooler and swilled a big mouthful. This one was fruit flavored, not her favorite. "The zombies can sort of hibernate, especially when they find shelter. We've found nests of them clustered around food sources, waiting for more supplies to come along. General Winter will take his share of the enemy, but he isn't going to do our job for us."

"Which general is that, Specialist Astroga?" Jackson asked, shrugging on a previously discarded camo jacket, warding off the breeze that had steadily increased all morning.

"General Winter is the Russian name for harsh climate that helped defeat the Nazis when they invaded in WW2," Booker replied confidently, causing Astro to pause with her mouth open. "The Germans had such a hard time working in the winter conditions which the Russians were used to that they were easier to defeat. So—General Winter."

"Was he asking you, Books?" Astro said tartly.

Booker twitched.

"But he's right," Astroga went on, taking another swig from her can, while giving Booker a gimlet eye. "A lot of Nazis died in the Russian winter snow, one way or another. Same thing, same place—more or less—happened to the French about a hundred years before that. The lesson is that when you're defending your territory, you use every advantage you can get. There's no such thing as fighting too dirty."

She drained the can of energy drink and dropped it back into the cooler with a rattle.

"Ah," she said reflectively. "I'm really going to regret it when I finish the last one of those."

"You're running out, Specialist?" asked Booker.

"Why, yes I am, Books," Astro said, eyeing another can before deciding to ration herself. Apart from her lack of resupply, she knew that while she could have a couple without a problem, three or more would make her jittery and lose her temper. Several RipIts in a row could create *interesting* side effects. Jitteriness and anger were the least of it. There was the potential for... explosive digestive issues. Stories of legendary RipIt races, where bored privates vied to solo a complete case of the chemical-laced drinks first, often ended messily. She'd heard Gunner's tale about being trapped in the upper turret of an armored Humvee during an alert that had interrupted his RipIt race. The soggy officer and his driver, pinned by incoming fire inside the truck with him, had not been amused.

She closed the cooler with a snap. "Nobody is making any more of these delicious cans of liquid rocket fuel, the elixir that powered a thousand patrols in the 'Stan and Iraq. There's only one other limited source of RipIts in the entire Cumberland Valley, and he's not sharing. And, in case you haven't noticed, *Private*, I can't swing down to the corner megastore and pick up a case, or any one of a hundred things that we're used to."

"No coffee," Wormsley said. "Just shoot me."

"Are you kidding?" Recruit Private Bill Ritch interrupted. "We've got instant coffee coming out of our ears."

"Instant. Is. Not. Coffee," Wormsley replied firmly. She, like many of the survivors, was a frustrated connoisseur.

"What we aren't going to have much longer is fresh bread," Ritch countered. "As soon as the grain stocks run out, we're screwed."

"Plenty of corn around here," Booker offered.

"I mean wheat flour," Ritch replied. "Pie crusts, biscuits and gravy. Pasta!"

"Don't forget chocolate," Astro interjected helpfully. "I'd trade a pallet of chocolate for a couple more cases of RipIts."

"Aah! Why did you have to use the C word, Specialist Astroga?" Wormsley said, raising her voice a bit. "I'm down to my last few bags of Cadbury's!"

"Specialist, I don't much care for energy drinks," Booker said, cutting across the reminiscing. "But there's an entire barge full of Army drinks just like the ones you have there."

"Say that again, Books!" Astroga demanded, the range evolution forgotten.

"When I took my folks' boat out of Chattanooga, you know, when everything came apart, it was crazy. I hid overnight on an island just above Chickamauga dam, Specialist," he replied diffidently. "There was a couple of CONEXs, you know, those big shipping containers they used to put on ships and barges. They were washed up on the beach. I opened one up and it was chock-a-block with cases of that stuff. I drank some because I didn't trust the water," he went on, making a face. "No offense, but they taste awful."

"You've fallen victim to one of the classic Army blunders, Private!" Astro said, trying to tamp down her excitement. "Not the first, which is to never get involved in a land war in Asia, but the second, which is that privates should never, ever volunteer information which might lead to extra duty. However, if you're telling me you know where there is literally a golden CONEX full of RipIts, I may permit you to survive with only a minor flesh wound. Are you sure of this?"

"Um, I'm sure, Specialist," Booker said, nervously eyeing his squad leader's grin and the various gazes of his fellows, which ranged from curiosity to anger.

"Alright everyone, collect your brass and your gear and head up to the warehouse," Astro ordered. As the group moved into action, she added, "Not you, Books. You and I have a hot date with a map."

"Specialist Astroga, didn't the sergeant say that we shouldn't patrol outside the fenceline?" Ritch asked, as the four members of the party quietly paddled along the edge of the island, just north of Chattanooga. Astro had "borrowed" an aluminum skiff for proficiency training and they were well downriver, nearly an hour's drive south of their camp, and that was in pre-Fall time.

"Indeed he did, Retch," Astro replied confidently. "Which is why this isn't a patrol, but a reconnaissance in force. We're not trying to clear infected. We're just checking the possible location of life-saving supplies."

"RipIts are life-saving supplies?" Jackson followed up.

"Sure are, Hickory," Astro replied. "For example, as long as we find some, they're gonna keep me from tossing you to the zombies and starting over. Hooah?"

"Hooah, Specialist."

"I think maybe I can see a CONEX!" whispered Booker excitedly as the little group cleared another point of land. "It's too dark to be sure."

The quartet paused, straining to make out their surroundings on the brush-covered island. The post-Fall world was so quiet, that all that could be heard was the gentle slap of very small waves against their aluminum boat and the sound of their own breathing.

"I can't be sure, Specialist," Booker continued.

The quarter moon was battling cloud cover. Astro had planned for that, and had further cadged the temporary loan of two sets of night observation devices, or NODs, for "troop familiarization," pledging the pound of flesh nearest her heart as collateral. There wouldn't be a problem as long as she had them back the next afternoon for scheduled inventory. The irreplaceable little headsets were mounted to rubber head straps and could swivel up and down.

"Flip down your NODs, Books," Astro said, and immediately regretted it as the unhandy recruit managed to whack Jackson with his oar before dropping it with a clatter. The movement of the two privates caused their flat-bottomed craft to teeter precariously for a moment.

*Here lies U.S. Army Specialist Cathe Astroga, Combat Administrator, drowned by her own recruits while making an unauthorized scrounging run in a stolen boat.*

She hissed her profanity-laced reproof and the group settled down as the boat drifted. Astro lowered her own monocular. The goggle was fed by a single tube that projected snoutlike from her face. NODs gathered ambient light and amplified it on fuzzy green screens inside each eye piece, restoring human vision even on the darkest night. Pre-Fall, they cost thousands of dollars. Now, they were effectively priceless. Her NODs were filled with the rectangular shapes of tumbled shipping containers, partially obscuring her view of the shoreline. She hadn't realized just how close they were.

"I see them!" Booker confirmed. "But there are a lot more than I saw the last time I was here."

After easing the boat up to the muddy bank, Astro scanned again while her little group assembled next to her. As their boots stirred up the mud at the water's edge, the redolence of rotting vegetation and other less savory things filled her nose. Their path took them past the decomposing carcass of a drowned cow, identifiable by the distinctive horns. Her goggles turned the initial scattering of containers on the island into dozens of units. Up close, the ubiquitous shipping boxes that were used to move goods the length of the Tennessee River were the size of single car garages, much taller than a man and five times as long. Sealed examples were buoyant, nuzzling the shoreline. Some had been deposited high on the island by the flood levels of previous storms. The double doors on others were cracked open, leaving a few partially sunken, extending into the river.

"Man, this is like looking for the Ark of the Covenant in that big warehouse, only on a tiny green window instead of the big screen," Booker said.

Unsurprisingly, there wasn't a big neon RipIt arrow conveniently pointing at a particular box. There was nothing for it but to look inside a few. Fortunately, there weren't any zombies in view, either. Astro figured that this made sense since this was an island, and while the infected congregated around water sources, they weren't known for their swimming prowess.

"Alright... Retch, you keep your hand on my shoulder and step where I step," Astro ordered in a low voice. "Books, you and Hickory pair up the same way. No white light—use your goggles. Remember, we're looking for the already open container that Books found."

Astro, Private Ritch in tow, squelched forward toward the closest container and found the doors sealed. And the next, and the one after that.

"Damn, this smells bad!" Ritch said in a low tone.

"Shut it, Retch," Astro ordered. "This isn't too bad."

After months of exposure during their trip out of New York, she'd gotten used to breathing through her mouth, avoiding the worst of the smells. It would take a really awful odor to shock her n—ugh! Okay, this was getting bad. Really bad, like cesspool mixed with rotting corpses bad. Must be another cow.

The CONEX ahead was resting at an angle, partially sunk into the mud of the shore. The unsealed doors were closed, and

Astro told her partner to open it. Ritch braced himself in order to swing one open against the slant, fighting gravity. At the halfway point he lost control of the weight and it clanged open, startling everyone. Astro decided to not shoot him. It was close.

"If there were zombies here, Retch, you just rang the dinner bell!" she said angrily.

"Sorry, Specialist." came the contrite reply.

Keeping one hand on her rifle's pistol grip, Astro waved distractedly, since the first thing that she noticed was the increased odor. The stench was so thick that it had a taste. Ritch stumbled back a step in olfactory shock. In a world now dominated by putrid odors, this miasma was beyond notable. To her regret, Astro had become an expert in bad odors, and this one was dominated by the smelling of decaying meat, overlaid with a strangely sweet smell. Astro suppressed her gag reflex as she took in the interior. Jumbled cartons lay at all angles, filling the container halfway to the ceiling. Could this be it? The smell was momentarily forgotten. Astro had to take a big step up onto the open lip of the tilted container and she risked a shielded red penlight.

What she'd initially thought were boxes were in fact drink cases shrink-wrapped together. The distinctive shape of aluminum cans under the shrink-wrap made her pulse start to pound. The colors of the packaging were distorted in her red light but the logo wasn't.

"RipIt - Energy Fusion," Astro said, pronouncing each syllable name reverently, the stench utterly forgotten. Her excitement continued to grow. This was. The. Mother lode. She might have enough RipIt to last forever. She flashed the light around a bit, excited, trying to count the boxes. She was the RipIt Queen!

"Alright!" she exulted, pumping one fist into the air. "Books, get the other two over here. We can squeeze a lot of this into the boat and retu—ack!"

Even strapped with her plate carrier, rifle, pistol, machete and other miscellaneous tactical kit, Astro's towering five-foot-two-inch height limited her total mass, with gear, to under one hundred fifty pounds. Well within the strength range, as it turned out, of a liquid rocket–fueled, insensate, cannibalistic infected human. Which was exactly what grabbed Astro's upraised arm and yanked her up and across the nearly head high stack of energy drink cartons and into the back of the dark CONEX.

This was getting beyond bad, even by Astro's admittedly jaded standards for the zombie apocalypse. However, the zombie was fighting from the uncertain footing of tumbled cartons and cans. It overbalanced, and fell, pulling Astro on top of itself. The resulting crash dropped them both onto the rear container floor, which was covered with several inches of mostly liquid... stuff. Horrible stuff, the vilest stuff, Astro realized in a split second. The stuff that a zombie made when it had been feeding exclusively on RipIt energy drinks for some undefined but extended interval. The zombie struggled with hysterical strength, biting Astro's combat harness. Stunned by the shock of the sudden encounter, the impact with the floor and the OMIGOD WHAT IS THAT SMELL, Astro was still elbowing the living crap of the zombie behind her. Each impact created a further sloshing of liquid that stirred the... stuff even more, releasing still greater waves of putrefaction.

Rocked by the wave action generated by the fighting but invisible in the pitch-black CONEX, what must have been thousands of Astro's beloved but empty RipIt cans jangled in a rustling metallic soundtrack to her struggle for life.

"Oh you sorry cocksucker!" Astro said furiously, trying to free one hand from her tangled rifle sling. Straining, she reached for the thick-bladed machete at her waist. Even through the surge of adrenaline, she could already feel a cramp coming on from keeping her head cranked forward, protecting her neck and scalp from the zombie's snapping jaws.

"You did not just ruin the last batch of RipIts in the world all by yourself!" The fighting duo was splashing around and Astro had just got her hand free when another heavy weight landed on her.

"Alright, we've just crossed into suckage territory." She gasped angrily, *still* working on getting her hand free. "I'm so going to murder you to death!"

Fully absorbed by the focus of life-or-death combat, Astro hadn't paid attention to anything else, but her faithful recruits had come to the rescue. Ritch landed first, making some kind of warbling scream. Unfortunately, his knees landed on Astro, driving the breath from her lungs with a gasp. The private had also landed facedown in the filth, abruptly cutting off his war cry. As his knees slithered off her chest, the sound of retching provided a nice counterpoint to the gargling growls of the infected *still* at her back.

*We've reached maximum suckage*, Astro thought. She managed to roll to one side and kicked backward in the pitch-dark container, driving the frenetic infected off her back for a moment.

A case of her beloved drink fell off the pile between her and the door of the CONEX, clipping her shoulder, just as she was about to swing the machete.

*Here lies U.S. Army Specialist Cathe Astroga, Combat Administrator, drowned in RipIt diarrhea, stunned by falling privates and eaten by an over-caffeinated zombie!*

"Specialist, do you need help?" Booker yelled from atop the stack. Then he lit the interior with his weapons light.

"Jesus Fuck, Books!" Astro yelled, completely blinded. "Get the light outta my eyes!"

She stumbled in the now well-lit muck, looking for her machete and nearly tripping over Ritch. Astro glanced at him, but quickly dismissed him as a source of aid. He'd found his feet and was fumbling with his M4, but his nearly continuous vomiting was precluding his ability to operate his firearm. That was probably for the best since she didn't trust the recruit to not shoot the wrong target in this suckage. In the other corner however, was the infected, still combat-effective. The relatively healthy, naked young male held its arms up, shielding itself from the light. Astro could see the infected's limbs vibrating, powered by a near terminal overdose of taurine, caffeine and L-glutamine. She knew the feeling. Understandably enraged by the interlopers and fueled by the almighty elixir of the U.S. Army, it lunged past her, reaching for Booker, the nearer of the two potential meals that it would then no doubt wash down with another helping of RipIt.

"Oh no, you don't!" Astro screamed. "No eating my recruits!"

She snap-kicked the infected in the knee, dropping it to the muck. She pinned it in place with one beslimed, thick-soled combat boot and made a quick draw of her sidearm. Ignoring the frenetic scrabbling at her leg and crotch, she carefully placed a single shot. The round slammed the zombie's jerking head backward, and she watched as its wire-taut muscles relaxed into limp finality. Booker's light, now aimed at the white-painted CONEX ceiling, scattered enough illumination that the gasping combatants could make out details of the disgusting scene.

Astro looked over at Ritch and then glanced down. They were both coated head to toe in a thin, yellow mustard–like liquid that smelled like soured fruit blended into rotted meat. Ritch's convulsive, involuntary heaving continued to agitate the small sea of gashed yet still floating RipIt cans. Their red, purple and green highlights shone through the yellow muck as they gently rustled around their feet while the ankle-deep ... stuff slowly surged back and forth.

"Retch, you alright?" she asked, spitting out some filth.

"Specialist Astr—" Ritch began, before continuing to spew his own contribution across the scene, further dappling Astro's uniform.

"Jesus, Retch!" Astro inquired, squinting upward. "Yeah, can I name them or what? Books, how about you?"

"Specialist Ast—" Booker began, then twitched and turned his head to the side, joining Team Vomit.

"Right, right. You're both fine," Astro replied, carefully holstering her pistol. "Let's get organized. Books, stop yacking all over my RipIts and tell Hickory to pull security. There could be more of these assholes around, island or no. Retch, enough puking. We're sure as hell not gonna leave without bringing back as much as we can, so start passing me cartons and we'll head back to the barn."

"You lost what?" Astro sputtered disbelievingly? "When?!"

"Specialist Astroga, I'm sorry, I just found out they were missing a minute ago!" Booker said guiltily. "I ran back to the skiff right away but they weren't there either."

"What's not there?" Wormsley asked, poking her head into the little warehouse classroom that Astro had appropriated as their orderly room. The female recruit immediately wrinkled her nose. "What is that smell?"

"Worms, fetch Hickory and Retch right now! I don't care if they're taking a dump. Everybody drops their gear here and we go through it item by item until we find Books's NODs."

It didn't take long for Astro to verify that the goggles were, in fact, missing. In a world where she wasn't required to immediately return the goggles to the perpetually angry, Tennessee Valley Authority engineer from whom she'd borrowed them, the look of abject terror on Booker's face would've been entertaining, funny even. However, in the real world, Worf was going to have her ass. A glance at her watch confirmed Astro's guess. Their plunder-laden skiff had been a struggle to get back upriver, and the trip had taken long enough that it would be light in less than an hour. Going back and searching the CONEX during the day was impossible without risking questions and certain discovery.

Maybe if she could reach some kind of understanding with Sarah...

"Tell me why I care, Astro," Sarah Shikenjanski said flatly, slapping her bench with one palm. The racks behind the TVA engineer were covered with bits and pieces of high-value electronics, and the benchtop in front of her looked like an in-progress autopsy of a heavily damaged tactical radio. "You lose it, you pay. See this? Another of you Army yahoos managed to run over one of my remaining reliable handsets and now I get to fix it with spit and bailing wire. What you people do to electronics is criminal! I used to manage nearly a thousand miles of power lines, and now I'm reduced to being the local Radio Shack. And...and what is that smell?"

Astro had thoroughly showered and changed, but the faint ambiance of eau de CONEX persisted. She glanced around for inspiration, but all she saw was Booker swallowing nervously as he looked fixedly at Sarah's chest. Astro followed his gaze. The engineer *was* totally stacked. Astro usually appreciated that sort of thing but this wasn't the time or place. Booker noticed his boss's angry glance and twitched.

"Sarah, the NODs aren't lost," Astro pleaded, returning to the matter at hand. "I know exactly where they are, but I can't get them till tonight. It's just one more day. Maybe I could trade you something for some more time?"

"What it is, Specialist Astroga, is inventory day tomorrow," the now stone-faced woman replied. Clearly, she'd noticed the byplay. Wonderful. "There's only one thing I need, and I can't imagine that you have it."

"Anything, Sarah." Astro was between a rock and hard place.

"Fine," Sarah replied firmly. "I need a new sports bra. And not any old bra. As your rude friend noticed, I'm big up top. So if you want one more day, it's going to cost you a 40F sports bra. Wide straps. And new! None of this 'lightly used' crap."

"Deal."

"Hey, Astro!" Warrant Officer Terri Harry, USN (Supply Corps) genially waved her coffee mug at Astro as she approached the window to the storeroom. The front of the very large space was cordoned off by floor-to-ceiling chain link, behind which Astro saw the familiar racks of clothing, medical consumables, canned goods and general supplies retrieved by sweep teams. Harry had been shanghaied from retirement by Astro's boss's boss after they'd saved Spring City. The warrant's background and temperament lent themselves to managing inventory. "How they hanging—wait, what's that smell?"

"One higher than the other, Warrant," Astro replied, ignoring the second question. Next to her, the meticulously prebriefed Booker kept his mouth shut. "Got a sec? I need a favor."

"Spill," Harry said, before taking a sip from her mug and frowning.

"Seeing as you run the inventory for every last thing that our recovery teams bring in, I wonder if you could check to see if you have a sport bra, size 40F."

"You need a 40F?" Harry asked, with a quizzical look at Astro's own sleek frame.

"I owe a favor."

"Ah, not too many 40Fs in camp, so Shikenjanski must have something you want," Harry said, green eyes sparkling over her coffee mug. "Well, everybody wants something. A year ago, anyone could have it, too. But here, now? Nope. Sarah's been in here before, asking, but she already has plenty of bras. She just has designs on that hunky Texan that wandered in last week. If she wants a sexy new bra to impress Fike, she can go look for one on her own."

"I'm in bit of spot, Warrant," Astro wheedled gently. "If I were to owe you a favor, would you maybe happen to have one in stock?"

"Well, let's see." Harry tapped at her laptop for a few moments, before staring across the brim of her coffee mug with a smile. "Yeah, I might have something. But the answer is still no."

Astro studied the thick enameled mug, sporting the silver bar and two blue squares of a Navy warrant office.

"You still drinking instant?"

"Does the pope wear a funny hat, Astro?" Harry replied, frowning into her mug. "That's all there is."

"What if I could scare up a pound of Jamaica Blue Mountain?" Astro asked. "Whole beans, none of that instant crap. Would that be worth the sports bra?"

"The McCoy?" The warrant sat her mug down, and held very still. "Here, now? We don't joke about things like that, Specialist."

"A year ago, anyone could have it," Astro answered. "But here, now? Yep. Still vacuum sealed in the original foil bag, in fact."

"I'm listening."

"So you caught your ass in a smelly crack, Astro." Doug Goodall smirked without looking up from his Xbox. "Heard one of your scrubs dropped something important doing Army training."

He raised one hand to make half of an air-quotes motion while he pronounced "Army training."

Astro declined to rise to the bait. During her "geeks with glasses are hot" phase, she and Goodall had been a thing briefly. Apart from a love of RipIts, they shared nothing. Eventually, she got bored. He got angry.

"Hi, Doug," she responded easily, noting a can of *sugar-free* lime RipIt on the floor.

*Poseur.*

"Yeah, I kinda did. In fact, I need a favor."

"What?" Goodall replied, setting down his controller. He picked up the can and swirled it around a little before taking a drink. "The all-go, never-quit, so-important Specialist Astroga needs a favor from little ole' me?"

*Here lies U.S. Army Specialist Cathe Astroga, Combat Administrator, convicted by court-martial for murdering an annoying civilian to death, and then shot by firing squad at dawn, beloved Citrus RipIt can in hand.*

Astro bit off the first three responses that suggested themselves. With a little luck, Doug didn't know the specifics of *why* and *how* she'd lost the NODs and she could make her offer before the size and nature of her haul was public knowledge.

"Remember how you made me breakfast a few times?"

"Uh-huh," he said with a leer.

"Remember that awesome coffee you brewed?"

"The Jamaican," Doug said. "Single estate. Mild roast."

"I want to trade you for some," Astro said. "Five cases of RipIt, all I have left, for a pound of that coffee."

"*Five?*" Doug said before recovering his cool. "I mean, I don't know..."

"One-time offer, Doug," Astro replied confidently. "All those RipIts to go with your gaming. Going, going..."

"I'll take it."

"I knew you would."

The snarling of a Tesla coil caught Astro's attention. She glanced up from her book to the monitor before confirming the kill on the tally board. She looked down at the cooler resting by her feet, but decided against popping another can of dewy cold RipIt. The door creaked open, and her boss strode into the powerhouse.

"Specialist Astroga, a moment of your time?" he said with unusual formality.

"Sure thing, Boss." Astro put her feet down, and sat a little straighter.

"How are the recruits shaping?" Worf asked. "Any standouts?"

"They're actually pretty solid," she replied. "Booker is a bit smarter than he looks. All four did well on shooting, navigation and communications. We've completed the first training sets and we're ready to move on."

"Glad to hear that you got in some good training, Astro," Worf said easily, sitting on the built in desktop. He reached toward the cooler and paused. "You mind?"

"Nah, help yourself," Astro said, watching Worf select a can of F-Bomb flavor. "Uh, I wanted to give you a heads-up on something, though."

"Yeah, what's that, Astro?" Worf said, pulling the tab on his RiptIt and hastily guzzling the soda that began to hiss out too rapidly for comfort.

Astro thought about it one more time and then took a breath.

"The reason that I'm so comfortable with the new privates is that I put them through a bit of a crucible." Astro went on to sketch out the intel from Booker, her RipIt run, dropping and then finding the NODs. She ran down after a couple minutes and looked at Worf, who'd withdrawn a small notebook from the breast pocket of his ACUs and scribbled notes here and there as she talked.

He meditatively pulled at his can.

"Let me rewind this for a sec," Worf said. "You traded five cases of RipIts to Goodall, before he learned about the newly discovered supply, just so you could take advantage of Warrant Officer Harry's coffee dependency, in order to break"—he consulted the notebook—"a size 40F sport bra with wide shoulder straps loose for Ms. Shikenjanski in order to help her get a date with Fike and buy yourself another day to collect the NODs that one of your recruits dropped"—he consulted the notes again—"and I notice that you carefully don't say *which* one—while you were on an unauthorized gee-dunk run, outside the wire, specifically against my direction to the contrary? And that during this little adventure, you borrowed mission-essential equipment without logging it and, lastly, the unit under your command engaged in close combat with at least one infected. Is that basically it?"

"Yes, Sergeant," Astro confirmed in a very small voice.

"Well, Astro, I gotta say," Worf said, standing up, "that's one of the finest pieces of E-4 Mafia skullduggery I've ever heard of."

"Really?" Astro couldn't believe her ears. No doubt the ass chewing would start in a moment.

"Yep, except for one thing."

"Well, I considered holding back the payment for Gooda—" Astro began.

"No, not that," Worf cut her off, making a chopping motion with one hand. "You told me about it! That violates every tenet that the E-4 Mafia holds dear! Whatever happened to the simple beauty of, 'Gee, I don't know Sergeant,' or 'First I've heard of that, Sergeant'? The E-4 Mafia *never* spills their guts like that! Why did you break the caper to me?"

"Um, well, it's like this, Worf." Astro stayed seated, but she twisted her hands together. "I realized that the job that you gave me was important. The trainees did get some good training, but I took some chances and it could've gone pretty bad. People that have fought together and shared risks like you and I, well, they share a certain way of looking at things. That builds trust. I figured that you needed to hear it from me before you gave me another job."

For a long moment, they looked at each other.

"Astro, what you just said is pretty much the textbook definition of integrity," he said, sighing and sitting back down. "As much as it pains me, there has to be repercussions, you understand?"

"I understand, Worf," Astro said quietly. She knew what was coming, and the free-falling elevator sensation in her gut was just an added bonus.

"You can't keep that specialist's tab, for one thing," Worf said, extending one hand, and making little "give it to me" motions with his fingers.

Astro's hands flew protectively to the specialist insignia on the front of her blouse. Then she reluctantly peeled the little Velcro square bearing the subdued, cone-shaped rank symbol from her uniform. She held her arm out and dropped the hard-won rank tab in Worf's hand. The elevator was accelerating downward, if anything.

"Here, you'll need this," he said, extending his other hand and passing her a cloth object. She accepted it numbly, and then turned it over. She stared blankly at the black-embroidered insignia in her hands and the elevator jerked to a halt.

"What's this, Worf?" she asked, looking up from the new sergeant's chevrons that he'd passed her.

"Astro, I know that you thought you were hot stuff as the chairwoman of the E-4 Mafia," Worf said expansively as he reached down for a second can of RipIt. "But you forgot that I was doing E-4 Mafia shit while you were still peeing down your leg. I just can't stand seeing it being done so badly. Now, you're part of the NCO mafia, and you're going to have another set of problems. Welcome to the club, Sergeant Astroga! Oh, and by the way—I'll bring by the next batch of recruits this afternoon. Try not to get any of them bit, alright?"

# Mike Massa

**Mike Massa**'s writing encompasses SF, Mil-SF and Fantasy as well as nonfiction. His most recent novel, with John Ringo, is national bestseller *River of Night* (July 2019) and is set, in part, just outside Chattanooga, TN. Since 2016 he has written two novels and his work has been included in ten anthologies. Mike received his first novel contract at LibertyCon 29 in front of a packed house inside the Chattanooga Choo Choo's main auditorium—LibertyCon will always be special for him!

# THE LIBERTY CON

I have been part of the science fiction community for forty years. I have known Tim and Anna Zahn for much of that time. First, as a fan in the early '80s when Tim was just starting to sell short stories, then later as one of the editors who got to publish him in book form at Baen Books, and finally in the twenty-first century as the publisher of his Cobra series and many other works. I saw Tim and Anna's son, Corwin, grow up at conventions. And I could do that because LibertyCon and others like it were friendly places for families, friendly places for young fans to congregate, let their hair down, and enjoy the company of others who loved science fiction. That, too, is part of Uncle Timmy's legacy.

—TW

# The Liberty Con

## Timothy Zahn

Pretty much everyone on New Vipitti hated the Benevolent Uncle's elite Political Compliance Enforcement Agents. On some days, PCE Agent Rafe Bosphor agreed with them.

Today was one of those.

"June 24, 8:33 a.m.," he murmured as he peered through the window from his café street-side table, watching the waitress bustling back and forth between the tables inside. "Subject has been at work for forty minutes. No unusual contacts."

"Never mind the subject," his controller's clipped voice came back over his earbud. "We'll pick her up later. Is the target in sight?"

"Negative," Bosphor said. "But there's no need to pick up the subject. She hasn't done anything."

"Everyone's done *something*," the controller countered. "Doesn't cost anything to pick her up. If she's not worth the paperwork, we'll cut her loose."

With an effort Bosphor unclenched his teeth. Yes, they'd cut her loose...but afterward she would spend the next days or weeks in a state of quiet fear, anticipating and dreading the day when they'd again come for her. "I don't think you need to bother," he said in his most diplomatic tone. "Unless I witness her in a criminal act, or she has contact with a known criminal, it would just be a waste of everyone's time."

"Time is cheap," the controller said. "We'll see. Keep an eye on her. If she contacts the target..." He left the threat unfinished.

"Acknowledged," Bosphor said. "I'll watch her."

"You do that." There was the faint click as the controller broke the connection.

Bosphor took a sip of his coffee and watched the waitress deliver two cups to a couple at one of the tables. Not everyone on New Vipitti was a criminal. Bosphor knew that, though he sometimes wondered if the PCE bosses did. This waitress certainly wasn't one.

The man who called himself Uncle Timmy, on the other hand...

Bosphor glared into his mug. With burglars and thieves, at least, the victim knew they'd been robbed. With con men, sometimes they never figured it out. That was what made that class of criminal so despicable, and what made Bosphor determined to nail this one. As far as anyone could figure out, he'd been conning people for at least five years, maybe longer.

As for the whole Uncle Timmy moniker, that could only be a deliberate dig at the Benevolent Uncle's title. To some people, Bosphor supposed, that might edge the man into folk-hero status. To the PCE, it just meant that much more incentive to nail his hide to the wall.

The waitress paused by one of her tables, pulling out her reader for the payment. Bosphor watched, staring at the back of the customer's head, wondering if he would even know Uncle Timmy if he saw him. Every victim PCE had found—and there were a *lot* of them—had given them a description of the man who'd taken their money. The problem was that none of the descriptions matched any of the others.

Timmy was large, slender, tall, short, bearded, clean-shaven, bald and sported a retro mullet. He had a weakness for Jack Daniels whiskey, Starline coffee, cola, white wine, and never drank anything except water. He had a western accent, a southern accent, an Old British accent, and spoke only in a thick Creole dialect.

The one thing everyone's bank accounts agreed on was that he'd taken a lot of money from them.

Five years. New Vipitti was a well-populated world, with plenty of cities and midsized towns where a person could hide. But in an era of chips and IDs and bounce-scanners it shouldn't be so hard to catch even so accomplished a human chameleon.

That Timmy was still on the planet was a given. The Benevolent Uncle had long-since vacuum-sealed his world, creating unbreakable restrictions on who could come and go. There was no way Timmy could escape.

So he was still here. The big question was *where*?

The customer finished with his reader, and with a last inaudible exchange of pleasantries with the waitress he got up and left the café, using the side door away from Bosphor's table. The waitress slipped her reader back into her side pocket and headed back to the serving window to pick up the next order—

Bosphor felt a jolt run through him. Her *side* pocket? But all the rest of the café staff kept their business readers in their apron pockets. So did she, for that matter—he'd seen her pull it out twice while he'd been sitting here.

She hadn't been taking the man's money. *She'd been giving him hers.*

Bosphor kicked back his chair and raced out into the street. But he was too late. The customer had already disappeared into the crowd of pedestrians. He continued on for another minute anyway, craning his neck in search of the shirt collar and back of the head he'd seen through the café window.

Nothing.

Cursing under his breath, he turned and headed back. The customer was gone, but the waitress would still be there. Maybe he could finally get a clear take on Uncle Timmy's face.

The waitress was clearing a table near the door when Bosphor returned. "There you are," she greeted him cheerfully as he walked over to her. "For a minute I thought you'd skipped out on the bill."

"Just trying to chase down your last customer," Bosphor said, looking around. None of the other patrons or waiters seemed to be paying any attention to them. "I need to talk to you."

"All right," she said, a slight frown creasing her forehead. "Can it wait? I'm kind of busy right now."

"No," he said flatly. "It can't." Turning his back to the rest of the room, he twitched aside his jacket to show the gold PCE badge glinting on his belt. "Right here will do. Sit down."

She swallowed visibly, her hand fumbling for the back of the chair. He waited until she was seated, then sat down across from her. "What's your name?" he asked.

She swallowed again. "Linda. Linda Vannucci."

"How much did you give him?"

Her eyes widened. "How did you—?"

"Answer the question," Bosphor cut her off. "How much?"

She lowered her gaze to the table. "Twenty thousand."

Bosphor felt his own eyes go a little wider. "Twenty *thousand*?"

"My aunt left me some money," Linda said, a little defensively. "He said..." She trailed off.

"He said what?" Bosphor prompted.

Her shoulders hunched. "I... don't remember."

"Of course you don't," Bosphor said with a quiet sigh. Once again, one of Uncle Timmy's victims was showing an inexplicable reluctance to spilling the truth. "Let me make it easy for you. He said if you gave him all the money you had that he could get you off New Vipitti."

She looked up again, her throat tight. "How did you...?"

"Because that's what he told all the others," Bosphor said. "All seven hundred of them."

"All seven *hundred*—? *That* many?"

"That many," Bosphor confirmed. "He's been running this scam for at least five years."

"I didn't..."

"No one ever does," Bosphor said, suddenly tired of this whole sordid thing. "Unlock your reader and let me see it."

Silently, she pulled out the reader, scrawled the unlock pattern and handed it across the table. Bosphor keyed for transfers and pulled up the most recent.

Twenty thousand, all right. This time, Timmy had had her send the money to an account simply called *Rowland Liberty*. Shifting Linda's reader to his left hand, Bosphor pulled out his own reader and keyed for backcheck.

The track went nowhere, of course. Timmy's money slipped in and out of dummy accounts like magic. So far the forensic accountants hadn't been able to sift through it all and find where the money actually ended up.

But from the talks PCE had had with the victims they'd managed to identify, it looked like the con man had scored at least five or six million. That money had to be *somewhere*, and PCE was hell-bent on finding it.

"Are you going to arrest me?" Linda asked in a low voice.

Bosphor looked up at her. Her face was rigid, her eyes haunted. "Do you deserve to be?" he asked.

"I—no." Another hunch of the shoulders. "But I heard once that people who fall for scams can be arrested."

"The law states that anyone involved in a money scam above a specific threshold is in violation of the law," Bosphor said. "Twenty thousand is well into that range."

"But I'm the *victim*."

"The law doesn't make that distinction."

And in fact, Bosphor knew that at least ten of Timmy's victims had indeed been thrown in jail for a couple of weeks while PCE interrogators tried to figure out whether they were victims or secret accomplices. That was the reason the law had been written that way, not simply because a frustrated Benevolent Uncle had specifically targeted Timmy and his persistently successful and highly embarrassing operations.

Those ten victims had subsequently been released for lack of any evidence, though two of them—Baggott and a particularly feisty woman named Knowles—had annoyed the investigators enough that they'd been held a full month longer than everyone else.

But just because they were back on the streets didn't mean PCE had forgotten about them. Sooner or later Timmy would be run to ground, and when that happened those ten men and women—and probably every other victim PCE had found—would be hauled back in for further questioning.

And, more than likely, made public examples of. One more kick in the teeth to go along with all the money they'd lost.

Bosphor should arrest her, he knew, or at least log her name. There were strict protocols PCE agents were supposed to follow, and this came under them.

But he'd been an agent long enough to have found a few cubic centimeters here and there where some personal discretion could be coaxed out of all that carved stone. "I'm not going to charge you," he told Linda. "But in return, you need to promise that if he contacts you again you'll call me immediately. And I mean *immediately*."

"Of course," Linda said. "I—thank you." Her nose wrinkled. "Don't know why he would come back. He already has all my money."

Bosphor suppressed a grimace. There was that, of course. Once Timmy had worked his scam there was every reason for him to make sure he never saw her again.

But maintaining the fiction that he might come back would allow Bosphor to keep her off the record, at least for a while.

"You never know," he said. "My number's on your reader. Call me right away if you see him or hear from him."

"I will," Linda said. "Thank you."

"You're welcome."

He started to stand up. To his mild surprise she reached over and clutched at his arm. "What happens now? My money—that was all I had. Am I going to get it back?"

"I don't know," Bosphor said. "We'll do our best, but I can't make any promises. A lot depends on whether we catch him before he spends it or squirrels it away where we can't find it."

"But how will I live?"

"You've got a decent job," Bosphor said, making a small gesture at the café around them. "And you're good at it—I saw how you handled customers. You'll keep this one, or get a better one. While there's life, there's hope."

"My mother used to say that." Linda sighed. "Okay. Thank you."

"You're welcome." Bosphor hesitated; but he had to say it. Timmy had offered her false hope in exchange for her money. Bosphor might not be able to return the money, but he could at least make sure no one else played on that same false hope. "But do realize that this was a complete scam. There's no way you can get off New Vipitti without official documents and personal permission. Not for any amount of money, cleverness, or fast-talking. Transports, passenger ships, freighters, personal yachts—none of them can leave without complete scrutiny of passengers and crew."

Linda lowered her eyes again. "I know," she said in a small voice. "But I thought . . . like you said, while there's life, there's hope."

"Hope is good," Bosphor said. "False hope is bad. Just hold on to what you've got, Ms. Vannucci. Things on New Vipitti are going to get better—really they are. There's talk in the Committee about easing restrictions and opening up more opportunities. Just be patient a little longer, and there won't be any need for you to try to leave."

"I hope you're right." Linda gave him a sort of tentative smile. "Thank you."

It hadn't been much of a smile, Bosphor reflected as he walked along the street toward his car. But it was more than he usually got from members of the public since the Benevolent Uncle rose to power.

It was certainly more warmth than Bosphor was about to get from his controller.

✧     ✧     ✧

"You just let her *walk*?" the controller asked, his tone incredulous. "You didn't even get her *name*?"

"Of course I got it," Bosphor said, trying to sound indignant. "The reason I didn't log it is that I'm using her to set a trap. If Uncle Timmy thinks we haven't tagged her he might try to contact her again."

"Kindly do not refer to him by that name," the controller said icily. "If he wants to make a mockery of the Benevolent Uncle, that's his business. But we don't have to assist in his attempted subversion. Regardless, what does a trap have to do with logging this woman's name? You seriously think Timmy has access to official PCE databases?"

"I don't know what he does or doesn't have," Bosphor countered. "That's part of the problem. None of our usual techniques have worked. I thought it was time to try something different."

"Did you, now," the controller said. The sudden calmness in his voice sent a chill up Bosphor's back. "Perhaps you're unaware of this, Agent Bosphor, but the Committee has had its eye on you for some time now. And they're not entirely pleased with what they see."

The chill went a little colder. "I find that remarkable," Bosphor said carefully. "My success rate is certainly on a par with the PCE average."

"It's not your performance that concerns them," the controller said. "It's your attitude. They're not convinced you have the proper degree of respect for the Benevolent Uncle."

"I've never said anything against him," Bosphor protested. "Nor have I ever criticized the Committee or any of the rest of the New Vipitti leadership."

"Words are cheap and obvious," the controller said. "It's the more subtle attitude and actions that show true intent. This business of letting the waitress go without logging her into the system, for instance. Did you do that because you were setting a trap, as you claim? Or did you do it because you thought the system would be unfair to her?"

"I already told you," Bosphor said. "If you think there's no chance my trap will work, say so now and I'll log her in."

There was a brief silence. "No, it's not a completely worthless idea," the controller conceded. "I personally think it's a waste of effort, but you can have a few days to see if it works. Uncle knows nothing else has worked."

"Thank you," Bosphor said between stiff lips.

"But if it doesn't," the controller continued, "you'll bring the waitress in—*personally*—and hand her over to the interrogators. Understood?"

Bosphor glowered. "Understood."

"Good," the controller said. "Good luck, Agent Bosphor. For your sake, I hope this works."

Bosphor had been through all the records of Uncle Timmy's activities, both the ones PCE knew he'd been involved with as well as the more ambiguous crimes that had been tentatively attributed to him. His next step was to sit down in the records section and go through all of them again.

Five years at least. Seven hundred victims at least. Five or six million at least. A hell of a lot of people, and a hell of a lot of money.

Every narrative and tale the same: promising the victim a way off New Vipitti.

A part of Bosphor, the part that had grown up on this world, the part that had stood proudly and taken the PCE oath, wanted to be surprised at that. But the deeper, more honest part understood it completely. Life on New Vipitti had slowly become harder and more restricted under the Benevolent Uncle's rule. People yearning for a better life would naturally look past New Vipitti's atmosphere toward Old Vipitti, or Greater Leptra, or any of the other worlds of the Expansion.

Which was what had made Uncle Timmy's scam so successful. Promising people an escape had hooked into a lot of yearnings and hopes, emotions that tended to shut down the brain's logic centers and suppress the recognition that escape was impossible.

Bosphor hadn't been overstating the case to Linda. Passengers off New Vipitti were few and far between, and every single one of them was scrutinized, vetted, and approved before they ever got within sight of any of the planet's three spaceports. Cargo ships were likewise guarded, their crews undergoing the same scrutiny, and before lift the ships were scanned for possible stowaways. Diplomatic ships had their own restricted landing area, and underwent the same set of inspections before being allowed to leave the planet.

And that was it. Unless Uncle Timmy had a magic beanstalk

stashed out in the jungle somewhere, there were no other ways off the planet.

Everyone knew that, or at least everyone who paid attention to the newsfeeds knew it. The occasional and universally unsuccessful attempts were certainly publicized enough, as were the punishments for the people who tried and failed. The only ships on the planet were isolated, restricted, well-guarded, and unreachable.

And yet, somehow, Uncle Timmy continued to persuade his victims that such a thing was possible.

Had everyone on New Vipitti started taking stupid pills?

He was at his desk, going over the list of Uncle Timmy's victims yet again, when the alarm sounded.

Kirby, down in forensic accounting, answered on the seventh ring. "What?" she growled. "I'm busy here."

"What's going on?" Bosphor asked.

"Do I *look* like your controller?"

"My controller doesn't know jack," he said. "You're the only one who ever knows what's going on."

"If I didn't know better, I'd say that sounded like a compliment," Kirby said with a snort. "Fine. Someone just spotted a red flag that a thousand hunting rifles had been delivered to three General Merch outlets near the spaceports: the stores in Cartwright, Phillips, and Cochrane. We don't—"

"Which spaceport?" Bosphor interrupted.

"*All* of them," Kirby said. "I just said that. Anyway, the flag went up, the Committee went slug-slime crazy, and everything that can fly has been kicked into defense mode around the ports. We've got fighters and helos stacked ten deep up there, and the army's on its way to cover the ground."

"Yeah," Bosphor said, wincing as he called up the schedules. Three freighters were on their way in, one due to touch down in each of the spaceports within minutes of each other. "How come no one noticed the weapons purchases until now?"

Kirby snorted. "Remember that burglary in the documents office two months ago?"

Bosphor winced. Like anyone was going to forget *that* fiasco anytime soon. Nearly fifty official form templates had been stolen, and up to now no one had been able to figure out what the thieves planned to do with them. "One of them was a weapons purchase and transfer authorization?"

"It's a little more complicated but yeah, that's basically it," Kirby said. "We're damn lucky we spotted it at all—if a glitch in the date field hadn't flagged it we'd never have known about them at all."

"Really," Bosphor murmured as a sudden, horrible thought struck him. "Do you know where the money came from?"

"Still working on that," Kirby said. "Look, I've got to go."

"Yeah, thanks," Bosphor said. "Do me a favor, will you? Check and see if any of the money came from an account labeled *Rowland Liberty.*"

"I thought that was your neighborhood con man's account."

"It is," Bosphor said grimly. "Just do the check, okay?"

"When I can get to it," Kirby said. "Just watch yourself, Bosphor. If this is a full-on insurrection, things are going to get bloody."

"That's why I want the money trail," Bosphor said. "As fast as you can get it to me."

He keyed off. For a few minutes he gazed at the window, the now-muted alarm echoing through his brain. *Things are going to get bloody...*

It was probably futile. But he had to try. Pulling out his reader, he keyed for the number he'd lifted from Linda Vannucci back at the café while he was giving her his.

"Hello, Ms. Vannucci," he said when she answered. "This is PCE Agent Bosphor. I was calling to see how you were doing."

"I'm fine, Agent Bosphor," she said, her voice wary. "I'm afraid I haven't been able to think of anything else I can tell you."

"That's all right," Bosphor said. "I need you to do me a favor."

"What kind?"

"I need to talk to Uncle Timmy right away," Bosphor said. "Tell him you've found someone new who wants to give him money."

"What are you talking about?" she asked, sounding bewildered. "I don't know how to find him. How would I even know that?"

"He called and arranged this morning's meeting, right?" Bosphor said. "That means you've got a contact number."

"But what if he doesn't—? Please, Agent Bosphor, this is crazy. Even if I find him, he'll never believe me."

"You need to make sure he does," Bosphor said, letting his tone go dark. "It's important."

She sighed audibly. "All right. I'll...try."

"Thank you," Bosphor said. "Let me know when you've arranged a meeting."

An hour later, she called to tell Bosphor that Timmy had agreed to the meeting, and gave him the place and time. By then Kirby had found the Rowland Liberty link to the hunting guns that Bosphor had known would be there. An hour after that, Bosphor slipped out of his office and headed to the place Linda had specified.

Hoping fervently that he wasn't too late.

Given the disturbingly wide range of the victims' descriptions, Bosphor had no idea what to expect. It was therefore something of a surprise, perhaps even a bit of a disappointment, to find a rather ordinary-looking man waiting for him at the deserted end of the park. With his dark hair and ruddy face, his white-flecked beard and cheerful eyes, he had the look of a man who'd spent his life making a living and collecting friends. Not exactly the smooth, refined look most con men nurtured.

He was also undoubtedly not alone. Any of the bushes, stands of waist-high flowering grasses, or clumps of trees offered good possibilities for a concealed sniper or two. Con men as successful as Timmy didn't spend five years on PCE's radar without taking precautions.

"Uncle Timmy?" Bosphor asked as he walked up to the bench.

"Yes," the man said, cocking his head to study his visitor. "Agent Bosphor, I presume." His eyes flicked around. "You came alone?"

"Every bit as alone as you are."

Timmy smiled, his whole face crinkling behind the beard. "Touché," he said. "Linda said you were a clever one. Please; sit down."

"So Linda *was* working for you," Bosphor said as he lowered himself onto the other end of the bench. "I had a feeling she was."

"Did you figure that out before or after she arranged this meeting?"

"Before, actually," Bosphor said. "Though it wasn't until I ran her bank records half an hour ago that I confirmed she was transferring other people's money to you in the café this morning and not hers."

"Interesting," Timmy murmured. "I thought I'd covered that. Yes, she's been with me from the beginning. And don't bother to call it in. She's safely beyond PCE's reach."

"I'm not here to rain fire on you or your people," Bosphor said. "Even if there was anyone left in the district for me to call."

"Really?" Timmy asked, his face and tone gone all innocent. "Where could they all be?"

"I think you know," Bosphor said grimly. "I came here to tell you to call it off. Now."

"Or?"

"Or someone's going to get killed," Bosphor said. "And if they do, you're the one who'll go down for it."

Timmy shook his head. "I think you're laboring under a misapprehension, Agent Bosphor."

"Am I?" Bosphor retorted. "Bad enough that you dangled your little escape con game in front of people and gave them false hope. Bad enough that you took all their money. But this is way over even those lines. To buy guns and send people off to try to hijack a freighter—"

"Whoa," Timmy interrupted, holding up his hands palms outward. "Who said I gave anyone any guns?"

"Oh, stop it," Bosphor growled. "We found the link to the Rowland Liberty account. You ordered the guns from General Merch. How the *hell* did you talk people into wasting their lives like that?"

"I don't know if I'd call it a *waste*," Timmy said. "There are a lot of people out there willing to take a chance to be free from the Benevolent Uncle's boot."

"This isn't a chance," Bosphor bit out. "This is a slaughter. The defenses are already in place around the spaceports, with fighters and helos stretched out twenty kilometers. I don't know what this part of the game is, but the people you're sending into that meat grinder haven't got a chance."

"And so they shouldn't even try?"

"When the end is absolutely certain death, no, they shouldn't," Bosphor said. "Especially when all they're doing is providing a distraction so that you can slip away in the confusion with the rest of their money."

Timmy blinked. "Is *that* what you think this is about?"

"I took another look at the templates stolen from the document office," Bosphor said. "One of them was authorization for offworld frozen-cargo shipments. I figure it shouldn't be hard to rig something that looks like it's running subzero temps while still staying warm and cozy in the middle."

"Really, Agent Bosphor," Timmy said reproachfully, waving

at his ample girth. "Do you really see all *this* squeezing into a packing crate?"

"This isn't a laughing matter."

"It will be in a minute," Timmy assured him.

"Listen—"

"There aren't any guns," Timmy cut him off.

The rest of Bosphor's threat caught in his throat. "What?"

"There aren't any guns," Timmy repeated. "There never were."

"What the hell are you talking about? I saw the order."

"Oh, there's an order, all right," Timmy said. "But it was nothing more than a paper trail we set up to kick the Council into scrambling everything they had to defend the spaceports that we're supposed to storm and the freighters we're supposed to steal. Provided the troops don't accidentally shoot each other, no one's going to get hurt, let alone killed."

"Lovely," Bosphor growled. "So you didn't even have to drop any of the money on guns. You get to leave with all six million?"

"It was closer to seven million, actually," Timmy said. "And, well—" He pursed his lips. "Well, yes. I guess, technically, we *are* leaving with it."

Bosphor stared at him. The man *seemed* rational enough, and a madman could hardly have conned so many people. But what had started as a straightforward con game was suddenly not making any sense at all.

"As I said, you're going to laugh," Timmy continued, staring back with the same intensity that Bosphor was giving him. "But a question first, if I may. I said there were people willing to risk everything for freedom. What about you, Agent Bosphor? What are *you* willing to risk?"

"Are you trying to con me?" Bosphor demanded.

"You're the one who told Linda you wanted in," Timmy reminded him. "But no, I'm not talking about a buy-in. The whole reason you're here is to talk me out of wasting lives. That tells me you care about the people of this world. That, plus you didn't turn Linda in when you knew you were supposed to. So if you want to come, you're welcome."

A cold knot formed in the center of Bosphor's gut. "It's not a diversion," he breathed. "You really *are* going to try to steal a freighter."

"Good heavens, no," Timmy said, sounding scandalized. "We

agreed we don't want to get people killed, remember? Besides, why would we try to grab a ship? We already have one."

"You—?" Bosphor broke off. "You *what*?"

"Where do you think the seven million went?" Timmy asked. "We bought a ship, piece by piece, and spent the past five years putting it together. Not entirely from scratch, of course," he amended. "We started with the hulk from the Djeven crash. The thing's not pretty, but my people assure me it'll get us where we want to go."

"You built a ship," Bosphor said, still trying to wrap his brain around that. A small fact tapped his shoulder—"The freighter liftoff permission form. *That's* what you broke into the documents office for."

"Exactly," Timmy said. "We just took the others to muddy the waters. You haven't answered my question. Do you want to come with us?"

"If I say no?"

"We say good-bye and go our separate ways," Timmy said.

"What if I don't let you go yours?"

"Is that a threat?"

"It's a question."

Timmy shrugged slightly, the first hint of concern creeping onto his face. "Then my people leave."

"Without you?"

"They have their instructions," Timmy said. "This is our one and only chance, while all of the Benevolent Uncle's gunships are busy guarding the spaceports. By the time anyone notices that our ship is lifting from somewhere besides an official field, it'll be too late for them to get enough firepower out here to stop us."

"It's still going to be for nothing," Bosphor said. "Even if you make it off New Vipitti, no other world in the region will take you in. Everyone within reasonable range has strict refugee laws."

"Don't worry about that," Timmy said. "We have a lot of professionals aboard, with good and highly marketable skills. We'll work out something. Once we're into the general population, we'll be able to blend in and disappear."

"Maybe," Bosphor said. "But you're going to be a bit higher on everyone's radar than the rest of your people. The government won't like you talking about them."

"All the more reason for me to go," Timmy said. "The Benevolent

Uncle's stranglehold relies on neighboring systems turning a blind eye to what he's doing. The less they're able to pretend they don't see anything, the faster New Vipitti will be free again."

He raised his eyebrows. "That might happen even faster with a former PCE agent along to confirm our stories of the government's abuse of power."

Bosphor snorted. Finally; there it was. "So *that's* why you offered me a spot? Because you need me?"

"Don't you want to be needed?"

"I don't want to be used," Bosphor said. "You've used too many people. I won't be one of them."

"Good," Timmy said gravely. "Because you won't be. I'm offering you a spot because you have integrity, and because you care about your people and your world."

"And because you need a PCE agent's voice."

Timmy's face crinkled in another smile. "Actually, we already have two PCE agents," he said. "No, Agent Bosphor. We want you solely for yourself. No strings, no obligations." He cocked his head. "The question is whether you have too much pride to accept a free gift."

Bosphor smiled back. He'd warned Linda about false hope. False pride was an equally dangerous affliction. "Not at all," he said. "Besides, I figure the story will play better with *three* agents telling it."

Bill Zielke, Uncle Timmy's pilot, was not only highly competent, but also had a flair for the dramatic. As he took the crowded ship around on its spiral path toward freedom, he ran their vector so as to make New Vipitti create a brief eclipse of the sun.

"Let's hope we can take the Benevolent Uncle's reign into its own eclipse," Timmy commented. He frowned at Bosphor. "What's so funny?"

"I just realized something," Bosphor said. "You really *are* a con man, aren't you? Except that you weren't conning these people. You were conning everyone else."

Uncle Timmy chuckled. "I told you you'd laugh."

"Yes," Bosphor agreed. "You did say that."

And so, for the first time in months, he did.

❧

## Timothy Zahn

My first recollection of Uncle Timmy was meeting him at the 1982 Kubla Khan in Nashville. He was hanging out, as always, with a bunch of friends—you were always one of Timmy's friends, whether you'd known him twenty years or twenty minutes—and we all got to talking. Anna and I were new to the whole convention thing, and when the conversation turned to conventions he told us about Chattacon and invited us to come down to next year's extravaganza.

We were interested, of course, but in those days I was a very struggling author and discretionary money was a pretty thin. That didn't bother Timmy. He simply made a point, over the next few months, to offer some quiet assistance in that area. We did indeed make the 1983 Chattacon, followed by many more; and when Timmy started LibertyCon we were ready, able, and enthusiastically willing to once again make the journey to Chattanooga (and to join the tradition of Chinese Blizzards).

Oh, and I was wrong earlier about everyone being Timmy's friend. Somewhere along the line, so smoothly that we never noticed the transition, we were upgraded from just being friends to being family.

Because that, too, was Uncle Timmy's way.

—Timothy Zahn

**Timothy Zahn** is a Hugo award winner and author of the #1 *New York Times* bestseller *Heir to the Empire* and several other novels in the Star Wars universe. Born in Chicago, Zahn earned a B.S. in physics from Michigan State University and an M.S. in physics from the University of Illinois. He sold his first story to *Analog* magazine in 1978 and immediately attracted attention as a new writer of science fiction based on real, cutting-edge science. Other Zahn works include the Conquerer and Dragonback series and now the Manticore Ascendant series, cowritten with David Weber. He is a frequent and popular guest at Star Wars and other conventions. His author page on Facebook has received over 50,000 likes and can be visited at http://www.facebook.com/TimothyZahn.

# AN ARIZONA WEREMYSTE IN CHATTANOOGA

David B. Coe is an accomplished writer of epic, historical, and urban fantasy. He is erudite, intelligent,
and passionate about his writing, the writing process,
his family, and the world. He is great on a panel,
fun at the bar but, most of all, just a great guy.
Who, I am compelled to say, has never turned in a
manuscript late to me. He is local to the Southeast,
and one of those people without whom LibertyCon
would not be the same. I'm very glad to bring to
you this story featuring one of my favorite fantasy
detectives, set in a world that I got to publish first.
—TW

# An Arizona Weremyste in Chattanooga

## David B. Coe

Stepping out of the terminal at Chattanooga's Lovell Field was like diving into a bowl of soup. The air was so hot and thick it was barely breathable. I sweated through my shirt long before I found my rental car and could crank up the AC. And we were halfway through September.

I was used to heat. I'd lived in Phoenix all my life. This was different, and far worse. I'd always laughed at people who dismissed Arizona temperatures with a facile "Yeah, but it's a dry heat." Slogging through that parking lot, though, searching for the white Corolla with Tennessee plates I'd be driving for the next few days, I had to admit that those people had a point.

I carried a license for the firearms still packed away in the strong box I'd checked through from Sky Harbor Airport. I carried a PI's license as well, although it was issued in Arizona and didn't really do me any good here in Tennessee. And, of course, I had a license to drive this gutless little car I was about to steer off the lot. The only thing I didn't have a license to do was cast spells. Not that I'd let that stop me.

I was a weremyste, like my father before me, and had been since I was a gangly adolescent messing with powers I didn't quite understand. I could conjure in a hundred different ways. And during a phasing—the full moon and the nights before and after—I succumbed to moon-induced madness: a psychological hellscape of delusion, paranoia, and hallucination. I was scheduled to fly home no later than the day before the phasing began. I really hoped I wouldn't have to extend my stay.

77

Most of my investigations were confined to Phoenix. Every so often, I needed to drive into a neighboring state—Utah, New Mexico, California. Once I drove down into Mexico for the three days of the phasing. That was wild. Buy me a couple of shots of tequila—the good stuff, please; Don Julio 1942 or one of the high-end Patróns—and I'll be happy to tell you all about it.

Trips as far from home as Chattanooga, Tennessee were rare for me. Jobs like this one—for clients I'd never met, offering me scads of money to take on inquiries I didn't know anything about and wasn't legally sanctioned to conduct—were rarer still. But I couldn't afford to turn down pay equal to all my earnings from last year. And, I'll admit, the mystery surrounding the offer intrigued me. Billie Castle, my partner, girlfriend, significant other, or whatever the current term was, thought I was nuts for taking on this case, even after I told her how much I'd be making. Of course, that didn't stop her from ordering me to bring her back a box of MoonPies and a fifth of Gentleman Jack.

I realized I was being watched the moment I left the terminal, but at first I didn't do anything about it. My trackers were a young couple in a silver sedan. Art on his neck and bare arms, sunglasses masking his eyes; she had short, dark hair, art on one bare shoulder, and sunglasses as well. Nothing, though, could hide the telltale blur of their faces. They were weremystes, like me. They tried to pretend they weren't interested in what I was doing; he checked his phone and adjusted his mirrors while she fiddled with the car stereo. I wasn't fooled for a minute. This was my profession, and I was much better at it than these two. I walked on to the car rental lot, but I never lost track of them, even after they circled the lot, appearing to anticipate my destination.

I got into my car, made my own adjustments to the seat and mirrors. And when I was ready to drive out, I cast my spell. Three elements, as easy as you please: their front tire, an invisible nail, and, to power the spell, the heat rising from the baked asphalt. I heard the blowout from where I sat. Heard him swearing as well. I was laughing as I left the lot.

Once I was on the road, my drive didn't take long. My client, Colonel Kevin Fotovich, lived in a gated community west of the airport—he had sent me the gate code ahead of time. This late in the day, I had to contend with some traffic, though nothing like what I was used to in Phoenix. Within a half hour, I was climbing out of the car in front of a home that would have fit in with the most expensive mansions of Scottsdale or Paradise Valley.

The man who walked out to greet me was nothing like what I expected. I'll admit it: Tennessee, colonel, money—I figured a guy in a white suit with a black string tie and a taste for fried chicken.

The problem was, I had little else to go on. Fotovich had managed to avoid media attention, despite his money and military career, and he had no social media presence to speak of. I tried to do my homework before getting on the plane, but could find next to nothing about him. A couple of mentions in articles about his philanthropic work, and others mentioning his retirement from the military, but that was all. He paid the first half of my fee with a bank transfer, the money securely in my account before I left home. No information, no glitches. To be honest, it made me a little suspicious.

The colonel was hale, tall, broad in the shoulders. He carried a cane and walked with a limp, and his hair had as much silver as red. In every other way, though, he looked more like a retired football player than a patrician cliché. I would have liked to get a good look at his face, but that was the other surprising thing about him: Like the mystes at the airport, his features were obscured by magic.

I could judge a lot from the degree of blur in a weremyste's face. Neither of the two I'd left at Lovell Field with a flat tire had been particularly powerful. The blur on Colonel Fotovich was much more pronounced. I had a vague sense of his appearance: clean shaven, square-jawed, eyes of hazel or brown. Mostly, though, I saw power. This guy had some serious mojo.

Given the amount he was paying me for "consultation," as his emails had put it, and the urgency of his invitation to fly east, I had assumed he was desperate for magical help. Seeing him now, I wondered what I could offer in that realm that he couldn't provide himself.

"Mister Fearsson," he said, extending a strong hand.

"Colonel Fotovich. Please call me Jay."

"And I prefer Fritz. Come in."

He motioned me up the stone stairway leading to his door. I followed him, glancing toward the garden and the distant river— the Tennessee, I assumed—which was gilded by late-day sunlight.

The foyer gleamed, its white marble floors reflecting light from an enormous crystal chandelier that probably cost more than my car. Beyond the entry was a living room that dwarfed my entire home. Wood floors, tasteful art, furniture that should have been roped off like pieces in a museum. I wished I'd asked for a larger retainer.

"This is a beautiful house."

"Thank you," he said, sounding uncomfortable rather than flattered. He offered me a drink—I accepted water—and asked me about my flight and the drive over. Small talk. I could tell he was stalling, and also that he was as intrigued by the blur of my face as I was by the smudge of his. We were like unfamiliar dogs sizing each other up, unsure yet of whether to bare our teeth and flatten our ears.

As we talked, I wandered the living room, sipping my water. Military memorabilia and antiques adorned the walls. Old firearms, what looked like Civil War–era sabers, a framed, tattered U.S. flag with forty-five stars. I wondered what war it was from. At one point I found a framed picture of a younger Fotovich in uniform. And beside it, also framed, a purple heart and silver star mounted on black velvet.

"You were in the Gulf War?" I asked over my shoulder.

"Beirut, a decade earlier."

I didn't know what to say. I had heard about the bombing of the Marine barracks, and the horrors of the aftermath. I could hardly imagine what this man had been through and what he might have had to endure to earn that medal.

"I'm...I'm sorry."

He opened his hand in a small gesture. "Thank you." Again, I sensed that he didn't want to have this conversation. "Finish that water and have a beer with me."

That was an order I could follow. He opened two bottles from a brewery I'd never heard of—wheat beers, good ones—and led me to a glassed-in room that offered an even better view of the river than I'd had outside.

We sat, and for a few minutes neither of us said a word. At last, I shifted in my seat.

"Colonel—"

"Fritz."

"Yes, sir. You offered me a lot of money, flew me out here

despite the fact that I'm not licensed in Tennessee, and managed to hide the fact that you're a weremyste. It wasn't to have a beer with me. And with the full moon coming, neither of us wants me to stay much past next Tuesday. So why don't you tell me what this is about and let me get to work?"

My eyes had adjusted some to the effect of his magic, allowing me to see his wry grin through the blur. "Spoken like your father's son."

I had been raising the bottle to my lips again, but I stopped, staring at him. "You know my father?"

"He worked my wife's murder back in the late '90s and, once he was convinced I didn't do it, we became... maybe not friends, but cordial acquaintances. It was one of his last cases before he lost your mom. He was a good cop, a good man. How is he?"

"About like you'd expect for an old weremyste," I said.

He winced, needing no more of an answer. Old weremystes tended to be crazy weremystes. Those phasings—monthly descents into insanity—took a toll over the course of a lifetime. My dad wasn't helped by his alcoholism, or by the trauma and scandal of my mother's death. I found myself wondering how this man—who must have been in his mid-sixties—had remained sane for this long. Assuming he had.

"I started taking blockers several years ago," he said, as if I'd asked the question. "That's why I'm better off than he is."

I nodded, on my guard now. "What I can I do for you, Colonel?" I asked again.

He didn't correct me this time. "Find my daughter."

"You think someone's taken her?"

"No, I wouldn't say that."

It wasn't hard to do the math in my head. "Forgive me, Colonel, but I'm guessing she's too old to be considered a runaway. So if she hasn't been kidnapped—"

"She's caught up in dark magic, Mister Fearsson. You of all people should understand the danger."

It seemed my reputation had spread east of the Mississippi. Over the past year or so I'd had more than my share of run-ins with weremancers and their friends. As he said, I knew the danger, better than most people. "Yes, I do."

"Then you also understand why I need your help. The police won't get involved for the reasons you've already mentioned. And

I'm not the most popular member of the runecrafting community here in Chattanooga."

"Why is that?"

He took a long pull of beer and set the bottle on the table beside his chair. After eyeing me for a moment, he stood and walked to the window. "The magical community here is controlled by two runecrafters: Randy Walker and Elayna Little Cook. They're good people, and they're as vigilant in their opposition to dark craftings as anyone. A few years ago, though, they asked to use this property as a sort of refuge, a place for weremystes to gather on the nights of the phasing." He faced me. "We're a small community, and we're feared throughout this city. Many runecrafters in Chattanooga—and throughout the South—are shunned by their families, at least on those nights when their minds are weakest. They're certainly not welcomed or even tolerated in public parks and the like. Fear of magic and witchcraft runs deep in this part of the world, Mister Fearsson. It's not easy for our kind anywhere, but here in particular..." He trailed off, lifting a shoulder and letting it drop.

"You refused their request?"

"You have to understand, I had just started taking blockers. I was trying to get away from the phasings. I didn't want to spend my last years..." He looked away.

"Like my father."

"I didn't mean—"

"It's all right. Go on."

"Yes, I turned them down. They accused me of being a traitor to all runecrafters. Some of their followers threatened me, said they would use their power to make my life a living hell. Randy even suggested that by refusing I was helping dark runecrafters spread their influence."

"So it didn't help that your daughter was using dark spells herself."

"Actually, at the time, she wasn't. That came later, long after I'd become a pariah." He hesitated, but not for long. "The worst came when another local runecrafter was assaulted during a phasing. This was two years ago. Almost three now. A young man—his parents ordered him from the house, and he wound up taking shelter in Coolidge Park downtown. In the middle of the phasing, he was ranting, acting strange, and a group of...I don't know. Someone. They were young, stupid, drunk. He scared them and so they beat him. He wound up in a wheelchair. Randy, Elayna, and the others blamed me."

I sipped my beer, considering what he'd told me. On the one hand, I sympathized with his decision. If I had chosen to take blockers, to give up runecrafting for a life without the phasings, I'm not sure I would choose to have dozens of crazed weremystes descend on my property every full moon. On the other hand, the guy had a huge property and resources beyond imagining.

"Tell me about your daughter."

"Nora—that's her name. Nora Pieper. She's divorced with a couple of kids. She kept the last name for their sake. She's headstrong and fiercely independent. After her mother died . . . she and I butted heads a lot. She moved out as soon as she could. She keeps in touch, again for the sake of her children, and for me as well, I suppose. But we barely speak."

"How do you know she's involved with dark magic?"

He slanted a glance my way, his expression turning guarded. "I know."

"Do you have runecrafters spying on your behalf, Colonel? Were the man and woman I spotted at the airport working for you?"

Alarm sharpened his gaze. "You were followed?"

"No. I'd imagine they're still waiting for Triple A. They weren't yours?"

The colonel shook his head. "You need to be careful. To answer your question, I do have runecrafters working for me, keeping tabs on Nora. She's involved with a dark conjurer."

"A weremancer," I said. "Do you know his name, or anything about him?"

"Matthew Fanny. He's an investment consultant in the city. He makes decent money, drives a pricey car, and he likes to play with blood magic and rituals that are more frightening than anything I ever tried, even in my youth."

"It sounds like you know a lot about him. Why fly me out here?"

"Because you solved the Blind Angel case. Because you've taken on dark runecrafters and lived to tell about it."

"There may be nothing I can do. She's breaking no laws." Even as I said this, I wondered if the runemyste, Namid—Namid'skemu, the reincarnated spirit of an ancient A'shiwi shaman, who had been my magical mentor for more than a decade—would disagree. As far as I knew, she'd broken no laws of the non-magical world. Magical law, though, was an entity unto itself.

"She's harming herself," Fritz said. "She might be harming her children. And depending on where she and her friends get their blood, she might well be breaking a slew of laws. I can't explain all of this to the local police, but surely you can appreciate the stakes here."

The truth was, I could. I asked him a few more questions, got his daughter's address and a few suggestions as to where I might find Walker and Cook, and left him with a promise to be in touch as soon as I had more information.

A brief check of an online map told me that a bar the colonel mentioned as a weremyste hangout—the Moon Flower—was only a stone's throw from Coolidge Park. I took that coincidence as a sign, and drove into the city through a sudden and intense thunderstorm. I parked just off Frazier Avenue, near that omnipresent river, and walked to the bar. The street smelled of lightning, fresh rain, and motor oil, all underlaid with the slight sour of dead fish and thick mud. Clouds of cigarette smoke hung over clusters of people huddled outside in the lingering drizzle.

The Moon Flower reminded me of the New Moon, a weremyste bar I frequented back home. My kind weren't all that imaginative with names for our hangouts, mostly because we wanted them to be easy for people to find. Ours were insular communities. Despite what the colonel had said, prejudice against weremystes ran deep just about everywhere. Simply having a bar of our own could make a big difference in the life of a runecrafter. This one was a little classier than the New Moon, but it still smelled of cooking grease and stale beer. The Allman Brothers' "In Memory of Elizabeth Reed" played through the overhead speakers.

I sat at the bar and placed a crisp twenty on the polished wood. The bartender, a tall black woman with short, tightly curled hair and a pronounced blur to her features, eyed the money and then me.

"Can I get a beer?" I asked. "Whatever IPA you have on draft."

She made no move to take the bill. "Where are you from?"

"Visiting from out of town."

Through the magical blur I saw her quirk an eyebrow. "Not really what I asked."

"Phoenix," I said. "I'm in town on business."

She didn't reply, not even to nod. But she picked up the twenty, pulled a beer for me, and set it down on the bar, along with my change.

As she started to turn her back on me, I said, "I was wondering if you know—"

"Don't." The look she gave me could have frosted my glass. "You're here from out of town. Leave it at that."

The threat was as naked as a blade. "Or?"

"Just leave it at that."

I held her gaze while sipping my beer.

"This is good. Thanks."

She dipped her chin and broke eye contact, her glance flicking to something, or someone, behind me.

I tensed and placed my glass on the bar once more. I turned slowly, not wanting to provoke anything before I read the situation. A smart move, probably my first since entering the bar.

There were six of them, arrayed around me in a tight arc. Two I recognized from the airport. Magically speaking, they were the weakest of their gang. The faces of the others—three women and a man—were smeared beyond recognition. All of them were tall, muscular, and bearing art of one sort or another. I whispered a warding spell, felt magic settle over me like a cloak. I figured my new friends were warded as well. I didn't think I should test the theory.

"Hi," I said, fixing a smile on my lips. "Can I help you?" Before any of them could answer, I turned to the couple from the airport. "Sorry about your tire."

"Bullshit," the woman said.

"Finish your beer," said one of the other women, her words shaded by a slight Southern accent. It only occurred to me then that Colonel Fotovich hadn't sounded Southern at all. "And then go home."

"Well, home tonight is a Hampton Inn, but that sounds like..."

I trailed off. She was shaking her head. "Go home," she said again. "No Hampton Inn, no stops at all. Just get on a plane and go home."

"I'm afraid I can't do that. Someone paid me a great deal of money to come here, and I haven't finished my work for him."

"You're on the wrong side of this, Fearsson, and you're going to get hurt."

I narrowed my eyes. First the colonel knew my dad, and now these people knew my name, though I was sure I'd never met any of them.

"How do you—"

"Leave Chattanooga. Leave Tennessee. You're not welcome here. That's all you need to do, and all you need to know."

I eyed each of them, turned slightly to take a long drink of my beer and return the glass to the bar, and then faced them again. This was not going to end well; all of us knew it. I thought my best bet was to use an attack spell on the couple from the airport and hope I could break through their line there once those two were down.

Before I could cast, I felt a whisper of magic on my skin. The next thing I knew, I was pummeled to the floor by a series of attack spells. I didn't think any of them did what the mystes intended—my warding held. But they pounded on my magical shields like two-by-fours, leaving me addled. Before I could recover, two of the mystes grabbed my arms and hoisted me to my feet. I saw the punch coming, but could do nothing to defend myself. The impact left me dazed. The second brought darkness.

The smells reached me first: stale beer and fried food. I was still in the bar, or at least in the building. I opened my eyes to dim yellowish light and wood paneling, an old leather couch that stank of cigarettes and whispered conversations that ended as I stirred.

"Have some water," a woman said.

I sat up, winced. My stomach turned an uneasy somersault. I regarded a glass sitting on a low wooden coffee table, and then the woman sitting opposite me. She was the one person I didn't recognize from before. Shoulder-length wheaten hair and another face hazed by powerful magic. She wore a business suit, elegant jewelry, shoes with a Gucci logo. I was guessing they weren't knockoffs.

I dropped my gaze to the glass again.

"If we wanted you dead, you'd be dead. The water's fine."

She had a point. I drank it all, my jaw aching, but my stomach settling. When I was finished, the woman reached forward, took the glass from me, and held it up for one of the other weremystes, who carried it from the room. In a room filled with runecrafters, a good tumbler could be a lethal weapon. The weremyste returned a moment later, the opening of the door letting in the bar's din.

"I take it you're Nora Pieper," I said, my voice thick.

"That's right."

"You father's looking for you."

"No, he's not."

The other weremystes in the room watched me. I was adjusting to the blur of their features, and I could see that they considered me with unveiled contempt. I assumed my warding was still in place, though being knocked unconscious could do weird things to protective spells. I didn't dare conjure again, though. I thought it likely that at the first brush of magic these folks would unleash every ounce of their power.

I faced Pieper again. "I realize that you might not want to see him, Ms. Pieper, but—"

"My father's dead, Mr. Fearsson."

That stopped me short. For about ten seconds—which is a long time when facing down dark conjurers—I could think of nothing to say.

At last, I found my voice. Sort of. "I saw him just— What happened?"

"What did he tell you?"

I glanced at the others again, drawing a thin smile from Pieper.

"It's all right," she said. "I have some idea. You won't be punished for telling me the truth."

"All right," I said, exhaling the words. "He told me he was worried about you. He believes—believed—you're caught up in blood magic, that a man you're involved with has turned you toward dark conjuring."

"That's all?"

At my hesitation, she said, "He's dead, Mr. Fearsson. Certainly there's no further need for secrecy."

"His death doesn't end my professional obligation to him."

"The confidentiality of your conversations with a client."

"Exactly."

"And what if that client was lying to you the entire time?"

"You deny that—"

She smirked. "My denials have nothing to do with it. Though yes, I do." She indicated one of the weremystes, a tall man with brown hair and biceps the size of my thighs. "This is Matthew, my fiancé. The man who allegedly led me astray. I'd guess you were told he works in investment, because that makes him sound heartless. He handles finances for a local university, helping them manage their endowment." She indicated the others in turn. "You recognize Ann Davis and Mark Paulk from the airport. Ann is a schoolteacher, when she's not following private detectives and changing tires. Mark is an EMT. This—" She pointed to a woman, tall and willowy, her black hair streaked with blue, her eyes ghostly pale. "This is Leigh Smith. Leigh runs a shelter for battered women in one of the rural counties outside the city." She waved a hand at the last two. "Elayna and Randy, who are probably the most influential conjurers in this area, are both priests in the Episcopal Church.

"None of these people is into dark magic, and neither am I. They contribute to their community, they do their best to improve the lives of other people. Several of them have families. All of them are my friends."

"Your father didn't say that all of them were doing blood magic. He said only that he was a pariah in the magical community, and couldn't turn to them for help. The only two he accused of being dark conjurers were you and Matthew."

"Interesting," she said. "According to him, he and I are estranged. He and the magical community are alienated from each other. The poor man's an island. Didn't any of this strike you as odd, or convenient, or contrived?"

I stared back at her. By now, I'd adjusted to the effect of her magic and could see her face more clearly. She had a straight nose, high cheekbones, full lips, small lines around her green eyes. She was attractive, but severe.

She was also right. I had accepted Colonel Fotovich's story without question. Was that because he was rich, or a veteran, or a weremyste, or an old white guy, or all of those things?

"It should have struck me that way," I admitted. I lifted a shoulder. "He flew me out here, he paid me a lot of money, he went to great lengths to secure my help. I just assumed... But I have to tell you Ms. Pieper, your father's concern for you—"

"That wasn't my father," she said, her voice rising and shaking slightly. "My father has been dead for more than a month."

Again, I had no idea what to say. Except, "Then who did I meet today?"

She blew out a breath, trying to compose herself. "We're not entirely certain. He looks and sounds and acts much like my father did. We believe he's... some malign magical entity who's taken my father's place."

"And how did your father die?"

"We don't know that either." She continued to meet my gaze, as if daring me not to believe her.

The truth was, I didn't know what to believe.

The smile that flickered across her face conveyed so much: grief, frustration, resignation.

"You think I'm lying."

"I'm a little lost, to be honest. I'm trying to make sense of it. If what you're telling me is true, why would this... this entity bring me here to find you?"

"A fine question. I have no answer. My friends believe he sees you as a potential ally. They point to your recent victories over dark magic as proof of your ambition. You're not a hero, they tell me; you're a rising power. Someone we should fear. Someone we need to stop. You're not making the world safer so much as clearing the field of potential rivals."

I actually laughed. I couldn't help it. Over the last year, I'd nearly gotten myself killed more times than I could count, each time at the hands of some dark magical force—weremancers, a necromancer, the Blind Angel Killer. To think that I was in their league, much less in league with them... It was ridiculous. And yet, I understood how someone could make that leap. The magical world was at war with itself, identities shadowed on both sides. Rampant paranoia was just one of many unintended consequences.

"You think this is funny?" asked Davis, the woman from the airport. She sounded truly pissed.

I sobered quickly. "There's nothing funny about what Ms. Pieper has been through, or about her father's death. But the idea that I'm some vengeful dark runecrafter taking out potential rivals so that I can conquer the world? Yeah, that's amusing, not to mention totally insane."

She bristled, as did others in the room. I turned to Randy Walker and Elayna Cook, the two the colonel, or whoever he was, had identified as the leaders of the local magical community.

"Why do you think the colonel was killed?"

They exchanged glances.

"We wouldn't know."

"I'm asking your opinion. I'm not accusing you of anything." Before they could answer, I went on. "Look, I came here under the impression that I was tracking down dark runecrafters. All of you think the same of me. That's probably not a coincidence. Someone wants us at odds. Maybe they want us at war. In which case, we might all be better off trying to trust one another."

Davis and most of the others didn't appear to be moved by this. Walker and Cook, though, shared another look.

"You want us to say he was killed for this," Cook said. "To get you here and force a conflict. I'm not sure I believe that."

"I don't want you to say anything. But yes, that possibility crossed my mind." I considered the question myself, trying to put together all they had told me, and all I had gleaned from my conversation with Pieper's "father."

"I should have asked this earlier. How powerful a runecrafter was your father?"

Pieper shook her head. "Not very. He could cast a few spells. Nothing truly challenging. And in recent years, as his mind started to go, he lost even that. He was most valuable to the community here for his wealth, and his property, which could have been a haven for us during the phasings."

That, at least, had been the truth. But the rest...

"So he wasn't taking blockers?"

She frowned and shook her head. "Not that I knew of."

The blur I'd seen on Fotovich had been that of an accomplished weremyste—not at all the man she was describing. No one with that much power who didn't take blockers could have maintained his sanity so late in life. The man I'd met today was no ordinary runecrafter.

I didn't think of myself as a power, as someone important enough to draw the notice of others in the magical world. But maybe I was being naïve. The necromancer Saorla had done her best to destroy me, and her followers still harassed me, months after her death. Long ago, Namid, and the Runeclave to which he belonged, had decided I was worthy of attention and training. Maybe blood-magic users here in the Southeast had come to the same conclusion.

"The weremyste—or whatever he was—who I talked to today had some serious power," I said. "He couldn't hide it."

"Meaning what?"

"I'm not sure yet. Why would runecrafters using blood magic be interested in you and your father?"

"I don't know," Pieper said. "My father was very wealthy, which, I suppose, means I am as well. Neither of us is particularly skilled with magic."

"You have power," I said. "I can see it."

She canted her head, acknowledging this. "Maybe, but not enough to draw the kind of attention you're asking about."

"What about after the beating?" Cook asked her. "That might have been enough to draw some notice."

The tension in the room ticked up a notch.

Pieper weighed this and turned back to me. "She's right."

"He told me about this," I said. "The one posing as your father. A weremyste was beaten by a mob during a phasing, right? Wound up paralyzed?"

"It wasn't during a phasing. And it wasn't a mob. Nearly two years ago, a weremyste was attacked in Coolidge Park. Yes, he was beaten, but he was also attacked with spells. His back was broken, and that was the least of his injuries. He was in a coma for six weeks. He never woke up."

"And after?"

"After, we took steps to guard against similar attacks. We started keeping tabs on those we suspected of using blood spells. And we managed to drive a few of them out of this area. They're still out there, of course, probably terrorizing some other city. But we wanted them gone, if for no other reason than to honor Rory, his memory and his sacrifice."

"And you were involved in this effort?" I asked her.

"She led it," Walker said before she could answer. "She's been great."

Others in the room echoed this.

"That could be it, then," I said. "That might be why this... this being wants to pit us against each other. We're both enemies of dark powers and their weremancers. I managed to defeat a necromancer in the Southwest not so long ago. You've had some success here. They're weakened. And maybe they saw an opportunity to weaken our side with minimal risk to theirs. They don't care which of us wins, because either way they gain."

"'Our side'?" Pieper repeated. "Does this mean you believe me?"

"I do," I said. "And I'm terribly sorry for the loss of your father."

She nodded, seeming to struggle to hold my gaze. "Thank you."

"I'd like to help you. And I'd like to return the money I've been paid. It came from your father's fortune. It's yours."

A faint smile crossed her lips. "Again, thank you. We can talk about that when this is over. For now...Yes, I'd welcome your help."

Something loosened in the room, as if the truce she and I had just forged extended to the rest of them.

"Does either of you have an idea of what we should do?" Davis asked.

"Actually," I said, "I think I do."

Pieper slanted a look my way. "Give him what he wants?"

I grinned. "Exactly. He hired me to find you, to bring you back to him. Maybe that's just what we should do."

Nora's fiancé, it turned out, worked in theater when he wasn't doing finance. He contacted a friend who specialized in make-up effects, and together they made Nora and me look like we'd been through an epic magical battle. I got a bloody gash on my forehead and another across the side of my neck, just missing the jugular. It made me look like I was lucky to be alive.

They gave her cuts, bruises, a hideous slash across her thigh—ruining a perfectly good pair of slacks—and a ghastly burn on one side of her face.

We warded ourselves with as many shield spells as we think of, and we took the added precaution of placing wardings on each other. I had seen this guy's power written on his face; we weren't taking any chances.

Once we were shielded and looked suitably brutalized, I drove her back up to her father's mansion. The others followed us, at a distance and in separate cars. As we neared the house, I pulled out my phone and dialed his number. He picked up on the second ring.

"It's Fearsson," I said. "I have her and I'm almost there."

"You're bringing her here?"

"That's what you told me to do."

"No, I didn't! I wanted you to—"

"It doesn't matter. I have her, and we're almost there."

I hung up without waiting for him to say more.

Nora watched me from the backseat, our eyes meeting in the rearview mirror. Her face was a mess, and a different sort of pain lurked in her eyes.

"He wanted you to kill me."

"He's not your father. Not anymore. It doesn't matter what he sounds like."

She nodded.

"When we get there, I'll bear you in as if you can't walk, as if you're not even conscious. As the others arrive, we'll attack."

"Yes, all right."

By now we were close. She lay down on the backseat and I steered us into his driveway.

He stood at the door, the lights from within the house shadowing his face. I parked, got out of the car, and pulled Nora from the backseat. Draping her arm over my shoulder, I dragged her toward the house.

"You shouldn't have brought her here," he said, still standing in the doorway, blocking our way.

I continued toward him, nerves prickling. "What should I have done with her?"

He faltered. "You look terrible. Both of you. Is she even alive?"

"She's alive. But she put up a fight. She claims she's not involved with dark magic at all. Her fiancé said the same."

He looked past me to the car. "Where is he?"

"Dead. I killed him. Can you let me in? She's heavier than she looks."

After another moment, he backed into the house and let me pass. I took her to the living room and started to lie her down on a couch.

"Wait, let me get a blanket." He hurried away.

As his footsteps receded, Nora opened one eye. "I'm heavier than I look?" she whispered.

"Would you have been happier if I'd said she's not as heavy as she looks?"

We heard him returning, and she closed her eyes again. He covered the sofa and I set her down.

"You've got her back," I said, straightening. "Alive if not well. She should be fine before long. Just the ending you were hoping for, right?"

"Of course." He stared down at her.

"She accused me of using dark magic," I said. "Why would she do that if she was a dark runecrafter?"

His lips twitched, but his gaze didn't waver. "A ruse, I'm sure."

A car door closed outside the house and his gaze snapped to the nearest window.

"Who is that?"

"Now!"

I threw a spell at him that should have hit him like a baseball bat to the back of the head. I drew on the electricity in the walls—a trick I'd learned not so long ago—and I knew it worked because the lights in the room flickered and the nearest bulb exploded. I felt Nora's spell as well, a wave of magic that should have landed on him like an ocean breaker.

He didn't stagger or sway or even flinch. He turned back to us, the movement fluid and unhurried, and smiled in a way that chilled my blood. I was certain that the real Fritz Fotovich had never smiled that way in his life.

"Fools," he said, his voice level. "Children."

Nora climbed off the couch to stand beside me. "What did you do to my father, you son of a bitch?"

"Your father is gone. This body is mine now. He's better off, believe me. He was weak, old, near the end of a pitiful life. I'm none of those things."

"You bastard." Tears streamed down her face. I sensed her spell, though I couldn't tell what kind it was. It hardly mattered. The casting never touched him. He laughed.

Then he cast. The air around us crackled with power, the way it would just before a lightning strike. Magic smashed into me. I felt myself lifted off the floor, heard Nora cry out.

I hit a wall. Air left my body in a rush and my head snapped back against plaster. I collapsed to the floor.

My first clear thought was to wonder what his spell would have done to me if I hadn't been warded. My second was that I didn't want to chance a second assault.

"You haven't done any of this the way you were supposed to," Fotovich said, advancing on us.

The front door broke in and weremystes streamed into the house. The man—or whatever he was—turned, still in no hurry, and threw a spell at them. They went down like bowling pins.

Two slammed into the wall beside the door. Three others tumbled out onto the walkway.

He faced us again. "You're a great disappointment to me, Mister Fearsson. I thought I could at least count on you to kill the woman and her beau." He raised an eyebrow. "I take it that was a lie and he's alive."

"Why not do it yourself?" I asked.

"Why do you think? Power like mine draws attention. The last thing I need is a runemyste, like your friend Namid'skemu, growing curious."

"So you tried to set us against each other."

"That's right. It was worth a try to get one of you. But if I can kill you both, and her friends as well, that might be worth the risk of revealing myself."

Power feathered over me, my only warning. His spell scythed through my defenses like a winter wind through cotton. Pain flared in my chest, searing and sharp, as if he'd pierced skin and bone with a white-hot poker. I howled, clutched at my heart. But I clung to the image, imagined myself melting his steel with fire of my own. Again I pulled power from the wiring in the house, from the residue of the day's heat still radiating from the drive-way and the roof. I drew on everything I could, poured all my magic into the spell, knowing that if it failed I was a dead man.

The poker seemed to melt away. Fotovich growled his frustration.

Using those same sources as fuel, I cast again. Not a direct attack. I knew I didn't have the skill or power necessary to defeat him head on. Instead, I aimed my magic at the floor beneath him. A hole opened and he fell, was trapped up to his hips. A spell from Nora lifted a chair off the floor and dropped it on him. He bellowed, rage and pain in the sound. The chair exploded into fragments of wood and tufts of cloth and stuffing.

By then, though, I had grabbed one of the swords from the wall. Before he could cast again, I leapt at him, swung the blade like it was baseball bat.

His head flew free, collided with a lamp and knocked it over. Where it had been, there was no blood, no bone, no gore. The body was empty. Hot, putrid air swept up from the hollow, accompanied by an inhuman wail that spiraled, crested, and then faded.

Nora stared at the shell of what had been her father, fresh

tears cascading over her cheeks, horror etched on her face. Before I could say anything to comfort her, Matthew called her name from the door. They ran to each other and she threw her arms around him.

I tossed down the sword, closed my eyes briefly. Footsteps made me open them again. Nora had returned. Matthew had an arm around her, protective, still a little wary of me.

"I'm sorry," I said.

She shook her head. "Don't be. You did what you had to. I didn't want that . . . that thing in my father."

"Is it dead?" Matthew asked. "Did you kill it?"

"I don't think so. We drove it off, deprived it of the . . . well, for want of a better word, the 'vessel' it was using. But a power like that can't be killed with a normal blade."

"So it'll be back?"

"Maybe. It might return here or come after me in Phoenix. It might go elsewhere. We can't really know until it shows up again. Are you hurt?" I asked Nora.

"I'm fine. I'll be sore tomorrow, but nothing serious. You?"

"I'm all right. We were lucky."

She looked around the house, her gaze settling on the corpse. "Yes, I suppose we were."

The other weremystes joined us. A couple were hurt, but none seriously. They debated calling the police, but decided not to. This was weremyste business. They would handle it.

Eventually, Nora approached me again. "How long will you be staying in town?"

I shrugged. "I have an open ticket. Unless you need to me to stick around, I'll leave tomorrow."

"That's fine. And as for the money he paid you, there's no need for you to give it back."

"He paid me a lot," I said.

She asked how much and when I told her, her eyes widened. "Well, maybe you could pay back half, then."

"Or two-thirds?"

She grinned. "Half is fine."

We agreed that I would send a check once I returned to Phoenix, and she thanked me for my help.

"I'm sorry you had to go through this," she said, "but I'm not certain we could have defeated him without you."

I wasn't sure I believed that, but I thanked her in turn, said my goodbyes, and left for my hotel.

It was late and the roads were nearly empty. The rain had moved on, leaving a hazed quarter moon low in the western sky, its glow muted, its pull on my mind subtle but already insistent. A preview of the phasing to come.

I'd be in Phoenix well before it began, which came as a relief. I could see the allure of this city, but my home and my heart lay to the west, beneath that moon. I was eager to fly back to both.

ॐ

## David B. Coe

I've been writing professionally for twenty-five years and have put out, as either David B. Coe or D. B. Jackson, about two dozen books and as many short stories. I attended my first LibertyCon back in 1998, a year after the release of my first novel. Timmy ran the show back then and he greeted me as if we were old friends. He made me feel at home and checked in all weekend to make sure I was having fun, which, of course, I was. But he teased me about writing epic fantasy and made it clear to me that as long as I was writing only that, he wasn't going to read my books. Timmy had me as a Special Guest in 2008, and Brandy made me a Special Guest of Honor ten years later. And Timmy remained true to his word: As soon as I started writing urban fantasy and historical fantasy, he dove right in to my work. But not the epic. Never the epic.

—David B. Coe

**David B. Coe** is the author of many fantasy and contemporary fantasy novels and stories. He was the winner of the William L. Crawford Award for best first fantasy series, awarded at the International Conference on the Fantastic, for *Children of Amarid* and *The Outlanders*, the first two novels of the LonTobyn Chronicles. His series Winds of the Forelands began with *Rules of Ascension* and continued with *Seeds of Betrayal*, *Bonds of Vengeance*,

*Shapers of Darkness*, and *Weavers of War*. Coe is a founding member of the well-regarded writing blog MagicalWords.net. His contemporary fantasy series The Case Files of Justin Fearsson begins with *Spell-Blind* from Baen Books. Coe lives with his wife, Nancy Berner, and their two daughters in Sewanee, Tennessee.

# LIBERTYCON 100

I've had the pleasure of meeting Bill Fawcett twice, if I am not mistaken. The first was at my second LibertyCon where he would do half-hour sessions with some of us new authors to give advice. I remember him saying that it looked like I was on the right path and that I should keep doing what I was doing. The second time was at the DragonCon 2018 Dragon Awards reception where I was sitting in a corner with a dazed expression on my face as I looked around the room at legendary writers. He must have noticed the dazed expression because he came over and said, "You do realize we're all just older nerds, right?" I was thrilled when he said he would love to do a story for this anthology.

—CW

# LibertyCon 100

## Bill Fawcett

The day was cool for Chattanooga in June, barely 105 degrees, and the sky clear. Jack smiled as he leaned against a brick wall and watched the Correction Corps building across the street. The current chairman of LibertyCon was in his early thirties, tall and beginning to get a bit overweight with black hair and blue eyes. The federal building sat on the site once occupied by the Choo Choo Hotel. Some bureaucrat had ruled part of the property a historical building so the high-roofed, twentieth-century train station remained intact, if badly needing repairs. The actual ten-story federal offices were contained in a blob of glass and steel, standard architectural plan C1, that squatted like an obese troll over and behind the former station. Most of the stores across the street were closed. So were most small retail stores everywhere in the Unified States of America. These storefronts were likely empty because no one wanted to be too close to the CC. Any annoyed C Corps officer who didn't like how his coffee tasted could have you on a bus to the Alaskan mines by merely checking a single box.

Jack had waited only a few minutes when he saw a likely candidate. The young man wore the red, white and blue striped coat of a CC agent, but his lapel badge said he was a junior grade in the information revision division; a pencil pusher.

"Did you drop this?" Jack asked, walking up behind the young CC agent and holding out a small envelope.

"Huh?" The young man stopped and looked around worried. Change of your routine was a problem. It was something to be avoided and this situation was new.

"Sorry to disturb you, Officer," the con chair assured the

somewhat confused agent as he held out the envelope. "I noticed this on the ground as you passed and thought you had dropped it." He held the envelope so the name written on it was visible: Senior Agent Michael Madigan. There was no address. "I imagine the senior agent will be grateful to someone who brings him his lost mail."

What may have even been a thought glimmered for a moment in the bureaucrat's eyes as he slowly accepted the envelope. Since few Americans outside the bureaucratic class were literate, the young man assumed, since he gave the correct name, that Jack was one of their own, just out of uniform. The young agent's eyes glassed over once more as he turned, still clutching the envelope, and ambled into the CC building without a word.

Jack smiled. He figured he had about ten minutes before Madigan reacted, so he settled back against the empty chocolate store to wait.

In his office on the top floor, the thin-faced and balding Senior Agent showed surprise when his assistant, Debbie Gants, brought in the envelope. She entered his office hesitantly, as the head of the CC for the Southeast was notoriously irritable. This time, she escaped with only a grimace and a curt gesture for her to leave. She dropped the envelope on his desk and fled, having scheduled to be off that afternoon. The senior agent could not see the small smile that emerged as she walked away and just kept walking.

It was three minutes before Madigan, scion of one of the most powerful bureaucratic clans in the nation, finished reading. With just initials, he approved the request from the Fairbanks Correctional Mines for three hundred more prisoners. Such requests had become routine. Providing workers for the state mines would be easy. He simply had to tighten one of the Patriotic Correctness Guidelines in Atlanta again without warning. It would also keep the fear level raised, always a benefit. Then, he frowned at the envelope.

The tan envelope wasn't federal issue, which was unusual. Since literacy had been ruled to interfere with patriotism and happiness, few but the bureaucratic class used written correspondence. The envelope's single use showed Madigan that yet another education campaign on the dangers of reading was needed. With as much annoyance as curiosity, the top agent carefully opened it. When he saw the contents, only annoyance remained.

Inside was a flyer, yellowed and brittle, announcing LibertyCon 28, to be held at the Chattanooga Choo Choo Hotel. The "28" was crossed out and "100" written over it.

Madigan ground his teeth. The LibertyCon family had been an obsession and embarrassment throughout his entire career. Twice they had made him the laughingstock of the annual Capital Conference: once by splashing him in blue dye the day before it started and once when they invited all the VIPs from the meeting to a party he was supposed to be throwing but didn't know about until the next morning. The rebels were always a minor annoyance. Less than a month earlier the so-called LibertyCon family had the audacity to pass out literacy training pamphlets at the official government market where the meat rations were being distributed. It had taken days for his agents to visit every family who had been there and recover what he hoped was all of the subversive literature.

There was a SAM number at the bottom of the flyer, not a name. That was a bit of an anachronism. Even the improved bureaucratic SAMs, a device derived from the cell phones of a generation earlier, such as he carried for communications and entertainment, no longer had a keyboard. Everything was voice-activated. Good bureaucratic instinct told the agent that something new was wrong. The LibertyCon family had been nothing but trouble for years. Worrying that he was going to regret it, Agent Madigan ordered his own SAM to call the number.

"Welcome to Madiganistan," Jack answered on his own less fancy, but certainly CC-monitored SAM. He smiled. He knew Madigan wouldn't be able to resist calling. A low growl answered and then silence fell. "Press the Green button to talk," the young con chair offered helpfully.

"By the authority of the Clinton, I order you to surrender," Madigan snarled.

"Oh, good, you can talk." Jack found himself smiling widely. "I was afraid all those boring public announcements had been dubbed." He waited for a reaction, but heard nothing. "Just wanted you to know, we are going to hold another LibertyCon this year. I'm the convention chairman! We plan to hold it in the original site, about ten stories below you. It will have a retro theme. There will even be a panel discussing citizen's rights. You know, about back when they had some."

"Not likely." Controlled anger was obvious in the Correctness Agent's voice. Jack realized no one ever talked this way to a senior CC agent, since a senior agent held the power to imprison or execute anyone they designated as an enemy of the Unified States of America. Jack didn't care. He was already committed; he might as well enjoy the ride.

"You are welcome to attend," he continued, keeping his tone light since he knew it would enrage the senior agent. "Let's see... this is Thursday, so you have a week to clear your schedule. If you look in the envelope your minion delivered, you will find a complimentary badge."

"Gnnnxxx!"

Jack paused, impressed. He had never heard anyone grind their teeth so loudly that you could hear it over a SAM.

Finally, Madigan spoke again. He was obviously using his "I am in control and will sound reasonable" voice.

"Look, you and your group are disruptive. It is the duty of the government to regulate every patriot's life so that they will be safe and happy. You know it is in the old Constitution that your group likes to quote, 'life and the pursuit of happiness.'"

"What about liberty?" Jack snapped.

"We have found that individual thought and actions lower the general level of contentment. That interferes with happiness, so of course that was edited out three versions ago." Madigan sounded comfortable repeating parts of the speech Jack used to hear him make almost daily. "Unnecessary information and thought just make patriots unhappy. Why do you want to make the patriots unhappy? Most will just resent it."

"Then why does the bureaucratic class still have schools?" Jack countered.

Madigan was ready with an approved reply; this was all right out of the Q&A section of the manual. "We sacrifice some of our happiness for the good of all. It is our Unified Duty."

"Which is why you live on a two-thousand-acre estate in a mansion filled with good little patriot servants?"

That question was not in the manual. Jack kept talking. "What if something happened at LibertyCon 100 that caused ten thousand or a hundred thousand of your patriots to start to think and question?"

"They would never dare!" Agent Madigan spat out the words.

"You'll see," Jack responded in a teasing, lilting tone. "You will see. But for today, look out your window."

Jack spotted Senior Agent Michael Madigan as the skinny bureaucrat went to his window and looked down. The tall, dark-haired man on the cracked sidewalk waving his arms stood out among the cowed patriots moving listlessly by. He stood out even more when he made a series of gestures, all obscene and none at all retro. Jack closed the connection, but the sound of a fist slamming into and cracking the poorly made window of the senior agent's office was still loud ten stories below.

The moment he hung up, Jack hurried around the corner and stretched out on a bench. They could trace him using the SAM he had called on. The SAM was the government's connection to every patriot. One was given to every resident of the Unified States when they turned five years old. It served as a telephone and text messenger as well as a connection to the state-controlled internet. No matter what you asked it gave you the party line. If you asked about a banned topic, it responded with a lecture on patriot obedience while alerting the CC. The use of any other device to access data had been illegal for twenty years. The SAM could only connect to the approved government database. It contained everything any viewer might want to know about the entertainment shows and the Clinton News Network, but no technical or scientific information at all. Not that there was much new science to report. Humanity had begun settling planets around other stars, but the revolt of America's colonies had led to cutting off contact and a total proscription of all scientific research or even education. To Jack a SAM was generally useless, but he conceded it had a good schedule listing for all nine entertainment channels and CNN. Jack found most of the shows boring, but CNN did generate the occasional laugh when watching how the reporters twisted themselves into knots in order to explain how another decrease in food production or shortage of fuel benefited all patriots.

Everyone accepted that their SAM was being monitored. Continued queries of non-approved topics almost always initiated a visit by Correction Corps agents. But the LibertyCon family survived because they had a solution to that problem.

"Goddess," Jack spoke into his SAM.

"Hi, J.R," a deep, rich, lilting female voice responded. Some said that the Regina all family members had imbedded in their

SAMs was modeled on one of the first family leaders. A few suspected that an aging Regina had herself downloaded into a computer. The topic often sparked a heated debate at the annual gatherings. The Regina refused to answer all questions about its origins. But she was the only one who called him "J.R."

"Regina, I need you to show my SAM moving toward the Marriott building."

"Easy peasy," the hidden AI responded.

From a few blocks in the other direction Jack watched a dozen identically dressed agents pour out of the CC Building and rush off toward the old hotel. He waited just long enough for them to arrive.

"Regina, now show me on the tenth floor of the Marriott." Jack chuckled, getting a startled look from a person passing by. Few people laughed or did anything to draw attention in public, but this was just too much fun. There hadn't been working elevators in the old hotel for years. Only the first six floors were ever used, but they remained the best accommodations in Chattanooga. He waited a moment. "Okay, now show me on floor fourteen." He could picture the agents chugging up fourteen flights of stairs, winded and angry. For the next ten minutes, Jack waited on his bench, appearing asleep to any who passed. Assured the agents had likely reached the fourteenth floor and were searching in vain for him, Jack addressed the Regina again.

"Can you show me jumping from the fourteenth floor to the ground outside, then cut off the monitoring signal of this SAM?"

"Splat," said the AI.

"Nice job. Goddess, notify the Uncle Timmy phase one is complete."

"Wilco."

He swung off the bench and strode down the street, away from the government building. Moving to one of their safe houses, an old abandoned home on a hill whose door never closed correctly, the current con chair of LibertyCon made himself comfortable and waited. He knew that the next few hours were going to be stressful.

After a few hours, Jack was sure that things would have calmed down. Someone would have filed a false report saying they had found a body on the sidewalk just to keep Madigan and the other higher-ups from blaming them for his escape. Time for phase two. He changed into the uniform of the Federal Maintenance

Brigade. He was now dressed as a janitor and carrying a bucket, a small bag, and a spray bottle that had been specially prepared by Debi Chowdhury, the family chemist. Forcing himself to walk slowly Jack once more approached the CC Building. He did not have to fake a worried look. Too many things could go wrong this close to the enemy.

The building seemed calm. Waiting for a lull in the foot traffic, Jack took the silkscreen from his bucket and unrolled it. He then taped the edges to the largest glass pane on the front of the building and sprayed the highly acidic and colored solution all over it. Jack noticed his hand shook a little and his shoulders tightened when the door thirty feet away opened. Three agents exited, but they paid no attention to the nearby janitor. Jack could hear his heart thumping as he pulled down the silkscreen and walked away, trying hard to slow down his pace.

Behind him at eye level the glass was etched a quarter inch deep and four feet across:

COMING SOON

LIBERTYCON 100

FEATURING MUD PIES

GUEST OF "HONOR"

AGENT MICHAEL MADIGAN

Turning at the corner the young rebel finally relaxed a little as he walked. He wondered how Madigan would deal with the poster. He rather hoped the senior agent would be angry enough to break the glass. Jack then wondered how Madigan would explain the need for a second expensive, replacement window to his superiors.

"Goddess, notify Uncle Timmy phase two is successful."

"Wilco."

Once well out of sight of the building, he began to walk faster. It would take him almost an hour to reach the location they had prepared, but taking one of the CC-monitored vehicles was too much of a risk.

"Goddess?" Drenched in sweat, Jack used a hidden switch to turn his SAM back on as he settled into a cool corner of the empty, dark candy factory. The windows in the almost acre-sized plant had been painted over. A wide aisle five yards across ran down the long center of the candy plant. Lining it on both sides at its center were ten elevated vats that had once held the candy mixtures that fed onto the long assembly belts to either side. A faint odor of chocolate and sugar remained among the musty smell of a too-long-abandoned building.

"What is the nature of your medical emergency?" his Regina answered. He had seen all of the forbidden *Star Trek* episodes and knew the reference, but was nervous enough to ignore it.

"I need you to spoof a call to the CC switchboard," the LibertyCon chairman said. "Make it appear to come from the office of Brandy Kelly. Have her report seeing me at this location." The Kellys still managed the only remaining SAM news service for Chattanooga. Their family had held the newspaper position for three generations. While appearing to be the most patriotic of citizens who released only approved news and propaganda, they had also managed to hide among their reports a steady stream of coded messages for the whole LibertyCon family. Using Brandy's line would add credibility to the tip, and if things went as planned, there would be no risk to her. If not, Jack shrugged, it wouldn't matter for any of them.

"Wilco, J.R."

The whole family had been preparing the old candy plant for weeks. Two of the more mechanically talented family members, Randall Pass and Jason Bolgeo, had spent hours diverting the local water main back into the building. Then, being careful to not be noticed, a dozen family members under Ann Darwin had brought in several tons of good old red clay. He had helped and it had been backbreaking labor that had involved a lot of sleepless nights. Still, if this worked, it should have the desired effect. Not to mention be fun to watch. All he had to do now was wait, and welcome his honored guest.

As he hoped, the thin, aging senior agent led his men into the building. Jack had to grin. Madigan was preceded only by his own information specialist catching his every heroic act on video. He hoped they had lots of room on their drives. Even if they didn't, their tech expert, Karin Harris, had four cameras in place.

"Goddess, start the cameras," Jack ordered in a low voice. There had to be thirty agents with Madigan, all armed. Not many resisted the CC, much less seemed a danger to it. He was probably the biggest threat most of them had encountered in their careers. He would have given good odds most of them were scared witless at the thought of an actual confrontation.

As they entered the far side of the factory, several spread to either side. That could be a problem, the con chair worried. As he had hoped, the senior agent did stride down the aisle ahead of his men. Barked orders from a visibly angry Madigan punctuated the echo of their footsteps.

Exposing himself to all those guns was intimidating. But Jack had to stop the procession in exactly the right spot. The con chair tried to slow his breathing, reminding himself that no matter what happened to him, this was for the good of the whole family. Two generations had grown up in the Unified States of America and the vise holding the nation's citizens had only tightened every year. They had no hope of defeating a million bureaucrats. They had to take this one chance for disruption or go under.

The agents moved closer to the center area and suddenly Madigan left the wide aisle to talk with his agents on one side. The young con chair mumbled a couple of curses at himself about making plans that require the enemy to do what you expect. Then, to his relief, the senior agent returned to the aisle and majestically led his men forward. He even smiled for his minion's camera. Their footsteps seemed to come from all over and get louder fast.

So far so good, Jack promised himself, then stifled a chuckle as he remembered the old joke about falling off a building.

The agents reached the center of the factory. Jack took a deep breath and stepped out, holding a control box at the end of a thick cord.

"Madigan!" he yelled. "Time to surrender."

Most of the CC agents froze and looked to their boss.

"Kill him!" Mike Madigan screeched, his thin, pale face flushed from rage.

A few shots pinged near the young rebel. Jack ducked. Shards of concrete from a near miss stung his arm and side. He almost dropped the switch, but his other arm convulsed, closing the connection.

The gigantic mixing tanks fifteen feet above and on every side of the CC senior agent emitted rusty rumbles, and opened. Torrents of thick, muddy water poured out, flooding the aisle. The force knocked most of the armed men from their feet. Those not being mudded looked on in shock.

"MoonPies for all," Jack bellowed. He let the control box drop and fled. He retreated toward what looked like a concrete wall, but actually concealed a short tunnel that a team under the resourceful Agatha Jean had dug. He could see her initials in pencil where he needed to push. Hearing footsteps hammering toward him, he slid into and pulled the wall panel closed behind him. The prospect of crawling fifty yards of a claustrophobic three-foot-by-two-foot tunnel had earlier terrified the young con chair. Jack had never liked close spaces. Now, full of adrenaline and bleeding from half a dozen gouges, he had no problem scurrying through it.

Once safely hidden in a forest that had long ago been a park, Jack again summoned his Regina.

"Can you edit the videos to their greatest effect?" he asked the computer intelligence.

"Already have," Regina replied. There seemed to be a strange sound to the AI's voice. Could an AI... giggle? The Regina sure sounded like she was. Before he could react, the edited takes from the four video cameras the family had set up appeared on the screen of his modified SAM.

Jack watched with pleasure. The video montage opened with him seemingly surrendering and Madigan ordering his men to shoot. Then, there was a close shot of the tanks opening, pulling back to a wide angle as the muddy water poured out over the cluster of agents surrounding their boss. This was followed by a tighter shot of the senior agent throwing his arms high and falling into the pouring sludge. When Madigan emerged, covered in filth, Regina had cut to a close-up of his thin face and thinning hair dripping with mud as the agent spat out a mouthful of the red colored filth with an expression of disgust and anger. In another wide shot, the senior agent began yelling angry orders and waving his arms wildly, only to lose his balance and end up sitting, startled, in the clay sludge. The video ended with a ten-second commercial for the long-gone snack "Moon-Pies." He wondered if Madigan had known that they had once been made at that very factory. Jack wasn't sure in what remote database his Regina had found the commercial, but it made a perfect ending.

"Wonderful! Can you send this to the Kellys' outlet and get it running immediately as a demand announcement on as many of the Southeast's SAMs as possible?" Jack requested.

Jack's own SAM pinged a few moments with the special announcement. A minute later he could actually hear laughter in the distance. Some upright patriotic citizens were enjoying the discomfiture of their chief overseer.

"Goddess, connect me to the Timmy," he asked, then added a "please." A stout man with rusty hair and beard grinned from the screen at him.

"Phase three complete in spades," Jack reported. They didn't think the CC was monitoring the side band they communicated over, but everyone spoke in general terms as much as possible out of habit.

"We saw it, Jack," the current Uncle Timmy replied. "He will be frothing."

"That was the idea," the young rebel agreed. "How goes it?"

"The last tests are positive," the elected head of the LibertyCon family assured after a thumbs-up from Ann Darwin, the travel coordinator. "We are gathering the last of the attendees. Everyone should be in place within the hour."

"Good news." It was a relief that there would be no delays. "I'm not sure how much longer I can stay ahead of the CC."

"On your signal, then," the Uncle Timmy agreed and closed the transmission.

Twice as he walked back to the center of Chattanooga, passing autodrive cars full of CC agents forced Jack to dive for cover. His side ached from his bruises and his left shoulder was a bit numb. Blood had stopped dripping from the half-dozen shallow but jagged tears in his skin. The initial sting turned to real pain as he walked. Finally, he reached a room hidden in the back of an empty gas station that had been in Phil Schultz's family since before the first LibertyCon. There he cleaned and bandaged the wounds the concrete shards had made. He suspected they would infect later, no matter what he did.

The rebel changed into another uniform, this time a pale green Pilots and Teamsters Unified Union jumpsuit complete with the American Eagle patch covering most of his back. Jack hoped the small wounds would not bleed through. He took three aspirin and waited on a folding chair. He had almost an hour before leaving to start the next phase.

The Regina came alive, something else he did not know the AI could do.

"Hey, J.R, you want to see this," she said. "It's a bulletin the Correctness Corps put out."

Jack watched it with growing unease. It featured a short video taken from the camera over the door of the CC Building earlier that day of him in the maintenance uniform. It was not a very clear likeness. The official voiceover, which sounded a lot like Madigan, enjoined all patriotic citizens to turn in the disruptive man if they saw him. Jack suspected a lot of janitors were about to get hassled that afternoon.

Three times while he waited nervously, multiple sirens wailed by the building. He presumed the CC cars were responding to reported sightings of the "maintenance man." None stopped near his hiding place.

Getting to the airport was no problem. Jack used one of the other family member's cards to summon an autocab and had the Regina blur its internal camera. Anyone monitoring would see a blur wearing a pilot's uniform and, he hoped, do no more than register the autocab for repair.

Once at the airport, Jack used legitimate and correct paperwork that had been prepared by a family member who had penetrated the bureaucracy to schedule a small, fast helicopter. His uniform and the flight bag he carried were equally authentic, donated by other family members. While the loss of trained maintenance personnel had grounded most jets, the government maintained a fleet of smaller aircraft. There was a constant stream of announcements over the big video on one wall. The vandalism to the CC building was the most excitement the town had seen in years. No one paid any attention to the new pilot. He even sat with a few of the clerks and watched the grainy footage of himself in the janitor's uniform. He worried for a moment, but after few seconds he relaxed. No one was looking past his clothes, and two were openly chuckling at someone else's mention of mud pies. Twenty minutes later, he was in the air.

"Goddess, the Uncle Timmy, please," the young con chair requested. He was still a little unnerved by the AI's new behavior.

"How goes it?" the current family head asked when he answered.

"On my way," Jack assured him. "How's *Travis* doing?"

"Great. All aboard and ready to go. We just need to get past those last three as planned." The family head sounded worried. This would be the riskiest part of the whole plan. "Are you sure you can help?"

Flying slowly in an arc around Chattanooga, Jack felt the

weight of the whole family on his shoulders. He just hoped he had both the skill and the courage to make their plan work. Nearly a thousand descendants of the original LibertyCon attendees were counting on him. He wouldn't let them down.

"I'll distract them," he reassured his friend.

"Ten minutes, then?"

"Ten, starting now," Jack agreed, glancing at the time on his SAM. Then he turned the helicopter toward the downtown and CC Headquarters.

Two minutes later, he was hovering over the CC Building. Locking the autopilot on hover at one thousand feet, he proceeded to empty the flight bag out the window. The slight breeze took the five thousand invitations to LibertyCon 100 and spread them across most of the city. The part about "Guest of Honor Senior Agent Michael Madigan" was even embossed with silver lettering to make it more special. Jack returned to the controls and watched agents scramble to gather up the flyers that fell just outside their building and then give up in frustration as they realized just how many there were and how far the flyers had spread.

He checked the SAM. Three minutes to go. It was time to tweak the senior agent, again.

"Goddess, connect me to Madigan and make sure he can't trace our location."

"What?" Madigan answered the SAM with a belligerent question.

"Con Chair here." Jack tried to sound cheerful as he spoke. "As you can see, we have made you our guest of honor. I hope you feel the promotion for the con has been sufficient."

Madigan snarled. "I'll take you down, rebel! You'll spend your last moments in a re-education camp on starvation rations!"

"Okay, then, I guess it was *not* enough." Now Jack was genuinely cheerful. Something about tweaking the pointy-faced bureaucrat was most satisfying. "Tell you what, I'll just pop over to the capital and drop the other batch."

Although he was now flying twenty miles northwest of Chattanooga, the rebel suspected that he might have heard the bellow that followed.

It was only an hour flight to the new national capital in St. Louis. The centrally located city had been chosen when the rising ocean returned the District of Columbia to the swamp from which it once rose. Madigan might spin his way out of problems in Chattanooga, but once the flyers dropped over the capital buildings the bureaucrat was as good as banished to counting seals in the Aleutians.

"Catch me if you can. Nah nah nah," Jack sang as he flew on, really enjoying himself now. On the other side of the Cumberland Plateau, he dropped to barely a hundred feet above the rolling landscape. This meant normal radars could not see him.

"They are scrambling all the aircraft for a thousand miles," the Regina informed him.

"Satellites?" the con chair asked, suddenly worried. Without Madigan using them the family's plan would fail. "What's going on with the satellites?"

"Two on you," the Regina replied, then paused. "Okay, now all three." Jack let out his breath in a relieved gush.

Once dozens of global positioning satellites circled over the Unified States. With the mandated decline in learning and loss of technical skills, the government was soon unable to launch any new rockets. Over time, most satellites had failed until now only three kept a top-down radar watch over the eastern half of the country. And in his effort to find and stop Jack, the senior agent had requisitioned all three.

"Tell them," Jack snapped as he pulled the helicopter hard to avoid a small mountain ahead. It was twelve minutes since he had turned toward Chattanooga.

"You are clear to go," the Regina informed the Timmy. She kept the connection open.

"Launch," came the single word from the Uncle Timmy. A hum rose from the open channel. Jack waited nervously. "*Travis* at ten thousand feet, twenty, fifty, exiting atmosphere."

To Jack, the Timmy's count was painfully slow. The gigantic spaceship could rise at only a few miles an hour at first. It was then the ship was most vulnerable. Even a small disruption could have disrupted the magnetic launch field and brought the hijacked vessel down.

"Approaching the space station... no response from it. I guess it really is abandoned.... *Travis II* is clear!" the Uncle Timmy's voice sang out with triumph. "No pursuit possible! Thank you, con chair."

The FTL ship was accelerating quickly. In minutes, it was already far enough away that Jack barely heard the weak signal.

"Toast me at LibertyCon 101," the rebel replied. He felt triumphant, but lonely, too. It was all over. His family was on its way.

For months, the LibertyCon family had been working in secret on the last FTL ship in the world. The *Travis II* had been on display at the long-closed Huntsville Space Museum. Everything had remained in place because it cost money to clear it off the land.

Once it was decided that they could not reverse the damage being done to their nation and the world by the Unified bureaucrats, the LibertyCon family had decided there was one further hope: escape. A free human colony lay twenty-eight light-years away, four months' flight. But to launch safely meant that they had to get away from the most vicious and competent sociopath in the entire Correction Corps, Madigan, the one who controlled fighter aircraft and ground-to-air missiles and could thwart their attempt to escape. Jack had come up with the plan to distract Madigan and appointed himself head and sole member of the LibertyCon 100 committee. Every other descendant of those who swore at LibertyCon 56 to uphold the old values were on board, moving away from Earth at a steadily increasing rate of speed.

Jack realized there was no purpose to continued running. His mission was over; he had succeeded. It had cost him his family, his friends, and left him alone in a hostile world.

Still then, Jack thought, resigned, no worries. I will likely be dead soon. The screen on his Regina showed about fifty military jets closing in from all directions. Still, Jack was not one to give up easily. He shifted course and scanned the ground.

"Goddess, what's our status?"

"Three aircraft are two minutes out," the Regina warned. "All weapons hot."

A small lake appeared to the south and Jack turned toward it. On impulse, he grabbed the flight bag and scrawled on it with his free hand "Return to D B Cooper."

"One minute," the Regina counted down, "Fifty seconds, forty..."

Hovering fifty feet over the lake, the rebel prepared the autopilot and opened the door. As the former con chair pushed ENGAGE he jumped, barely clearing the landing rods. The helicopter rose high over his head, turned north and accelerated at its fastest speed. Jack's first thought as he fell was the realization that he had no idea how deep the water below was. There was a crash of thunder in the distance as the missiles impacted his former ride. Then he hit the water, hard, and it was cold.

✧     ✧     ✧

Former Senior Agent Michael Madigan's replacement had agents searching that area of the Tennessee mountains for weeks, and divers continued to search the deep cold lake until it froze over the next winter.

No trace of the LibertyCon 100 con chair, John Ringo Correia, was ever found.

ॐ

## Bill Fawcett

After attending LibertyCon for many years my best memory may be riding in the cart with Uncle Timmy the year Jody was GOH. He was obviously enjoying himself and it was a fun ride from the back of the Choo Choo.

—Bill Fawcett

Timmy, when his mobility was impaired in later life, would use a golf cart to get around the several acres of grounds of the Chattanooga Choo Choo Hotel and Convention Center, of blessed memory. (And yes, it was indeed a repurposed train depot. It is mostly condos now, far more upscale than when we fans inhabited it for our cons.) But Timmy made the best of this situation, making sure that anyone who needed or wanted a ride, got one. He remembered the lessons of Samanda Jeude, an early crusader for handicapped accessibility at conventions.

—TW

**Bill Fawcett** & Associates has packaged and edited over four hundred science fiction novels, two oral histories of the Navy SEALs, and other military titles. He coauthored the official Mycroft Holmes Mysteries and has written almost a dozen nonfiction books, many on Great Mistakes in History. He was a founder of Mayfair Games. He hopes you enjoyed his homage to Eric Frank Russell and, as Timmy would have encouraged, that you seek out his works, too.

# HIDDEN, A FAIRY TALE

Mr. Drake is one of the authors I have never met in person but if I were adding how many of the books I have read by the man, it might take a higher math skill than I possess. I've read a lot of them. Some of my favorites were coauthored with Eric Flint. The Belisarius series was fantastic. Hammer's Slammers is the go to when you talk about mercenaries. When one of us writing about mercs is compared to the Hammer's Slammers series, it is the ultimate compliment. I spent more years than I want to think of swapping books with my brother. Every time one of us found something new by David, we would get it to the other as quickly as possible. I was ecstatic when I found out he was going to do a story for the anthology. I consider it a bonus that I got to read it before everyone else. Sorry, Brisco, you have to wait.

—CW

# Hidden, a Fairy Tale

## David Drake

I heard Trieber, the sergeant of the guard, open the door at the head of the stairs to the lower level. They were steep so he came clumping down carefully, setting his right foot on each step and bringing the left one down beside it. He was checking up on me, but I was glad to have the company.

When Trieber was in public he had a crested helmet and a halberd with a star worked into the blade with brass wire. Right now the only sign of his position was his red and blue tabard. He was breathing hard.

"You've got the postern open," he said as he came out into the corridor. "Who told you to do that?"

"It doesn't offer much either of view or ventilation..." I said. It gave onto the twisting alley at the back of the palace. "But at least with it open I don't feel so much like I'm in prison myself."

"Well, you shouldn't leave it open," Trieber said. He stepped past me and reached for the postern.

"Look!" I said. "This creature, whatever it is, walks right through stone walls, right? That's what they say, anyhow."

"That's what they say," Trieber said, gripping the edge of the panel. It was iron-strapped oak and hard to swing even if the hinges hadn't been so stiff. "But this stays bolted anyhow."

"If you want me awake, Trieber," I said, "then leave it open. Otherwise you may as well just lock it and figure that the creature doesn't *really* walk through stone. Which is what I believe and you do too."

Trieber paused and looked at me. "Look, smart-ass," he said, "if you go to sleep, this critter'll just tear your throat out if it *does* come through stone!"

I shrugged. "If it really walks through walls, it will, yeah," I said. "But I'm telling you, there's no way I'm going to stay awake for a dark-to-dawn shift if you close me in this room."

He swore but left the postern open and stepped away from it. "You're a smart-ass," he said. "Look, anybody else comes around, you shut it, right? I guess you'll have plenty warning on these bloody steps."

"Like you say, Sergeant," I said. "On my oath."

Trieber walked back to the door to the steps. "Smart-ass," he repeated under his breath.

He could've had me flogged, I suppose, which I didn't want, but Trieber was a decent enough fellow and he knew that I was telling the truth that I couldn't stay awake during the watch down here if I didn't at least have the postern open. It was hard enough as it was, carving linden branches into unbroken chains.

What I really wanted was to be released from Count Heber's service, but that wasn't likely to happen till they caught the creature or the Count decided it'd gone somewhere else. It'd attacked during the full moon for the past three months. The Count laid on extra guards and watchmen, but I think that was mostly to calm people down rather than because he thought they were going to catch the creature.

Nobody'd even seen it for sure, just the bodies it left behind. They'd been alone and were found bled out with the throats torn open. There was nothing the watch could do if they didn't see the thing, and we extra guards—well, if we were placed alone the way I was, we were just more for the creature to attack. That might've been what the Count had in mind: he wouldn't miss a stableboy like me.

It was getting about time for Burbey to take his shift and spell me. I had a shard of stoneware pot in my wallet. I gave my whittling knife a couple strokes on it to bring one side of the double-edged blade back to a wire edge and stuck it into the sheath. I picked up the halberd and stepped outside to see how bright the sky was.

It grated on me that the halberd shaft was such a piece of crap. I'd been apprenticed to Master Hendren, a bodger. I was with him for three years. I wasn't good enough to make a chair by myself yet, but I could've turned a spearshaft on one center—instead of three, like the shaft on this halberd.

Hendren's brother was a bodger too. When the brother died, Hendren took Gerry, his brother's apprentice, and set me loose with the bit of cash he had on hand. That sounds pretty harsh, but Hendren was really a good guy. He had a daughter, though, and Gerry was interested in Cathe as I surely was not. I guess Hendren figured the way I did: that there wouldn't be many men interested in Cathe, so she'd better jump at Gerry.

I went to the inn in town on Palace Square because I'd helped Hendren deliver a set of chairs there and I figured Pierre might remember me. It turned out that he did, and besides that his hostler had recently vanished with a maid from the palace. Later word got around that a necklace from the effects of the late Countess had also gone missing.

I'd cared for Hendren's team and I got along with horses, but I wasn't anything like experienced enough to run an inn's stables. Regardless, Pierre hired me and with the help of Cisca, Pierre's daughter and housekeeper, it went along pretty well.

Then folks started getting their throats torn out and the Count decided he needed more armsmen. I wasn't given a choice. Until something changed I was pulling dusk-to-dawn shifts for what was supposed to be ten pence a week. In the two and a half months I'd been doing it, I'd gotten seventeen coppers. I didn't expect that was going to change in a good way.

I kept working—and eating, and sleeping—at the stables. Pierre had a succession of old men and young folk helping now, but I still did all the heavy work. Pierre had been good to me; I wasn't going to leave him in the lurch even if it wasn't my fault.

I heard somebody shuffling in the alley, long before they came into sight around the bulge of the wall on the other side of the passage. I straightened and waited. The sound was coming from the right but I even looked back the other way to make sure it wasn't a trick to hold my attention in the wrong direction.

It was Burbey, my relief, with another man behind him. There was enough light to make out the new man's face but I didn't know him.

"You took your time," I said, nodding up to the graying strip of sky between the walls.

"Keep your shirt on, kid," Burbey said. "There's somebody here wants to meet you."

I thrust the halberd into Burbey's hands; there was only one weapon for the man on duty, so the halberd stayed here. I didn't know what this was all about but I wasn't going to let Burbey stick me with a double shift. He was fat, old and sodden, which is why we shared this wretched post where nobody would see us.

The stranger looked me over. I glared back at him. Burbey must have brought him around by the alley instead of coming the usual way through the palace to avoid being seen.

"With a tabard and a cap, you'll do," he said. "Look, kid. How would you like to be on duty midday to dusk and then off till tomorrow night? That's six hours for twelve, a good deal, right?"

It seemed like a good deal, sure, but I was so tired I'd probably think it was fine if somebody told me to jump in a well with a millstone. "I need sleep," I said.

"Sure, get some sleep," the stranger said. "Just be back here before midday. Burbey'll have the outfit for you. Then you're up to the front hall till dusk, then off till tomorrow night."

It probably had something to do with a woman, but that was none of my business. I also figured Burbey was getting paid something, but the six fewer hours were better than cash for me.

"All right," I said. "I'll be back here before midday."

There were two guards wearing tabards and caps in the entrance hall. I guessed I'd be taking the place of one of them this afternoon. Their halberds seemed at a glance to be better made than the piece of crap I shared with Burbey but they didn't have anything fancy about them.

If I'd seen Sergeant Trieber I'd have said something to him—he must know more than I did about what I was supposed to be doing this afternoon—but I didn't see him and I didn't go looking for where he may have gotten off to.

Instead I walked across Palace Square to Pierre's inn. I went into the taproom, which was pretty near empty at this time of day. Old Eric was behind the bar talking to somebody I took for a drover. His legs were covered with road dust, and he was using the inn's best vintage to wash more of it from his throat and mouth.

"Oh, it's terrible!" Eric said. He sounded more cheerful than he usually did, to tell the truth. "Each of the past three full moons a monster has torn the throat out of somebody in the city and drunk every drop of his blood! And tonight is the full moon! Two on the street, you say, but Dame Curlee was behind locked doors and six sturdy men in the house!"

I said, "Is Cisca down yet, Eric? I thought I'd take care of anything heavy she had for me before I catch a couple hours' sleep. I'm back on watch at midday."

The victims had been a drunk in a door alcove and another behind a dram shop near the west gate. As for Curlee, she lived on the fourth floor of her house but everybody knew that she invited young men up the back staircase when she was in a mood for company. Was the window casement always locked after they left? Maybe, but I wouldn't swear to it.

As I spoke, Cisca came bustling down the stairs from the two upper floors. "Oh, Hap," she said. "Would you like some broth along with your bread and cheese this morning? I saved some scraps from last night's roast hen."

"That'd be great, Cisca!" I said. I was happier just to see her more than I was at the thought of broth to dip my bread in. Cisca was especially pretty when she smiled, and she smiled most of the times that I saw her. I thought she liked me, which was good because I surely liked her.

She gave me another smile and went back through the kitchen door. Old Eric went on with the horrible details about the monster's attacks. Some of them were new to me and were probably things Eric had made up for the occasion.

A stranger came in from the street. He was dressed with city taste, but he struck me as more flash than quality—sort of like a copper coin with a silver wash on it, if you know what I mean. I looked at him and looked away, like I would from a dog taking a dump.

He set his arms akimbo and looked around the big room, then focused on Cisca, who'd just come back with my food. "Well, there's something worth seeing in this wretched town after all," he called. He made a half bow in the direction of Cisca.

"How may we serve you, sir?" Cisca said. It was her job the way hanging out the bedding was, but the whole business didn't best please me.

"To begin with," the fellow said, "you can bring me bread and broth and a cup of what you think is the best wine in the house. I am Dressan, Lord Quarmal's man."

He said that last bit like it was supposed to mean something, which it didn't to me.

"Pleased to meet you, I'm sure," Cisca said, "but I'm afraid that's the last of the broth. Is there something else we can get you?"

"No problem," Dressan said walking over to the long table where I sat. "I'll just have this one."

He reached for the mug. I caught his wrist as he reached past me. I squeezed. I don't have the muscles of a blacksmith, but forking up hay and muck gives me pretty good arms and shoulders.

Dressan tried to reach down for the poignard hanging by straps from his belt. It was a real fighting knife, not the usual work knife that pretty much every peasant carries.

He tried to force his hand down against my grip. I squeezed harder and smiled up at him.

He jerked himself away. He looked at me—really *looked* at me—for the first time and snarled, "You stupid yokel! When my master scotches this monster of yours, he's to marry Lady Isobel. The Count has no male heir, so Lord Quarmal will succeed him—and *I* am his chief man. What do you think of that, hobby?"

"*I* think..." said Eric, who'd been listening from behind the bar, "that people before your master have tried to kill the monster and none of them got so much as a sight of it. But it's here anyways, and the bodies prove that."

Dressan realized he was massaging his wrist with his left hand and jerked it away. "Well, I shouldn't expect peasants in the provinces to know any better," he said. He had a nasty, whiny voice. "My master has brought a great scholar from the faculty of Theology and the Arts in Paris, Doctor Carolus. He'll infallibly search out the place where your monster lurks!"

With that, Dressan turned on his heel and went back into the street. I let out my breath and tried to relax. My muscles were trembling from the strain they'd been under since the business started with Dressan. I sopped all the broth I could with my bread crust and swallowed it, then bolted the rest of the bread.

"Cisca?" I said, hearing my voice wobble. "I've got an early shift and need to get a bit of sleep. Can you make sure I'm up and out of here before the last stroke of the midday bell?"

She nodded. She was looking solemn. I suspected I did too—unless I was simply looking scared. I didn't want to leave my place, and I was pretty sure I'd have to if things worked out the way Dressan said they would.

I wasn't sure I'd be able to get to sleep after the fuss with Dressan, but if Cisca hadn't shaken my foot, I wouldn't have roused till midday started to ring. I went to the postern like usual, but Burbey surprised me by having it half open. Usually he barred it and went to sleep so sound that I had the devil's own time waking him from outside the thick panel.

"I was getting worried about the time!" Burbey said, handing me the gear.

"You've never had to wait for your relief," I said. "I wish I could say the same."

The tabard was just two half-red and half-blue panels linked together front and back. I stuck my head through the opening in the middle and didn't even bother tying the tapes at the bottom.

The cap was too small for me. It balanced on the top of my head when I stood still, but if I had to run somewhere it'd fall off for sure. I didn't figure to be doing much running.

"Go up the back here and draw a halberd from the arms room," Burbey said. "Hans knows you're coming."

I shuffled up the circular staircase. The arms room was in the corridor just behind the stairhead. I'd never been in it before, and actually didn't enter now: the top of the half-gate was open. Hans had a face like a weasel, and his graying russet hair increased the resemblance.

He thrust the butt of a halberd over the gate to me. "Bloody well time you got here!" Hans said. "The nobs are due any minute! I thought I was going to have to cover for you myself!"

"But where?" I said.

"Out in the main hall, you bloody fool!" he snarled. "You're here for Graeme, aren't you? Get out there now!"

There was no point in saying that nobody'd told me anything; it always seemed to make people angrier when they saw the problem was their own fault. I went through the short corridor to the main hall, tilting the halberd so the point didn't catch in a crossbeam. From the look of the ceiling, not everybody had been so careful.

There was a fuss going on at the entrance and the half-dozen people in the hall were looking that way. There was another guard in livery standing close to the wall. When I moved close to him, feeling relief, he turned his head and snarled, "The other side, you bloody fool!"

I trotted across the hall, trying to hold the halberd upright. I stood near the wall and hoped nobody would notice me.

The Count came in with another noble, who wore maroon velvet. There were several pages. Two of them belonged to the palace, but Dressan was there too. The man in academic robes must be Doctor Carolus.

The group paused close enough to me that I heard the Count say, "So, Doctor Carolus? How do you propose to begin?"

"Before we worry about methods..." said the gentleman who'd come in with the Count, "perhaps you should introduce me to your daughter Isobel so that I can satisfy myself that she is as you described her?"

"Do you doubt my word, Lord Quarmal?" the Count snapped.

"Not at all," said Quarmal in a tone that seemed pretty doubtful to me. "But there's no better time than the present, don't you think?"

The Count bent and spoke into the ear of one of his pages. Leo scurried down the cross-corridor on my side of the main hall. Nothing further happened until the page returned with a worried expression.

"She says she's not coming, your lordship," the page said.

I expected the Count to shout. Instead his face got almost white. He drew his sword and strode down the corridor. I heard him hammering on the door to his daughter's suite. Only then did he bellow, "Isobel, come out this instant or I'll have you dragged out by your heels!"

For a moment there was nothing. Then the Count shouted, "Guards, come here and—"

Before I could act, I heard a door open. The Count said toward it, "Out here to meet Lord Quarmal."

The Count returned to the main hall, gripping his daughter by the shoulder. Her maid, Ayesha, followed them wringing her hands. Her dark face was frozen.

"Isobel..." the Count said. He still had his sword out. "Make your courtesies to Lord Quarmal. He's here to rid us of the monster that's been troubling our nights."

As angry as Lady Isobel seemed to be, I wasn't sure how she'd react to her father's direction, but training carried through and she made a polite dip and flourish. She was a small girl and looked even smaller in the full dress she was wearing.

"Well, my dear," said Quarmal, "you're truly as much a little doll as your father says, aren't you?"

He turned and nodded approvingly toward the Count, then faced back around to the girl. Quarmal was about forty and in good health. He wasn't fat, but I thought of grease every time he spoke.

"And your father says you're a woman now," Quarmal said, "so you need to think of marriage. When I dispose of this monster, you'll wed me. How do you like that, my pretty little thing?"

"I don't like that at all!" Isobel said shrilly. "But it doesn't matter because nobody's been able to find where the monster hides!"

Quarmal reached out, I suppose to pat Isobel's cheek. She jumped back with a look of desperate fury. Ayesha put her arm around the girl's shoulders, and Isobel buried her face in the maid's robe.

"You've raised a spirited one here, Count Heber," Lord Quarmal said. He smiled when he turned to the Count but I didn't like the look I caught in his eyes. "No matter. That's easily cured after I've dealt with your monster."

Doctor Carolus stepped forward—toward Lady Isobel, I thought, but he pointed in Ayesha's face and said, "You! Arab! What are you doing here?"

The maid straightened and thrust Lady Isobel behind her. "I am not an Arab!" she said fiercely. "I am a Kabyle. A Moor if you wish, but never an Arab!"

"She's my daughter's nurse," the Count said. "My late wife chose her before Lady Isobel was born, thirteen years ago. There's never been a problem in all that time."

"Hasn't there?" said Doctor Carolus. "Perhaps you haven't been looking with the eyes of art, then!"

His face was turned toward the Count but that must have been misdirection as he watched Ayesha from the corner of his eye. His left hand shot out suddenly and snatched the thong hanging around the maid's neck. Carolus pulled the medallion hanging from it out of her clothing. The maid's head jerked forward for an instant before the thong broke.

Carolus held the medallion in the air as he rotated to display it to everyone in the hall. It was a disk of bright red crystal carved with a round design like a sun disk with inward-pointing rays. A sun disk, or a lamprey's open mouth surrounded by teeth.

"Do you think it nothing to worship demons, my lord?" Carolus said.

Ayesha sprang at his back with her fingers spread like the claws of an angry cat. Maltach, the Count's personal bodyguard, caught her by the arm before she reached Carolus, and a moment later Dressan had her other arm. Lady Isobel put her clenched fists to her mouth and began a high-pitched scream.

"Ayesha!" the Count said. "What does this mean?"

The maid mumbled in a language I didn't know. Doctor Carolus said—to Lord Quarmal rather than to the Count, "I'll need a room with an overhead beam to question her properly. And perhaps a charcoal brazier."

"We'll go into the large council room here," the Count said, gesturing down the cross-hall. The room was across from Lady Isobel's suite. "Leo, get a brazier from the kitchen. And Eric—" the other page "—get a twenty-foot rope from the stables. That should be enough for a strappado, don't you think, Quarmal?"

"More than enough," Doctor Carolus said with a nod.

The company moved to the council room. Isobel continued screaming until the Count carried her into her own suite and slammed the door. She may have kept it up even then but the door was thick and I couldn't hear her.

Unfortunately the Count left the council room door ajar when he joined the others. I didn't like torture much better than Isobel did, but nobody was interested in my opinion either.

Ayesha stayed quiet even when they tied her wrists together behind her back and then tied the separate rope to them and tossed the other end over the ceiling beam. Carolus kept asking questions about the monster. She didn't speak until Maltach pulled the free end of the rope and her feet came off the floor. Even then Ayesha only screamed.

Doctor Carolus continued to repeat his questions. To my surprise Dressan and Lord Quarmal came out of the council room. "Don't let anyone interrupt!" Quarmal said to his servant loudly enough for me and probably the other guard to hear clearly. Dressan drew his long dagger and smirked at me.

Quarmal crossed the hall and pulled open the door to Lady Isobel's suite. He slipped inside. I didn't like it, but it still wasn't any of my business.

Dressan smirked again and said, "That hoity-toity girl's going to get her first lesson in the duties of a wife."

I said nothing. If I looked straight ahead, I didn't have to see Dressan's face. I couldn't close off the memory of Lady Isobel shrieking over her shoulder as her father carried her away, though.

The cry of agony was loud in the hallway despite the suite's thick door. I started for it. Dressan wiggled the point of his dagger toward my eyes and snarled, "Stay where you are, hobby!"

I rotated the shaft of my halberd and smashed the butt into Dressan's crotch. He doubled up with a *Whoof!* His dagger clanged on the stone floor.

The door to the suite wasn't locked. It was so heavy, though, that I dropped the halberd behind me to use both hands to open it. Lord Quarmal had a sword, but that wouldn't matter until after I'd pulled him off Lady Isobel. That was as far as I was thinking.

I stopped. Lord Quarmal was sprawled on his back at the foot of the bed. His throat had been torn out. Blood splashed the room.

Lady Isobel lay on the bed. The light dress she'd been wearing when her father dragged her to the room was beside her on the coverlet, ripped as it came off. She'd stopped screaming; her face had a glazed expression.

Maltach pushed in past me. He too stopped when he saw the situation. Apparently he didn't have any better idea of what to do than I did.

More people crowded into the suite, but they all made way for the Count. He too stopped when he saw his daughter.

"Isobel!" he said. "What's happened? Are you all right?"

The girl sat up straight and tugged a corner of the coverlet over her torso. "It was awful! It came through the stone wall. It was all teeth, Papa, but the man was covering me and it bit him and there was so much blood! Blood everywhere and I fainted."

"Who saw what happened?" the Count said, looking around. His eyes didn't rest on me, but Maltach was likely to say I'd been here before him.

I said, "My lord? I heard the scream and ran over to the door. When I pulled it open, everything was just like it is now."

Dressan could vouch for where I'd been when Lady Isobel screamed—if it was her and not Quarmal—but I figured he'd say whatever he thought would hurt me worst, so I hoped nobody would decide to question him.

Doctor Carolus squeezed into the room. People got out of his way when they realized who it was.

"What this shows us, your lordship," he said to the Count, "is that the demon has the cunning of its master Satan! It has attacked his opponent Lord Quarmal unawares and fled back to its lair. We must all be doubly cautious until we've winkled it out."

"I guess it also shows us that Ayesha isn't the monster," I said. It was dumb to say something, but I'd been feeling sick already. Almost sprawling over Lord Quarmal's body had really cut my common sense loose.

"Really?" Doctor Carolus said. He drew the word out long enough for three. "May I ask what university do you lecture at, sirrah?"

I looked at the floor, wishing I were someplace else.

Thank the Lord God, Carolus decided to let the business drop. He turned again to the Count and said, "Your lordship, I'm sure that your demon-worshipping pagan will shortly tell us all she knows."

"Later, Master Carolus," the Count said. "For now, I need to get Lord Quarmal laid out in the chapel and send off to his people. And—"

He looked toward Lady Isobel, still cowering on the bed.

"—I need to tend for my daughter."

I picked up the halberd and went back to my post in the hall. Palace servants, none that I knew well enough to talk to, carried Quarmal's body off, leaking blood. Several of the female servants took Lady Isobel away, I suppose to the late countess's suite. Those rooms had been unused since the Countess died over a year ago.

Lady Isobel hadn't allowed any servant but Ayesha to be close to her for as long as I'd been in the city. She had a dazed expression now, though she wasn't fighting her attendants.

Doctor Carolus and the male servants went back to torturing Ayesha. He called the monster "your familiar spirit" and demanded to know where it was hiding.

I couldn't hear what Ayesha answered or if she even did. Her screams were only faint whimpers.

At sunset, a guard I'd never met appeared with his own halberd. He said, "Hans says they caught the monster. What happened?"

"Better ask Hans," I said. "I don't know anything about it."

I carried my halberd back to the arms room. I'd thought it was going to be pretty useless as a weapon inside the palace, but it had done just fine on Quarmal's man.

Dressan was with Carolus now, torturing the maid. I couldn't help that.

When Hans saw me, he asked enthusiastically, "What did the monster look like, then? Did Lord Quarmal kill it?"

I thrust the butt of the halberd over the counter, making Hans jump back. "Quarmal and Lady Isobel are the only people who saw the monster," I said. "Maybe some of the blood in the room came from the monster. I don't know."

I heard Hans babbling to my back and I went down the staircase. He hadn't been my friend before, and I sure wasn't going to chatter with him about a business I didn't understand and didn't want to think about.

One thing I did know for sure: Lord Quarmal's sword was still in its sheath on that chair where he'd thrown it with his belt before he assaulted Lady Isobel. He hadn't injured the monster.

I guess I knew something else as well. A lot of Quarmal's blood had sprayed the room when his throat was torn out, but his body hadn't been drained the way the first three victims had. Perhaps I'd startled the monster away when I'd burst in so quick. If that was so, the creature might still be hungry.

My shuffling down the stairs didn't rouse Burbey. I had to shake him by the shoulder to wake him enough to take the tabard and cap from me. He didn't know anything about what had happened to Lord Quarmal, so I could just unlock and open the postern instead of listening to him talk.

Now I realized it was true that the creature could walk through walls and they were no protection. I wasn't sure that Burbey could have done much about it even if he were awake, though. I wasn't sure that I could either.

I slipped into the inn stables by the side door instead of going through the common room like I usually would. The girl, Vonn, was there to take horses and to return them to any guests leaving. She hadn't heard about what had happened in the palace so I could just send her off without listening to a lot of questions.

I wanted to sleep, but I wouldn't be able to do that without settling down. I watered the horses, then mucked out the stalls, moving each of the six horses in at the moment to an empty stall.

That's real work but it always makes me feel good to do it. The muck fork is as good a piece of craft as the halberd is crappy. The hickory shaft is as smooth as an arrow, and the head and tines are oak. Horse dung is pretty dry so you don't need to use elm like you'd want in a cow yard.

When I had a pile gathered in the center aisle, I opened the left half of the big door into the yard in back. I shoved today's pile out and forked it as high onto the main pile as I could toss it.

When I finished, I'd had the workout I'd needed. It was time to turn the pile—there was enough space in the yard to do that—but I didn't need to do it right now. Another day or two—or week or two—would be plenty soon enough.

I closed the door and hung the rake up on its pegs, then climbed to my cubby in the upstairs loft. I figured I'd be ready to sleep.

I wrapped my spare tunic around an armful of straw as a pillow and stretched out on the rest of the straw. I was asleep before I had time to wonder if I'd be able to.

I woke when the bell in the church rang twice for the second watch, the middle of the night. The moon was coming in through the front door and the vents under the eaves in the back. No light came through the sides because those were solid masonry, as sturdy as the walls of the palace.

The horses were quiet. The one that belonged to the drover I'd seen in the common room whickered in his sleep, but that wasn't a problem as soon as I realized what it was.

It made me think about the monster, though, which I'd forgotten until then. The Lord God knew I wasn't going to go back to sleep with that on my mind, so I got up and climbed down the ladder.

I opened the back doors. Brilliant moonlight flooded the yard; it was plenty bright enough to work. Turning the muck heap would be a better way to spend the time than lying on the straw, remembering that the creature had climbed to the fourth floor to drain Dame Curlee's blood. I put my clogs on, took down the fork, and got to work.

My moving around disturbed one of the horses. She started to whinny, so I closed the back doors.

Doctor Carolus would probably have laughed to hear me say it, but there's right ways and wrong ways to do any job—including turning a muck heap. I'd just started lifting down the top layer and spreading it on the bare flagstones at the right side of the yard when I heard sounds from the stable in back.

It froze me. That shows how scared I'd been by what I'd seen in Lady Isobel's suite. I hadn't really thought about the attacks until then. Sure, I knew they were happening, but there's lots of ways to die—freezing to death on a cold night was pretty damned common in the winter, especially if you had money enough to drink yourself sleepy before you started home.

I'd never worried about that, though I'd seen men dead in the gutter.

Well, now I'd seen a man with his throat torn out by a monster and the body was still warm. *That* had made me believe.

What I'd heard was a voice. It was calling, "Hap?"

I jerked one of the doors open. Cisca, holding a basket, stood at the bottom of the ladder and called up. She jumped away with a little *Eep!* when I swung the door back.

"Oh, Hap! It's you," she said, lowering the basket that she must've thrown in front of her face for protection.

"Sorry, I didn't know you'd be coming," I said. "I'd have left the doors open if I had."

"My fault," she said, though she hadn't done anything wrong I could see. "You hadn't eaten dinner and I thought I'd bring out some food and, well, make sure you're all right."

There was a pair of wooden trestles in the yard. I brought them in. They weren't comfortable seats but they were better than standing up, which Cisca must've been doing all day.

"I'm all right," I said. "I just wasn't hungry. There was a messy business in the palace this afternoon and I didn't want to eat then."

The basket had a quarter loaf, a wedge of cheese, and several plums. I popped a plum into my mouth and realized I'd certainly *gotten* hungry. "This is good, Cisca," I said. "This is good of you."

I paused and looked at her. "You're a good person," I said.

I'd never really thought about how pretty she was, but she was that too. The moonlight coming in through the open doors set off her looks.

"Thank you, Hap," she said, looking away. "I'd heard people talking about what happened in the palace, and when you didn't come into the inn I . . . well, I worried that there was more than they were telling."

"There's not much to tell, really," I said, pulling out my knife and using the side that I hone to a wire edge to cut slivers from the cheese and lift them onto the bread. "The creature came through the wall of Lady Isobel's suite and killed Lord Quarmal right in front of her. I don't think she got a good look at it, at least not that I heard. Then it went back through the stone wall before anybody got there."

Before I got there, but I didn't say that.

"That's *awful*," Cisca said.

"Yeah," I agreed. "Quarmal won't be missed, but Dame Curlee wasn't a bad sort. The other two were pretty much like anybody else. Pretty much like me."

"I'm glad it wasn't you, Hap," Cisca said, looking away from me.

I thought she was going to say something more, but she stood up instead. She said, "Make sure you come in for porridge in the morning."

I was off duty tomorrow, but I didn't bother to say that. I'd check in when I got up if that was what Cisca wanted.

I lifted the fork, wondering whether to hang it up or get back to work on the heap. I'd done enough that I'd be able to get to sleep again, and besides—a meal and chatting with Cisca had put me in a better mood. I'd turn the muck heap another time.

I lifted the fork to put it back on its pegs and I heard something behind me. I spun around.

It was Cisca, returning from the street. She gave me a big smile and said, "I almost forgot my basket."

She reached for the handle, and as she did blackness came through the stone sidewall just like fog flowing down the street on a winter evening. Cisca didn't know about it till it started to wrap around her throat. Then she screamed. The creature either hadn't seen I was there or didn't care.

I just did what went through my mind, same as I had when Dressan tried to stop me after Lady Isobel screamed: I stabbed the shadow with the fork, putting my shoulders into it. The creature was bearing Cisca down and pretty much covering her head, but this was risky and if I'd had time to think I'd have hesitated. There wasn't time, to think or hesitate either one.

The oak tines crunched. The blackness came away from Cisca's body and slid back across the flagstones like the loads of manure I'd been pushing. The fork hit the sidewall and *that* stopped me.

I jerked the tines free and backed away, gasping for breath. I was ready to prod the thing again or anyway get between it and Cisca if it came for her again.

There was a notch out of the eaves where the thatch had fallen away from the frame of withies. The creature was dying. Moonlight fell across its head. For an instant I saw a circuit of wedge-shaped teeth like those on the crystal medallion Ayesha had been wearing.

The blackness flowed and changed. It became a human face.

Cisca was standing beside me. She gripped my shoulder, I think to steady herself. In a small voice she said, "That's the Lady Isobel."

I swallowed. "It wasn't her a moment ago," I said.

The wooden tines had punched through the top of the young girl's chest, flesh and ribs alike. One of the wooden pegs had started to split and ought to be replaced. Isobel's blood had pulsed for a moment as I pulled the fork back, but now it just oozed from her dying body.

"Lord God," I said. "Save us Your children."

I'd never been much for praying but I meant it now.

"Look," Cisca said, pointing with her free hand.

On a thong hanging from Lady Isobel's neck was a medallion like Ayesha's. I'd been feeling sorry for the maid being tortured in the palace, but even though she wasn't herself the monster who'd been stalking the town, she must have known the truth about what was happening. I didn't think she would ever tell Master Carolus what that truth was, but the way he was trying to learn it no longer bothered me.

"Who do I tell what happened?" I said, swallowing again. I looked at Cisca and added, "I won't mention you. Go back to your room and don't let on you were down here."

"It was coming for *me*," Cisca said. "It saw me when I left the stables and followed me back. You saved me, Hap."

"Cisca, keep out of this!" I said. "If you don't, they'll burn *both* of us alive because they'll never believe us!"

"No!" said Cisca. She jerked away her hand and looked up at me. "What were you doing when I came in? Turning the muck heap?"

"Yeah," I said.

"Well, we'll finish the job now with that"—she nodded toward the body—"at the bottom of it. Before it's turned again there'll be nothing left to tell it from any of the children's bodies buried in muck heaps over the years. I'll get the shovel and help you."

"What about the medal?" I said.

"Especially the medal!" said Cisca.

"Right," I said. "Then we'd best be at it, because I want the pile at least waist high before the sun's up enough for anybody to take a look at what I'm doing."

## David Drake

I was never a fan. I was an SF reader from grade school, and by high school was trying to write stories, mostly fantasy. I had no contact with fandom, however, until 1974 when I attended DisCon II with Stu Schiff.

It was a horrible experience. I knew nothing about the milieu or the culture, and it was a lot of people in a relatively small space. I was recently back from Nam and had a degree of PTSD.

I'd sold stories by then, but I was a complete unknown. Not only were the people I met generally unwelcoming, a few were actively hostile to a Nam vet.

I attended a few other cons following that, but it wasn't until my first LibertyCon that I found one which was generally welcoming to everybody, me included. That was Uncle Timmy's doing. LibertyCon was a family, and I was privileged to be a part of it.

—Dave Drake

**David Drake** was attending Duke University Law School when he was drafted. He served the next two years in the Army, spending 1970 as an enlisted interrogator with the 11th Armored Cavalry in Vietnam and Cambodia. Upon return he completed his law degree at Duke and was for eight years Assistant Town Attorney for Chapel Hill, North Carolina. He has been a full-time freelance writer since 1981. His books include the genre-defining and bestselling Hammer's Slammers series, and the nationally bestselling RCN series including *In the Stormy Red Sky, The Road of Danger, The Sea without a Shore,* and *Death's Bright Day.*

# LIBERTY FOR ALL

Jody Lynn Nye is a consummate professional. I've worked with her since the early '90s, and been pleased also to consume the fruits of her baking for much of that time. She has been there, done that, in the industry, from writing gaming modules, to collaborating with Anne McCaffrey and Bob Asprin, to writing all sorts of SF and fantasy, and on to running the DragonCon writer's workshop. She and her husband, Bill Fawcett, have been attending LibertyCon, often on their own dime, for many years—because it's fun. So's this story—about modern-day superheroes.

—TW

# Liberty for All

## Jody Lynn Nye

"Welcome to LibertyCon," said the sixtyish man, looking up from the registration desk with a smile. The big, gaudy nameplate on his colorful T-shirt said ROBERT GANTS. "May I have your ID, please, sir?"

"Jerry Rivers" shot him a cautious glance, then looked over his shoulder at his partners. He clutched the canvas bag hanging by a thick strap over his shoulder. "Why do you need my ID?"

"Well, so I can look up your badge," Robert said, reasonably. "You don't want me to hand it to someone else who claimed they were you, isn't that right? We like to keep everything straight so this convention runs smoothly." He held out a hand. "You don't have to give me your secret identity unless you want to."

With a forced chuckle, the tall, clean-shaven man reached into his pocket for the false billfold that Covert Inspection Operations had prepared for him. He flipped it to the clear plastic window with his newly minted Maryland driver's license. Robert didn't try to take it. He only nodded and scrolled down the tablet on his desk. Once he found the name, he handed over a badge similar to the one on his chest.

"Welcome to LibertyCon, Mr. Rivers. We hope you have a fine time here. Ma'am, can I help you next?"

One by one, the other Secret Service operatives displayed their credentials and received badges, program books, and sticky-backed red, white, and blue ribbons that said FIRST LIBERTYCON!

"Hotel check-in's over there," Robert said, pointing out of the glass doors and up to the right. "Programming already got started. Dealers Room is open, and you can go over to the con suite for snacks. Enjoy yourselves!"

"How did he know about our secret identities?" "Lois Nelson" whispered, her hazel eyes full of concern.

"I dunno," said "Gregory Scott," sticking close to Jerry's shoulder. He lowered his dark brows over his nose. "Our briefings were all top-secret need-to-know, coming down from the highest level!"

"Shh!" Jerry cautioned them, with a curt wave of his hand. "No more talking until we set up the soundproof wave generator in the hotel room."

Robert waited, a half smile on his face, until the trio had gone out the glass doors and up the steps toward the grand entrance hall. He spoke into the badge on his shirt.

"Uncle Timmy, this is Knowledge Base. They're here and wired for sound."

"Got it," the hoarse voice of The Nucleus replied from the tinny little speaker. "Scott, Bobby, y'all hear that?"

"We did, Uncle Timmy!" two more male voices replied in unison.

"This is gonna be fun," Scott Richardson said. He was a relative newcomer to LibertyCon, but had already achieved trusted status.

"Now, don't blow it!" Uncle Timmy warned him. "We went to a lotta trouble to lure these people here."

"No problem," Uncle Bobby Bolgeo said. Uncle Timmy's brother was built on the same lines as The Nucleus himself, big and broad, with a round face.

"No way!" Scott replied, but Robert couldn't restrain a chuckle. He traded a wink with Doris Manning, a large lady with graying brown hair piled in a bun on top of her head, sitting casually at one end of the registration tables. Yes, indeed, some fun.

"They'll all do fine," Doris said, with a knowing smile.

Surrounded by a dampening field that had been developed for the department by DARPA for use in high-risk areas, Jerry studied the other two agents. He had worked with each of them on other missions, both in and out of the country. All three of them had qualified with the necessary hardware and techniques. Both Lois and Gregory passed all necessary psychological training and had spotless records. They were loyal to the government of the United States.

"You've been given a basic overview of the mission, but not

the full details," the tall man said, handing them each one-use digital viewers with profiles and photographs of all the known subjects from his equipment bag. "You get that now. This so-called annual convention has been pinpointed as a training ground for disruptive elements. At the heart of LibertyCon is the founder, Richard Timothy Bolgeo, aka Uncle Timmy." He paused as the other two found the image of the craggy man with silvering beard and hair and wildly curling eyebrows, and nodded. "He's a former electrical engineer with the Tennessee Valley Authority who even decades ago displayed an interest in subversive literature such as science fiction, and has since been named as a secret master of a wide group of fellow devotees. Most, if not all of them, are here this weekend.

"You already know that the people upstairs suspect that they recruit from a small but select population with ties to law enforcement, military intelligence, advanced science backgrounds, literary personalities, and other groups that have been tagged as potentially divisive and dangerous to the interests of the United States. Many of the attendees have been observed and photographed in overseas and domestic locations that had been hotspots of unrest, like the Afghani border, Hong Kong, Liberia, Haiti, and so on. If you scroll down through the files, you'll see certain names popping up again and again, and all of them have ties to LibertyCon and Uncle Timmy."

"Did they stir up the trouble?" Lois asked. The slender woman, straight, sable-black hair cut just above her collar, sat perched on the edge of one of the identical, cushy queen-sized beds with which the suite had been furnished. She scrolled through the data on the small backlit screen. "This part was in my initial briefing, but not the outcome. The dates don't all look as if they match."

Jerry frowned. He had gone over the briefings numerous times himself. The contradictions had stood out to him, but he put it down to hasty transcription by a clerk. "I'm afraid that it's not clear whether they came before or after the riots and disease outbreaks had been quelled. The matter at hand is *how* these agents happened to be in those places at those times; more importantly, why and who sent them? Investigations have proven that it was this Uncle Timmy."

"But how?" Gregory asked. "How would he know to dispatch one of his 'fans' to those locations?"

Jerry shook his head. "Bolgeo seems to be at the center of some enormous web of information. The brass don't have a clear understanding of how he gets classified data; they have only proved that he does obtain it and make use of it. Therefore, he is suspected of endangering US interests in numerous locales. On more than one occasion, he has undermined the government's ability to control situations to our advantage. Our mission is to take him out. You have been issued the appropriate equipment, and been trained in its use. Sometime during this weekend, one or more of us will get the man alone and carry out our assignment. Once the spider is gone, the web will fail."

Lois and Gregory only nodded. Wetwork wasn't for squeamish wimps.

Jerry himself had twelve years of experience in the field. He didn't think of himself as particularly brave. He was only doing his job. When it came to protecting the country and its liberty, he could be absolutely fearless. What kept him going into danger on behalf of the United States with a clear mind was the knowledge that behind him was the best wife in the world, and the ten-year-old daughter with whom the two of them had been blessed. As long as they were safe, and they were watched over by other members of the Secret Service when he wasn't in country, he could do anything. With them to protect, he was inexorable and incorruptible. To succeed in this mission was vital; this threat lay too close to home.

A small population of fewer than seven hundred people didn't seem as though it could have so much influence, but it wasn't up to Jerry to make that determination. The upper-ups had declared that the careful manipulation by government organizations to restrict the liberties of the American people to what could be easily controlled seemed to go haywire. His immediate superior admitted that they couldn't pin anything directly on these attendees or Bolgeo. Still, rumors of black magic, computer hacking, and other things were reported to be going on there. Nobody wished to admit that such things were possible, but if the Russians had a Department of Psychic Phenomena, America was not going to be caught out by mystical wrongdoing, oh, no!

"This event seems to be so normal," Gregory remarked, as they walked through the convention center. "Apart from things like that." He gawked at a man in an articulated suit that sort of looked like Iron Man's. "Man, that's pretty dope."

"Look at that one," Lois said, glancing toward a woman in a brocade medieval gown complete with tall headdress. "I love that!"

"Act casually," Jerry warned them. "We have to look as if we fit in."

"Hey, there!" A lovely young woman with short black hair and flashing eyes came up to them. Her badge said CO-CHAIR. "You're new! Welcome to LibertyCon! I'm Brandx Spraker."

"Nice to meet you," Jerry said, putting on the false effusiveness he had practiced in front of a mirror. It seemed natural to ask questions, so he did. "Er, what's with all the costumes here?"

Brandx laughed. "That's cosplay. When you're here, you get to be the person you are deep down inside that no one ever gets to see. You get to be the real you. We think that's very important. You can borrow some costumes or masks if you want them."

Lois looked as though she wanted to take her up on the offer. Jerry let out a peeved cough.

"Uh, maybe another time," Lois said, nervously. Brandx patted them on the arm.

"Sure. Opening Ceremonies are about to start. Y'all come and see it. We introduce all the guests and you newcomers, too!"

"No!" Jerry exclaimed. Brandx gave him a sympathetic glance.

"It's okay. We're all friends here. It helps you to get to know everyone."

*We don't want to get to know anyone,* Jerry thought, impatiently. It didn't matter; the names under which they had registered weren't their own anyhow.

"Threepeat, any problems?" a very tall man asked, coming up beside them. His badge stated that he was Mike Bast.

"None," Brandx said. "It's all going right as it should be. Mike, these people are new. You want to help them out?"

"Sure. Glad to do it."

"Threepeat?" Jerry asked, in spite of himself.

"Aw, you know, an old nickname." She smiled at them. "Well, I gotta go pull myself together before Opening Ceremonies."

Jerry watched as she walked away. Two more women came out of a side corridor and joined her. They had lush, dark hair and convention T-shirts identical to Brandx's. In fact, they looked remarkably like her.

Suddenly, the light in the hallway flashed, almost blinding him. When it cleared, he could see only Brandx. The other two were nowhere in sight.

The young woman glanced his way as she was about to turn the corner, and gave him a smile. He couldn't put his finger on what seemed so strange, or where the other two women had gone.

"Come on," Mike said. "I'll help you find seats in the auditorium."

Following Uncle Timmy's instructions, Mike kept close behind the three newcomers as Opening Ceremonies broke up. From there, they wandered into the Dealers Room. Mike was amused by the combined expression of fear and disdain on the face of the leader. If he hadn't known what they were at the convention for, they'd have seemed like any mundanes visiting fandom for the first time.

"Why would people even want to wear a toy dragon on their shoulder?" Jerry asked the man selling handsome handmade bronze *objets d'art*, including tiny dragons with opal eyes.

"Because real ones will burn your hair off," the man replied, calmly.

Mike almost laughed as the three newcomers retreated hastily into the hallway.

The shorter, dark-skinned man was looking over the program book. Mike took his opportunity to approach them and do a quick scan on them.

"Can I help you all find something?" he asked again, putting his hands on the men's shoulders. Before the tall man automatically flung him off, he sensed weapons: handguns tucked into their socks, knives secreted in their belt buckles, and glass vials of some kind that practically gave off a blue, radioactive glow. Uncle Timmy had been right: they were loaded for bear.

"We want to see the Guest of Honor panel," the shorter man said. The way he pronounced it sounded kind of momentous. "We don't know where this room is." He indicated the name next to the panel description.

"Well, the Guest of Honor happens to be right over there, near the door of that room, so that just got easier," Mike said, guiding them with hands in the middle of their backs. "Dr. Bova!"

Mike waved to the slim, tanned man in the bright blue shirt, who gave him a nod. Ben Bova was always a favorite of the LibertyCon crowd.

"Oh, my God, is that Ben Bova?" Lois cooed, looking thrilled to her bones.

Mike took her arm. Her aura radiated compassion, curiosity, and fascination with what was going on, almost overwhelming her sense of responsibility. He liked her at once. Uncle Timmy had chosen well, as usual.

"Y'all are newcomers. Let me introduce you to our GOH. Dr. Bova, we've got some new people here who want to meet you."

"Good to meet you," Dr. Ben Bova said, extending a hand to each of them.

"How are you doing, sir?" Lois asked, her eyes wide. The writer scientist gave her a kindly smile.

"Fine. A little tired. I just flew in from Florida."

"Um," Gregory ventured, looking for something to say. "What airline did you come in on?"

Bova looked at them blankly. "Airline?" Mike shot him an urgent look. "Oh, it was a private flight."

Gregory nodded.

Mike felt a surge of relief. Sonic Wing almost blew security too soon. He looked around frantically for Doris, who was due in the corridor just about then. She was supposed to have tipped off Dr. Bova so no one else could hear her. As Little Birdie, she could put thoughts into other people's minds as if she was whispering in their ears. It didn't mean she could will them to obey her. She had trained for years to try, but that didn't work. Still, minor powers were just as valuable as major powers. Otherwise, LibertyCon would have only a few heroes attending instead of over seven hundred.

Uncle Timmy was one of those major powers. He seemed like an easygoing good old boy who loved his family and science fiction fandom, but every strand of that thick, wavy hair of his extended off into the ether, listening in on the bastions of power all over the world. A lot of world leaders and people of influence had received a mysterious call from The Nucleus warning them not to impinge on people's liberty. He probably had a hundred assassination contracts out on him, but he knew where every would-be killer was at all times, and it was the pleasure of his fan base to drop in unexpectedly on those operatives and remind them that they weren't working in a vacuum. The free world needed defenders. LibertyCon was at its center, and Uncle Timmy was its heart. Mike was proud to be a part of his cadre.

The three newcomers seemed as clueless as anybody attending their first con, but he'd seen enough FBI, CIA, SEALs, special forces, foreign agents, and serving or retired military from every major country in the world to know what they were dealing with. It made him uneasy to have them in the house during their most vital meeting, but Uncle Timmy assured him he knew what he was doing with these three. Watching the woman go all gooey over meeting their Guest of Honor told him they could be cracked. All they had to do was find their vulnerable spots before they tried to do something stupid. Meanwhile, they had to get them out of the way while the main meeting took place. Once the GOH panel was over, and Dr. Bova's escort came to take him to the boardroom, Mike would lure the intruders away to the trap they had set. He hoped it would work. That leader of theirs was pretty suspicious. Mike didn't want them to figure out what they were doing. Sure, these agents thought LibertyCon was concealing stuff from them. They just had absolutely no idea of what or how much.

He all but tag-teamed Uncle Bobby and Doris Manning, who had finally made it down to the function area.

"Can they hear us?" Mike asked Little Birdie.

"Sure can." Doris made herself comfortable on a chair just outside the door of the panel room. The subject, expounded on at length between author John Ringo, otherwise known as Sentinel, and a number of the other guests, was about surveillance and counterintelligence tactics. Citing one of his novels, Ringo deliberately had introduced the concept of blood-bound oaths and fatal consequences for breaking loyalty. Regular fans knew it was one of those way-out theoretical discussions that was more fun over half a dozen beers, but the three visitors didn't. They hung on the edge of their seats with their eyes wide, occasionally touching the places where Mike had detected they were carrying armaments.

*Taking over now*, Little Birdie said in his ear.

Mike grinned at them, and went off to report to Uncle Timmy.

"I have confirmation," Gregory murmured to the others as they joined the crowd leaving the panel. He glanced up from what looked like an ordinary smartphone, yet was anything but.

"An important meeting with all the principals is going to take place in the ballroom in about twenty minutes. We'll have just enough time to plant listening devices there."

"If anyone questions us, look clueless," Jerry cautioned them. "They appear to be forgiving of any casual behavior. Make sure we are not being followed."

"I'm seeing the same forty or so people in convention T-shirts around us all the time," Lois said, taking a quick glance around. "I can't tell if they're following us or not. That Brandx seems to be everywhere we go."

As the three agents went by him, Uncle Bobby raised his voice.

" . . . You know there's gonna be a lot of blood spilled up there on the roof," he said. Out of the corner of his eye, he spotted the tall guy stiffen.

"It's okay," Doris said. "We brought plenty of sand. That'll absorb it until we can move everything back down again."

"From the roof?" the stout man asked, enunciating his words very carefully.

"From the roof," Doris confirmed.

"I hope that virgin don't back out again," Uncle Bobby said, shaking his head. "She promised she'd show up last time, too."

*Blood*, Little Birdie sent whispers into the ears of the three agents. *Blood! Death! Satan!*

"We got the keys to the roof door. It's all gonna start in about twenty minutes," she added aloud.

"Don't forget the marshmallows for the s'mores roast over the body," Uncle Bobby said, helping Doris to her feet.

"I'd never forget a thing like that!" she assured him. "I haven't had a good blood sacrifice in more than a year. You got to do these things right."

*Blood! Murder! Black magic!*

The expressions on the faces of the agents were everything they could have hoped for. Doris giggled as Uncle Bobby helped her get away.

"They're plotting a murder!" Lois said, horrified, watching them go. "We can't ignore that."

"Our mission is to gather information and stop Uncle Timmy," Jerry said, firmly.

"Look, he's not going anywhere!" Lois said, lowering her voice and pulling her two colleagues aside from the stream of T-shirted humanity flowing past them. "We can prevent an innocent victim getting killed and still do our job. We can get Uncle Timmy any time this weekend."

"The sooner the better," Jerry said, slowly, "but I agree. The more evidence we can collect about the anarchy going on here the easier it will be to shut this whole place down forever."

Like most hotels, the roof staircase on the top floor was clearly marked with an EXIT sign. No one was in sight as the agents approached it.

"Locked," Lois said, trying the handle. "Hurry! It's already been fifteen minutes."

Gregory stepped forward and inserted a small, highly classified, computerized device into the lock. A few muted clicks later, the door sprang ajar.

"Weapons ready," Jerry murmured, drawing his Glock from the hidden pocket in his shirtfront. In spite of his controlled exterior, he felt a rush of adrenaline. Who knew what horrors lay exposed to the sky?

One by one, the agents slipped into the stairwell.

At that moment, Jerry's cell phone vibrated on his hip. *Not now!* he thought at it. But he couldn't stop himself from looking. The message on the glowing lock screen said, "Walter Reed." His heart sank. He wanted to call his wife, but the mission came first. He understood that. *She* understood that. It didn't help. The butterflies in his stomach doubled in quantity.

The sun beat down on their heads as they crept out of the stairwell. Gregory eased the door quietly toward the jamb, but it yanked right out his hands and slammed shut. The agents jumped. Jerry frowned. There was no wind up there. Lois tried the metal handle, then tugged hard on it with both hands.

"It's stuck!" she said. "There's no lock on this side."

"Call the desk," Jerry said. "We may need emergency services in a minute."

"All right." Lois took her smartphone from her pocket and phoned the Marriott hotel main number. "Hello?"

At the convention registration desk, Robert picked up the call on the first ring. The Nucleus had intercepted the call and rerouted it to his cell phone.

"Good afternoon!" he said, putting on a smooth, professional voice. "How may I assist you?"

Lois breathed a sigh of relief.

"We're assisting someone who got hurt up here on the roof," she said, keeping her voice low as she watched Jerry and Gregory edging along behind the air-conditioning unit. That stretched the truth a little, since they hadn't found their victim yet. "We'll probably need paramedics. Can you send someone to help us get her down?"

"Right away, ma'am," the man's voice said. He didn't ask how they had gotten onto the roof. Undoubtedly, such things were common at this conference. "You all just stay calm, and we'll get to you as soon as possible."

"Yes. Thanks. Bye." Lois switched off and put the phone away. Crouching low, she hurried to catch up with the others.

Robert hung up, then promptly went to the hotel bar to tell all the concom members waiting for the real meeting that it could go off without interruption.

*They're coming*, Little Bird's voice said in Heather Booker's ear.

"...Dark and stormy night," Heather intoned, her voice wailing up and down the scales like a banshee as she recited memorized passages from *Paul Clifford* by Edward Bulwer-Lytton. The pink highlights in her short blond hair twinkled like stars. "The rain fell in torrents—except at occasional intervals, when it was checked by a violent gust of wind which swept up the streets (for it is in London that our scene lies), rattling along the housetops, and fiercely agitating the scanty flame of the lamps that struggled against the darkness..."

"Blood! Blood! Blood! Blood!" chanted the other players.

She knelt on the big round rug spread out over the pea gravel covering the tar-paper roof. Black and red candles burned at the points of a massive pentacle that had been carefully limned on it in white chalk. Matt Fanny sat at one side, humming into a didgeridoo. The rest of the robed role-play gamers crouching in a circle around her swayed from side to side, their arms in the air.

"Roll your saving throw!" she commanded Cisca Small. The freckled young woman shook a handful of colored crystal dice and cast them into the center of the circle. They rolled over and over. Cisca looked at the total and let out an anguished scream.

"You failed," Heather stated. She raised a toy dagger over her head with both hands. Cisca threw herself down full length on the rug. "Now, die!"

From behind the air-conditioning units, two men and a woman hurtled, holding guns at the ready. Not changing her pose an inch, Heather fixed them with an owlish gaze. They stopped, staring at the woman lying in the middle of the pentacle, moaning and writhing.

"Stop!" the leader commanded, pointing the gun at Heather. "Drop the weapon!"

Heather let it dangle from her fingers, making sure they got a good look at the green plastic blade and the big Lucite gems in the handle.

The sight of the toy brought them up sharply.

"It's fake," the woman said, blinking.

"Of course it is!" Heather said. "A real one would cost a fortune."

"What are you doing to her?" the dark-skinned man demanded.

"Me?" Heather asked. "She did it to herself."

"I cannot believe that I put my drow up against a troll!" Cisca wailed, holding up a tiny painted statuette. "Forsythia, I *betrayed* you!"

"Wait, what?" Jerry asked, trying to retrieve his wits. "What's happening here?"

"Fifth-edition D&D. What's it look like?" Heather asked. The three agents swayed, uncertain. Uncle Timmy had told her to lay it on thick. Looked as if her Fascinator mojo was working just as it should.

"Um," the tall man said, completely taken aback. He blinked hard. "Um. Nothing. Nothing." Hastily, he holstered the gun. Looked like a classic Glock. The others put their guns away with the same speed. Heather and the others pretended not to notice. Everyone up there was more heavily armed, and probably just as well trained.

"Y'all want to play?" Heather asked, pouring on the persuasion. "We just lost our dark elf. They're trying to infiltrate the Central Temple of Chattamonganutricata. We could use some people who are good at *covert operations*." She gave them a cheeky grin.

The three froze. They had been Fascinated.

"Um, sure," the shorter man said, ignoring the shocked look on his tall colleague's face. "Can anyone lend me some dice?"

"Wasn't that fun?" Gregory almost chirped, two hours later, as they trooped down the stairs. The roof door had magically unlocked itself during the game and swung open without a problem. "And we fit right in. I thought you made a great Dwarven King."

"Shut up," Jerry said, feeling abashed to the core of his soul. Playacting like a little kid! This wasn't going into the report for HQ.

"It was the only way to recover from bursting in like that," Gregory continued. "We interrupted an innocent game. They were only having fun. Even the Defense Department uses RPG as a training device."

"All right!" Jerry interrupted him, with a curt swipe of his hand. "It *was* innocent. We responded to bad information. It won't happen again. Focus on the task at hand! Nothing else matters. We fulfill our mission and get out of here, if we can."

Lois was shaking her head.

"Why did Central think there was something out of the ordinary going on here? Apart from games and costumes, I'm not seeing a thing that wouldn't happen in any high school."

"Not *my* high school," Jerry protested. He glanced at his watch. "Dammit, we missed the meeting."

"I'm sure there will be follow up," Lois assured him. "Uncle Timmy and the central structure of this organization must want to disseminate information to the rest of their cadre."

Jerry shook his head. "I'm shocked at the number of former or serving military here. How could this group have poisoned the minds of so many of our armed forces and trusted personnel?"

"What if . . . ?" Gregory began, then hesitated.

"What if *what*?"

"What if our intel was wrong? It came from an informant in the WorldCon committee. They've always given us good info."

"Did anyone check against their personal agendas?" Lois asked, reasonably.

"Not that I know of," Jerry said. He felt betrayed by his associates. He intended to report both of them when they returned to HQ. How could they get so distracted by the outward appearance of this organization? Their job was to follow orders!

His cell phone buzzed again. NATALIE'S IN ICU, the message read.

Resolutely, Jerry put it aside. He forced himself to ignore his concerns and concentrate on the mission. This was a high-profile case with ramifications that rolled throughout world government and spheres of influence. Once this task was dispensed with, he could request leave.

"There he is," Gregory said, pointing across the room. Jerry peered over. Sure enough, the heavyset man with thick hair and beard sat in his golf cart rolling toward an elevator. This time he was in reach.

A fit, middle-aged woman in a striped T-shirt walked beside him, almost like a bodyguard. According to their briefings, she was Melissa Sleeman, retired Air Force. Sleeman was on their radar, one tour of duty seconded to an intelligence group in Syria, then returned to the Air Force. The report said that she had managed to escape from a dire situation, facing almost certain death against sixteen enemy insurgents. No one had a clear picture of how she had managed it, but she got a commendation and a medal. She was undoubtedly a fierce and canny fighter, but Jerry had come out of some sticky situations himself. He was confident that they had experience and stealth on their side.

"We can take care of this *now*," Jerry said. He touched the hidden pocket with the syringe in it. The others surreptitiously checked their own weapons. Once they injected the toxin, it would take effect in seconds. They would confirm death, then get out in any way they could. If challenged, Gregory carried a poison gas grenade large enough to blanket the first floor of the hotel. All of these operatives had been treated with the antidote.

The crowd in the elevator lobby was large, but not so dense that they couldn't move close to their target. Jerry had the syringe out, its point within a hand's breadth of Uncle Timmy's meaty upper arm. He slid the hypodermic toward the old man's flesh.

Then, the elevator in front of him chimed.

"Let 'em out!" a number of the fans chorused. Jerry found himself shoved backward by a wave of soldiers in white Star Wars armor. He tried to sidle in between them to get back to his target. Before he could make his way through, the golf cart rolled into the elevator, followed by Melissa Sleeman and Brandx, who came out of a side corridor at the last moment.

"Never mind," Gregory said, observing Uncle Timmy's escort's finger stabbing at the indicator panel. "They pushed three or four. We can get up the stairs and meet the car."

Jerry gave him a curt nod. They ran up the two flights to three, and arrived just as the chime announced the arrival of the elevator. He assumed a casual stance next to the door. It slid open.

The car was empty.

"Wait a minute, we saw them get on here!" Gregory exclaimed.

Jerry cast around. Over the rail of the balcony, he saw the golf cart back on the ground floor again, trundling away from them toward the convention center doorway. The tall woman with military bearing ran ahead to open it for Uncle Timmy. Jerry couldn't stop himself from goggling.

"How did he do that?" Lois asked.

"I don't know," Jerry said. Convinced more than ever that he was dealing with advanced technology that could aid and abet the enemy, he considered vaulting the rail to catch up. Instead, he made purposefully toward the stairs and thundered down them.

Once they emerged from the stairwell, though, he saw no sign of his quarry.

"Y'all trying to find something?" asked a man whose name tag identified him as Uncle Bobby. They had seen him before, near the panel room.

"Um," Lois said, "we wanted to talk with Uncle Timmy. He was, uh, just here."

The man grinned.

"You gotta keep on the move if you want to catch up with my brother." He looked at the face of his cell phone. "I bet he's gonna be at the private reception on the second floor in a while. Come with me. It's invitation only, but you're first-timers. I'll get you in."

Jerry hesitated. Too many witnesses. Yet, to refuse was to draw unwanted attention to the group. They couldn't be seen as not eager to experience everything at this conference, illicit though it was, but with Uncle Bobby, he found it impossible not to be enthusiastic. He shook his head. This place was getting to him.

"Thank you," he said. "That would be helpful."

"Do we have to dress up?" Lois asked Uncle Bobby. To Jerry's dismay, the idea seemed to appeal to her.

"No, not if you don't want to. Most people are going to go casual."

✧    ✧    ✧

Jerry carefully observed who bundled into the elevator with them to the limited-access venue on the second floor. The effusively friendly attendees seemed to consider it a sport to see how many people could get into one car without setting off the weight alarm. It was an annoyingly large number. Most of them did seem to have bathed during the present century, except for one very big man in blue and red spandex. The three agents' eyes watered as if they had been to a funeral. The costumed man not only smelled like the latrine house during Jerry's army days, but Jerry could have sworn he could aim his body odor. He couldn't be doing that on purpose. Could he?

Jerry peered at the large man out of the corner of his eye. The big man grinned.

Perhaps he was.

Uncle Bobby aimed an equally surreptitious glance at Smello-zone. It was like the dude did it out of spite. Timmy was gonna have to have words with him later. They were too close to the finish to wreck it now. If all the hard work everyone had been doing fell through, they'd be years trying to get it all set up again.

The time had come to arrange the confrontation. Bobby got the trio off the elevator and quickly aimed them toward a bunch of the professional guests, their biggest powers. They all knew about the intruders and were prepared to deal with them. Red Pen had a table with a view of everything in the reception area. Sword Thane immediately noticed Bobby and his guests, then went back to his discussion with Sonic Wing. Sentinel, Spite, and The Voice were laughing it up near the food. Three of the protective powers, Panther Mom, Safe Haven, and Mother Nature, huddled over a cell phone, trying to look nonchalant. Mother Nature, who never missed anything, sized up the visitors as they went by. She glanced meaningfully toward Doc Rocket, Point Man, and Solar Sailor. Bobby nodded. Nobody here was going to be caught off guard.

Despite Uncle Bobby's assertion that it was a party limited to a small number of the convention-goers, Jerry counted over a hundred and fifty of the seven hundred members in the space. A woman with collar-length dark brown hair and oversized glasses held court at a small table near the buffet. The man who had been introduced to them as Dr. Bova stood near the window with a taller man with brush-cut brown hair and a mustache. By their hand gestures, they appeared to be discussing aerodynamics. A man of medium height with a silvering crewcut, tinted eyeglasses and a wide grin shared a raucous laugh with a huge, broad-shouldered man with prominent black eyebrows and beard, but a shaved head, and a tall man with a Van Dyke beard and mustache whose straggly blond hair was caught back in a ponytail. A pale-skinned woman with dark brown hair and eyeglasses balanced on top of her head showed cat pictures from her phone to a very pretty, petite woman with blue hair and army boots and a buxom woman with shoulder-length bleached hair. Two men, movie-star handsome and broad-shouldered, one blond and one brunette, joked with a slim, balding man with glasses perched on his large nose.

"Oh, my God," Lois breathed, as they walked around the huge open space. "I can't believe all these people are here!"

"They're potential traitors to America!" Jerry growled.

"They're literary royalty!" Lois said. She stared at a big bearded man in a motorized scooter. "Look, there's David Weber! Let me at least get his autograph."

Jerry surveyed Weber, and observed that he was wearing a full uniform with a chestful of medals that was not authorized dress gear for any American armed forces. He had clearly pledged allegiance to some foreign power, no doubt one hostile to the land of his birth. These people were showing their true colors, now. They intended to undermine the legitimate government and sway weak minds into believing in separatist and anarchist claptrap. This nest of dangerous vipers had to be wiped out, beginning with the spider at the center of the web.

"Focus, Agent," he hissed at her. "Remember what you're here for."

Lois blinked the starry expression out of her eyes.

"Yes, sir," she murmured.

Gregory tapped him on the arm.

"There he is."

Jerry glanced up. The golf cart trundled around the rim of the circle and came to a halt at the buffet tables. The man in the striped shirt began to fill a plate for him.

"Now's our chance," he said, then raised his voice. "Sir! Uncle Timmy!"

The older man lifted his head and peered at Jerry.

"Hey, there," he said. "Don't think I've met you yet."

"No, sir," Jerry said, planting an eager expression on his face. "Jerry Rivers. This is our first LibertyCon." He held out a hand, hoping to palm the syringe, but Uncle Timmy reached for his plate of food instead.

"Welcome! Hope it won't be your last."

*Perhaps not*, Jerry thought, annoyed to be thwarted, *but it will be yours.*

"So, what can I do for you?"

"Well, sir," Jerry began, holding his shoulder bag forward, "we do a podcast on current events and cultural trends. We've never had a chance to talk to someone who has created such a successful and long-running multimedia conference like this. It must be unique in American culture."

Bolgeo sat back in his motorized carriage and gave him a narrow-eyed glare. Everyone in the immediate vicinity turned to stare at them.

"Don't BS me, son. You never did an episode of any podcast in your life."

*Abort! Abort! Abort!* All the alarms in Jerry's brain went on high alert. He began to look for the nearest exit, wondering how many of these people he was going to have to take out to make his escape. He was so flustered that he almost didn't hear the next sentence.

"...Y'all want me to be the guest on your *first* episode, don't you? You don't have to sell me a load of crap, son. Just ask me!"

Jerry sent out mental hands to grab all of his scattered wits and put them back where they belonged.

"Um, right, sir. That's what we wanted to do."

"We...felt shy about asking you, sir," Lois said. Bolgeo laughed.

"Well, come on! How long an interview you want?"

"Twenty minutes?" Jerry suggested.

"Good. Let's get it done now. We'll use one of the function rooms. Then we can come back to the party."

Uncle Timmy steered his golf cart toward the elevator, with Melissa striding alongside. Jerry had to run after them to catch up. After a frustrating day, everything was falling into place. The victim was deliberately taking them into a private location and isolating himself from his support structure except for Ms.

Sleeman. She wouldn't be any problem. Jerry signed to Lois to neutralize her as soon as they reached the room. The plan was working!

Uncle Timmy took them to the same conference room where the discussion about blood oaths had been held earlier in the day. He rolled up to the table at the front and waited. Jerry made a big show of setting up the technology he had with him, including a recorder and a camera. The brass wanted absolute proof of success.

"If I can just attach this mike to your shirt, sir?" Jerry said, holding out the small, black alligator clip. Gregory positioned himself close to Melissa as Lois closed and locked the door. He gave a nod.

Jerry leaned close to Uncle Timmy's collar, slipping the syringe out of his sleeve and placing his thumb on the plunger. *Too easy*, he thought. *It was just too easy.*

Gregory lunged toward the woman in the striped shirt, but his hands closed on nothing. Suddenly, she was in between Jerry and his target. She grabbed the agent's wrist and twisted it. Jerry grunted with pain. The syringe dropped into her open hand. She showed it to Uncle Timmy.

Bolgeo's eyes went wide. "What the hell do you think you're doing with that?"

Jerry grabbed for the needle, but missed. The woman vanished and reappeared twenty feet away. Jerry vaulted over rows of chairs in pursuit of her. She disappeared again. Jerry spun. Once again, she stood on guard before the golf cart.

"How the hell are you doing that?" he demanded. "Never mind! I don't need it!"

He put his shoulder down and charged, intending to go through her to his target. Gregory leaped to close the distance as well. Instead of connecting with the golf cart, they crashed into each other and dropped to the ground. Uncle Timmy and Melissa reappeared across the room. Jerry sprang to his feet.

"What is your problem, man?" Bolgeo asked. "Not having a good time here?"

"It's you!" Jerry shouted. "You've been sending these people, these *attendees*, on foreign missions counter to the interests of the United States. For the good of the people, you have to be stopped!"

"You're not going to touch me, son," Bolgeo said, with a confident smile.

His complacency made Jerry's blood percolate with fury. He and the other two hurdled chairs, trying to catch up with the golf cart, but it bounced all over the room like a giant basketball. Jerry was almost insane with frustration.

"Knock it off!" he said. "Just stand still so I can kill you!"

Uncle Timmy gave him a long-suffering look from across the room.

"Son, I don't know who gave you your information, but I'm not your enemy. Neither is anyone else at this convention."

"You're an agent working against the United States!" Gregory blurted, vaulting over the table toward him. Melissa grasped the canopy of the golf cart, and it moved again.

Uncle Timmy just shook his head. "That's a lie. I love my country. Everything I do is in the interests of the United States and its Constitution. We operate in secret because most people wouldn't get how we work."

"How else would we have found out what you're doing?" Lois asked.

Uncle Timmy's mouth formed a smile. "Because I let you find out about it. You don't have the slightest idea what we're doing here."

Jerry gawked at him. "You think you lured us here?"

"I don't think, I *know*. I wanted you to come here because you're an E-13, and we need your help."

"Never," Jerry spat. "We would not give aid and comfort to an enemy of the United States!"

"Neither do we. None of us."

The wall containing the door simply vanished, leaving a jagged hole thirty feet across. The three agents leaped back in shock.

"Jericho, I told you!" Uncle Timmy scolded Scott Richardson. "We're not gonna get our security deposit back now."

"Sorry, Uncle Timmy," Scott said.

Jerry was horrified as the room flooded with people, including the big man in red spandex, who sounded off a major fart as he passed Lois. She blanched.

Jerry cast around for escape. He found himself surrounded by fans and committee members. He reached into his bag for the poison gas grenade attached to the back by a strap. They would take out some, but he would fall with them. He had to complete the mission. His hand scrabbled for the snap.

"You don't want to do that," the blonde from the roof said, holding up a calming hand. Jerry's hand faltered. He tried to force it to open, but he couldn't. "Just let it be. You'll be fine. Listen to Uncle Timmy."

Jerry had no choice. He couldn't move. By the terrified looks on their faces, neither could Lois or Gregory.

"Take it easy, son. Let me introduce everybody to you," Uncle Timmy said.

"I saw them at Opening Ceremonies," Jerry snarled.

The old man nodded. "Yeah, but you only heard the names on their driver's licenses. Now you get to hear their secret identities, and why you can stop being afraid of us."

"Doris Manning, Little Birdie," said the heavyset woman with the bun on her head. "I warned a high-level tech executive that his personal assistant was planning his assassination. The assistant wanted to sell out his corporation to China, and had all his personal technology bugged. Now he's on our side."

"Heather Booker, Fascinator," the dungeon mistress from the roof said, with a toss of her blond hair. "I persuade people to cooperate. My last assignment was pulling the peace talks back together in Sri Lanka."

"Melissa Sleeman, Longstep," said the woman in the striped shirt at Bolgeo's side. "My previous mission was pulling a journalist being held hostage out of a prison in North Korea. His reports embarrassed the dictator. It helped to start loosening his hold on his people. Worked out well for our diplomats."

"Crystal Ritchie, Spoonful of Sugar," said an attractive redhead dressed all in purple. "I took care of the victims of a gas explosion in Sebastopol in April. My best barbecue," she added with pride.

"Scott Richardson, Jericho," said the tall man whom Uncle Timmy had scolded. "I got sixty people out of a factory during a fire in Chicago."

"Bobby Bolgeo," said the heavyset man. "You can call me Emphasis. I made a bad political employee resign her post in South America. Communism's on a downward cascade there now."

Jerry felt as though the man's words echoed in his chest like thunder. He had to get out of there! The brass didn't have a clue how weird everything really was at LibertyCon!

The tall man who had taken them to Opening Ceremonies cleared his throat. "Mike Bast, Touchpad. I knew you were basically good people. You're just a little out of your depth."

"Robert Gants," said the older man who had issued them their badges. "Good, maybe, but you're not as smart as you think you are. Neither are your bosses. Knowledge Base."

One by one, the others introduced themselves. If half of what they said was true, they had been at touchpoints around the world doing things beneficial to the United States. Jerry fought against believing anything they said.

"This is all just talk," he choked out. "That woman is just causing optical illusions with some kind of advanced technology. There's a logical explanation for it!"

Brandx stepped forward. This time, no light blinded Jerry, but suddenly there were three identical young women standing before him. He gasped at them.

"Threepeat," said the first one. "I was supposed to be triplets."

"I'm Brandz," said the second one.

"And I'm Brandy," finished the third. "We help Dad keep this convention going. Sometimes it's handy to be able to be in more than one place at a time."

"And I keep track of 'em all," Uncle Timmy said. "I'm The Nucleus. If anybody's been on the news, or on the net, I can listen in on 'em. Like you."

Jerry felt dread. "I've never been on the news!"

"You were when you were on the presidential motorcade. I saw you running alongside the limousine when Clinton was president. I've followed you ever since. This young lady here started out in the Richmond, Virginia, police force. Got a couple of commendations but no promotions, even though she deserved them."

Lois started.

Uncle Timmy waved a hand toward Gregory. "And this guy worked security for the Nuclear Regulatory Commission when Martin Sheen and his buddies tried to storm a New Mexico nuclear power plant."

"My God, he's right," Gregory said.

"Sure I am." Bolgeo grinned. "You can't see what I do, but I let you catch on to a little bit of it. We're all patriots here, like you. I work in the best interests of this country. Always have. Once I found I had this little ability, well, that made it easier."

Jerry stammered, trying to find an explanation he could live with. "Y-you worked in nuclear energy. Was it...some kind of accident in the plant?"

Everyone laughed.

"Like Spider-Man? Nope. I always had it. Then I started finding people like me."

"So, some of the people here are...superheroes?" Even thinking the word made Jerry feel foolish.

"No, son, *all* of the people here are superheroes," Uncle Timmy said, tenting his hands on his belly. "All of them have abilities of some kind. A few of them are world class. Most of 'em are low-level, but they are all good at something. We think the three of you have some small talents, too. We'll help you figure out what they are.

"You're worried about the US being taken over by hostile powers. We don't want that to happen either. If we could get you and some of your colleagues on our side, we could start to move our own people into positions where we could do some real good over there. Make contact in real life with some of the heroes I've been corresponding with. As agents, you could open doors for us."

"No! This is too weird! We're leaving." Jerry started to push his way through the crowd toward the broken wall. He could call in a major strike on this location. The resulting fireball would be seen from miles around, but they would make it look like an accident. He could still pull this mission off. Ten minutes, and this hotel would be a smoking hole. He'd go with it, but this cancer on humankind would be gone!

He reached for his phone. In a twinkling, Longstep appeared at his side and hit his wrist. The phone fell into her hand. Jerry tried to grab it back. Longstep vanished and reappeared behind Uncle Timmy. She handed him the phone.

"You don't have to do that," Uncle Bobby said.

"You're a fellow gamer," Heather said to Gregory. "Someone moves. We counter. They try again. They fail. We win because we never lose sight of the objective."

Gregory frowned. "I don't know..."

"You play *Settlers of Catan*?"

"Of course!"

She grinned. "I figured."

"You studied us," Jerry accused Uncle Timmy. "You use people's secrets against them."

"Once in a while. But mostly we do it to help them. Like now. Spoonful!"

Crystal went to Uncle Timmy's side. She had a plate of cookies with her. Longstep took her hand. They disappeared.

Jerry almost fell toward the spot where they had been standing. Jericho grabbed him and held onto him.

"Easy, man."

"What is going on?"

Uncle Timmy sat back in his seat and closed his eyes.

"They're there. Uh-huh. Looking good." After a few minutes, he opened his eyes and looked straight at Jerry, then held out the phone. "You're about to get a phone call. Answer it."

His cell phone erupted. The lock screen told him it was his wife calling. The lead agent glared at Uncle Timmy.

"What did you do? My wife never did anything to you."

"Just answer it."

Still glaring, he thumbed the green dot.

"Honey, are you all right?" he asked. His wife's voice burbled out of the phone.

"Jerry, this woman gave Natalie a cookie. She ate it, and... Jerry, she's walking. And breathing normally. It's a miracle!"

"Honey, you can't let a stranger give food to our daughter."

"You don't understand! It *cured* her."

Jerry let his arm drop, with his wife still chattering from the speaker. "I don't believe it."

"We can't cure everybody in the world," Uncle Timmy explained, "but Crystal's been working hard on that recipe ever since I found out about your daughter. Your worry about her has been your weak spot. Now you can be strong for this country and promote the cause of liberty all over the world. Join us. We need people like you."

"You really do help," Lois said, wonderingly.

"You better believe it. For more than thirty years, now."

"I'm in," Gregory said, hoarsely.

Jerry glared at him. "I'll see you in federal prison. Traitor!"

"Jerry, they did you a miracle. They're not asking for anything we wouldn't give to the department."

Lois straightened her back. "I am in, too. Jerry, they're not what we thought!"

"No!" Jerry shouted. "You can't do this! It's against our training, our loyalty!"

"It's not," Gregory said, his voice hoarse. "LibertyCon is a good thing."

Jerry shook his head. "I . . . I've got to get out of here, think this through!"

Hands balled into fists, he pushed through the crowd, feeling blindly for the door. The crowd made way for him.

Lois started after him, but Uncle Timmy caught her arm.

"He'll come around," he said. "They always do."

🙢

## Jody Lynn Nye

**Jody Lynn Nye** lists her main career activity as "spoiling cats." She lives near Atlanta with three feline overlords, Athena, Minx, and Marmalade; and her husband, author and packager Bill Fawcett. She has published more than 50 books, including collaborations with Anne McCaffrey and Robert Asprin, and over 165 short stories. Her latest books are *Rhythm of the Imperium* (Baen), *Moon Tracks* (with Travis S. Taylor, Baen), *Myth-Fits* (Ace), *and Once More, with Feeling*, a short book on revising manuscripts (WordFire). She teaches the annual DragonCon Two-Day Writers Workshop every Labor Day weekend in Atlanta, GA, and is a judge for the Writers of the Future Contest. She attended ChattaCon some years ago as a Special Guest and LibertyCon as Literary GoH and has come to LibertyCon most of the years since. She had the fun of walking around the London World Science Fiction Convention (2014) with Uncle Timmy and a couple of his friends and getting to hear his philosophy of con-running. She especially appreciated his sense of humor and love of family, as well as the excellent conventions he helped run.

# OR GIVE ME DEATH

The first time I met Chris Kennedy was in Raleigh, NC, at a convention called HonorCon. He was set up at the table next to mine and we spent some time talking between panels. He was just beginning his work with Mark Wandrey on the Four Horsemen Universe and I don't think he expected what would come of that. After he and Mark had seen my books and talked with me, they invited me to join the other authors they had approached to write in their series. I haven't regretted that moment for a minute. One of those novels took me to the 2018 Dragon Awards. Chris is a great guy and he has proven to be a very good publisher. I have started a similar deal with him on The Fallen World series and we plan to work on that series for a long time to come. He was the first of the authors I invited to the anthology, and Toni was pleased to find that he was already on board when she got involved.

—CW

# Or Give Me Death

*A Four Horsemen Universe Story*

## Chris Kennedy

### Pat's Patriots Mercenary Unit, Auckland, New Zealand, Earth

"Hey, boss?"

Pat Smythe looked up from his slate, happy for the distraction. The numbers weren't working out, no matter how he fiddled with them. "What's up?" he asked his executive officer and best friend, Lieutenant Taylor Hoch.

"We just got a comm from an alien named Zon. I think he said he's a Caroon or something like that. Apparently, he's looking to hire someone for a contract they have."

"The Merc Guild has an injunction on contracts at the moment. Did you tell him he'd have to wait?"

"Yeah, I did, but he said they can't wait. He doesn't care that it won't be guild-sanctioned; he needs mercs, and he needs them now."

"Let me guess; he's got handfuls of red diamonds that he can use to hire us, too."

"As a matter of fact, he does," Hoch said. "How'd you know?"

"Because, like many things in life, it's too good to be true." He held up the slate. "Without a new contract—or something to bring in some money—we're going to be bankrupt in two months. And now—lo and behold—an alien comes along with red diamonds, looking to hire us under the table."

"I can call him back and tell him you aren't interested," Hoch replied.

"No, no; don't do that," Smythe said quickly. "It's the only prospect we've got, so it's worth at least talking to him about it.

167

Maybe we can get a few of his red diamonds and get them assayed, too, and make sure he's on the up and up." He tossed the slate back onto the desk with a grunt. "Did he say where he was staying?"

"Down at the Auckland Harbor Hotel," the XO replied.

Smythe shook his head. "That fleabag?"

"But it's all suites," Hoch replied, humming the hotel's jingle.

"That you can rent by the hour." Smythe shrugged. "Grab your sidearm. We'll also take Waller and Fike."

"Don't want to go down there without backup?"

"No, would you?"

"Hell," the XO replied, "I don't want to go down there *with* backup."

### Auckland Harbor Hotel, Auckland, New Zealand, Earth

Smythe drew his hand back to knock on the door but paused.

"Rethinking leaving Waller and Fike with the APC?" Hoch asked.

"No, I think you and I can handle ourselves, and the APC's a lot likelier to still be there when we get back if they stay with it."

"What's wrong, then?" Hoch asked. She smiled as realization dawned. "It's not like the future of the company rests on this or anything."

"Yeah," Smythe agreed. "Nothing like that, at all." He straightened his shoulders, took a deep breath, and rapped on the door.

They could hear movement inside the room, and then an alien opened the door. Generally mammalian in appearance, the Caroon looked like an oversize, bipedal anteater with a long nose, droopy ears, and long, sharp claws on the paw that held the door open. Smythe had done some research on the race; they had a reputation for being excellent diggers and miners. What the GalNet didn't say was that they also smelled—badly—and he had to cough to keep from gagging.

"Is it time for maid service already?" the alien asked as he opened the door. "For the life of me, I just can't figure out the way your clocks work. Who bases a system of time around the numbers sixty and twenty-four? It's very strange."

"No, actually, I'm not the maid. I'm Captain Pat Smythe and this is Lieutenant Hoch. We're from Pat's Patriots Mercenary Unit, and we're here about the job."

"Oh!" the Caroon exclaimed. "Yes! In that case, come on in!" He held the door open, and a stench rolled into the hallway, the likes of which Smythe had never before scented—and he very much hoped he never would again. It was something like an Amish farm sitting in the middle of a landfill at noon on a sunny, summer day.

His eyes watered, and he coughed again. "Sorry," he said when he could breathe, shallowly. "Allergies." He walked into the room, followed by Hoch.

He didn't remember a tornado-type waterspout hitting the waterfront, but *something* had to have hit the alien's hotel room. Furniture was overturned, rocks covered many of the surfaces, and clothes were everywhere—and the alien barely wore any. He shook his head in confusion. "Were you...uh...robbed?"

"No, why?" the Caroon asked.

"Uh, no reason..." Smythe replied, his voice trailing off. He picked up a couple of large rocks from one of the chairs at the table and set them on the floor so he could sit down. Hoch joined him after picking up a chair and righting it. The Caroon took a chair across from them, sitting on the edge so his tail could flip off to the side, and a second Caroon came and joined them from the small kitchenette.

"We have read all of your planet's history," the first alien, who introduced himself as Zon, said. "Well, all of the info that was on the GalNet, anyway, which admittedly wasn't much. Your race is a new member of the Galactic Union, after all, and not much has propagated to the rest of us."

"Oh?" Smythe asked. "And what have you learned?"

"We love your spirit of independence; it is much like ours. When you broke away from England and had all of those great speakers like Thomas Jefferson...it gives me shivers."

"Uh, that's not our country."

"It's not?"

"No. That's America. Cartwright's Cavaliers is from there, but we aren't. We're from New Zealand."

"Where is that?" asked the second Caroon, whose name was Con.

"It's right here; you're sitting in it. America is on the other side of the planet."

"Oh," Zon said. "I thought we were in America. Your geography is most confusing, just like your system of time. We came here to hire Cartwright's Cavaliers, but they said they weren't currently taking any contracts."

Smythe frowned. "Why would you rather have the Cavaliers than us?"

"Because if they are American, they are the most like us," Con replied. "We started as a colony, but now we are ready to be independent and make our way on our own, just like America. The American Revolution was something to behold." The two gave each other blissful smiles, which looked...odd...on their overlong snouts.

"So you're still looking for a unit to hire to help gain your independence?" Smythe asked. "If you're fighting a planet's worth of troops, we're probably not the best unit for the job, as my company is only platoon strength."

"Yes, we are looking for assistance, since we were unable to hire the Cavaliers," Zon said. "You are the first Human mercenaries we have spoken to since they turned us down. We like your name. 'Patriots.' Do you fight for your homeland? Perhaps, since you are also from Earth, maybe you share a similar spirit as the Americans?"

"I'm sure we do." Smythe was a fan of independence about as much as the next man, but if there was a paycheck involved, he was willing to be *very* independence-minded. "So tell me about this contract."

"So, did you believe them?" Hoch asked as they drove back to the hangar.

"What'd they say?" Gunnery Sergeant Zach Waller asked. The driver of the APC, he had to pause in the middle of his question while he avoided a roadblock that had been set up, dodging into the oncoming traffic and then back into his lane. "Damn thugs are getting worse and worse down here," he muttered.

"Apparently," Smythe said, "they are members of some sort of colony or commune or something. They set up a mining facility on a planet out toward the end of one of the galactic arms. After about a hundred years, they decided to declare their freedom, but the company that had sponsored the original mining operation sent in mercenaries to put down the revolution."

"What race?" Sergeant Teresa Fike asked from the turret.

"Xlatan," Hoch said.

Waller grunted. "Never heard of them."

"They look sort of like Bengal tigers, but with six legs. They can run on four of them, and fire a gun with the other two."

"So, kind of like a tiger centaur?" Waller asked.

"Yeah," Smythe said. "They're some of the dumbest-looking mercs, but they're tough and fast." He shrugged. "Anyway, it appears the mercs didn't keep to the contract—or maybe they did; I don't know. In any event, whether sanctioned by their employers or not, the Xlatan began 'disappearing' some of the miners. Our employers aren't sure whether they are being taken off-planet or just killed, but over one-third of the people have gone missing and the rest have been relocated from their homes into a tent city. At first, it was just the dissidents who disappeared; now it's anyone that questions them. Ask a question? Poof—you're gone the next day, never to be seen again."

"And we're supposed to kick the Xlatan off-planet?"

"We are," Smythe agreed. "They wanted us to kill them all, but I told them we didn't do slaughter contracts."

"Even for slavers and murderers?" Waller asked. "I might be able to make an exception for them."

Smythe nodded. "Even for them. It's a bad reputation to have. It's hard to get people to surrender to you if they think you're going to kill them, and you take unnecessary casualties because of it."

"So, kill or capture the tigers?" Fike asked.

"Yep."

"How many of them are there?"

Smythe looked out the window. "A lot," he finally said.

"About a company's worth," Hoch said.

"Shit," Waller said.

"No way," Fike added. "Unless we're hiring more people. Are we? You know? Hiring more people?"

"There isn't time to hire anyone else and get them trained in time," Smythe said. "They want us to leave tomorrow. Their transport leaves tomorrow, and we're either on it or we're not."

"On the good side, we have CASPers, and they don't," Hoch said.

"Shit," Waller said again.

## Cargo Bay, Trading Ship Independence, Hyperspace

Smythe rubbed his eyes and checked the countdown clock on the wall. They had just over eight hours until the Caroons' ship emerged in the T'praken system. Time to go over the plan one more time and then get a little rest before arrival. It had taken most of the seven-day trip through hyperspace—after a frantic day of loading and departure—to come up with a suitable plan. "All right," he said, "let's go over the plan one last time.

"Here's our target area. It consists of three main objectives: the mine, located under this mountain; the domed town to the east of it; and the tent city, located just to the south. All three of these are connected by tunnels."

"Busy little bees," Corporal Greg Eden noted.

"They've been here for over a hundred years," Smythe said. "They've had time to work."

"We also don't like being wet," Zon said. "We built the dome over the town to keep us dry, and tunnels to keep us dry as we went to the mines and back. When the Xlatan arrived, they took over our nice dry town and forcibly relocated us to a tent city outside it where they could keep an eye on us."

Smythe nodded and pointed at the model. "After we come out of hyperspace, we'll do a HALD drop on the back side of the mountain from the town." The high-altitude, low deploy insertion as they came around from the opposite side of the planet would keep them out of sight, he hoped, or the mission was going to end really quickly.

"It'll take us one night to cross the mountain and get eyes on the target. We'll attack on the second night, as Zon says most of the Xlatan sleep at night. It'll be a three-pronged attack. First, Lieutenant Hoch will take the majority of First Squad to the mine, where she'll deal with any of the Xlatan she finds there."

"There are normally three or four per shift there," Zon interjected.

"Right," Hoch said. "With ten CASPers, we shouldn't have any issues with the kitties, but we need to get in and neutralize them before they get the word out."

Smythe nodded. Hoch's men had been upgraded to the Mk 8 version of the Combat Assault System, Personal—giant mech suits that could deal out death and destruction through a number of weapons systems, including ones which shouldn't alert the main body of the Xlatan. They also were a little smaller and would be better able to move about underground.

"At the same time," Smythe said, "I will be leading Second Squad to the tent city, located here, just south of the town. Once we take out the sentries, we'll get the women and children into the tunnels and Corporal Wormsley will lead them to the mine so we can protect them. After they are safe, Second Squad will take up positions and either kill the Xlatan as they come out of the town, or we will assault into the city if needed. Our employers would like to minimize the destruction of their town if at all possible, so we'll try to catch them on the plains.

"Finally, Gunnery Sergeant Waller will take Corporals Green and Chapin, will link up with Zon and Con, and will go into the tunnels to drop the one from the city to the mines and camp. *This is the key,* as it will force the kitties to stay on the surface where we can out-see and outgun them, and the tunnels can then be used as a sanctuary for the dependents. This *must* happen."

He looked at Waller, their demolitions specialist, who nodded. "Got it."

"I'm counting on you, Waller. This has to happen, on schedule, or we're going to have a lot of pissed-off felines in the tunnels with the dependents. We can *not* allow this to happen. We can beat them on the surface, but if they get into the tunnels, it's going to be messy."

Waller nodded again. "I know." He glanced at Green and Chapin, who each gave him a thumbs-up. "We've got this."

"Good." Smythe looked around the group. "After that, it's a matter of killing enough of them that the rest surrender. Waller will come join Second Squad, and we'll trap the rest of the Xlatan between us. They will likely have armor on, so everyone will be armed with shoulder-mounted heavy MACs, and the Mk 7s with me will also have a rocket pod for killing them in the open."

He nodded as he looked around the platoon. Everyone seemed focused. "They outnumber us two-to-one but we have CASPers and surprise. The key is to get the civilians out of the way first, so we can give them a liberal application of explosives and even the odds. Shock and awe, people! By the time they know what's going on, we'll have them trapped, and they'll either surrender or die. Any questions?"

Seeing none, Smythe nodded again. "Good work, everyone. Go get some rest. The techs will prep our CASPers while we sleep, and we'll meet back here one hour before emergence to do final checks. Ready, break!"

### Cargo Bay, Trading Ship Independence, Descending to T'praken

"All right, boys and girls," Captain Smythe said as the jump light went from red to yellow, indicating their imminent release, "here we go!"

Smythe was the first to drop, and he was slammed around in his suit as the launch module began kicking out the CASPers. Encased in drop shields to get them through the atmosphere, Smythe's arms were locked at his side, and he was a prisoner of the system until it reached the deployment altitude. He held his breath as he watched the rest of the platoon's mechs deploy on his system, and then he released it when everyone's status indicators showed green.

The *Independence* was coming in to land, so his launch had been from lower than normal, and it wasn't long before the CASPer's shield began to glow pink and then cherry red from the atmospheric friction. He reached deployment altitude, and there was a tiny explosion as the eight petals of his drop shield flew away. Designed to fool radar by simulating extra targets, they flew far enough away that he wouldn't either run into them, or get hit in a weapon's blast radius if they got targeted. As they were behind the radar horizon of the Xlatan's antiaircraft systems, the latter wasn't an issue, but it was still nice to have them far enough away to avoid a collision and have them damage any of his systems.

"Successful deployment," the onboard system declared as it began searching for the target zone and applying braking and steering thrust from his jumpjets to get him to the designated area. With the shield gone, the CASPer was also able to start building the battlespace on the Tri-V display in front of him, and he checked to ensure the suit was following its preset route of flight. He nodded to himself; he was coming down on target, and he could see the other members of his platoon following him in. A couple of them were having to input some manual commands, but all were on course.

The last bit of the drop shield—a cone at his feet to help with aerodynamics—fell away, and he rode his jumpjets the rest of the way to touchdown. Two seconds after he reached the planet, Gunnery Sergeant Waller landed, and then another trooper landed every two seconds until Lieutenant Hoch at the end of the stick. He released the breath he didn't know he'd been holding. HALD drops were sometimes more dangerous than the combat that followed them. Thankfully, he had a good set of technicians to keep the suits well maintained; they were worth every penny he paid them...and hoped to be able to pay them after this mission.

"All right, Gunny," he said. "Let's get everyone rounded up and headed over the mountain so we're in place and hunkered down by daybreak."

"Yes, sir," Waller said. "Sergeant Johannesen, you're point. Let's move!"

### Four Miles West of the Target, T'praken

The platoon traveled for an hour, reaching the beginning of the mountain's back slope, when Johannesen came to a sudden stop. Although she didn't indicate a stop, everyone held their positions while they waited for her to assess whatever she had found in front of them. "Captain Smythe, I think you're going to want to see this," she said finally.

Smythe moved forward, and, after a second, Hoch followed him. Smythe's senses strained to the maximum, trying to determine what had set the sergeant off, but he couldn't see anything dangerous.

"What is it?" Smythe asked as he came to stand beside her.

"Look," she said, pointing down into a small ravine.

It took a moment for Smythe to adjust his low-light sensors to get a good picture of the narrow valley, but then he could see the area was full of bodies and—more often—pieces of bodies. After a couple of seconds, he saw one with a long nose and droopy ears, and he realized what he was looking at.

"Well, shit," Smythe said.

"Yeah," Hoch agreed as she came to stand next to him. "I guess we found the missing miners."

"Looks like they must have killed them and then dropped the bodies out here where no one would find them."

"Yeah..." Hoch replied, her voice trailing off. She walked

a few paces to the side and stopped next to what Smythe had originally thought was a rock, but now could see it was part of a Caroon. "Did you get the brief on the local flora and fauna?" Hoch asked.

"Yeah. Nothing indigenous bigger than about the size of a kakapo. Why?"

"Come look at these teeth marks. This body wasn't gnawed on by scavengers; I think the miners were eaten by the Xlatan."

"Those bastards!" Corporal Christine Chapin exclaimed. Smythe knew she'd spent a lot of time talking to Zon and Con during the trip through hyperspace and had gotten close to them. "That's just sick! Those are *people!*"

"Take a look, everyone," Smythe said, loud enough to be heard by all. "Take a *good* look. Here's why we came—to stop this shit. You've met the Caroons; they aren't overly bright, but they're good folks. They just want to mine and have peaceful lives. Instead, they got"—he indicated the ravine—"this."

He couldn't see the faces of his troops through the steel canopies of their CASPers, but he was sure they all wore the same look of grim determination he had on his face. This was no longer about a paycheck, this was about doing what was right. The Xlatan would pay; he would see to it.

### One Mile West of the Target, T'praken

Smythe increased the binocular's magnification and looked out over the tent city in the last light of the evening. He had left his suit behind to sneak forward and get a better look into the valley beyond. The Caroons' enclosure was surrounded by barbed wire, and even from a mile away, he could tell the beings inside it were miserable. The tents had holes in them big enough to see from where he lay, and the area was in a depression between two hills; there was more standing water among the tents than there were dry areas.

"Why didn't you put the tents on one of the hills?" Smythe whispered.

"They wouldn't let us," Zon said. He'd sneaked out late in the afternoon through an unused tunnel to join them. "They know we don't like to be wet—they don't like it, either—so they made us build the city where we would always be damp and miserable." He looked away from the tent city and added, "*We are your huddled masses, yearning to be free.*"

Smythe nodded slowly as he scanned the rest of the area. Four Xlatan patrolled the exterior of the enclosure in pairs, and there were two more at the entrance to the mine below him and to the left about a half mile. There was a lot of motion inside the dome of the former Caroon town, with the Xlatan walking around; he hoped they would settle down once it got dark as Zon had indicated they would.

"It looks pretty much the way Zon described it on Earth," Hoch said from the other side of him.

"Yeah, I know," Smythe replied with a sigh. "That's what bothers me."

Halfway through the planet's night, the platoon moved down the south slope of the mountain, following Con and Zon, and two other Caroons who'd come to guide them, Gron and Plon. "Why are we going this way?" Smythe asked with his suit's volume set to minimum.

"There is a new tunnel on this side that the Xlatan don't know about," Zon said. "They finished it while we were off-planet. It will let us sneak into the tunnels undetected."

"You're sure the Xlatan don't know about it?" Smythe asked.

"Yes, yes, it was only dug while they were sleeping."

"Okay," Smythe said. Changing the plan in the middle of a mission wasn't something he liked doing, and it sent a shiver down his back. "Lead on."

The Caroons took them down the slope and then paused.

"Why are we stopping?" Hoch asked.

"Because we are here," Gron said. He pointed to a large rock. "If two of you could roll that away?"

"Eden, Cook," Smythe said. "You heard him. Move the rock."

The two corporals rolled aside the massive boulder, revealing an opening leading underground.

Gron stepped up to the entrance and waved theatrically at the cave mouth. "After you."

"No," Smythe said, "we don't know where we're going. You lead."

The CASPers had to duck to get through the opening, but then were able to stand up normally. The ceiling was only about eight feet high, though, so they only had about six inches of clearance. They walked about fifty feet through the new passageway, and then it joined into a larger, well-lit one in a "T" intersection.

"Hey," Gunny Waller said, pointing to the wall across from them. "I know this passageway is new and all, but did you put a camera on it, or is that courtesy of the Xlatan?"

"What?" Gron asked. "Where?"

Waller crossed the passage and pointed to a small Tri-V camera high on the wall.

"That's not ours!" Gron cried. "I don't know where it came from!"

"Shit," Waller said. He reached up and smashed it with a metal fist, then turned to Smythe. "They know we're coming, sir. What do you want to do?"

"This is still our best chance," Smythe replied, knowing that his chances for a bloodless takedown had probably just evaporated. "We continue, but hurry. Don't waste time on stealth that would be better spent trying to control the tunnels. Split up and let's get this done!"

Lieutenant Hoch grabbed Plon and spun him to the left, toward the mine. "Show us where we need to go!" she exclaimed. "Hurry!"

Plon scampered off on all fours, with First Squad hustling after him. Smythe turned to Zon. "We don't have time to waste! Go! Go!"

Zon, Con, and Gron hurried off to the right, with Smythe and Second Squad racing after them. The tunnels were generally straight, but slowly winded enough that Smythe couldn't see more than sixty or seventy feet in front of him. Smaller side passageways branched off on both sides periodically.

After about ten minutes, the Caroons stopped at a side passage that was larger than the ones they'd passed periodically. "This leads to the town," Zon said. "Con and I will take the group that is blowing up this tunnel. Gron will lead the rest of you to save our people."

"Are you good?" Smythe asked.

Waller, Green, and Chapin all gave him a thumbs-up. "Yeah," Waller said. "We're good. We've got Con and Zon to show us where we need to go. We'll set the explosives and rejoin you as quickly as we can."

"Good luck," Smythe said. He turned to Gron. "Show us the way to the enclosure where they're holding your people. Hurry."

"It would be my pleasure," the Caroon said. "Follow me." He turned, dropped to all fours, and scampered off, and Smythe and Second Squad hurried after him. They'd only gone about fifty yards when the XO reported she'd made contact. They heard MACs firing from behind them right after. It was on.

Lieutenant Hoch led her squad as it chased after the Caroon. When the little aliens wanted to, they could actually run pretty quickly, and she had to spend most of her time watching where she was going and not looking at the Caroon. She was unprepared when the Caroon stopped all of a sudden, and she had to dodge to avoid him. She slammed into the wall and rebounded, just as a grenade went off behind her, throwing her back up against the wall.

A number of her systems went yellow in her monitor, and she was able to right herself in time to see several Xlatan down the corridor at the next intersection begin firing their laser rifles haphazardly. With a thought, her laser shield deployed from her left arm, and she held it up in time to redirect the first well-aimed laser bolt. She unclipped a K-bomb from her side, armed it, and tossed it into the intersection. The blast from the mech-sized grenade knocked her back again, and brought down part of the ceiling at the intersection. It also thoroughly shredded the Xlatan firing at them.

She looked back at the Caroon—it was pulling himself toward Hoch with one arm, while leaving a stain of red behind it. "Medic!" she yelled as she ran over to the alien.

"Entrance...to the right," Plon said pointing to the intersection, then he collapsed to the floor.

The medic, Corporal Jeremy Cook, ran up. He gently turned the alien over, but even Hoch could see there was no hope; the initial grenade blast had ruined his entire chest cavity.

"Sorry, ma'am," Cook said. "I—" Whatever he was going to say was lost as another laser blast speared through his chest, and his icon went red on Hoch's display. Hoch dove to the side, and a second laser bolt went past her.

Her magnetic accelerator cannon rotated into place, and she drew her reticle onto one of the two new Xlatan that had taken cover at the intersection. The MAC fired and the round removed the enemy merc's head. A second round from Sergeant Teresa Fike killed the other.

"Forward and right!" Hoch yelled. "We have to keep them from getting into the tunnels." She jumped to her feet and raced forward, followed by Fike and the seven remaining members of the squad.

Hoch reached the intersection and turned right, only to run into one of the Xlatan. She had a glimpse of the tunnel mouth about sixty yards away, but it was obscured by the ten or twelve Xlatan in between her and the entrance.

The collision almost stopped her in place—she hadn't realized how big the Xlatan were, especially in armor—but then she commanded her sword to deploy on her right arm, and she stepped forward to skewer the alien in front of her. Fike and Private Granger appeared as if by magic next to her, and the three waded into the mass of the enemy troopers.

Hoch slapped away a rifle pointed at her and slashed down on the alien holding it. The Xlatan fell backward as his arm dropped to the floor.

"Help!" Fike exclaimed, and Hoch spun to find her holding off two of the aliens with her sword, while a third aimed a laser rifle from behind them. Granger took a bolt to the chest at the same time, and his icon went red; he wouldn't be any help.

Hoch slashed back across one of the Xlatan fighting Fike while her MAC swiveled across to target the alien with the laser rifle, but the cannon was too slow. The Xlatan got a shot off which speared through Fike before the round hit the alien in the chest and blew him backward.

Fike went down, and two more of her troopers stepped in to take Fike's and Granger's spots. The other members of the squad began sniping carefully with their rifles from behind them, and the Xlatan fell back.

"Drive them to the entrance!" she said as she slashed down, cutting a laser rifle in half. The return stroke nearly took off her enemy's head. She killed two more, and, as the last one dropped, she realized there weren't any more in front of her; the tunnel entrance was theirs.

She had just started to celebrate when a laser beam flashed from the darkness outside. It pierced straight through the mech's armor and then through her head.

"We need to go a little way down this tunnel," Zon said as he raced off. "That way, we don't collapse the other tunnel as well."

Corporal Christine Chapin followed Green and Waller as they

ran off after the alien. The Caroon ran for about a minute, until he came to a spot on the wall that was labeled with a large "X," where he stopped.

"Here," Zon said, pointing at the mark on the wall. "This is where our engineers said to do it."

"Shit, that's not obvious at all," Corporal Andy Green said.

Chapin chuckled. "No kidding."

"Here goes nothing," Waller said. He toggled his canopy open and raced down the boarding ladder to the stowage compartment in his suit's right leg. He had just opened it when the tunnel lights went out. "Dammit," he said with a snarl. He climbed back up to the cockpit and turned on his suit's floodlights. "You two give me some cover while I do this," he added as he began pulling explosives out of the compartment.

"You got it," Chapin said. She waved Green to follow her and went to stand on the other side of Waller. He had just attached the first load of C-12 to the wall when the first blob showed up on her infrared system. "I've got movement coming down the passageway."

"Well, don't give them a chance to shoot me," Waller said. "Move down there a ways and shoot them first!"

The two troopers walked another fifty feet down the tunnel, and their infrared systems showed a mass of targets just before the tunnel went around a curve a hundred yards away.

"Damn," Green said. "That's a lot of fucking kitties."

"Let's thin them out, then," Chapin said, "shall we?"

Both began firing their MACs down the passageway. It was hard to tell if or how many of the Xlatan were hit, but the rounds impacting in their midst galvanized them, and the entire pack raced forward.

"Fuck," Green said. "Maybe that wasn't such a good idea."

Both troopers fired as fast as their MACs could cycle, but they could tell it wasn't going to be enough, and their sword blades snapped into place at almost the same time.

"Hurry!" Chapin called to Waller. "I don't know if we can hold them."

"Going as fast as I can," Waller yelled back. "I'm playing with plastic explosives here; you don't need to rush me!"

The lead Xlatan jumped at Chapin, trying to knock her mech down, but she braced herself for the impact and slammed a fist down on the alien's head. The Xlatan fell to the floor and she stabbed it with her sword. "Well met and farewell, you bastard," she said.

After that, she didn't have time to talk as the remaining Xlatan hit them, and it was all she could do to hold them back. After what seemed like an hour but was probably only a minute or two, the remaining Xlatan turned and fled. She took a breath and turned, just in time to see Green's mech collapse with several holes through its chest.

"Green!" she yelled.

"I'm done," he said. "As long as...I took several with me."

Judging by the pile in front of him, he'd taken more than several, Chapin saw.

"More coming!" Zon said. He'd come to see what had happened to Green but was now looking down the passageway.

"Get back!" Chapin said and snapped out her laser shield.

This time, they were smart—they didn't rush her. Instead, they stayed back in a firing line and volley-fired their laser rifles at her. Despite the shield, she still took several hits, including one to the right knee joint that put it out of action. Locking it in place, she began working her way back, dragging her right leg as she went, while still firing back at the Xlatan.

Her suit took several more hits, and she realized the Xlatan were pushing forward.

"How much more time do you need?" she called to Waller.

He didn't respond.

Chapin widened out her field of view to look behind her. Waller was underneath the explosives he'd wired to the wall. He'd taken several laser beams to the chest; it didn't appear he was getting back up again.

She could see the initiator box on the dashboard inside his cockpit. The button flashed red—it was ready to activate. She turned to grab it, but a laser burned through the side of her CASPer, and she fell to the ground on her left shoulder.

"They're coming!" Zon screamed.

Green was down, Waller was down, and Chapin couldn't feel her legs. She had no idea how she was going to get the initiator box. Movement caught her eye; Zon was dragging himself behind Waller's mech.

"Zon," she called. "I need you to go up into the cockpit of

that mech. On the dashboard, there's a box with a flashing red light. I need you to press the button."

"What?" he asked.

"Now!" Chapin yelled, as much as she could. She could feel her strength slipping away with every breath. "Before they come!" She coughed and a red spray hit the metal in front of her. She wasn't a medic, but she knew that wasn't good. "Hurry!" The last was a gasp; it was getting harder to breathe. The laser must have holed one of her lungs, and it was filling with blood.

Zon looked down the passage and jumped, then started up the boarding ladder. His left leg wasn't working, and he had to pull himself up the rungs. Chapin could just see him pick up the box at the corner of her display.

"Push...button," she gasped.

"Are you sure about that?" Con asked weakly. He lay against the wall and had a laser hole through his stomach. He pointed up to the explosives over him. "Gonna kill...you, too."

Zon took a deep breath as the first laser bolts hit the mech next to him. "I am," he said. "When discussing Freedom and Liberty, you cannot ask someone else to do something that you are not prepared to do yourself. Freedom that isn't bought with the blood and sweat of true Patriots isn't as meaningful as the Freedom which is just given to you."

Chapin could hear the capital letters in the way Zon spoke. Liberty. Freedom. They were often unappreciated, until you didn't have them anymore.

Zon looked down the passage at the Xlatan racing toward him and smiled. "As the American, Patrick Henry, said, 'Give me Liberty, Con, or give me death!'"

He pressed the button, and Chapin saw the flash, then nothing else.

The ground rumbled under his feet, and Smythe smiled grimly. The three icons for Waller's, Green's, and Chapin's suits had gone red, but at least one of them must have gotten out and set off the explosives in the tunnel. At least he wouldn't have to worry about the Xlatan coming up from behind him.

He'd also gotten a call from Corporal Hilliard. Although they'd lost Hoch, Fike, Granger, and Cook, they'd taken the mines and were holding them. All he had to do was rescue the hostages.

"Here!" Gron shouted. "They're right up here!" The Caroon pointed to a ramp in front of them leading up into the night sky.

Sergeant Inga Johannesen led the charge up the ramp and into the night, with Smythe and the rest of the squad right behind her.

They came out to their worst nightmare; the four Xlatan guards were at the gate to the compound where the Caroons were being held, and they were firing into where the anteater-like aliens huddled at the other end.

"No!" Johannesen screamed. She toggled her jumpjets and roared over the fence. She touched down in the pen, and her laser shield snapped out. Immediately, she became the target of all four Xlatan.

"Follow her!" Smythe roared. He fired his own jumpjets and landed next to Johannesen as she staggered. He deployed his laser shield and stepped in front of her as the other seven members of the squad touched down around him. Smythe had time to target one of the Xlatan, and then the squad's MACs all roared, and the aliens were blown backward.

Johannesen's icon went red, and he turned to see her mech fall forward onto its face. A number of holes had pierced all the way through her back, with many having a red trickle coming from them in the starlight.

"They're coming!" Corporal Jeff Wormsley yelled.

Smythe turned back toward the town and could see at least a platoon of Xlatan loping toward him. "Fire!" Smythe commanded. His rocket launcher and MAC rotated up to his shoulders, and he began firing. Hitting a dodging Cat in the open was hard, but not impossible, and several of his rockets blew up the charging aliens.

Fewer than ten remained as the Xlatan reached their line, and, as a group, launched themselves through the air to slam into the CASPers. Smythe ducked as his sword blade snapped out, and he gutted the Xlatan that attacked him as it flew over him. It landed in a heap behind him when it hit.

He spun back to the fight and saw two of the aliens on Wormsley's mech. He fired his MAC and the round swept both of them off, but not before one of them fired down into Wormsley's mech. His icon went red.

Corporal Greg Eden's icon went red, and he turned to find the mech had stabbed one of the Xlatan. As Eden pinned the creature to the ground, though, it had fired its rifle up into the mech. Both were dead, and Eden's mech collapsed into his enemy's lifeless arms.

Smythe scanned the rest of the battlefield. All the Xlatan were down, and the rest of his people appeared to be okay. He turned back to the Caroons, who were un-piling themselves. Although a few on the outside of the group appeared to be dead—victims of the Xlatan's laser fire—the overwhelming majority appeared to be fine. They'd done it. Let freedom ring.

## Town Square, T'praken

"And so it is with great appreciation," President Gron said, several days later at the award ceremony, "that we honor all of our saviors in this fight. First, to our Human friends. While there are many who will say, 'But they only came because of the pay,' I know better. I saw Sergeant Johannesen sacrifice herself to save the lives of the Caroons. She could have easily stood to the side and shot them, but more Caroons would have been killed so she did not. She put her life on the line to help us, and she paid the price. Similarly, other Terrans gave their lives to help us, even though they did not need to. We greatly appreciate their sacrifice.

"But it was not just the Humans that bled for our freedom. Our very own twins, Con and Zon, aided the forces that made our freedom possible. I was in radio contact with them as we led the Humans through the tunnels, and I remember Zon's last words. He knew he was going to die, but he also knew his actions would save hundreds, if not thousands of us."

Gron stepped forward and pulled the sheet off the new statue that had been placed in the center of the town. On it, a Caroon in bronze pushed the initiator button on a small box. "Zon gave his life that we should live, and I am extremely thankful for that sacrifice. Unlike Zon, we will go forward with our lives, and I think it's imperative that we always keep his words in our thoughts and close to our hearts as we do. As Zon said, 'Give me Liberty, Con, or give me death!'"

⁊❧

# Chris Kennedy

Although I have been to LibertyCon several times, I never really had much experience or close contact with Uncle Timmy. The times I saw him, he was always surrounded with people, and he was obviously loved by many. While I can't comment on Uncle Timmy, himself, I can, however comment on his legacy—LibertyCon. It is without a doubt my single, most favorite convention of all the ones I have attended. It is a great place to meet your favorite authors, discuss with them their books or whatever they had for breakfast, and otherwise have a great time with people you love to be around. It was once described to me as "a family reunion with people you actually like," and I wholeheartedly agree. You can't choose your family, but if you could, mine would be the family Uncle Timmy brought about—the staff and attendees of LibertyCon.

—Chris Kennedy

A Webster Award winner and three-time Dragon Award finalist, **Chris Kennedy** is a Science Fiction/Fantasy/Young Adult author, speaker, and small-press publisher who has written over twenty-five books and published more than one hundred others. Chris's stories include the "Occupied Seattle" military fiction duology, "The Theogony" and "Codex Regius" science fiction trilogies, stories in the Four Horsemen and In Revolution Born universes and the War for Dominance fantasy trilogy. Get his free book, "Shattered Crucible," at his website, https://chriskennedypublishing.com.

Called "fantastic" and "a great speaker," he has coached hundreds of beginning authors and budding novelists on how to self-publish their stories at a variety of conferences, conventions and writing guild presentations. He is the author of the award-winning #1 bestseller *Self-Publishing for Profit: How to Get Your Book Out of Your Head and Into the Stores*, as well as the leadership training book, *Leadership from the Darkside*.

Chris lives in Virginia Beach, Virginia, with his wife, and is the holder of a doctorate in educational leadership and master's degrees in both business and public administration. Follow Chris on Facebook at https://www.facebook.com/ckpublishing/.

# "LIBERTYCON ODDITY"

"LibertyCon Oddity" was my way of saying "Thank You" to the convention for letting me be part of it. I had wanted to attend LibertyCon for a number of years, but it had never worked out...then in early 2016 I got a call asking me to be the Master of Ceremonies! The scheduled MC had canceled due to a family matter, and somehow my name had come up as an alternative. It was nice to be thought of, but also a frightening proposition because I knew that LibertyCon meant a great deal to the fans—and because some very talented people had performed as MCs in the past. Ultimately, of course, I said, "Yes!"

Having said yes, I then needed to figure out something I could do that perhaps other MCs hadn't done. That came down to including something musical in the Opening Ceremonies, and my thoughts turned to one of my favorite musicians who had recently died: Keith Emerson, of Emerson, Lake, and Palmer. I seriously considered doing a takeoff on "Karn Evil 9"— in particular, the "Welcome back, my friends, to the show that never ends" portion. But that seemed hopelessly complex for me as only a mediocre guitarist, so I turned to another influential musician who had also recently passed: David Bowie. And, "Ground control to LibertyCon" seemed a pretty natural fit to "Ground control to Major Tom." I took it from there.

I don't know what people were expecting when I picked up my guitar to start the Opening Ceremonies. I hadn't told anyone about the song, and I introduced

it "in memory of David Bowie" and started playing...
at which point a couple of people groaned and
someone said, "Oh, no," loudly enough for me to
hear it on the stage. But after the first line, when
my version turned out to be about LibertyCon itself,
nobody complained anymore.

—Gray Rinehart

# "LibertyCon Oddity"

## Lyrics by Gray Rinehart

*To the tune of "Space Oddity" by David Bowie*

Ground control to LibertyCon
Ground control to LibertyCon
Take your bourbon shots and put your Jayne hats on
Ground control to LibertyCon
Commencing countdown, costumes on *(10, 9, 8, ...)*
Check ignition and may God's love be with you

This is ground control to LibertyCon —
    It's time to start the show
And the vendors want to know what shirts you'll wear
Now it's time to leave the Con Suite if you dare

This is LibertyCon to ground control —
    We're stepping through the door
The fen are floating in some most peculiar ways
It's just a normal fannish weekend, wouldn't you say?

    *For here are we in a hotel that was once a train (station),*
        *with friends from everywhere*
    *Romulan Ale is blue, let's have another drink or two*

Though we've read our favorite books a hundred
        thousand times, we've barely just begun
Because we're fans, and we can never get enough
I'm glad my wife puts up with all my fannish stuff

Ground control to LibertyCon, are you ready to go,
        or is something wrong?
Can you hear me, LibertyCon?
Can you hear me, LibertyCon?
Can you hear me, LibertyCon? Can you ...

  *Here are we in a hotel that was once a train (station),*
        *with friends from everywhere*
  *Romulan Ale is blue, let's have another drink or two*

# THE TUCKERIZING

I have never had the pleasure of sitting down and talking to Larry Correia. I have met him on a couple of occasions. My sojourn to the reception at the top floor of the Marriott for the Dragon Awards was the first. I was still in my daze when I happened to be in a circle of writers that included Larry. The second time was at a panel at the same convention concerning the Four Horsemen Universe. He had come and sat in the audience for the panel. I'm not sure if it was to watch the panel or just to be ready for the next one, which he would be participating in. A question was asked by Charles Gannon about where we would like to be in two years. When the time for my answer came I said, "I'd like to purchase a mountain." Larry laughed and said it took five. Larry is one of those guys we, as self-published authors, can look at and see possibilities. Five years. It's been one and a half years since that day.

—CW

# The Tuckerizing

## Larry Correia

*In the multiverse, rifts between realities are considered especially heinous. Across infinite alternate dimensions, the dedicated agents providing the highest quality customer service belong to the elite insurance company known as Stranger & Stranger.*
*These are their stories.*
*Dun Dun*

"What are you doing back there, Jimmy?" Tom Stranger asked.

"I'm putting together a cool-sounding intro, so we can get all the folks who've never heard of us before up to speed about what we do, protecting our clients from other dimensions crashing their place and wrecking their stuff and all that. So they'll know you're like a super-dedicated, serious badass professional, and I'm the new guy...who is also pretty badass."

Though inept, goofy, clumsy, easily confused, and usually hung over, Jimmy meant well, but he was only an intern, and not yet properly trained in the arts of customer service. "There is no time for such frivolity. We are almost at our destination."

Jimmy unplugged his VR headset and went forward to look out the cockpit window. Ahead of them was one of the many Earths that they did business on. "I'm afraid, Mr. Stranger. The last time we went to a sci-fi convention, it got a little crazy, what with the zombies and that balrog from hell eating dudes, and stuff."

"Do not worry," Tom Stranger assured his intern as he piloted their giant battle mech toward the planet. "That convention was amateurishly run in comparison to a LibertyCon."

"That's a relief!"

"Indeed. The staff here would be more than capable of handling

193

mere demons without our help. However, should one of the brilliant yet unhinged minds which are drawn to LibertyCon decide to bring about an apocalypse, it would be nothing so cliché as opening a portal to hell. That is rather dull by their mad science standards."

"Wait...what?"

"Yes, Jimmy. We are here preemptively because LibertyCon brings together writers and their boundary-pushing ideas, with genius industry leaders who can make those ideas come true, as they consume staggering amounts of alcohol together. There are vigorous debates between competing philosophies, and much fun is had."

"Fun is good."

"Yet 'fun' is something which various nefarious beings in the multiverse find very offensive. They meddle when they think anyone is having fun incorrectly. Their unholy crusade against wrongfun has destroyed many conventions. However, LibertyCon is a refuge for creators who would make art without constraint. This event is a conflux of raw probability, beautiful yet deadly. It is a rare and special occasion to have this much creative energy gathered in one location, and as you know, Jimmy, that often causes a clash among realities from across the multiverse."

"Uh yeah...I, likc, totally knew that."

"The claims paperwork for LibertyCon-related events are always epic in scope. Our Actuary has peered into the future, and there is a 97.4 percent chance that our services will be required there this weekend."

"Okay. Gotcha. I'll do my best to protect our clients." Jimmy nodded solemnly. "I'm cool with the drinking lots of booze part, though."

"Not while you are on duty, young intern."

"Awww, man."

Like most interdimensional insurance agents, Tom Stranger loved his job. There was no better feeling than providing quality customer service to his clients. When realities collided, Stranger & Stranger would be there to set things right. As long as said realities were covered, of course. Normally an interdimensional insurance policy would cost billions of dollars, but long ago LibertyCon's wise founder, Uncle Timmy Bolgeo, had the foresight to bundle a Stranger & Stranger Bargain Umbrella policy with his car insurance. Plus he'd had a really good coupon for excellent savings.

The Stranger & Stranger battle mech smoothly descended into the atmosphere of Earth 845-9017B at a leisurely five thousand miles per hour.

"Behold. Chattanooga."

"It seems nice."

Tom checked the info-link implanted in his brain. The Chattanooga of this dimension was above average as far as the two million cataloged Chattanoogas of the multiverse went. It did not have a plesiosaur infestation—as was common in most Chattanoogas—and this one had a very good diner that served excellent cakes. Tom liked cake.

"Yes. It fits the parameters of nice."

He parked the giant battle mech in the lot next to the hotel. Thus far the establishment did not appear to be on fire, under siege by warlords, or sucked into a rift, so that was a good sign. Tom and Jimmy debarked. They were met at the entrance by two of the volunteer staff, who were dragging what appeared to be an angry gremlin, kicking and screaming, from the facilities.

"Get in there, you little bastard!" the female volunteer shouted as she tried to force the little green creature into a burlap sack. "Oh, Tom's here!"

"About time," the man said as he managed to close the bag.

"REEEE!" screeched the goblin.

Tom recognized them from previous events. The humans, that was. He had not met that particular gremlin before. "Greetings, Tish and Rich Groller. How goes your science-fiction-and-fantasy-themed social event?"

"One of the writers claimed a mogwai was their service animal. But then somebody fed it after midnight and tossed it in the pool," Rich said as he held up the thrashing sack. "So we've got these friggin' things everywhere now."

Tish sighed. "People just don't realize how much work the volunteers do to keep this con running smoothly."

Tom nodded thoughtfully. "If only there was some way attention could be directed toward the vital yet unsung efforts of the volunteers who make beloved events like this successful."

"Maybe we could get one of the writers who come here a lot

to do a story about the volunteers being a bunch of badasses?" suggested Jimmy.

"Do not be absurd, Jimmy. Such a work of satirical fiction would be very silly."

"Bummer."

A muffled voice came from within the gremlin container. "Am I being detained?"

"Nope." Then Rich hurled the sack into the dumpster and dusted off his hands. "Anyways, Tom, glad you're here."

Tish's radio crackled. She listened for a moment, frowning. "Uh oh. There's a Kzin on the third floor marking its territory, one of the fantasy authors misplaced his Elf Stones, and the con suite is out of Coke Zero."

"We've got to move. The guests get uppity when they're uncaffeinated for long," said Rich. "See you, Tom."

As the two volunteers ran off, Jimmy the Intern turned to his boss. "Gee whiz, Mr. Stranger. It sounds like this place is off the hook."

"I am unclear which hook you speak of, or why anyone would want to dangle upon a hook in the first place. However, early indications are that this will be a busy year. All three of those things originate in other planes of existence, thus are fully covered."

"Even the Coke Zero?"

"Especially the Coke Zero."

There was a roar as a spaceship did a low pass overhead. Someone from another dimension was showing off his new solar sails, probably to make Les Johnson envious. Such flagrant displays of technologies that hadn't been invented here yet could cause all sorts of trouble.

"We are off to a busy start." Tom reached into his coat pocket and pulled out something for Jimmy. "You should take this in case we have to split up."

"Whoa! I get my own Combat Wombat?"

The ultra-lethal CorreiaTech Combat Wombat was the state of the art in personal firepower, capable of obliterating up to Godzilla-sized threats. Tom always kept one on his person for insurance-related emergencies.

"Oh no, Jimmy. Of course not. The last time I entrusted you with a weapon of mass destruction it did not work out well." That was a bit of an understatement, since Jimmy's joyride in a suit of manatee power armor had doomed an entire Earth. That had required a lot of paperwork. "This is a Junior Training Wombat. Think of it as a doomsday device…with training wheels."

"That explains the Hello Kitty stickers on it. So no missiles or death rays, but what are we talking? Can it still wreck the state?"

"No."

"The town?"

"Negative."

"The hotel?"

"Not even close."

"A hotel room?"

"Perhaps if the room was filled with extremely flammable material. Do not worry about that right now, Jimmy. Our clients need us. Let us get to work."

Jimmy hid his Junior Training Wombat beneath his Chico State hoodie as the two of them entered the building.

Inside was a bustling and excited crowd on their way to attend various panels on interesting topics or engaging in lively conversations. Groups of fans were clustered around individual authors as they "held court." Which was a colloquial term used in this dimension to describe authors sitting on a couch bloviating on various subjects, a few of which they even knew things about.

"Everyone seems happy," Jimmy said suspiciously.

"It is a popular event. According to my info-link this year's memberships sold out in 16.6 seconds. There is quite the waiting list."

A young male volunteer approached them. "Excuse me, are you the insurance guys who handle alien invaders and crap like that?"

"In laymen's terms, that is approximately correct." Tom paused to read his name tag. "How may we assist you, Alex Spraker?"

"Friggin' Posleens, man. They're eating guests again."

"On the bright side those openings will be good for some of the folks on your waiting list," Jimmy said. "But, Alex, dude, you look like a jock. You're way more jacked than most sci-fi peeps, why don't you just kick the crap out of these pos-whatevers?"

"Yeah, bro, naw. Imagine wrestling a carnivorous centaur crocodile."

"Oh. Gotcha. They're *bitey*."

"Way bitey," Alex confirmed.

Tom just shook his head at his intern's naivete. This would be a valuable learning experience for him, provided he didn't get devoured. "Jimmy, go with Alex and deal with the Posleen. Make sure you pick up all their eggs too, or we will soon be troubled by ferals."

"On it, Mr. Stranger! What're you gonna do?"

"I will go to Operations Command and see where I am most needed."

"Sweet. Look out, horse-gator dudes, Jimmy the Intern is on the case!"

LibertyCon's command center was inside a high-tech bunker on the third floor. Tom knocked on the steel vault door, and waited to be let in. After submitting to a retina scan, a DNA test, and a credit check—Tom Stranger had a perfect 850—he was let inside.

A group of volunteers were hard at work in a space that had been made to look suspiciously like the bridge of the *Enterprise* (original series, not *Next Generation* obviously), so lots of blinking lights and random noises. There was no sign of Supreme Commander Brandy—she would have been easy to spot, what with the Valkyrie wings and her usually riding in a flaming chariot pulled by a team of unicorns—but she must have been busy elsewhere. The volunteers were frantically checking the monitors and sticking tacks into a map of the building.

"What's our situation at parking?"

"Under control for now. That meteor missed the garage. But we've got another Code Red in the hospitality suite. Max?"

"Again? How can human beings eat so many chips?" A volunteer whose name tag read "Poddubny" closed the helmet on his suit of power armor, gathered up a giant box full of Chex Party Mix, and leapt into action.

"Ahem." Tom politely interrupted the volunteers. "Can I be of assistance?"

One of the chairs spun around, revealing a woman Tom had worked with before. Currently Shannon Souvinette was wearing a beret and had a treecat sitting on her shoulder.

"Yay! Tom's here. Yes, you can help."

"Hello, Shannon. Last time we met you were the art show director."

"Now I'm serving as Brandy's personal bee-yatch. And it's a good thing you're here. Check this out." She spun her command chair back around. "Michelle, put the *anomaly* on screen."

"Aye aye, bee-yatch." A brunette volunteer punched some

commands into her terminal and the big display came on. It showed a flickering, purplish blob, floating in one of the conference rooms.

"That is a Class Five Dimensional Rift!" Tom exclaimed.

"Shoot. I figured it was at least a six." Shannon took out a dollar and handed it to Michelle. "You win the bet."

"Told you it was only a five."

As they watched, aliens from various universes and other copyrighted intellectual properties spilled through the portal. So much creative energy in one place always attracted beings from other universes. LibertyCon drew such illustrious guests that they were all in danger of being crushed beneath the sheer weight of the worlds they had created.

"This is very serious," Tom stated grimly.

"Meow," agreed the treecat.

Fortunately, treecat was one of the 685 languages Tom was fluent in. "Indeed. If we do not act quickly then all of Chattanooga may be sucked into another dimension."

"Plus, we need that room clear for the Midnight Mad Scientists' Panel," said Shannon. "It's one of our most popular events."

"A rift of that size could only be caused by an extreme fluctuation in the equilibrium of the space-time continuum. What could be causing it?" Tom looked to the treecat for answers, but it had gone back to licking itself.

"I think I know," said Michelle as she quickly typed. Numbers and wave forms flashed across her screen. "From these readings it appears that the rift was caused by too many Tuckerizations at one time."

"Hmmm..." Tom was not familiar with that term. "What is this *Tuckerization* you speak of?"

"The practice is named after Bob Tucker, who was actually LibertyCon's toastmaster for many years. It's when an author uses a real person's name, likeness, or other characteristics in a work of fiction, usually as a homage or in-joke. We are seeing a spike in them right now for some inexplicable reason."

"Do these foolish authors not realize that an alternate branching dimension is automatically created to hold each of these new realities? Too many of these Tuckerizations at once would cause a great a strain on the fabric of the multiverse and doom us all."

"Absolutely," said Michelle. "By the way, my last name is Farenci. My friends call me Chelle."

The entire hotel shook. Sparks flew from the consoles as volunteers were dramatically hurled across the command deck.

"Whoops."

Tom noted that the purple blob on the screen had grown larger. "Now it is a Class Six."

"Sweet. Gimmie my dollar back."

"If you will excuse me, I must close this rift before it destroys us all." Tom Stranger left the bunker by sliding down the conveniently located, Batman-style firepole.

Tom could not let the con get engulfed. Not just because that would be providing unsatisfactory customer service, but also because LibertyCon was one of the last bastions of freedom in fandom, from the time before fun was forbidden.

He came across Jimmy along the way. The intern's clothing hung in ragged, bloody tatters. "Hey, Mr. Stranger. About those alligator-horsie dudes, it turns out they weren't super intimidated by my Junior Combat Wombat." Jimmy held up the weapon. When he pulled the trigger it made a *Weeeee* noise as bubbles and sparkles shot out.

"You need to take the safety off," Tom explained patiently.

"Do you want to be my friend?" the gun asked in a high-pitched voice.

"No. Not right now. Bad gun. Bad!" Jimmy turned back to Tom. "If this one volunteer hadn't jumped in and put that horsie dude in a chokehold I woulda totally got eaten."

"Those aliens can wait, Jimmy. I am afraid we have a far more pressing problem. We have to stop all these authors from Tuckerizing the LibertyCon staff at such a rapid pace."

"I don't know what any of that means, but okay." Then Jimmy nodded at the young lady who walked up beside him. "Oh hey, this is the volunteer who, like, saved my life from the horsie dudes. She put this one jerk in a headlock, and was all, like, pow, right in the snout!"

"I've seen worse," she said modestly.

"Mr. Stranger, this is—"

"Jimmy, no!"

But it was too late. Jimmy was already finishing his introduction. "—Cecil Curlee."

An earthquake rocked the hotel as yet another Tuckerization attacked the delicate space-time continuum. The guests were mildly discomforted as gravity temporarily reversed itself. A great many drinks were spilled.

"It is vital we do not introduce any other people, Jimmy. Some of the authors here are haphazardly taking people from one reality, and inserting them into different, fictional realities. I do not know how much more the multiverse can take of this."

"Got it!" Jimmy hoisted his weapon. "Shoot the writers!"

"Yay!" said the Junior Combat Wombat.

"No. Do not shoot any authors. Some of them are paying clients. We merely must stop their insane rampage through any means necessary."

"Cool, cool. Okay. See ya, Cecil."

"Good luck, weirdos."

By the time the intrepid insurance professionals reached the rift, it had consumed all of one conference area and expanded into the game room. The volunteer in charge of the videogame area was a tall, thin man who seemed mildly annoyed at the chaos.

"Hey, you're that insurance guy. I really could use a hand here," the volunteer said as the rift behind him vomited forth unspeakable terrors.

"Do not introduce yourself. Do not let me see your name tag or we will all perish."

"Whatever you say. I just want to wrap this up so I can go back to watching anime."

The earth shuddered beneath them. Cracks appeared in the walls. "No personal details either, please."

The wind was howling like a hurricane, lightning crashed along the ceiling. At this rate Brandy would not be able to get back her cleaning deposit.

"Mr. Stranger, look! That's got to be our guy!"

There were several author guests nearby. "Which one?"

"The overweight bald one with facial hair, eating Cheetos!"

That described half the sci-fi authors in the world, but Jimmy pointed to where an author was sitting on a nearby couch, typing on his laptop. It made sense. The other authors were all fleeing, but this one was wearing headphones, so had not noticed the looming apocalypse. Tom rushed over to the man—who would remain unnamed, to protect the multiverse from more cross-dimensional pollution—and snatched the headphones from his head.

"What the hell, man? I'm up against a deadline. Hey, what's

my insurance agent doing here?" Then he noticed the giant purple hole in space-time. "Huh...Didn't notice that before. That's what happens when I get in the zone."

"I must know what you are working on. Quickly. Speak, author."

"It's a story for this anthology that's a salute to the awesomeness of LibertyCon and the fantastic people who've made it one of the best things in all of fandom."

This had to be the source of their trouble. "I do not delight in such impolite behavior, and I will understand if you give me an unsatisfactory customer review for destroying your property, but I must hurl your laptop through that rift in the next few seconds or all of Chattanooga will be sucked through time and space and deposited who knows where."

"So, like *1632*." The author handed over his computer. "I didn't pack my time travel boots. Carry on, then."

Tom took the laptop and tossed it like a Frisbee into the center of the purple blob.

Nothing happened.

The author frowned. "That's the part where I would have put *insert explosions here* in the rough draft."

"Hmm...It appears I must have miscalculated," Tom mused as the rift continued to grow. More of the game room was being sucked to who knew where. "The catalyst is gone, but the damage done by the Tuckerizations remain."

"Maybe you just need to, like, reset the quantum hypernode," the author suggested.

"Now you're just making up words!" Jimmy said, as he tried to hide beneath a table to escape the expanding cloud of purple death.

"Quit yelling at me. I'm more of a fantasy guy than a hard sci-fi type, okay?"

The volunteer in charge of the gaming area had wandered over to see what was going on. "Is there anything I can do to help? Because this is really cutting into our MechWarrior time."

That gave Tom an idea. The computer with all the dangerous Tuckerizing was now inside the rift. If he could disrupt the maelstrom, they might still have a chance. "What is your name, Game Room Man?"

"Uh, I'm David. David Robards."

*CRACKBOOM!*

The laptop detonated. There was a mighty *whoosh* of wind and flash of light as a chunk of reality turned inside out.

When Tom could see again, the purple blob was gone. Chattanooga was saved. Unfortunately, the area that had been immediately inside the rift had been replaced with another reality. There was a forest inside the hotel now.

"Is that Oz?" asked David the Volunteer. "Because this is the videogame room. Munchkin goes in the regular game room."

"No. I think it is Narnia."

Jimmy shrugged. "If we don't say anything maybe the hotel won't notice."

But Tom just shook his head. "No, Jimmy, leaving a magical fairy-tale land inside this establishment would not be providing the best possible customer service. I will start the paperwork." He turned to the author. "And I certainly hope that you learned your lesson. Next time you use real people in a work of fiction you should be more subtle about it."

"But I suck at subtle!"

"Everyone knows that," Tom agreed. And they all had a good laugh.

The rest of the weekend went smoothly, thanks to the hardworking volunteers who continued the vision of the wonderful man who had founded LibertyCon.

## Larry Correia

I first met Uncle Timmy Bolgeo at LibertyCon. I was a brand-new author and that was my first-ever convention outside my home state, and only my second or third total. I didn't really know what to expect. So of course I immediately screwed it up.

They give you these printed name tags to stick in front of you when you're on panels so people in the audience can know who you are. I was on a panel in the morning the first day and didn't realize I was supposed to take my name tag with me, so I just left it on the table.

The next hour they opened up the walls of that room to accommodate everyone for opening ceremonies. When I walked in I saw my name tag was on the panelists table. So *obviously* I thought that was where I was supposed to sit. At the time I didn't even get suspicious why some total newb author was sitting between one of the guests of honor and the toastmaster. So I'm there, between legends Eric Flint and Terry Brooks as the room fills up, and I'm feeling like hot stuff. These LibertyCon people must really like me!

Then opening ceremonies start. As I'm looking out over the audience, I realize that there are a lot of really famous people in the crowd...and I start to wonder why some new scrub like me is up in front. I'd only published a couple books. There's people who've written fifty books standing in back. Then it slowly dawns on me that this is the same room I was just in, only the interior walls are open, so it looked different.

A feeling of dread comes over me as I realize my name tag never moved.

Then as they are introducing all the super-dignified important guest of honor–type people, they get to Ben Bova...who is out in the audience. I look across the table, count the seats, and discover that not only am I not supposed to be up here...I STOLE BEN BOVA'S CHAIR!

Panicked, I looked to Eric Flint and whispered, "I don't think I'm supposed to be up here."

Eric snorted. "Too late now."

Afterwards I went to Timmy Bolgeo and apologized profusely. I was mortified. Except that was when I learned that Uncle Timmy was kind, understanding, and above all had a great sense of humor. I think my screwup made opening ceremonies a little more entertaining for him.

That was my first LibertyCon, but it wasn't my last. For many years afterwards I've gotten to visit with Timmy and the LibertyCon people. People talk about Southern hospitality, but LibertyCon lives it. Even after he turned over the reins, Timmy was still around, having a good time, and making sure everybody else was having a good time. We had some fun conversations.

It was obvious Timmy cared about making everyone around him feel welcomed.

He sure did for me.

—Larry Correia

**Larry Correia** is the creator of the *Wall Street Journal* and *New York Times* bestselling Monster Hunter series, with first entry *Monster Hunter International*, as well as the urban fantasy hard-boiled adventure saga the Grimnoir Chronicles, with first entry *Hard Magic*, and the epic fantasy series The Saga of the Forgotten Warrior, with first entry *Son of the Black Sword* and latest entry *House of Assassins*. He is an avid gun user and advocate and shot on a competitive level for many years. Before becoming a full-time writer, he was a military contract accountant, and a small business accountant and manager. Correia lives in Utah with his wife and family.

# PARTNERS

I can't remember which convention I actually met Kacey at. We both wrote in the Four Horsemen Universe on the first anthology they put out. I almost think it was LibertyCon in 2017. She's a helicopter pilot and a good writer. Her portrayal of alien races is right there with the best in the business. She was there the same year I was with a finalist for the Dragon Awards in 2018 with her alternate history, *The Minds of Men.*

I believe I met Chris Smith at LibertyCon that same year. He was at one of the parties held that weekend and carried a flask of liquor in a leather holster on his belt for "emergencies." Both of them are working with John Ringo on a new series and I was happy they decided to join us for this with a story from that universe.

—CW

# Partners

*A Story of Last Judgment's Fire*

## Kacey Ezell and Christopher L. Smith

Jack's chair creaked in protest as he leaned back. If the glances flying between his opponents were any indication, there were side bets going on as to how much longer he'd remain sitting calmly at the table as opposed to sprawling inelegantly on the mud-caked floor of the riverside saloon. However, his partner, Taylor, never let her cool, blue gaze waver as she watched him across the table. He appreciated that about her.

"Two," Jack said, placing his bid.

She didn't smile, she didn't react much at all, but her eyes warmed just a touch.

"Two," she echoed when it was her turn and, as she was the last to place her bid, that signaled the start of the hand.

Jack had played spades before, though it had been years. If he'd had his choice, he would have chosen poker or blackjack, but he was new to this knocked-together tavern set back on the bank above the Mississippi River. So he played the house's game.

For now.

"Where'd you say you came from again?" the muscular brunette on his left asked. She'd introduced herself as Katie Cochrane. Not Katherine. Not Kate. Katie. Nice girl. Pretty, but without a lot of makeup and with a steely glint in her eye. Jack had noticed that she carried a nice-looking 1911 inside the back waistband of her denim jeans, as had been the fashion before the Bug War twenty-five years ago.

"Atlanta originally," Jack said. "Further north most recently. You?"

"We're all mostly from the Tennessee Valley," Katie's partner, Mike Gants, said. Like Katie and Taylor, Mike and his daughter Alana were part of a riverboat crew that apparently stopped at the Proud Mary Tavern on the regular. "I didn't realize that people were living in Atlanta, still."

"I wouldn't call it living," Jack said with a sardonic grin that he knew didn't meet his eyes. "The Gants—beg your pardon, Mike, but you've got a damned unfortunate name, brother. Anyway, the *giant ants* still infest the majority of the downtown area, but people have crept back into the outskirts. There's just too much to salvage there, and communities spring up. Mine was one of those."

Mike Gants chuckled and leaned back in his own chair, one hand stroking his moustache as he grinned merrily up at Jack. Way up, as it happened. Jack knew he was a big man, but Mike was shorter than most folks. It didn't seem to bother him much, though. He wasn't as overt about it as Katie, but the way Mike carried himself told Jack that he was a man capable of handling himself in a tight spot.

Across the table, Jack's young, beautiful blonde partner laid down a six of spades, taking the first trick. Using neat, economical movements, she gathered the cards together into a stack and swept them to the side, and then smoothly laid down the two of spades from her hand.

"Bring 'em out, bring 'em out," Taylor sang softly, her breathy voice at odds with the heavy rhythm of the old song.

"Goddamn it, Taylor!" Katie said, tossing her head backward in disgust as she threw her card down. "Why do you have to be so cutthroat all the time?"

"Why play if you're not playing to win?" Taylor said, smiling coolly back at the other young woman before turning her gaze back to Jack. He felt the silent, steely challenge flowing from those icy eyes.

"Damn straight," Jack said, laying down his own three of spades before smiling back at her. The girl wanted to test his mettle as her partner? Fair enough. Challenge accepted.

"I play to have a good time," Mike said with a sigh as he put down a ten of spades. "Which I generally do whether I win or lose, at least in this crowd. You screwed me with this one, Tay."

"Sorry, Uncle Mike," Taylor said, turning to him with a grin.

"You don't sound sorry, young lady," he said, grinning back.

"I'm not," she admitted as she gathered up the cards yet again. "Not at all."

"That's my girl," Mike said with a wink, then let out a sigh as she led with a heart. "Are y'all hungry at all? I could eat a horse."

"Thought you were a Gant, Uncle Mike, not a dragon," Katie said with a snort.

"They both eat horses, kiddo. Alana!"

Jack looked up to see another young woman approaching the table. Her features resembled Mike's, but in a prettier, softer way.

"Yes, Dad?"

"Sweetheart, please find the bartender and order us some food. See if Linda's here. I'd kill for one of her pizzas." He looked up at Jack, then at the two women at the table before turning back to his daughter. "Make that two pizzas. And breadsticks."

"I don't have any cash on me, Dad."

"Tell the kitchen to charge it to the ship. Beth worked out a line of credit for us here, since we run their supplies so often."

"Really?" Alana's eyes lit up.

"Easy, kid," Mike said. "Your mother will murder me if you go buck wild. Stick to cider and only one dessert per day, got it?"

"Yes, Dad," Alana said with a sigh before turning away.

"You're welcome to join us for pizza, big man," Mike said. "What was your name again?"

"Jack," Jack said. "And thank you. I'll accept if you all let me buy a round for the table. Man should bring something to contribute if he can."

"Sounds reasonable," Katie said, smiling at Jack for the first time. He let himself smile back as he gave her a nod, even while laying down the Queen of Spades over top of her Jack. He felt a brief stab of regret as Katie's smile turned to a glare, but then he caught the corner of Taylor's mouth turning upward, and he winked at her across the table.

"Play to win," Jack said softly.

"Play to win," Taylor replied.

"Damn," Mike said, and gave a low whistle. "You're a cool one, Jack. I'll give you that. Will you be around long? I might have to quit playing Spades before I lose my shirt."

"Could be," Jack said easily. "Plan's not fixed yet. I like to keep moving, mostly."

"Us too." Mike let out a heavy sigh and began gathering the cards together. "But we're here till Taylor's dad can get the boiler fixed. It blew something... not sure what. Not my area."

"He'll fix it," Taylor said softly, steel in her tone.

"Wasn't a stab at your father, hon," Mike said with a smile. He reached his free hand out and gripped her fingers. "He's the best on the river, we all know that. But the *Sally* is a great lady, and she's been sailing a fair few number of years."

"Well, I'm out," Katie said. "Find someone else to scam if you want to deal the next hand. I've got better things to do." She shot a sour look at Taylor, then Jack as she got to her feet. Jack eyed his partner, who simply smiled sweetly at Katie in return.

Next to him, Mike sighed.

"The world would be so much easier if you women would just handle your rivalries like men do. Go have a fight, then have a beer. All done."

"That's not ladylike, Uncle Mike," Taylor murmured, then looked a challenge up at Jack.

He put up his hands and shook his head. Not his business.

"Lizard!" Mike called out. "Come sub in for Katie! We need a fourth to finish the game."

A woman approached them and smiled at the group. "You rang?"

"Liz," Taylor said with a smile. "Play with us?"

"Are you playing for money? You already cleaned me out, Taylor, and you know that."

"I got you covered, Lizard," Mike said. "Come on, I need a partner against these two hustlers. Jack," he went on as Liz smilingly pulled out Katie's vacated chair. "Meet Liz 'the Lizard' Rowland."

"Pleased to meet you," Jack said. "Quite a nickname you've got."

"Yes," Liz said, throwing him a wink. "It is."

Since she offered no further explanation, Mike set to dealing and the game continued. Jack found himself appreciating his partner's icy ruthlessness more and more as the hands stacked and the tricks were taken. In the end, he and Taylor reached five hundred points just ahead of Mike and Liz, and that ended the game.

"One last round for the table," Jack said, gathering his winnings in. "On me."

"Very kind of you, Jack," Mike said with a smile. At no point in the proceedings had the man lost his affable, hail-fellow-well-met demeanor, and Jack smiled in return.

"Good game," Taylor said across the table. Jack met her eyes and found her lips quirked in a tiny smile. "Thanks."

"The honor was mine, miss," Jack replied, trying to ignore the way that tiny curve of her red lips felt like someone punching him in the gut. Gods above and below, she was beautiful.

He abruptly became conscious that he was staring. So he blinked and turned rather hastily toward the bar, drawing in a breath to call out for the round.

He never made that call.

The flimsy wooden front wall of the saloon splintered with a deafening *crash*. One side of a giant mandible pushed the swinging wooden doors out of the way and clamped on to the wall, tearing it and the doors away as if they were paper. A Gant warrior, her head the size of a river dinghy, pushed through into the screaming mass of saloon patrons.

Jack stepped backward, pulling his semiautomatic pistol out of the holster nestled inside the front waistband of his trousers. Unless he hit an eye, his 9mm rounds wouldn't do much but piss the Gant off, but it was better than fighting barehanded. He'd leave that nonsense to the crazy Windfist monks and their violence-worshipping ways.

"Taylor, Liz, get back," Jack heard Mike say behind him. "There's a back entrance that leads down to the docks!"

"You go," Taylor said, and Jack looked down as he felt someone come up hard against his left side. "Jack and I will cover your retreat. Get Alana and Katie and the rest of the crew if you can. We'll be right behind you!"

Taylor had a shotgun in her hands, though for the life of him Jack couldn't imagine where she'd stashed it. The slim, blonde girl put the stock of the weapon up to her shoulder and fired three times, working the pump smoothly between each shot. The Gant warrior snarled and turned toward her, mandibles gaping. Suddenly, Jack had a shot at one of the warrior's compound eyes. He took aim and fired as fast as he could, emptying his magazine into the multifaceted domed surface the size of a dinner platter.

The warrior screamed and thrashed her head from side to side, knocking tables and chairs to the ground. The sharp, acidic scent of lemons flooded the air, and another warrior charged through the hole in the building her sister had made. This second warrior began attacking the not-quite-dead-yet corpse of the first one, and more screaming ensued.

"We need to fall back," Jack said. He dropped his empty magazine into his free hand, and shoved a full one home. Sometimes it was good to have big hands.

"Yep," Taylor said, then fired again at the second warrior. "I'll keep covering you. Back and to my left, there's a door that leads out to the privies."

"You're not staying," Jack said. It wasn't a question.

"Nope, I'm right with you," Taylor said. "But we gotta move now!"

Sure enough, a third warrior started crowding her way in, ripping out more of the front side of the saloon and pushing in to begin fighting for her share of the spoils. Jack let out a short, dirty curse and began slide-stepping backward, trying not to trip on overturned furniture or spilled drinks.

"Come on, sweetie," Taylor said, her voice soft and soothing. Jack glanced down to see her on one knee behind an overturned table. A young woman crouched there, her eyes wide with fear. Jack thought she might have been one of the bar's serving staff. "You gotta come with us now."

The girl shook her head, too terrified to leave her hiding place.

"Sweetie, you can't stay here," Taylor said, reaching down to grab the girl's arm.

"Tay, she's not coming," Jack said as the girl screamed and swatted at Taylor's hand. Her scream caught the attention of the warriors, who turned away from their internal fight, their blood-wet mandibles gleaming wickedly in the afternoon light. "Come on, we gotta go."

The girl swung at Taylor again, then turned and screamed her terror right into the face of the oncoming warriors. The first one to reach her was the newcomer to the building, and the girl's screams abruptly cut off with a wet gurgle as the ant's mandibles closed around her middle.

Taylor let out a soft gasp, and that was enough for Jack. He reached out with his free hand and caught her upper arm, then dragged her backward with him to the dubious safety of the exit.

He let her go as they pushed through the door and found themselves in a tiny island of calm in a sea of chaotic carnage.

Streams of giant ants poured up over the northern bluffs that marked the edge of this waystation along the river. The back door of the saloon opened onto a small hill dotted with low scrub. Jack crouched behind the concealment and took a moment to get his bearings.

"Mother of..." Taylor breathed as she joined him. Her eyes looked bleak.

"Swarm," Jack said grimly. "It happens sometimes. One of these took out the town where I grew up. We gotta get out of here if we can. Down the river would be best. Swarming Gants will chase survivors for miles. Where's your boat?"

"At...at the dock, but...the boiler isn't working. Dad's been... Oh my God. Dad!" Taylor's pale face went a few shades paler, and she spun toward the river so fast that she lost her balance and stumbled into Jack.

He swore and reached out with his free hand to steady her.

"If he's on the river, he's likely safe," Jack said. "Gants don't swim. I'm more worried about us right now. I see a sternwheeler down at the docks. That your boat?"

"Yes," Taylor said. "That's the *Sally*. But I don't know how we're going to get down there."

Neither did Jack. "Down there" meant descending down off of the small rise where the saloon overlooked the rest of the ramshackle little town that had grown up to support the needs of riverboat traders stopping for fuel and supplies.

"Town" was a bit grandiose, if Jack were being honest with himself. It was really just a collection of clapboard buildings clustered together with no organization, rhyme, nor reason. The "street," such as it was, was just a narrow dirt track that wound through the buildings. It would be a pain to navigate on a horse, let alone with a wagon...but that just might work in their favor.

"There's a stockyard here, isn't there?" Jack said suddenly, sniffing at the wind. "For ships carrying livestock?"

"A tiny one," Taylor said with a sniff. "We brought a few head of horses up here once, but never again, Beth said. The buyers here are poor and miserly compared to further upriver. Livestock's a pain on a boat anyway."

"Where's the stockyard, though?" Jack asked.

"Southeast end of town," Taylor said, turning to point. "Why?"

"Because we need a distraction if we're going to run through that"—he pointed to the boiling chaos of Gants milling around in the center of the town, bursting into buildings, fighting with one another, and chasing the few screaming inhabitants who hadn't already fled or been devoured—"down to the *Sally*."

Taylor looked from the town, to the river, then back up to him and nodded. He saw the muscle in her jaw jump slightly, and saw her eyes go steely and determined.

"Just stay with me," he murmured.

"I'm good," she said. "Let's do whatever we have to do."

"Get me to that stockyard," he said.

She nodded again and rose to a low crouch. She moved quickly, keeping as low a profile as possible as she skirted the edge of their little hill and headed down a rockfall on the southern side. Small stones rolled and slid beneath Jack's feet as he followed, and he fought to keep his balance centered. Being a big guy had its advantages, but it had its downsides, too.

They slid down the rockfall onto a gentler slope covered with pale, weedy grass and shielded by the back of the town's mercantile building. A single Gant scout rounded the northern corner of the building and froze as it caught their scent.

"Shit," Taylor said, and fired. The scout flinched, and wheeled around. Unlike the warriors, scouts didn't have oversized mandibles, and so she spun much more quickly than Jack expected. He fired at her as well, but she scuttled back around the building and out of sight before he could do more than harmlessly wing the rearmost portion of her carapace.

"Should we follow?" Taylor asked. "She might bring others looking for us."

"She *will* bring others," Jack said. "She's a scout, that's what they do. As you saw, they're also fast as the lightning they eat. Following her isn't a good idea. We just need to get moving and find that stockyard!"

"It's just up here," Taylor said turning back to the south and starting to move again. "Can't you smell it?"

Jack inhaled, and sure enough, a miasma of old shit thickened the air. It grew stronger, coating his nose and mouth as he and Taylor climbed up another small rise and saw the pens stretching out on the other side. Forty or so brown-streaked white barrel shapes clustered together near the closest rail fence. As they approached, the filthy things started to move in his direction, and Jack realized that these were the sheep he'd been seeking.

"They think we're going to feed them," Taylor said.

"Not exactly," Jack said. "But we are going to set them free." He walked up to the gate and lifted the latch, then heaved backward to pull the section-sized gate loose from the mud and muck that covered the ground.

"Guess I know why there's no lock," he grunted. Taylor nodded.

"Most people can't open this without a draft team," she said.

The sheep milled toward the suddenly open gate, then meandered slowly out. Jack cursed, then looked around.

"Damn," he said.

"What now?"

"Nothing, I was just hoping for a helpful border collie to appear and herd these dumb animals down toward town."

"Sorry," Taylor said, shrugging one shoulder. "Guess you'll just have to do it yourself."

"What about you?"

"This is your plan, bud," she said with a tiny smile. "Let's see how it works out for you."

Jack growled at her, then squared his shoulders and reached his arms out wide.

"C'mon, stupid sheep," he said, making his words sharp and staccato-sounding. "Go! Go that way! Ha!"

He waved his arms and kicked his feet and generally made himself as big as he could—which was pretty big, all things considered. Despite his confidence, he fought down a stab of surprise when it actually started to work, and the sheep began moving a little more quickly up the hill toward the town.

By the time they crested the rise, the town had all but been obliterated. No buildings remained untouched, and those that still stood looked moments away from falling down under the onslaught of carapaced bodies. The sheep started bleating, and backing away, but once again Taylor came to his rescue by firing her shotgun. *That* sent the bleating, milling mass into a panic, and they began to run down the slope of the rise toward the corpse of a town far faster than Jack had ever expected to see sheep run.

"C'mon," Taylor said then, breaking into a run herself and grabbing Jack's free hand as he watched his small herd spill down into the writhing chaos below. "They won't buy us much time."

Indeed, they didn't, but the sudden influx of new, tasty

morsels did grab the attention of the Gants long enough to let Jack and Taylor skirt what was left of the town and head down toward the docks. The wood creaked as their booted feet pounded the surface of the long pier that led to the *Long Tall Sally*. Jack's breath burned in his throat and chest, and it felt as if someone had stitched a very nice sampler in his side. *Home Sweet Home*, perhaps, or maybe *Home Is Where You Stash The Ammo*. Something like that.

"Taylor!"

Jack recognized Mike Gants's voice as they sprinted ahead. He very nearly stumbled as a gunshot cracked out over his head. This one sounded like a rifle. Another followed, and then another. Something thudded onto the pier. Something other than them. Something big enough to send vibrations rippling down under their feet.

"Come on, guys!" Mike called out. "You can make it! You're almost there!"

Jack looked up, blinking away the sweat that dripped into his eyes. Mike stood at the railing of the *Sally*, flanked by four women Jack hadn't seen before. All five of them held rifles. As he watched, one of the women put hers to her shoulder and fired at something behind them.

"I hope...they're...good shots..." he gasped.

A half-step in front of him, Taylor looked up.

"Best sharpshooters on the crew," Taylor called back. "They won't hit you by mistake, don't worry."

"Thanks..." Jack said. "That's...so...reassuring."

Despite his skepticism, the women proved to be as good as Taylor said, for they continued to fire, and based on the number of *thump*s he felt reverberating through the wooden pier, they continued to hit their targets. Meanwhile, he stopped worrying about being shot and started to think seriously about dying of an exploded heart.

Up ahead, a gate opened in the railing below Mike and the sharpshooters, and another group of women pushed a ramp over the side to thud down on the pier as well.

"C'mon, Jack," Taylor said, sounding almost as winded as he felt. "Don't leave me now."

Her plea shot adrenaline through his system, giving him the boost he needed to pick up his flagging pace and storm up the ramp just a second behind her. Once he passed the railing, he tripped and fell hard, only just managing to roll out of the way as the women hauled the ramp back in.

"Cast off!" one of them screamed. "Cast off! They're right behind them!"

Jack turned his head to look out between the railing supports and saw a stream of Gant warriors barreling down the dock. The *Sally* lurched, and then the tiny sliver of water between the dock and the boat began to widen as she drifted out into the current.

"Peg, did everyone make it back?" Taylor asked the woman who'd called for them to cast off as they wrestled the ramp out of the way and got the railing latched back up.

"We think so," a third woman said. "You were the last. Beth wouldn't leave without you. Said she couldn't do that to your father."

"She's right," Taylor said. "My father wouldn't have survived losing me, and then she'd have no one to fix her precious boiler."

Jack pushed himself up and got to his feet, fighting to slow his breathing down and appear like a man in control of himself in front of all these women.

"Ladies," he said. "I'm Jack. I must say, I appreciate the help. Especially from lovely women such as yourselves. The *Sally* is blessed in her crew, it appears."

"Ha!" Taylor said. "That's not it. Beth just doesn't trust men as much. Jack, these are KC Charland, Peg Smareker, and Monika Beeman . . . and Annastasia Webster, Linda Zielke, Sande Ankenbrandt, and Carol Hoch," she added as the sharpshooters appeared one by one, climbing down a set of stairs from the upper railing.

"And Mike and I have already met," Jack said, exchanging a nod with the only other man present as he followed the ladies. "I was just saying, I sure appreciate the rescue."

"How'd you get out of there?" Annastasia asked, her brow furrowed in worry as she continued to scan over the side for Gants. Personally, Jack thought she should relax. Everyone knew Gants didn't swim.

"Jack rescued me," Taylor said. "Got me out of the bar, and created a distraction so we could run for it through the town."

"You rescued me right back," Jack put in, turning his attention back to her. "So thank you."

"We're partners," she said, and her lips curved in a soft, real, genuine smile. And just like that, Jack felt his heart explode and his world flip upside down and reorient itself with this tall, blonde, breathy girl as its center.

"Yes," he said, his eyes serious. "We certainly are."

"Well," Mike said then, slapping Jack on the back and breaking the spell, "we appear to be safe for the moment. Shall we head belowdecks for a drink? Beth—that's Beth Spraker, the captain of the *Long Tall Sally*—will definitely want to meet you."

"I should go help my fath—" Taylor broke off when a deep, rumbling roar shuddered through the ship, and the sternwheel started a ponderous rotation. "Never mind," she said. "I guess I'll come with you to meet Beth, then, if that's okay with you."

"I wouldn't have it any other way, Taylor," Jack said, and to his secret dismay, he found that he really, truly meant it. If it were up to him, he'd never be parted from her again.

Damn it all.

❧

## Kacey Ezell and Christopher L. Smith

**Kacey Ezell** is a USAF helicopter pilot who writes sci-fi/fantasy/ alt history. She was a Dragon Award finalist in 2018 and 2019, and her stories have twice been featured in Baen's Year's Best Military and Adventure SF compilation. In 2018, her story "Family Over Blood" won the 2018 Baen Readers' Choice Award. She has had novels published by Baen, Chris Kennedy Publishing, and Blackstone Publishing. Kacey first attended LibertyCon in 2015 and was immediately welcomed into the "family reunion" atmosphere. She can literally trace every novel contract she's ever signed back to networking connections she first made at LibertyCon. Uncle Timmy and his family created something entirely, uniquely special; and Kacey is honored to play this small part in recognizing his legacy.

A native Texan by birth (if not geography), **Christopher L. Smith** moved "home" as soon as he could.

Attending Texas A&M, he learned quickly that there was more to college than beer and football games. He relocated to

San Antonio, attending SAC and UTSA, graduating in late 2000 with a BA in Lit. While there, he also met a wonderful lady who somehow found him to be funny, charming, and worth marrying.

Christopher began writing fiction in 2012. His short stories can be found in multiple anthologies, including John Ringo and Gary Poole's *Black Tide Rising,* Mike Williamson's *Forged in Blood,* Larry Correia and Kacey Ezell's *Noir Fatale,* and Tom Kratman's *Terra Nova.*

Christopher has co-written two novels: *Kraken Mare* with Jason Cordova, and *Gunpowder & Embers* with Kacey Ezell and John Ringo.

His cats allow his family and their dogs to reside with them outside of San Antonio.

Chris reports, "I didn't get to spend much time with Timmy, unfortunately. But what I can say is that the very limited contact I had with him made me feel at home at LibertyCon. I think we only met face-to-face two or three times, at most. Each time, however, he made me—a relative newcomer into the con and writing scene—feel like he had known me for years, and was so excited that I'd come to visit.

"LibertyCon is and always be my 'hometown' con, even though I'm not from Chattanooga. I can attribute this to Timmy's attitude and heart, which permeates his convention, and his legacy, which Brandy has carried on masterfully.

"I wish I'd been able to get to know him better in the short time I knew him."

# OPEN SEASON

It's always good to have Joe Buckley in an anthology.... (And for more information about the mythical and nonmythical Joe—who, when nonmythical, is a frequent LibertyCon attendee—please see *The Many Deaths of Joe Buckley* at www.baen.com, another project that goes to support charities.) I'm pleased Chuck included him. Chuck was another of the hardworking LibertyCon toastmasters—and I'm afraid he has spawned a whole new genre of "secret history" of convention stories, he having first planted this idea in his epic opening ceremony speech. Chuck himself is one of those "overnight successes" that were decades in the making. I got to publish his first collaborative novel and his first solo novel, and I am looking forward to many more years of publishing his work—so long as we can continue to fight the battle outlined in this story....

—TW

# Open Season

## Charles E. Gannon

Matthew Fanny poked his head through the door. "We clear?"

Don Puckett nodded slowly. "We have the room to ourselves. Except a techie, working behind the curtains in the back." He tapped a white-noise generator on the round table in front of him. "Whoever's there isn't going to hear anything."

Gerry Martin, who was typing furiously on his laptop, looked up when some distant laughter came echoing through the facility's hallways and in over Fanny's shoulder. "Did you find someone to fill in for Regina?"

"I did, though Ms. Kirby sends her regrets."

"Well, then bring in the replacement and close the door." Gerry stopped typing, looked up to see who had been added to their OpSec cell at the last minute. Regina Kirby's was arguably the hardest role to fill, especially at the last minute. There weren't a lot of people who were both outside the operation and who could be trusted to oversee its security and counterintelligence needs.

But Fanny just grinned confidently in reply to Gerry's eager expression and Don's tombstone stare. He stepped aside.

Joe Buckley slid sideways into the room. "Hi, fellas."

"Cool!" beamed Gerry suddenly. "Nice to meet you, Joe. I mean, officially."

Puckett just stared. "Well, I'll be damned." He nodded twice. From him, that was an enthusiastic gesture of approval.

Fanny slipped in, grinning. "Told you."

"You did," Puckett agreed. "I just didn't believe you."

"And what's new about that?" Matthew countered with a sly smile.

Puckett affected a mild glower. At least, Fanny *hoped* he was affecting it.

Joe had found a seat in the loose ring of chairs. "It's nice of you to let me help out."

"'Nice'?" Gerry echoed. "Joe, you are doing us a huge favor."

Joe scratched his head. "Well, I'm glad to hear that . . . but why did you need *me*?"

"Look," Matt said, grabbing the fourth and last seat in the council circle, "it's tough running OpSec for Operation Liberty. I mean, anyone could be trying to infiltrate us: government, foreign powers, contractors, corporations, tech spies, TVA—anyone. So we need a face we know. Not easy to come up with on short notice."

Gerry leaned forward. "That's why it's a huge stroke of luck that you're here—and a stroke of genius that Matt thought of you. I mean, who's been vetted more than you, Joe? Damn near every author here has killed a 'Joe Buckley' in at least one of their books. And, as a result, you know all the players, but are also one of the few people who hasn't been brought inside the Bolgeo 'crime family.' So, with Regina unavailable, that is exactly the background we need."

Don was frowning. "So why'd we lose 'Gina, exactly?"

"Conflicting event." Matt sighed. "Some kind of author reception. Or maybe she's helping provide transport to the regimental mess."

Don's frown deepened. "We call that the Baen dinner, Fanny. No exceptions."

Gerry looked up from the laptop when Fanny made a disparaging noise. "Don's right, Matt. Even referring to the unit violates basic OpSec."

"It's not even a full regiment," Fanny groused under his breath.

But not so low that Don didn't hear. "Doesn't matter. The unit remains unnamed and covert. If our existence was known, our mission would be over. And would get handed off to idiots. Who'd screw it up. And probably lose the planet."

"Yeah, yeah, okay. So I'll rephrase: 'Gina might be helping arrange transport for the *Baen dinner*. That better?"

Don simply nodded. "Might be another reason she's there, though."

"Why?" Joe asked.

Gerry shrugged without looking up. "Because she knows our

new person of interest pretty well. Well enough to keep chatting him up during an event."

"And so, keep an eye on him," Don added.

"And who's her handoff?" Matthew asked.

"'Handoff'?" Joe echoed uncertainly.

Don nodded. "When you're watching someone, you need to keep one of your operatives close. But it can't always be the same operative. That would make any smart POI suspicious. Fast."

Joe nodded. "Got it. So who's Regina's partner for POI-watching?"

"Fritz Fotovitch," Gerry volunteered. "He and Regina have been doing it as a tag team for six years now. Ever since he started coming steadily, in 2013."

Fanny frowned. "Shit. I just thought they were, you know, friends of his."

Don Puckett turned an "are you that gullible?" glare upon him.

Joe shrugged. "So who's the person of interest?"

Don sighed; there might have been a hint of regret. "This year's Master of Ceremonies."

Joe blinked. "Him? Why?"

Gerry stopped typing, looked up from under black, bushy brows. "You did hear his Opening Speech, right?"

"Yeah, sure. Some okay jokes in there. Some good ones, too."

Don's frown was back. "Too good. Too... accurate."

Joe blinked again. "Uh... what?"

"His jokes were too accurate. We've got to figure out what his angle is."

Joe Buckley shook his head. "Wait a minute; back up. Are you saying that... that—?"

"That LibertyCon is actually a cover for something else?" Fanny finished for him. "Damn straight."

"That's why you're here," Don said, staring at Joe Buckley. "We needed someone who's familiar with the con, with the players, and with the books. Who's got years of familiarity with them, but who isn't on the *real* inside operation. That's the only way an outsider can hit the ground running."

Joe looked like he might be on the verge of laughter, the shakes, or both. "But, but—if this is all true, then why have an outsider in your, uh, 'oversight cell' at all?"

Gerry was typing again. "Because an outsider is often the

best way of spotting a mole." When he got a blank look from Joe, he explained. "Almost all moles have a carefully groomed persona. They've been read in on all our operational protocols and objectives; they know how to respond at any given moment, to any given event, in a way that won't blow their cover. But outsiders ask unpredictable questions. They're a potential wild card for which the mole can't prepare. So here you are: the ultimate insider outsider."

"Gee. Thanks." Joe's voice was too surprised to hide the undertone of irony.

"Okay," Fanny said, "so let's get to it. Do his activities raise any high-risk flags?"

Gerry was scanning the POI's dossier on his computer. "None. Well, no more than the usual with the authors that come to LibertyCon. Writes mostly hard SF, so he's already trafficking in relevant topics: alien contact, invasion, technology. All of the latter being logically extrapolated from current science or firmly grounded theory."

Don nodded. "So, perfect cover if he's trying to infiltrate us."

"Yup," Gerry agreed, continuing to scan the files on his laptop. "He also traveled a lot as a professor."

"Professor of what?" Joe asked.

Gerry looked up slowly. "English."

Fanny winced. "Ooo. I'd forgotten that. Not good."

Don didn't react. "Actually, if he was like most English professors, that *would* be good news. They usually don't know squat about science, technology, or the military."

Fanny smiled. "You mean like the one who thought a covert extraction is when a dentist pulls your tooth in a dark alley?"

Gerry may have snickered.

Joe smiled. "Hey, that's a good one."

"But off topic," Don snapped. "Look: the guy consults with defense and intel agencies around the Beltway. So his having been an English professor doesn't change the risk equation. Is there anything else in his past that might influence our assessment? Have you heard any talk?"

"Well," Gerry sighed, "I've heard some folks mutter about his 'regional affinities.'"

"Huh?" Joe said.

"He was born, bred, schooled, and worked north of the

Mason-Dixon and east of the Mississippi. His whole life." Gerry didn't look up.

Joe blinked again. "I'm from Massachusetts."

Fanny was looking pointedly away, murmured, "I relocated from New Hampshire."

Don almost smiled. "Sasebo. Nagasaki Prefecture. Gotcha all beat."

Gerry tapped in a few corrections. "Sooo...I think we can put that variable aside."

Matthew Fanny frowned, voice fast and annoyed. "So what are we looking at, then? Was he suborned sometime after he first came to LibertyCon in 2010? Or during the two years before he returned? Or maybe he's a deep plant, a sleeper agent whose whole career was just a ploy to get him next to us?"

Gerry shrugged. "Or he might be a messenger from some of his pals inside the Beltway or the defense industry, here to give us a wink and a nod."

"But what's his message?" Joe asked.

Don's eyes glittered like obsidian. "That he knows what we actually do at this 'convention.' That someone is on to us. And that they want to talk to us. Privately. Otherwise, they would have simply revealed what really goes on at LibertyCon. Would have told the whole world."

"Okay," Joe said, hand on his forehead. "So which is he: suborned agent, deep plant, or messenger?"

Gerry shrugged. "No way of telling from his background data. Or his current activities."

Joe frowned. "So in other words, we've got no idea."

Don pulled a portable recorder out of his pocket, the kind used by reporters. "Not from what's in the dossier, no. Which means that the answer will be in what he said during the Opening Ceremony. Whoever he's working for, *they* want us to know what they've learned about LibertyCon. So they'll have worked it into his talk."

Gerry was looking at the recorder as if it might transmogrify into a pit viper. "You know, Don, once this opening speech gets out, we'll have bigger problems. *Much* bigger."

"That's why it's not getting out, Gerry." Don tapped the recorder lightly. "This is the only copy."

"What?" marveled Fanny.

"Yep. Thank Fritz for the fast thinking. He saw where the emcee's 'parody' was going and killed the live feed to Facebook. Made it look like a mistake. Meanwhile, the room's hidden cameras recorded the audience. So—thanks to the POI's being long-winded—we had enough time to scan the crowd, find any folks who might have been recording, and then get close when they left the hall. To scramble their phones."

"Were there a lot?" Joe asked, swallowing, his face transformed into a "shit-just-got-real" expression.

"Nah. Not a one. The con was only recording on general principle. Who else is gonna record opening ceremonies? Particularly if they're emceed by a has-been professor with a reputation for running on at the mouth."

"Good point," Fanny agreed with a sharp nod.

Don moved his index finger to the recorder's control surface. "The first time I heard it—just twenty minutes ago, with everyone else—I was too surprised to do anything but follow along with the audience. Laughing at the right places and such. Now, we need to listen for any clues indicating who sent us this message and why. Ready?" He was answered by three somber nods. He played the tape.

The emcee's predictable introductory palaver of welcoming con-goers and reeling off the list of guests had—mercifully—been edited out. A few harmless comic bits—well, *ostensibly* comic bits—had been left in. The emcee had employed one of the oldest schticks in live acts: to set up a catchphrase that the audience recognized and so, telegraphed when he was about to veer off into another, related gag.

Don stopped the tape. "I gotta say, this setup was pretty shrewd."

Fanny's face contracted into a mass of doubting creases. "You mean, the clichéd catchphrase? That kind of routine was old before there was vaudeville."

Gerry quirked an eyebrow. "It was old before Rome."

Don frowned: mere annoyance, this time. "No, not the routine itself, but the way he used it to both set himself up to reveal ninety-five percent of our operations and still give himself—or his handlers—plausible deniability."

Joe looked totally bewildered. "Sorry—what?"

Don turned patiently toward him. "The catchphrase—the line

he used to set up every gag—was, 'Now, I have a theory about this.' By calling it a theory, he's provided himself a perfectly innocent-sounding way to signal the parts that are his message to us. But the regular folks in the audience just hear it as the windup for another joke."

Joe nodded, frowned seriously, but still looked confused.

"Listen to how he uses it to make that shift here." Don reactivated the playback.

The emcee's voice rolled out of it: "Now, one of the most unique aspects of LibertyCon is the number of headliners, bestsellers, award-winners and rising pros who attend every year, *without any compensation of any kind*. So, a lot of folks wonder, 'How the heck do the organizers get all those pros to attend a con that won't even allow a thousand paying fans in the door? That's impossible!'

"The 'public' explanation is that these authors just like sharing their work and their love of science fiction and fantasy with each other and their fans. But of course, anything that straightforward, that open and agenda-free, beggars belief.

"So...I have a theory. A final theory, you might say. But I need your help to test it."

Don spoke quickly, getting his remarks into the pause where the speaker caught his breath—which seemed nearly inexhaustible. "This was a pretty ballsy move. Suckered the whole audience into a show of hands that revealed the Liberty Regiment's table of organization."

The emcee's voice was less conversational, now. It was more the tone used to give people instructions or to ask them for anticipated feedback. "Keep your hands up when you hear what applies to you. Military personnel?" A pause. "Civilian consultants and contractors?" Another pause. "First responders? Degreed scientists? Trained bladesmen and martial artists?"

A long pause. "Keep your hands up. Look around you. Damn near all of you have your hands in the air."

His tone shifted to ironic incredulity. "Sure. All at the same con. And not in a major population center like New York, L.A., or Chicago. No, it's in *Chattanooga*. At a con that *won't allow* more than seven hundred and fifty attendees. A con that has, as one of its oldest traditions, a pre-con meet-up for a friendly shooting event—but WAAYYY off-site where no one can observe. A con that is run by one family.

"All coincidence? Sure..."—the voice changed again, suggested the unveiling of a sinister conspiracy—"unless it's not a coincidence at all.

"Because there's a far more probable explanation: that at the same time every year, a group of alleged sci-fi 'fans' with a peculiarly optimized skill set gathers in Chattanooga"—the emcee's tone became strident, emphatic—"where they fight to close an interdimensional gate that's opened by alien invaders just after every summer solstice!"

Now he was on a roll. The audience was laughing; the four men gathered around the table were not.

"Hey," the emcee continued, "you think *Predator* was just a movie? That was a training film! Remember what we're told? That the aliens always come when it's hot? And humid?"

A moment of silence followed by hysterics.

Joe frowned. "I forgot: what happened there? Why's everyone laughing?"

Gerry, taking notes on his laptop, muttered, "He pointed."

"At what?"

"Toward the outside exit."

"What's funny about that?"

"Joe, have *you* been outside in the heat and humidity today?"

"Oh. Yeah. Sorry."

The laughter died down and the emcee resumed: "I mean, what else could explain the casual mustering of this multitalented reaction force which masquerades as 'con-goers'? And who'd really believe that they're all getting together for something called 'Liberty-con'? That's not the name of the convention: that's their secret battle cry!

"And now we know where the all-controlling Bolgeo crime family's power *really* comes from. They're the ones who discovered the interdimensional gate. That's how they fund this covert op. Think about it: Liberty Con...but never Liberty *Convention*. And now you know why: it stands for Liberty CON-traband. Wake up, people: this is all made possible by black-market alien goods. It's an off-the-books black op. This is Noogagate!"

It certainly didn't sound like anyone in the audience was suspecting anything fishy as going on—although a lot *should* have.

"And that off-site shooting expedition?" The sneer was evident in the emcee's voice. "Just cover for a refresher course in marksmanship, and a pre-op weapons check. And make no mistake: there are enough firearms to equip a regiment. Or, if Mike Williamson shows up, a light division. Support weapons included.

"All taken together, it beggars belief that this could just be a science fiction and fantasy con. That's my theory. And I'm sticking to it."

Don leaned over and switched off the playback. "So, what do you think?"

"I think we've been compromised," Fanny said sharply. "He gets too many things right. Hell, the part of the audience that is actually in the regiment probably figures he's secretly *been one of us* all along. That's the only reason they would have kept laughing—instead of rushing the stage, guns out."

"It's worse than being compromised," said Don, with a sharp shake of his head. "Because he doesn't just get 'too many' things right; he gets *everything* right. That's not your garden-variety opsec breach."

"Why?"

"Because," Gerry answered, "except for us, Uncle Timmy, his wife, Linda, and Moll-in-Chief Brandy, no one knows everything. The operations, the different action and security cells: they're all compartmentalized. So either there's a mole in every single cell—"

"Or it's one of us. Well, one of—of you." Joe ended the sentence on a stammer; apparently, he only realized the ramifications of his deduction as the words were leaving his mouth.

Fanny and Gerry looked suspiciously at each other. Don did something even more unprecedented:

He laughed.

Just one short bark, but he actually laughed. The others looked at him as if they thought he might have a stroke, undergo rapture, or both.

"What are you laughing about, Don?" Matt said cautiously. "Joe's right. The only answer is that it's one of us, or the original capos. No one else has all the intel that the emcee just rolled out."

Don did another unprecedented thing: he smiled. But it wasn't a pleasant smile. "I think you fellas forget who we've been fighting for over thirty years now. Aliens who can blend into any background. Whose tech is centuries ahead of ours. Or at least it was until we took some off their dead and reverse-engineered it."

Joe frowned. "What's your point, Don?"

"My point, Joe"—Puckett was smiling again—"is that we adopted one of the classic—and worst—bad habits of opsec groups."

"Which is?" asked Fanny with a frown.

"That we're looking for what we expect to find."

Now Gerry was frowning. "I don't follow you, Don."

"Really? Shucks, Gerry: what is it that we're supposed to provide for the Regiment?"

Gerry looked like he'd been scolded by a cherished uncle. "Operational security and counterintelligence."

"Right. So what are we always looking for?"

Fanny was frowning, but he was also nodding. "Signs that we've been compromised or sold out."

"Exactly. And because that's our task, we might miss other threats, other explanations for how the Regiment could be compromised."

Joe looked baffled again. "Such as?"

"That our enemy has ways to observe us, or hack us, that he's never revealed. Or has only recently developed." Don put his hands in his lap, leaned over the table. "It's a logical evolution of the conflict. We push 'em back every year. The few that make it back through the gate never get a look at our infrastructure, so they never bring any useful intelligence. Which means that, for almost a third of a century, the aliens have been operating in the dark when it comes to our numbers, our assets, our technology. Although, in the last ten years, survivors will have reported that we've reverse-engineered some of their technology. Which means—"

"Which means," Fanny picked up, "that they are fighting a losing battle. Well, a battle that they become more likely to lose with every passing year. So, yeah: they need intel on us. But doesn't that make it *more* likely that they'd reach out to someone on our side of the gate, to find a human—a traitor—to do exactly what the master of ceremonies did today?"

"Oh, I'm sure they'd like to be able to do that," Don agreed. "Except there's one little problem: *how* do they do that? They get one shot at breaking through to our world every year. Our job is to keep them from scoring that goal. And so far, we've been successful. Or so we've believed."

Now Gerry was nodding. "Sure. We've assumed that they're still working from the same old playbook: assault and attempt to hold a beachhead while they set up machinery to stabilize the gate, to make it permanent. But what if they changed their plans last time? What if some of them came through *intending* to be left behind?"

Fanny was on the edge of his seat. "Sure, sure. And if they came up with that plan a few years ago, they'd have spent that time adapting their chameleon tech so that they could pass as human. They'd stay here undetected, setting up data hacks and comm taps. That would explain how they know everything we do."

"It would," Don said, nodding. "But you're missing something."

"What's that?"

"Well, if the aliens put one of theirs through last time, one that we didn't see, what's that infiltrator probably preparing to do now, just a few hours before the gate opens?"

Gerry and Matthew stared. Gerry sputtered out his answer first. "Surprise attack. From *this* side. Hit us from where we least expect it. Cripple our defenses."

"Take down our comms—hell, our whole C4I. And—and our cadre!" Fanny jumped up. "We've got to warn—!"

Don waved him down. "Take a seat, Matthew. We have time. Some, anyway."

"We do?"

"Why, sure we do. Don't you agree—Joe?"

"Huh?" Joe said.

Don nodded. "I apologize. It's not fair to ask an outsider—and a newcomer—to speculate on that kind question. So let me ask you a simpler one." He jutted his chin at his recorder. "When I replayed the emcee's speech, why didn't you know what was going on when he pointed outside, the bit that got all the laughter?"

Joe smiled lamely. "Went to the bathroom at that part."

"Really?" Don leaned closer. "As I remember, it was a standing-room-only crowd. The doors were blocked, people backed up into the hall. Now just how did you not only get out, but then back in?"

Joe shrugged, looked confused. "Well, heck, Don, I know people. Pretty much everyone. Why *wouldn't* they let me through?"

"Well, I guess that's true enough. I'm sure those kind folks didn't want to keep you from hearing the end of Hannon's speech."

Joe smiled. "I suspect you're right."

All three men stared at Joe. He stared back, confused.

"Joe," Don said amiably, "you know our emcee, right?"

"Well, through social media. I don't think I've ever met him personally."

"That's a shame," Matthew Fanny said carefully. "Chuck *Hannon* is an okay guy. Even if he does talk a lot."

Joe paused, seemed taken aback by the way they were hanging on whatever he said next. "Hannon seems okay, yes."

Gerry's eyes were wide as he scanned rapidly through several files at the same time. "I thought you might have a grudge against him."

Joe frowned. "A—a grudge?"

"Yeah. You wrote that you felt that the way Gann—er, *Hannon* killed you off in his novel was the cruelest of all."

Joe Buckley looked around the group, puzzled. "Why is that important right now? We've got an invasion to stop."

"I quite agree." Don's nod was slower this time. "So just how did Mr. Hannon kill off your character?" When Joe didn't respond immediately, he added, "Surely you remember."

Fanny: "And what about how Ringo killed you?"

Martin: "And Weber?"

No one was surprised when Joe went for a gun, but he was fast—terribly fast. Faster than Fanny or Martin, as they grabbed after their own pistols.

But Don simply kept smiling as the tabletop erupted in multiple sprays of wooden pressboard, blasted upward by three .44 jacketed hollowpoints.

An eyeblink later, both Gerry and Matt double-tapped the alien, making sure he was as dead as he looked.

Don rose, waved off their amazed stares, growled: "And yeah, of course Han fuckin' shot first. Who wouldn't?"

Even as they approached, the image of Joe's corpse fluttered and dissipated, leaving a familiar, quad-jawed, talon-handed monstrosity in its place.

Fanny almost spat. "Great. So they *do* have mimic suits, now."

Gerry craned his neck to get a look at the weapon that had fallen out of the alien's hand. It looked like a ray gun from a bad 1950s sci-fi flick. Or *Mars Invades*. "Well, *that's* going to be worth some bucks at the interagency auction we'll hold one day."

"Keep dreaming about that auction," Don muttered, "but in the meantime, we have a much bigger problem. Right now and right here."

"What's that?"

Don nodded toward the black drapes at the back of the room, where the sound of tools on metal had stopped when the guns started firing. "Not everyone working for the con knows the full truth."

Fanny shook his head. "We should never have—"

As Don silenced him with a look, Gerry stepped forward. "I wonder who it is?" The curtains parted. A head popped out to look at them.

It was Joe Buckley.

Don hissed, "Well, shit," an instant before the three of them vented the hapless alien doppleganger.

Don didn't even have to prompt the other two with gestures; Martin checked the new casualty as Fanny re-crossed to the room's entrance and slid up alongside the door.

Ear cocked toward the hallway beyond, Matt muttered, "And what do we do about Gannon?"

Don was checking their comms; so far, they were still working. "What do you mean?"

"Well, he may have just made up all of that stuff for his speech—but he still knows too much. Even if he doesn't really *know* it. If you see what I mean."

"I do." Don moved on to Gerry's laptop; it was still running clean and secure. "So: recommendations?"

"Well... dead men tell no tales."

Don stopped, considered. Then: "Naw. Dead men also attract too much attention."

Gerry looked sideways as he went to the other side of the entrance. "Um... recruit him?"

"Seriously?" Don shook his head. "That guy can't stop talking."

"Fair point," Gerry conceded.

Fanny gaped. "So—we just leave him in place? Like a walking time bomb?"

Don shook his head. "Gannon's only a time bomb if anyone believes what he says. And hell, he doesn't believe it himself. He just made it up." Don joined the other two. "Sometimes, fellas, the best action is to do nothing at all."

There was a knock on the door.

"Shit," muttered Gerry.

"Never have a suppressor when you really need one," Fanny groused.

"Who is it?" Don asked in a voice that indicated he really did not want to know and was not about to open the door.

"Vonn. Vonn Gants."

Don sighed. "Did we make too much noise?"

"Not hardly. Not compared to the war films being shown just down the hall."

"Thank God for small favors," Gerry muttered.

"Vonn," Don said, "we have a 'situation' here. Only come in if you're on Regimental business."

"I am," answered Vonn as she opened the door. "Found someone Matt was looking for. To help with OpSec," she added, smiling as she entered.

She was followed in by Joe Buckley.

Who was shot where he stood. Eleven times, by three different calibers.

As shouting started farther along the hall, Don shook his head and gestured for the others—including the redoubtable Vonn—to follow.

"Guess it's open season on Joe Buckley," Fanny wisecracked.

"Yup," Don agreed, "and no bag limit. Let's go huntin'."

&

# Charles E. Gannon

My connection to LibertyCon and Uncle Timmy was a bit on the late side compared to a lot of other folks. I first heard about—and was invited to—LibertyCon in 2010 and discovered a convention unlike any I'd gone to before. There were tracks and panels—sorta. And you could tell the pros apart from the fans—sorta. But when it came to enthusiasm and engagement, there was no uncertainty whatsoever.

And that was why it was a bit difficult to tell the pros and the fans apart: because at LibertyCon, it just didn't matter a whole lot. David Weber—who would have been mercilessly swamped at any other con—was with a cluster of pros and fans playing Spades in the lobby. *In the lobby.*

Which exemplifies the core (and unique) nature of LibertyCon: a community of equals who sit on different sides of a panel table 'cause it's just more convenient that way. At other cons, you can often observe an almost feudal relationship between the "aristocrat" pros and "peasant" fans. Not only was that absent at LibertyCon: it was anathema. And in no small number of cases, reviled.

So, for me, LibertyCon was a little bit like discovering a home I had never known existed. I didn't grow up in fandom, so my reaction to the "stratification" evident at my first cons was that it was not just wrong and weird, but downright contradictory. I mean, these are science fiction and fantasy readers we're talking about. NO ONE accepts the idea that ANYONE is smarter or better than they are. And yet, at most cons, the divide between pro and fan was not only palpable, but reinforced at every step. So LibertyCon was an absolute breath of fresh air.

I don't remember my first encounter with Uncle Timmy. I know it was at my first LibertyCon, and that was followed by happy reunions at other cons and later Liberties. And over the course of those years and conversations, the thing about him that I remember best (and most fondly) was his enthusiasm. For the entire genre. For everyone in it. Which manifested not just among his boosters and supporters, but even with good-natured winks aimed (figuratively) at his detractors. Because, strange (inconceivable) as it might seem, Uncle Timmy had detractors. And I never heard him utter an unkind or angry word against them.

—Chuck Gannon

**Charles E. Gannon**'s Caine Riordan hard SF novels have all been national bestsellers, and include four finalists for the Nebula, two for the Dragon Award, and a Compton Crook winner. The fifth novel, *Marque of Caine*, came out in 2019 and a side series, Murphy's Lawless, launched in 2020. His epic fantasy series, The Vortex of Worlds, debuts with the novel *This Broken World*. He has collaborated with Eric Flint in the Ring of Fire series, written solo novels in John Ringo's Black Tide Rising world, and worked in the Starfire, Honorverse, Man-Kzin, and War World universes. He has also written a whole bunch of short fiction, designed and wrote RPGs for GDW, and was a scriptwriter/producer in NYC.

As a Distinguished Professor of English, Gannon received five Fulbrights. His book *Rumors of War & Infernal Machines* won the 2006 ALA Choice Award for Outstanding Book. He is a frequent subject matter expert on national media venues (NPR, Discovery, etc.) and for various intelligence and defense agencies. He lives in Annapolis, Maryland, with his wife and four (living) children.

# IN THE DETAILS

I met John Hartness in 2016 when my wife and I attended our first convention. It was a convention in Chattanooga called ConNooga. We were curious about the conventions and wondered if that was what we wanted to do. As I was working my way down the aisles he said something that gave me a look at who this guy really was. "Come on over, buy my shit!" Never having heard anyone approach sales quite like that, I went over and talked for a while with him. I asked advice on what I had done as an author and he didn't hesitate to get right into it and tell me what he had learned in the time he had been publishing. He's got a great sense of humor and is very good at the trade of BS. When thoughts of this anthology came up, he was one of the first I thought of.

—CW

# In the Details

*A Quincy Harker, Demon Hunter, Short Story*

## John G. Hartness

"You know it's literally never Satanists, right?" I asked as I followed Glory up the brick sidewalk to the unassuming ranch-style house just outside of Clarksville, Tennessee.

"You're right," said the angel. "It's never Satanists. And there's never any hint of real supernatural power."

I opened my mouth to ask her why the hell we'd just driven three hours in the pouring rain if she agreed with me, when she held up a finger.

"It's never anything," she said, turning to me. "Until it is. And when it is, it's usually too late to do anything about it. There are two people dead in that house. The first murders this town has seen in more than a decade, and there are symbols that have the police thinking there might be an occult aspect. So, we're going to go in there, wave our little federal agent badges around, offer up our services to the locals, get rebuffed because the last thing they want is a couple of Feds sticking their noses into local business, and then we're going to leave. But not before we get a look around. You good with that?"

I wasn't, really. The last place I wanted to be was anywhere near even a hint of magic, but when your guardian angel throws the keys to your pickup at you and tells you to drive her halfway across the state to look at a couple of dead suburbanites, you just do it. I held up my credentials to the patrolman guarding the door, and he took the wallet and looked at me.

"Homeland Security? This ain't no terrorist thing, man." He didn't tell me to leave in so many words, but I could tell he wanted to.

243

"Probably not, but my boss dragged me away from happy hour on Beale Street for this shit, so how about you let me look around, talk to whoever's in charge, and let him kick me out?"

The cop's eyes widened when I mentioned Beale, which wasn't a surprise given that we were better than three hours from Memphis. "Well, shit, man. If y'all come all this way just to be disappointed, I reckon you might as well go on in. You don't have to worry about booties or gloves, the crime scene guys left about ten minutes ago."

"Thanks, Officer..." I looked at the nameplate on his chest. "Woods. I appreciate it."

We stepped into the house, which was at least as boring inside as it was out. The front door opened into a small foyer, with a dining room to the right and a great room off to the left. I followed the buzz of conversation and stepped into the great room, stopping just inside the door and waiting to be noticed.

A wiry little cop with more hair on his upper lip than on top of his head elbowed a big burly man who stood in the middle of the living room floor munching on a white powdered doughnut. The big man turned and bellowed at us, spraying crumbs and confectioner's sugar all over the floor. "Who the heck are you and what moron let you in here? Woods! You're fired! You're fired, and when I get back to the station, your brother's fired, and if you give me any lip, your idiot dog's fired, too."

He stormed over to us, the little gnome statues on the mantel shaking with his every gargantuan step. "I asked you a question!" he practically shouted from six inches away from me.

I reached up, wiped a little speck of sugar from my cheek, and held my badge up between our faces. "Quincy Harker, Department of Homeland Security. We heard you had an unusual case and came by to see if we could lend our expertise."

"Well, if I need to stop a terrorist, I'll call you," he snarled, his lips curling in distaste. "But I think I can catch a devil-worshipping murderer without any *federal* help." He was tall, and thick through the shoulders and the middle. Probably a high school football stud who went into law enforcement when he realized that playing for Middle Tennessee State wasn't going to get him drafted into the NFL. He was almost certainly a pretty good sheriff. Good at handling people, good at breaking up bar fights, and good at dealing with husbands who slapped their wives around.

But this wasn't a small-town drunken scrap, and it wasn't an abusive asshole who needed to be taught to respect women. This was murder, and from the moment I stepped into the house, I knew it was my kind of case. I didn't even have to use my Sight to confirm it, I could *feel* the magic coating every surface in the place. Something seriously bad had happened here and whatever did it was not the kind of thing that was likely to stop on its own.

So, I couldn't let the second coming of Buford Pusser intimidate me, not that he ever had a real chance. I've stared down demons and Lords of Hell, and I learned to fight from Dracula himself. The day a redneck with a badge can stare me down is the day they throw the first shovel of dirt on my face.

"Sheriff," I said, working to keep my voice level. No point in shouting until it became necessary. "This is no more a normal murder case than you are a ballerina, and while you might not want any federal help, I'm pretty sure you don't have anyone in your department that can read those symbols painted on the wall over there."

I pointed to an intricate pentagram scribed into the drywall with a knife, then filled in with blood. Most of it had dried to a dirty brown, but there was just enough shiny red still that there was no question what it was. It was a summoning circle. A big one, with complicated warding. There was an inner circle, with symbols running clockwise around the perimeter, then there was an outer circle enclosing those, with another ring of markings, this one running counterclockwise.

The sheriff took a step back, because I sure as hell wasn't going to, and looked at the wall. "And you've got somebody who can make sense out of that gibberish?" He flapped a hand at the circle. "I've sent pictures to half a dozen professors and four preachers, and ain't none of them ever seen anything like this."

He was wrong, of course. One of the ministers he'd sent pictures to, a Methodist minister by the name of Dr. Ann Robards, recognized the language but couldn't translate it. So she sent the pics along to a Father Randall Hartwig, a Catholic priest in Nashville who just happened to be doing some important work with the homeless there. Important enough work, and in shitty enough neighborhoods, that the Host had seen fit to assign him a guardian angel of his own. When that angel saw the writing on the wall, he contacted Glory, who dragged me halfway across the state just so I could stand in the living room and have doughnut crumbs spewed on me by an overfed elected asshat of a sheriff.

"I do," I said, pointing at Glory. "Her. Sheriff...?"

"Shelton," he replied. "Gary Shelton." He didn't offer a hand-shake, which saved me the trouble of leaving him hanging.

"Well, Sheriff Shelton, meet Glorinda Jones. Glory is an expert on ancient languages and rituals from around the world. And I'm pretty sure she knows exactly what you're dealing with here."

"Indeed I do," Glory said, pulling her blond curls back into a twist and wrapping an elastic around her hair. It never fails. I can barely find my wallet, and Glory is never without a hair tie. I guess there are worse things to use your innate magic for. She walked over to the wall and put her nose right up to the edge of the outer circle. "This was scored deep into the wall. They really didn't need the blood to bind the circle, it was solid enough without it."

"But if you don't need blood, you don't need to kill people. And where's the fun without the killing?" I asked. One of the deputies, a slender black woman with a tight Afro, shot me a dirty look. I just shrugged. If Sheriff Gigantor couldn't scare me, one woman looking at me with disgust wasn't going to do it.

"How many victims?" Glory asked. "Two?"

"Yeah," Shelton said. "Emma Bosker and Dave Watson. They were married for a while but divorced a couple years ago. Decided to keep the house because they were upside down in the mortgage. Good people. They didn't deserve...nobody deserves what was done to them."

"They were tortured, weren't they?" I asked. I stood by the hearth, looking into the ashes of the burned-out fire. There were fresh scorch marks on the carpet several feet away, like someone had thrown hot coals at something. Or someone.

"Yeah," the sheriff said. His voice was different, all the bluster gone. I looked around and noticed this coincided with the last of his deputies leaving the room. "Look, I need all the help I can get. I've been sheriff for eight years, and we haven't had a normal murder, much less something like this. Worst thing that's happened since I took office was a bunch of bikers shooting each other up by a meth lab out of town, but none of them died. This? This is..."

"Fucked up," I finished it for him. The sheriff looked like a good church-going man, the kind of man who could win an election in a small town with more churches than houses. He didn't look like a man prone to F-bombs. Fortunately, I was there to pick up his slack.

"Yeah," he agreed. "Messed up."

"Can you walk me through the scene while Glory translates the text?" I asked. I didn't really give a shit how it happened. Everything we needed to know was written on the wall, including the name of the demon calling the shots. What we didn't know was who worked for it on this side, and how many more people were going to die before I caught the son of a bitch and sent him to Hell to join his demon boss.

The sheriff turned his back on the wall and its roadmap to Hell. He pointed to a blue and white–checked sofa and said, "Best we can tell, the victims were sitting here watching TV when the killer came in and slit their throats. We're guessing he snuck in through the kitchen, since that door was unlocked."

I looked around the den, confused. There was a healthy pool of blood on the floor, but it was all over by the wall with the circle on it. There were no arcs of blood to indicate an arterial spray, and the sofa had a few drops of blood on it, but not near enough for anyone who's seen even one episode of a cop show to think that two people were murdered there. When I looked back at the sheriff, something was very, *very* off about him.

He wasn't nervous. He wasn't upset, or distressed in any way. He didn't have a single drop of sweat anywhere on his face, and he was calmly eating mini-doughnuts out of a paper bag and sipping coffee, his stomach apparently undisturbed by the stench of blood that filled the room. For a small-town cop who had never investigated a murder before, he was remarkably calm. Even given his newfound willingness to let us help with the investigation, something was hinky.

"Okay, so then what?" I asked, moving around in front of the sofa. "The killer dragged the bodies over to the wall where he painted the circle with their blood, did whatever ritual he came to do, and left by the same back door?"

"That's pretty much what we figured. We got a good boot print in a clear patch of mud in the backyard, so we made a cast of that. The crime scene guys took samples of all the blood and are running it all to see if the killer cut himself while he was skinning the bodies."

"While he *what*?" I asked.

"He...he skinned them. Peeled the flesh right off 'em."

"You didn't want to lead with that?" I asked. I felt a slightly sick churn in my stomach, the complete opposite of the sheriff's calm demeanor. "Were the skins still here?"

"No. The killer took them. We figure he wanted them for trophies."

*Nope.* That was one hundred percent not what was going on. I had a theory, but it didn't involve some *Silence of the Lambs* re-enactor dancing around in the skin of his victims. "Okay, then. That puts a different twist on things. Can we meet you at the station later today? My partner and I need to go do a little research."

The sheriff looked confused at my sudden desire to leave. "O-okay. I reckon I'll be there most of the day dealing with reporters and paperwork and shit. Probably have to go over to the morgue and talk to the coroner this afternoon, but otherwise I'll be in my office."

"Sounds good," I said. "We'll check in with you in a few hours. We may even join you at the morgue, if that's alright."

"Sure. If you want to."

"Good. Glory? We need to roll," I said. "I've got a couple things I need to call the Regional Office about."

"O...kay." She started to ask a question, but when she got a look at my face she just nodded and followed me to the truck.

Once I turned the pickup around and got us pointed back toward the main road, Glory turned to look at me. "What was that about? Did something spook you?"

"Yeah, kinda," I said. "More confused than spooked. Did you notice anything funky about the sheriff?"

"Other than his doughnut fetish, not really. Why?"

"He wasn't nearly freaked out enough for a guy who found two skinless corpses just a few hours ago. He had just the right level of territorial pissed off for a small-town cop when we got there, but he shifted gears way too easily into helpful. And the rest of the officers? I expected to see cops puking their guts up all over the crime scene, but they all just seemed...detached."

"Or professional," she countered.

"Yeah, but like you said, there hasn't been a murder here in years. It's mostly breaking up bar fights and throwing drunks in jail overnight to cool off. This is big-time murder, with a serious gag factor. I mean, skinned corpses? I've seen those before. They're *nasty.*"

"Where have you seen skinned corpses?" Glory asked.

"New Mexico. I think it was '89 or '90. There was a nasty demon there skinning people and trying to blame it on the Apache living on the Jicarilla reservation. I convinced the local white people not to go messing with the tribe, and I tracked down the demon and sent it back to Hell."

"What were you doing in New Mexico?"

"Believe it or not, I was cactus farming. I had a couple hundred acres planted in agave, and I wanted to make tequila."

"You've...never struck me as the farmer type."

"I suck at it. Lost my shirt. I was only there a couple years, but long enough to make myself known to anyone with any kind of power in the area. When people started pointing fingers at the res, tribal leaders came to me and asked if I could help clear them. They figured a white guy would have a better chance of being heard than one of their medicine men."

"What happened?" she asked.

"Spoiler alert—it was a white guy who called the demon, lost control of it, and now the demon was running around skinning people and eating the skin."

"Okay, that's nasty. And a new one to me. Why the skin?"

"Do you really want to know?" She gave me a steady look, so I sighed and told her. "The demon said it tasted like pork skins, only chewier. It considered the skin to be the best part, because that's where all the scars and pain were stored. It felt like consuming the flesh gave it true dominion over the person."

"You're right, I didn't want to know. Do you think this is the same demon?"

"That depends. Your Enochian is better than mine. What was the name on the wall?"

"Malindor. It's not one I'm familiar with, so he either isn't old enough to be one of the Fallen, or he wasn't powerful enough back then to be part of the War." That was a first. Glory was usually really hush-hush on her time before she was my guardian. She'd never said anything about being part of the War for Heaven before.

"Yep," I said. "Same guy. That sucks."

"Why?"

"Because he's smart. And he knows me. That kills any element of surprise we might have. But we don't really have a choice. He's not going to stop killing people, and we can't just let a demon run around outside Nashville. Commercial country music is bad enough lately without adding demons to the mix."

"What's the plan?"

"We hole up in a hotel, do some research, and when it's dark we go back to the house and see what we can find without any interference from the locals."

"Does your research happen to include hot chicken?" Glory asked.

"Well, we are less than an hour from Hattie B's. And I'm going to have to eat *something.*" She laughed as I plugged in the address of the best chicken joint in Tennessee into my phone and pressed the accelerator down.

"If you get arrested, I am not bailing you out," Glory said as I put my hand on the doorknob to the Watson/Bosker home.

"No, you'll just do that angel thing where you 'poof' out and leave me to deal with the consequences on my own." I gathered my will and focused a tiny thread of magical energy on the lock. "*Apertum,*" I whispered, and released the magic. The tumblers on the lock clicked into place, and the door swung open.

I slipped on my Sight, peering around the house in the magical spectrum. Even with all the cops and crime scene techs who had been traipsing through there all day, there was still a thick slime of dark magic coating every surface. This place was going to need some serious cleansing before it was ever habitable again.

"What are you looking for, Harker?" Glory asked. "It's not like there are going to be any clues the crime scene guys didn't find."

"I'm sure they found everything they knew to look for. But I'm not looking for clues. I'm going to cast a spell to find Malindor's human minion." I navigated the dark living room by the red and purple glow of dark magic that hung on the walls and made my way over to the wall. The summoning circle was a void, just an absence of all light and energy hanging on the wall. The *wrongness* was palpable, and the closer I got to it, the stronger the stench of brimstone and fear became. Yeah, this was definitely the same asshole I'd met in New Mexico. Wish I'd been able to kill him, but all I could do then was send him back to Hell. Maybe if Glory could use her soulblade on him we could arrange a more permanent solution.

I dropped my Sight, slipping back into the normal visible spectrum, and put my hand on the wall, right in the center of the circle. I reached out with my magic, not invoking the circle, just tracing its lines, getting the signature of the caster fixed in my mind. I let a little more of my power eke out into the circle, just enough to activate it, but not enough to call the attention of anything on the other side. I hoped. I leaned my head against the wall, focusing on the magic used to summon Malindor.

It was new magic, and cast by a human. That was good. It meant that I could probably kill whoever I needed to kill to shut this shit down. If I was lucky, I wouldn't even have to tangle with the demon, but let's be real. I'm never lucky.

"Put your hands against the wall!" The flashlight beam cut through the living room along with the cop's sharp voice.

*Yup. Never lucky.* "Officer, I'm going to reach in my pocket for my—"

"You put that hand anywhere but on the wall over your head and I'm going to put four in your back before you can reach a damn thing!" Her voice was high, thready, and her words were coming out too fast. She was scared. Sounded young, too. She probably got "watch the murder house" duty because the worst thing that anyone expected to come sniffing around were neighborhood kids on a dare, not century-old wizards with their guardian angel. A guardian angel, I might add, who was conspicuous by her absence. She could have at least warned me. Angels are great backup when the cause is righteous, but when it comes to breaking and entering, they're shit lookouts.

I put my hands on the wall over my head and sighed. "This is not my night, is it?"

"Not when you decide to come back to the scene of the crime, asshole. They thought this was a cake assignment, so they gave it to the rookie girl. Let's see what they think when they see me perp walk the—"

"Federal agent," I said, cutting her off before she could actually accuse me of being the murderer.

"The what?"

"Federal. Agent," I repeated. "Now, I'm going to reach into my back pocket and toss my credentials back to you. You'll see that I'm actually a...never mind, you just take a look." I pulled the badge wallet out of my pocket and flicked it in the general direction of her voice. When I knew she'd be distracted, I spun around, took three quick steps across the room, snatched her pistol from her hand with my right hand, and put my left palm to her forehead. "*Somnus*," I said, pouring magic into her.

She slumped, immediately unconscious. I caught her before she landed in the still-tacky puddle of drying blood on the floor and carried her over to a mostly clean easy chair. I removed the magazine from her service weapon, cleared the chamber, and put the gun and the magazine on a table beside the chair. I didn't want to leave her unarmed, but just in case she woke up while I was still searching the house, I wanted a few seconds' warning before I had to start dodging bullets.

All that became moot the radio on her belt crackled to life. "Ling? You there, Ling? We need you at the Games R' You, corner of Liberty Street and Bolgeo Lane. We've got a mob of crazy Baptists threatening to burn the place down for promoting devil worship. Pastor Smith has his whole congregation riled up about Dungeons & Dragons and we need all hands on deck. Leave the house. Nothing's going to happen there tonight, anyway. Ling? I need you to confirm. Ling?"

Whoever was on the other end of the radio was still trying to get Ling to wake up as the door swung shut behind me. Thirty seconds later I was back in my truck and headed downtown to save the gamers from the Baptists. Or maybe the other way around.

Glory was still MIA when I pulled up in front of the game shop and hopped out of the truck ten minutes later. I couldn't actually see the front of the store, but I knew I was in the right place because it was the one with the cop cars and the angry white people out front. The head rabble-rouser, who I assumed to be Pastor Smith, stood on a small folding stool with a megaphone, which seemed overkill for the two dozen people, including cops, that were there, but it wasn't my riot so I figured I'd let him run his party his way.

He had a good rhythmic cadence going as he exhorted his followers to take a stand against the devil and his insidious dice games and demonic card-playing. Apparently Magic: the Gathering had been added to the "evil" list when I wasn't looking. "We canNOT tolerate this afFRONT to Christian decency in our comMUNity, brothers and sisters! We must stand STRONG in the face of Satan and let him KNOW he is not welcome here. Can I get an AMEN?"

At least twenty middle-aged white folks hollered out "AMEN!" with all the fervor of someone who's never actually, you know, *met* Satan. I have. He's a dick, and legitimately the scariest thing I've ever seen, and I've watched the odometer roll past the new century twice at this point, even if I was just a toddler in 1900. I took a good long look at the "mob," and figured they weren't likely to actually cause any trouble aside from annoying anyone in the store and hogging the good parking spaces.

"Where's your good-looking partner?" asked the sheriff as he walked up beside me. He'd switched from doughnuts to coffee at some point, and I picked up a weird hint of *something* in the drink, but it wasn't booze. Probably hazelnut or whipped cream or something.

"She had some leads of her own to follow up," I said. "What's this guy's story?" Sheriff Shelton hadn't been exactly welcoming this morning, but if he was going to be all buddy-buddy now, I might as well get some information out of him before he found out I decked one of his officers and left her unconscious at a crime scene.

"Pastor Angus Smith, age sixty-three, born and raised in Clarksville. Degree from Bob Jones University with a Master's of Divinity from the Southern Baptist Seminary over in Kentucky. He's got a small church on the edge of town, a couple hundred people in the congregation. Hates pretty much everything that even smells like a Democrat. Gays, Blacks, Hispanics, Women's Libbers . . . you name it, Pastor Angus will quote you a Bible verse about why they're the spawn of Satan. Pretty sure I'm the spawn of Satan, too, but God and the good pastor are the only ones who know why."

"I'm pretty sure the Bible never mentioned Hispanics anywhere," I said.

"You ever read the Bible, son?" I nodded. "Then you know that anybody with enough time and dedication to being a dick can prove both sides of any argument if they're willing to dig deep enough and twist words far enough. What started off as a guidebook to keep the Jewish people from getting exterminated turned into something more over the years, and God himself only knows what any of it means now. And I'm pretty sure Pastor Angus ain't got the man upstairs on speed dial."

I raised an eyebrow at the sheriff. He shook his head at me. "Don't go getting any ideas. We ain't friends now just because I think Angus is a butthole. If I had one bullet and both of y'all in front of me holding pistols, I'd drop you like a bad habit. But I don't have a whole lot of use for people that corrupt the words of the Lord for their own purpose, and if you take a look at Pastor Angus's home, he's decided that serving God is best done from a nine-bedroom house with a four-car garage on eighty acres. While his congregants live in single-wides with leaky roofs."

"So what can I do to help, Sheriff? I'm not very good at the standing around with my dick in my hands part of the federal agent game."

"I reckon going back to wherever you came from isn't an option I get to choose?"

I shook my head.

"Then why don't you walk up there and ask the good pastor to move along? Or go inside and make sure Tammie's okay?"

"Who's Tammie?" I asked.

"Tammie Darden owns the game store. Her and her cousin Alyssia Nixon opened it up when Alyssia moved back after a divorce. Been open about five years, and Pastor Angus has been on 'em ever since they opened the doors. Says Dungeons & Dragons opens up gateways to Hell, and they're corrupting the minds of our innocent youth with fantasy novels and demonic code words. I think he just needed someplace new to picket after the used-record store shut down and he couldn't yell at them about the evils of rock and roll no more."

I held back a chuckle. I've opened up doors to Hell, and if it was as easy as playing D&D, I'd just be rolling twenty-sided dice all the time instead of burning through my own magical energy and spell components. Candles and chalk start to add up after a while, and don't even get me started on how hard it is to find good eye of newt nowadays. PETA really made it hard on a wizard when they started screaming about every little dead animal.

"I'll go check in on the folks inside the store, but dealing with the rabid Baptists is on you, Sheriff. I haven't had my shots. Maybe if we can get this defused and I prove I'm not a total asshole, you'll share some crime scene photos with me, and I can help you catch a murderer." I had no intention of helping him catch anyone, but I did want a look at the bodies. There was no way I was going to put a small-town sheriff on a collision course with someone who summoned demons for fun and profit.

"Maybe," Shelton said, not committing to anything but another slurp on his strange-smelling coffee. I nodded, flipped up the collar on my duster, and headed toward the front of the store.

"Excuse me, coming through, excuse me, coming through, EXCUSE ME GET THE FUCK OUT OF THE WAY YOU FUCK-ING MORONS!" That last bit was when one particularly corpulent redneck stubbornly refused to stop blocking the door to the game shop. A hush fell over the crowd and you would have thought from the look on their faces that I had just taken a shit on a Dale Earnhardt poster and wiped my ass with the Confederate flag.

"What did you say to me?" the fat redneck asked, turning around, his hand drifting toward his belt where I assumed a pistol was concealed.

Mine wasn't concealed, though. My Glock was pointed straight at his left eye as I held my credentials up beside the barrel. It was too close for him to read anything, but I'm pretty sure he got the point. "I'd stop moving that hand if I were you. If you were to bring it up with anything in it that made me even the least bit nervous, I'd hate to see the mess that would end up all over that big glass window behind you."

"Y-you wouldn't shoot an unarmed man. You're a cop, you can't do that."

I leaned in closer, bending over until my nose almost touched his. I could smell the different kinds of engine and cooking grease that coated this hillbilly's life, overlaid with the rank stench of fear and maybe a little dribble of piss that he couldn't quite hold back. "I'm not a cop, dipshit. I'm not even *just* a federal agent. I'm Homeland Security, you stupid fuck. I'm the guy who renditions your ass for looking at me funny, then goes back in and erases every digital record of your useless life. I'm the guy who makes you fucking *disappear.* Now get your fat ass out of my way before I have to check on what the biggest-size jumpsuit is at Gitmo."

He opened his mouth to speak, and I just raised an eyebrow at him. His jowls wobbled and his teeth clicked together, and the suddenly mute moron took one giant step sideways, leaving the path to the doorway clear. "Thanks, citizen. Now go home before you do anything stupid."

"As you were!" I called back over my shoulder as I entered the game shop to an electronic *BEEP*.

A forty-ish woman with a brown ponytail and a T-shirt that read WHEN THE DM SMILES, IT'S ALREADY TOO LATE stood behind the counter smirking at me. "That was fun. Did Duane actually shit his pants, or is he just walking a little funny?"

"I think he pissed himself a little, but I didn't smell any crap," I replied. "You Tammie?"

"Yeah. Who's asking?" She looked a little more suspicious, but not too concerned. I figured the fact that her hands were close to a shotgun or baseball bat behind that counter might have had something to do with that.

"Quincy Harker," I said, stepping forward. I sat on a wooden stool on the other side of a glass-topped counter filled with multicolored dice, bags, and playing cards with astonishingly high prices on them. I chalked Magic up as another investment I'd missed out on. I passed her my badge, but she waved it away.

"I don't need to see that. I saw you talking to Gary, then you didn't let Duane give you no shit, so you must be okay. I'm guessing you're not here for the new Eberron sourcebook?"

"To be honest, I have no idea what you just said. I'm in town investigating the murders this morning, and when I heard about your little gathering outside on the police scanner, I thought I'd come by and lend a hand."

"Yeah, any time anything weird happens around here, Pastor Angus gets the congregation all spun up. If he's not picketing our place, he's out on Highway Forty-One hassling the kids at Sarah Martin's club. I guess she didn't have a band playing tonight, so we got lucky. If there'd been any flavor of metal act at Sarah's joint, Angus and his assholes would have been out there instead."

"Angus and the Assholes," I chuckled. "Sounds like a punk band." I looked around the shop. It was brightly lit, with a lot of tables and folding chairs with different board games set up. Tammie and I were the only souls in the place. "This place usually hopping like this on a weeknight?"

She laughed, a bright, cheerful sound. "No. Usually we get a pretty good crowd playing Magic or Yu-Gi-Oh, but I got a heads-up that Angus and his 'flock' were going to pay me a visit, so I sent everybody packing. No need in any of them getting into it with the churchies. A lot of our customers are kids in their teens or twenties, and you know how they get. One wrong word and they're ready to fight."

I didn't have a lot of room to talk since I'd literally scared the piss out of a man right outside her front door and knocked a cop unconscious less than an hour ago, but I just nodded. There would be better times to examine my own short fuse. Like half past never.

She jerked a thumb at the front door. "Well, look at that. Seems like you scaring the crap out of Duane took the wind out of Angus's sails. He and his people are packing up to go home." Sure enough, the Christians were dispersing like somebody had shouted "Lion!" in a crowded church.

"I guess I'll do the same, since it looks like I won't have to replace any of my windows this time. Thanks for that, by the way. It gets old, having to nail up sheets of plywood and sweep up broken glass just because your business has monsters in the windows."

I understood that. My business had real monsters, and I still wouldn't want to deal with the shit she went through on a regular basis. Of course, I also had a pretty good way of dealing with it; I could just blast the assholes to cinder. "I'll stick around while you lock up," I said. "Make sure nobody's hanging around your car."

"You don't have to do that," she said, but she smiled as she did. I felt a little flash of warmth at that smile, then remembered the woman waiting for me back in North Carolina. If life ever let me get back to North Carolina.

"I'm here. And if I let you get mugged on the way to your car, I lose all the hero points I earned scaring the fat moron in your parking lot."

"Okay, wait right here while I lock the front, then you can walk me out the back." I did as she asked, looking over the cards in the case with names like Mox and Karn and Polluted Delta. Given the art prevalent on the cards and on the walls, I could see how folks like Pastor Angus thought there might be something hinky going on there. But the only occult nastiness I'd seen in Clarksville was in a three-bedroom ranch with a nicely manicured lawn, not a strip mall game store with a few dragon and demon posters hanging up.

A couple minutes later, Tammie flipped off the lights up front and walked back to the counter by the glow of one strip of fluorescents that remained. She pointed to the back wall. "I'm parked back there. I'll give you a lift around front since you're being so chivalrous." There was a promise of something else in her smile, but she was going to have to be disappointed on that front. I'm a taken man.

I went through the door into the storeroom, pausing at the edge of the darkness. "Can't really see the path, love. Where am I going?"

"Just straight ahead, if you don't mind." Something in her voice rang false to me somehow, and I started to turn just as I heard something whistle through the air. I flung myself forward and felt an explosion of pain in my shoulder as Tammie laid me out with something hard and heavy. I sprawled on the concrete, rolling over to try and see what the hell was happening, but all I got was her in silhouette. She held a club or bat or something, and stepped forward to take another shot.

I rolled to my right and scrambled to my feet, trying to pound some feeling back into my right arm. I didn't think she'd broken anything, but it sure hurt like hell. "What the fuck, lady?" I yelled as I tried to get my bearings. Boxes and games clattered to the floor as I flailed around the small back room.

The overhead lights blazed to life as the door into the main part of the store swung shut, and my blood ran cold as I recognized the circle on the floor. It was a perfect copy of the one at the murder scene, only this one was painted on the concrete, not scribed with blood. Yet. Seems I'd found Malindor's human accomplice after all. "You? You're the killer?"

"Well, my lord Malindor did most of the work," she said. "But I helped."

"So the person running the wicked game store really was the Satanist. It's so cliché it's almost original. Too bad you fucked up this time," I said. I straightened up and called power. "You see, I'm not some nebbishy househusband or silly teenager you can terrify. I'm—"

"Quincy fucking Harker," came a new voice from the back door. "We know. That's why I told her just to shoot you and get it over with." Gunshots ripped through the room, slamming into my reinforced duster and knocking me to the ground again. "But no, she had to save you for Daddy Mal like a good little minion. Fucking humans. I tell you, if they weren't so damn tasty, I'd be in favor of just exterminating every last one of them." Sheriff Shelton stepped into the storeroom and pulled the back door shut behind him.

"Daddy Mal?" I gasped from the floor. His service weapon couldn't punch through the spell-reinforced Kevlar of my coat, but that didn't do anything to keep the force of the bullets from beating me to shit. "Goddammit, you're a—"

"Cambion, yes. And do you know how hard it's going to be to restock my supply of Nephilim blood after I kill you?" That explained the smell. Cambion, the offspring of demons and humans (never ends well for the human involved), show up like neon to people with magical Sight. Like me. But by smearing a little blood of a Nephilim, the offspring of a human and an angel (doesn't really turn out all that much better for the human, frankly) on themselves, or ingesting it, they can hide their true nature. Nephilim blood has a very specific scent, which Shelton apparently masked by stirring it into his coffee. I had to give him credit. He was clever, if evil as fuck.

"Why?" I asked.

"Why kill the two this morning? Or why you?"

"The others. You have to kill me," I croaked out. It's rare that you can get a bad guy to monologue anymore, but I needed a few more seconds before I could focus my mind enough to fling magic.

"It was supposed to start a whole chain of events that would strengthen Malindor enough to break through to this plane permanently. I kill Bosker and Watson, Angus leads his band of morons here, a riot ensues where Tammie kills Angus in self-defense, then one of his flock kills Tammie, one of my deputies kills a couple more of the Baptists, maybe one of them gets lucky and kills a cop, and before you know it, I've racked up a baker's dozen of souls and Dad cashes them in like green stamps to get a lifetime pass out of Hell. Then you came along and fucked it all up, so now I just have to hope that killing Quincy Harker will be enough for Lucifer to turn Papa loose upon the world."

"Wait a second," Tammie said. "Did you say I was supposed to die? That wasn't the deal we worked out. I was supposed to get to kill Angus, but it was self-defense so I wouldn't go to jail."

"Oh, don't worry," said the sheriff with a vicious grin. "You were never going to spend a single night in jail. Because we don't incarcerate corpses. Sorry, hon. Daddy needs souls. But look at it like this. Now that we're killing this bastard, you don't have to die."

"No, but you might, you double-crossing prick." Tammie raised the baseball bat and took two steps into the warehouse, only to drop to her knees with a surprised look on her face when Sheriff Shelton drew his pistol and put three rounds in her chest from ten feet away.

"Well, you could have lived through it," he said, turning the gun to me. "You, on the other hand..." He raised the pistol and fired twice at my head, but I'd recovered enough to focus energy around my left forearm into a shield, which sent the bullets careening off into the room.

I rolled to my feet and tried to fling magic at him with my right hand, but that arm still wasn't cooperating very well after getting smacked in the shoulder with a baseball bat. So I kept my shield up as Shelton kept shooting at me and just charged him, shield-first. We slammed into a big shelf full of inventory, and cardboard boxes rained down on top of us. Shelton definitely got the worst of it, not the least of which because I kept ramming my knee into his balls.

After a few seconds I saw the slide on his service weapon lock open and I let my shield go. I leaned into him with my right shoulder, pinning him to the shelf but sending bolts of pure fire down my arm. Between gasps of pain I focused just enough to call power into my left hand and press my fist into his throat right under his chin.

"Tell 'Daddy' I said hello. And to go fuck himself. *Incendium!*" With a word and my focused will, a column of white-hot flame streaked from the knuckles of my left hand straight into Shelton's neck, boiling his brain from the inside and turning his face into one of the Nazis from the last scene of that Indiana Jones movie. I jerked my hand back before melted asshole brains ran down my wrist, and stepped back as the sheriff dropped to the ground, his face and the top of his head completely blasted away.

"Well, that was enthusiastic," Glory said from behind me. I turned and saw her leaning on the door into the shop without a hair out of place. I had a busted shoulder and Cambion bits in my hair, but she still looked great. Somedays I really hate angels. But it was good knowing that she'd been there, ready to step in if I got in too deep.

"You know what I always say, right?" I asked.

"'Fuck you, you fucking fuck'? I don't really see how that applies to this situation, Harker."

"No, the other thing I always say: 'Go big or go home.' I mean, if I'm going to kill a half-demon sheriff in a small town, is there a better way than melting his face in the back of a game store?"

"Not that I can think of right now. You good to drive?"

"Have you suddenly learned how in the past three hours?"

"Nope."

"Then I guess I'm good. But we're totally going back to Memphis by way of Nashville."

"You think that chicken joint is still gonna be open when we get there?"

"Probably not, but I got the owner's phone number and superpowers. I think we can come to an agreement that gets me some spicy wings to go." With that, I stepped over the sheriff's steaming body and walked out into the night, my guardian angel in tow.

❧

# John G. Hartness

**John G. Hartness** is an author, publisher, and podcaster from Charlotte, NC. He is the author of multiple novel series, including the award-winning Quincy Harker, Demon Hunter series. He is also the co-founder and publisher of Falstaff Books, and a member of the *Authors & Dragons* Live D&D podcast. In 2019, John was honored to serve as the Master of Ceremonies for LibertyCon, a place where he has always been welcomed with open arms and loving smiles, no matter how many weird colors of hair he sports.

"Thanks to Timmy for creating such a welcoming family. We'll keep it going for you."

# FOR LIBERTY

Like the Zahns, Sarah and her husband, Dan Hoyt, put the "family" in family-friendly con. Though they live in Colorado and have far to travel, they have been bringing their two talented sons, Robert and Marshall, to LibertyCon for years. Part of the attraction is the atmosphere, part is the programming, heavy on the literature and the speculative science beloved by the whole family. Both Sarah and Dan became active in another venture close to Timmy's heart and in many ways inspired by LibertyCon, the Tennessee Valley Interstellar Workshop (about which more later), and both have stories in *Stellaris*, one of the anthologies that emerged from that conference. Sarah is a prolific author of novels and short stories in many genres. I'm happy to include this excellent H. Beam Piper–esque story in this volume.

—TW

# For Liberty

## Sarah A. Hoyt

"I don't believe you," I said.

Grigoris Florus smiled benevolently. He knew I didn't quite mean it, I think, and merely took my exclamation as proof of my shock. He was a small dark man, with incongruously bright blue eyes. The rumor had it that he was an actual ancient Greek, recruited by the Corps, but he never talked about it. No one ever asked. And the environment in which he'd chosen to work was more Victorian, English and Academic than anything else.

His office was as large as most living rooms, lined in oak bookcases filled with books. I'd never had either the leisure or privacy to look at the books in them. Casual glances as I walked past reveled the classics: Milton and Kipling, C. S. Lewis, Tacitus, Machiavelli, Shakespeare, Heinlein, Pratchett. But some of the titles were in alphabets I hadn't come across before. A natural side effect of the Corps and my job. After all, we worked in the multiverse. I was relatively new, and had only once served in a reality in which the Babylonians had developed a technological civilization. That was weird enough, but I was told there was weirder. And of course, it was important for the coordinator of operations to know a lot of the universes, even if not all of them. Considering they were uncountable, branching off from every significant event—and they weren't always what people thought of as significant—no one could know them all.

He smiled at my disbelief. I realized in retrospect that I'd been, if not rude, at least borderline so. But then, Director Florus was always indulgent with women agents.

"Is there anything about my statement you find particularly incredible?" he asked. Instead of sitting at his desk across the room with its back to a bay window and having me sit at one of the guest chairs facing it, he had chosen to sit by the fireplace at the other end, so that we faced each other, maybe four feet apart. He was almost lost, sitting in the deep leather chair.

I made a sound. "Science fiction conventions in the early twenty-first century in world C-23 were nests of neurotics and maladjusted. We studied it in psycho-history. They were all insane, and weren't even particularly involved with the classic writers remaining from that period, like Heinlein and Pratchett. Their entire literature had turned to belly gazing and victimhood."

Florus smirked. I hate it when my superiors smirk. "One should not believe everything one learned in school, my dear. What you are citing might be...enemy action."

I shifted uncomfortably in my chair. What he was saying... Look, when you work with time, you should be aware of when it's been manipulated. Every time agent was told, when signing, that one of our compensations for a life that promised little stability and even less ability to connect to the rest of humanity was that the implants we were given would make us very aware of when timelines had shifted.

It was necessary, since the time-jump invention was one of those that humans in all time lines, and in multiple times had invented and reinvented. Like paper, or the self-fluxing moustache waxer. Which meant that there were more time-terrorist organizations than there were known parallel Earths. Which is saying a lot. Some of them were obscure and strange, like the people dedicated to killing Shakespeare or the three time corps who had decided the source of all evil was George Harrison—lead guitarist for the Beatles in all known universes, except in 45-D in which he was a car salesman—and must be eliminated in all his incarnations, in every branch of history. We had managed to keep at least some versions of both alive, in different universes, but protecting them was a full-time—and tedious—job for entire divisions of time agents.

Which was why our implants needed to detect when history had been modified. But if what Florus had said was true, not only hadn't I been informed that our own über-timeline had been tampered with, but neither had my professors at Time-Corps-Training, who'd taught me that bit about science fiction conventions.

The hair attempted to rise at the back of my head. If they'd penetrated into the Corps, what hope was there for the forces of order?

Before I could answer, though, the door opened, and the proverbial Victorian butler came in, carrying a tray with a silver tea service. Florus smiled, "Ah. On the little table, please."

I realized the butler came with a retinue of grave young men, like him dressed in the formal black attire of a bygone era. Between them, they slid a small side table over, divested it of its load of books, and set the tea service down on it with all due formality.

There was an astonishing amount of food for two people, ranging from little triangular sandwiches on white bread, to a pyramid of cream pastries balanced on a white porcelain tray, and a bowl overflowing with fruit, some of which I lacked names for.

As the servers withdrew, Florus poured tea into a delicate porcelain cup ornamented with roses and asked me, "Sugar? Cream?"

Baffled, I assented to both, wondering exactly what this entire ceremony had to do with science fiction conventions in one of the analogs, or with the fact our Corps might have been corrupted by time terrorists. I felt my hair attempt to rise again and had that sense of when reality betrays you. It's like putting your foot out in the dark and not meeting the floor where you expected. Not meeting the floor at all.

I took the cup and saucer, and they rattled merrily against each other, like a pair of porcelain castanets, which made me realize just how unsettled I was. Time Corps is not just ineffective, but totally counterproductive, if you don't know which reality is the right one for that analog. We could effectively fight on the side of evil, and not know it.

"Just so, my dear," Florus said, and sipped his tea without the slightest tremor or break in etiquette. "But cheer up, it's happened before. And this time we might be able to head it off at the pass. This con, LibertyCon?"

"Yes?"

"Well, many of the people who organized it are retired time agents."

This was a shock to me, as I didn't know time agents could retire. He smiled and drank his tea. "You can retire, you know, in recognition of good service. Well, not many do. They were the ones who alerted me to something strange going on in their reality. And it appears the adversary, whoever it is, is making a final, all-out push in this reality in their convention."

"But why this convention? Why science fiction at all? Aren't they just fans of an odd subset of literature?"

"Yes, and no." Florus set the teacup down on the little table, picked up a pastry and nibbled at it. I set my own cup down, mostly untasted. "This particularly convention was started by a gentleman named Tim Bolgeo, aka Uncle Timmy."

I was glad I had put the cup down. "The former director? Or was that one of his analogs?"

"No, no. He was, like all other directors, the only one of him."

"Directors retire?"

Florus smiled. "Of course, you have to give us hope of having a life again, once we're done herding time-divided cats. You can say we may have a life, but in a way, we never do. Bolgeo didn't. Not really. He knew how crucial science fiction was for this universe, arguably for all universes and he—"

"Why?"

"Oh, my dear." He deployed the napkin to deal with cream on his upper lip. "Have you ever read any of it?" And to my head shake, "You should try it. It is at its best a literature of expansion, of... dreaming of the future, of dreaming of side universes, of being able to handle reality when it gets confusing. Many of our best operatives are fans. I'm surprised you aren't. Done properly it is the best help our people have in fighting the chaos that would destroy civilization in the multiverse. Which is why chaos has been attacking it."

"And apparently us."

He gave a nod halfway to a head shake. "Well, yes. Except that we had that node of retired agents at LibertyCon, and they alerted us to the intrusion. We thought we knew all their plans and that everything was under control, in fact we changed the date and hotel of this year's convention, in an attempt to thwart the enemy forces, but... Well, but then Director Bolgeo died."

"Of natural causes?"

Director Florus wiped his hands vigorously. "It's always of natural causes, isn't it?" He made a face. And I realized my question had been stupid. No matter who time terrorists wanted to remove, they always—always could go back and make the illness start, or set up the accident. Florus must have read my mind, or knew really well how I thought, because he sighed in pace with my inner despondence. "Unfortunately, he was the one coordinating the intelligence, and it all slipped. There are other agents there. Many of the regulars are retired temporal agents. But once his . . . shield was gone, their own implants stopped alerting them to the disruption.

"We don't precisely know what is supposed to happen. We just know what has happened, throughout a lot of the science fiction field, including other promising conventions. And that they are going to try it, possibly, at this convention. We could be wrong. You could go in, and just have a pleasant time—they have a range day, by the way—and nothing of any untoward significance will happen. Or—"

"Or? What has happened to the rest of the field operatives?"

"Or you could be caught in the attack, and have their device implanted in your brain. Of course, I don't know if they'd do that to a Time Agent or simply kill you."

I was suspicious. That "or simply" was deadly. "What does their implant do?"

"It makes you unable to dream. Not physically. Not at night. But those daydreams of which true civilization is formed. It's particularly sad when it happens to writers. Their stories become either pale echoes of other people's, or . . . well, speeches, not stories. And fans . . . well, they stop being able to appreciate stories of the imagination. Several worlds have already fallen to this infection, and science fiction has stopped existing in them." He cast a look at the shelf, and I noted it was the place where I'd seen the Heinlein books. "Which distorts their civilization and usually stunts it. They often stop all space exploration and their branches of time never develop time travel. Of course, that is the idea, as it leaves them vulnerable to every time terrorist and bandit in the multiverse."

"And what will the attack be like? Do they come in guns blazing and start pushing implants into people? How is this done, anyway? Our implants require surgery. I suppose they're not performing surgery in the middle of a science fiction con?"

"Uh . . . no. Not really. Not all implants require it. These seem to have a biological form. The problem is that we don't know which group is doing it. Part of sending you to LibertyCon is the hope that you will figure out who they are and thwart them, but also capture a prisoner. Or three. So that we can start fighting back."

And there I was in beautiful Chattanooga in . . . June. I supposed that was an improvement on what I was assured was their usual July meeting date.

For those not up on the ways of universe C-23, Chattanooga is a city in one of the States in the United States of America, which is the form taken by the former British colonies, which then proceeded to aggregate to themselves a good portion of North America. Yes, I know in most universes their rebellion failed. But never mind. That's what they are in C-23, having seceded from the mother country on a platform of life, liberty, pursuit of happiness and other natural rights. Very Locke, very improbable, but oddly inspiring. I'd slammed through implant-dumps on their history, their aspirational striving to live up to their unlikely birth. I'd even come to like their flag: a square of stars, white on blue, in the corner, and the rest taken up by broad, bold red stripes. In most universes, just the fabric would make some designer a fortune.

LibertyCon in fact referred to the founding of the country, since it was usually set around the fourth of July, their celebration of independence.

As I made my way into the hotel and to the registration table, I kept running into people who wore T-shirts with the symbol of past iterations of the con. Almost all of them were an image of the Statue of Liberty, which had been given by France to America. Never mind. Just go with it. It's the statue of a woman clutching a book to her breast, and holding up the lamp of freedom. Because of her placement, on an island off a city where most immigrants came in, it became known as a symbol of America. It was always, of course, a symbol of liberty itself.

Anyway, Tennessee was at the edge of the original colonies, new territory just broken at the declaration of independence from England. The Southern edge. For those of you at all familiar with what I'm talking about, you're probably flinching at the idea of meeting there in the summer. It was hot, humid, with a high incidence of mosquitos.

And yet, I'd read the story of the con. Many people traveled from all over the country to be here. And most of them were not retired Time Operatives. Which just showed how crazy these science fiction people were.

The lobby of the hotel was cool by contrast to the outside, but full of people, all greeting each other like long-lost family. It was very loud, and as I walked past various groups, I got the impression they were speaking almost in a kind of code. Like, there was some very large guy, in a beard, singing the aminoacids song. Other people were wearing kilts—who wears a kilt outside Scotland? In any universe?—and there was a repeated phrase, "Oh, John Ringo, no." I briefly wondered whether it was a terrorist code, but then I consulted my notes and realized "John Ringo" was the code name for a Time Operative who was still active. In C-23 he had an identity as a writer, and continuously baffled his fans by writing trilogies in three days, then suffering years of silence.

What can I say, serving in the Time Corps and thwarting terrorists can be a real PITA.

I'd also been given a list of people I could contact for recon on the ground. They knew what Uncle Timmy had suspected, had been briefed and brought up to date, and would be ready to assist me should I require it.

Of course, before I could be assisted I had to figure out what was going on.

The first order of business was to retreat to my room with the bag they'd handed me and decide what I'd do. The program book was invaluable in this. There were scheduled discussions, called panels. I carefully highlighted all the ones that mentioned time or multiple universes, and planned on attending or at least dropping in.

Then there was a dealers room, which was opening about now, and an art show. That too would give me clues. For one, if they were totally unimaginative, I'd know that the virus was already in place and go back to headquarters.

I showered and changed into a dark blue T-shirt with the silhouette of a woman holding what people in this universe would think was a ray gun, but which was in fact a nerve disruptor, in wide use in the ports. It said in gray letters, I'M WITH THE TIME POLICE. It was absolutely true, and perhaps it would flush someone out of cover. Also, it would pass completely unnoticed. I hadn't believed Florus when he assured me it would, but now

I'd seen some of the T-shirts these people wore. There was for instance the very tall guy walking around wearing a T-shirt that proclaimed I AM A DWARF.

I put on the safety of my nerve disruptor, in my left pocket, so I wouldn't disrupt my left foot. In my right pocket I had the injector with the antidote for these biological implants. It worked, I was assured, but would take years to take effect. I was also told to be very sure not to inject anyone who hadn't received an implant. We are the Time Corps. We do the impossible every day. We also often have the absolutely stupid demanded of us, but never mind.

I was about ready to open the door, when someone knocked on it. I looked through the bull's-eye and saw two faces I vaguely remembered went with the names on my list. Lissa and Richard Hailey were Time Agents who had retired to C-23, to Tennessee, and married. They had a child and everything. In other words, the happy story we all thought we'd given up when joining the Time Corps.

I opened the door, while keeping my hand in my pocket because you never knew. After all, the Corps had been penetrated, right? Or at least our implants had been rendered ineffective.

"Hi," Lissa said. "You're . . . Uh . . . You're . . ."

"I am Rozenn Millard," I said, extending my hand.

"With uh . . . The Tots Company?" Richard asked.

I almost said no, then realized what the initials were. "Indeed. Is there an emergency?" My hand was resting very firmly on the disruptor, my thumb ready to take the security off.

Lissa shook her head. "No. Actually . . . I just wanted to know if you knew anything? We've been coming to this con for years. I can't believe anyone would attack it. Director Bolgeo was really good at keeping this place safe. I mean . . ."

"I know," I said. "And he did alert us to a possible problem. The issue is that he didn't pass on more details. So we don't know for sure if the con will be attacked, nor who is doing all of this. Honestly, this is like mission impossible."

At this point they both made sounds . . . well, I think it was supposed to be music. Something like *Bam bam bam toodeeloo toodeloo*. I ignored it. All I could imagine is that they had gone native in this strange Science Fiction tribe.

They looked disappointed I didn't react, and Richard cleared his throat. "Well, we thought we'd give you our cell phone numbers.

It's . . . the communicators used here. So, if you need us, all you have to do is text, okay?"

I acceded, pulled my own cell phone—yes, I'd been equipped. It was weird of them to try to explain such basics to me, but as I said, I think they'd gone native—and took their numbers and gave them mine.

I then walked out of my room and down the hallway with them, keeping a weather eye, in case they turned out to be traitors. But they didn't do anything strange. Nor did any of the hundreds of people we passed. Most of them were in groups and minding their own business. Some waved at Richard and Lissa, who eventually got peeled off to join one of the groups. I continued, into the part of the hotel that connected to the convention center, where the actual discussions and program took place. Other than the dealers room there wasn't much place to go yet.

Halfway through the glassed bridge between the two structures, a blond woman detached from a group and came toward me, smiling as to a long-lost friend. Mel Todd. I remembered her from my briefing. "Hi," she said, and when she got close enough, lowering her voice, "I didn't know who you'd be. The shirt is clever. I presume you know who I am."

"Of course," I said. "Mel. Still-active agent, posing as a writer. There seem to be a lot of those here."

She shrugged. "I am a writer. I mean, it's a little more than posing. And yes, because it's so easy to have a double life when you're not supposed to go to an office every day, you know?"

"Yes. So, do you have any idea what is supposed to happen or when?"

She shook her head. "I have a vague impression that the bio implant is conveyed in food or drink. We've had operatives replace all the water in the containers provided by the hotel, just in case, but I don't sense that was it. I don't know what it could be."

"I see," I said. "Are you lead for the mission or am I?"

"I presume you are," she said. "I didn't get my orders from the Director himself." I wondered how she knew that, and she laughed, as if I'd spoken aloud. "We all know, of course," she said. "You know what the Time Corps is. Something whispered last night in Ancient Rome—"

"Will be known this morning in Mars Town. Yeah, I know. Have experienced it even."

A tour of the dealers room, with its fine complement of bladed weapons and various ... science fiction, fantasy, and alien merchandise was fascinating, but not enlightening. I was complimented on my shirt, and considered buying several. I mean, how freaked out would Florus be if I came back with a T-shirt reading MY OTHER T-SHIRT IS IN MY SPACESHIP? but decided against it.

Another of the agents on my list revealed himself. John Pieper. I had a moment of confusion when I first saw him, because though he wore a T-shirt—inscribed with DMS AREN'T GOD, WE WOULD NEVER GIVE PLAYERS FREE WILL—and jeans, I momentarily saw him wearing a cavalier hat and the ruffled, lace-trimmed outfit of baroque France. Then I blinked again, and remembered we'd met there, over l'affaire Richelieu. Honestly, that was one of the times when time terrorists had actually got one in, and we had never been able to extricate the evil bureaucracy that agent had introduced to France in this analog. I'd completely forgotten it was C-23.

"Roz!"

"John!"

We stood, not sure how to speak in a room crowded with strangers, not knowing how to talk about what we'd been through or how we'd met each other. Instead I cleared my throat and said, "I heard you ... ah ... changed jobs."

He looked equally confused. "Well, yes. The last one ... I mean ... when we didn't do, ah ... when I didn't meet management's goals, there was some fall out. But you know, I still come to this con every year, so I still ... uh ..." He seemed to run aground, then reached into his pocket and got out a little card, which he handed me. It said *It's a Time Thing, You Wouldn't Understand, Room 303.*

"It's a party," he said. "There are these parties every night, for various groups of fandom. No one will know we're not just ... I mean, we can talk about our particular fandom, then, right? Party tonight after the opening ceremonies."

I took that to mean there was reconnoitering and strategy to discuss, and we could do it in private there.

Fine. It wasn't the most ridiculous thing I'd ever done.

A visit to the art room made me raise my eyebrows. I mean, most of the art was fairly innocuous, but there were two or three pieces that made me wonder exactly what the policy was on drawing scenes no one in this analog had seen. Take the couple of people fighting a giant snake.

"I remember that," said a voice behind me.

I looked over my shoulder. It was Tara Urbanek, an operative I'd met at time school. "Is the artist—" I started.

She shrugged. "Not that I know," she said. "She probably just heard someone describe this in a no-shit-there-I-was late-night bull session." She smiled at my horrified expression. "Most people not read-in think they're just stories, you know?" She looked closer at the painting. "Though the name is familiar...Karen Comeau...wasn't she?"

"A computer specialist for...er...Tots Corporation."

It took her a moment to register, then she said, "Interesting, she hasn't made contact with anyone else, here, that I know. I mean, she hasn't tried to revive...Corporation ties."

"Some people are really disgruntled when they change jobs."

"Sure," Tara said. "But it makes you wonder precisely how disgruntled, doesn't it? Remember that corporation member who, ah...decided he hated Shakespeare in C-45?"

I remembered. That was one of the worlds where we'd lost Shakespeare, because the agent assigned to guard him had taken his nerve disruptor to the bard and fired and fired and fired until the poor man's heart had given out, all the while screaming, "We all owe God a death." No one knew why he had snapped, and in the end, we'd had to replace poor Will with a robot.

There was nothing else interesting in the art show. Or rather there were lots of interesting things, which meant these people were not under the effect of an imagination-killing bug, but nothing that helped my case. Okay, okay, okay. I confess I put bids on a pair of earrings, a beautifully decorated bowl, and a painting of a Statue of Liberty holding a rocket in one hand, with a field of stars behind her. Look, there's only so much I can resist native artifacts, okay? And we do get a forty-kilo allowance through the time gate, anyway. Deal. You can't really send a woman with money to a place where she'll have to check out the merchandise and not expect her to spend some. Also, I'd reimburse the Corps for whatever the expense was in real money.

Tara convinced me to go to the hospitality suite, saying at that time there would be few people there, and I met two more members of the Time Corps. Tyler Gants was a very young man, and a new recruit, obviously not retired, but he was, Tara explained, a native of this analog, and as such had been sent back, in case there was something he could do. He had been involved in swapping out the water, and was now helping in the kitchen of the hospitality suite.

He sat with us on the sofa by the window and spoke almost freely since the place was deserted, only without mentioning the Corps, or anything that wouldn't sound either everyday or like part of one of the games or novels everyone was discussing. He showed me the palms of his hands, where lights chased each other from some kind of subcutaneous implant. "It sends a shock if anything I touch has been contaminated with bio implants. Or at least it's supposed to. I'm not absolutely sure if it's working, because it hasn't triggered an alarm yet."

"I see," I said.

Janet Baggott was working in the back area. She was a retired agent. "I volunteer in the hospitality suite here every so often, though," she said. "And this seemed like a good year." She hesitated. "The one thing I can tell you is that I've seen a few people around here who are known to me. But they haven't come by or said anything, or acted like they know anything about the corps. There's Mark Walker, for instance. Why, we worked together in that thing in Mexico City, you know, with the cult?"

I knew. It was one of the Corps' great fiascos. The analog in T-61 had ended up with all of North America in the hands of a human-sacrificing cult.

"I'd thought he'd quit," Janet said. "But he's walking around, and there's a young woman with a name tag that ends in Walker with him."

"Wife?"

"Nah, too young. I'd say daughter."

"Uh," Tara said. "I also thought I'd seen Steve Bonaparte. I mean, it's pretty hard to mistake it. I think they still have his name on coins in H-52."

Steven Bonaparte, whom I'd met once, long ago, had a complicated history, having started out as the heir to the throne in a France that remained imperial well into the twenty-second century, and then—for reasons no one had ever explained to me—having left all that behind to become a Time Corps agent. Maybe because even with operations that ended in death or destruction as often as not, it was safer than dealing with all the would-be-assassins in the Napoleonic court.

"Has it occurred to you there are two Corps operations running?" I asked.

"What, like in that thing in Venice? The one that ended with the city burning? I mean, who manages to burn a city that's mostly made of stone and set in water?"

"Two teams," I said. "I remember that Matthew Bowman quit over that."

We left to attend the opening ceremonies, but there was nothing remarkable there. I'd swear Brandy Spraker, Director Bolgeo's daughter, had worked around the Academy but there was nothing new in that. Family of agents often joined the Corps, and that must go double for retired directors.

"She's bucking for being director someday," someone whispered in my ear. I turned to see Christine Dorsett. She'd been a year behind me at the Corps training, and we'd become friends. "She is already an agent, and I understand a very good one. Of course, she has to prove herself extra hard to prevent people from saying it's nepotism."

I nodded, as I watched the much-too-young-looking—or much-too-young-looking to have teen children—woman on the stage call out the names of every pro attending. Pro in the writing and art sense, in the music sense, and in the science sense.

I'd seen the listings in the program, but it wasn't till they read all the names, punctuated by people standing up briefly, or being called as "is in the bar." This line was followed by much laughing. Again I felt I was missing something.

At the end, people got up and poured out. I noticed our "fan party" hadn't been advertised with the others and turned to Christine. "Why wasn't our party advertised?" I asked.

"Well," she said, "because it's private. Do you have time to talk?" She came from a world where Canada and Mexico were the only nations in North America, and her accent retained a faint tinge of her native Canada in her native world.

"Sure," I said. I didn't add *I've got nothing but time.* "Where do you want to go?"

"Come with me," she said. I followed her and we seemed to be headed to the hospitality suite, but then veered sharply and she took a door with a sign that said something like OPEN ONLY IN CASE OF EMERGENCY.

Alarms didn't sound. It might have something to do with a badge she waved in front of it before pressing the bar to open. We walked briskly down a hallway that seemed like some sort of maintenance thing—being just tiled floor and white walls—and she opened another door. We went in.

It looked like the mother of all supply closets, with floor-to-twelve-foot-ceiling shelves crammed with every form of cleaner known to man.

Then she took a key out of her pocket, and opened a narrow little door at the back that looked like an actual closet door. She stepped aside to let me go in, but by then all my alarms were ringing. Look, I liked Christine. But if one were dealing with implants, which could do such far-fetched things as change one's ability to imagine anything new, what else could it change? And who was implanted?

She gave a small laugh and a sigh of exasperation at the same time, and went in ahead of me. I followed. And yes, my hand was on the button of my nerve disruptor.

"Sorry," she said, turning around. "I'd forgotten the paranoia inherent in the Corps."

The room was small, but appointed as a sitting room. There was some kind of covering on the wall that shimmered, vaguely metallic. I had a sense it was some form of tech I hadn't encountered before. The floor was bare wood, but polished. And there were chairs in a circle around the room. "This is the one place we're sure of not being heard, or spied on by time cams."

Time cams are devices you can send back in time. Since nothing nonsentient can time travel, these cameras have AI capabilities, and the ability to slip through the time-gate into any time needed. In most worlds, when first discovered—sometimes after, sometimes before actual human travel—they've been used first by scientists. To travel back in time and see the signing of the Magna Carta, or the building of the pyramids, or even the Crucifixion—although that one returned very odd results—and therefore unlock mysteries that had bedeviled the species forever.

But it didn't take very long till those with access to those cams were using them to spy on cheating spouses or unfaithful lovers, or even rival politicians.

At one time, after a king—Edward XIX?—of Great Britain was

proven a bastard by the cams, there was a move to try to make them illegal in that reality. It didn't work. It was easier to send the cams back in time to find some dirt on those who wanted to make them illegal, and then blackmail them than to try to hunt down every instance of illegal time-cam usage.

Most of us, since then, had chosen to proceed as though all our actions, and all our thoughts, were completely visible. "As in the great and terrible day of judgment, when every secret shall be laid bare." Sure every once in a while one of them snagged a Time Agent doing something like, perhaps, selling advanced tech to down-time savages. More often, it caught double-dealing on the part of our so-called elites, who seemed to have trouble remembering they were accountable to the people, and then there was a spasmodic convulsion. And then things resumed as they were.

Perhaps the cams weren't as used as they could or should have been, because the spies had secrets themselves—who knows? I know there were times and places in my life I wouldn't care to have aired in public. After all, I am human and was once young and foolish.

But the one thing the Corps didn't do was send time cams after its own agents willy-nilly. There was a process to do it, and a reason.

"I don't understand," I said.

She smiled, tightly. "No, I imagine you don't. Lissa and Richard went to check you out with a sensor, and see if you are contaminated, and you don't appear to be, though, so I'll speak frankly: Does this mission make any sense to you, Roz?"

I blinked at her. "Uh, not a ton." Understand, most missions, when we are sent somewhere, involve getting a specific target and a very specific mission. "Go to Elizabethan England and thwart the five hundredth assassin." Or perhaps "Go protect George Harrison." Or even "Go plant a small, discreet explosive device in this ship, so it sinks with all hands." That last type is rarer, and usually they pick agents with a certain moral flexibility. Or a strong stomach. Because, you know, not many people can face killing a boatload of innocents.

But the problem is that sometimes the history-changers or history-influencers don't kill people. No, they find the defect in the ship. They give it earlier warning of "Iceberg, dead ahead." And then, to restore the balance of reality to what it was, you have to go ahead and make sure those people are dead.

Every once in a while there are deliberations between the

governing bodies of various nations on simply slipping those people into an uninhabited alternate reality. But if that ever was done, I don't know. If there is such a reality, it's probably chock-a-block with various famous assassinated people from various realities.

And don't get me started on the jokers who implanted a healthy male fetus in Katherine of Aragon just as the divorce started. I think someone took the baby and had it adopted up time, while slipping in the corpse of a born-dead infant. But still.

Anyway, with all of this, yeah. This was a fairly weird mission. "It's strange," I said, "but Director Florus told me that we're dealing with an implant that corrupts our perception of reality and the working of the Corps implants."

Christine snorted. It was a very unladylike snort, not something I expected in such a gentle woman. "Perhaps the corruption is in the implant's programing?" she asked.

This froze me again. "But that would mean corruption in the Corps," I finally said. "Actually inside it."

"Think about it," she said. "Really think about it. There are either two teams here, and one team posing as retired or composed of disgruntled members, or ..."

"But that would imply ..."

"All the way to the top."

I was silent a long while. "What happened to Uncle Timmy?" I asked. I had studied his tenure as director, and he'd impressed me, not only with his ability to knit the Corps—which was best likened to fighting cats—into something like a family, but also by his inflexible belief in liberty. I also found he had come from this reality. He was an American, and he seemed to be a patriotic one. That thing about life, liberty and the pursuit of happiness? Those were the values he brought to the Corps and to the timelines in which we worked.

I tried to think, suddenly, of any values Director Florus brought in. Order? Proper, by-the-numbers action? I didn't know what else.

Christine made a gesture. "Natural causes."

"Was there any reason for him to have been ... ah ... removed?"

She made a face. "He had told a few of us he was concerned. Worried about—" She shrugged.

"The direction of the Corps?"

"Too many casualties. Too many lost operations. Too much.... Yeah."

"I see," I said again. I rubbed my hand on my face. What had I been fighting for, the five years in the Corps?

"Can you tell me what your status in the Corps is? Are you really retired?"

She sighed. "It's complicated. On paper I am."

"I see."

"One more thing," Christine said. "There really is an implant. Or a corruption of the implant. You are clean. We had Lissa and Richard check." She smiled at my expression. "Well, you didn't think they'd come to your room just to play welcome wagon, did you? But you resisted implantation, rather than it never having been attempted."

"Come again?"

"Someone tried to implant the bug to your implant. The bug that rewrites history, stops creativity and makes you a passionate defender of order. Your implant rejected it. For the record, the same happened to all of us, before we figured it out.

"I just wonder why he sent you here, and gave us to you as contacts. I wonder what's intended."

I did too.

We left the room by the same complicated route, and emerged into the hallway, we hoped unobserved. We parted and I assured her I'd go to the party.

On the way to my room I was assaulted. Fortunately something warned me and I was prepared. Okay, I know exactly what warned me. It was a movement of shadow on the floor where they should be no shadow. It was a deserted hallway since everyone was downstairs and working or playing. But there, as I approached a corner, I saw a shadow on the floor. As though someone had flattened himself to the wall just around the corner.

Instead of walking on, I knit myself to the opposite wall, until I could see that it was a man, taller than I, in great shape. Also, I knew him. His name was Brian Hair. He was a Time Operative who worked directly in Florus's office. What was he doing here? It was almost sure he was here for me. I mean, think about it. As thick on the ground as Time Agents were at this convention, the chances of one waiting for me just there . . .

"Hello, Brian," I said. And I had my hand on my nerve disruptor, in my pocket, had turned off the safety, and had aimed it all without removing it from my pocket.

He jumped. He jumped like a startled cat. He tried to paste

a smile on his face, as he said, "Roz," but the smile was not convincing, and his hand was diving for his pocket. Too late.

I looked at him, twitching on the floor, and thought, *Damn it. Now I have to drag him to my room.*

A quick look through his pockets revealed a pellet gun, a lethal toy whose aim is always to kill. And a link, cleverly disguised as one of the ubiquitous phones. Then I dragged him to my room.

He was alive, just passed out. Yes, the disruptors can kill, but you need to give a heavier dose and hold it.

Do you know how hard it is to drag a full-grown man two doors away down the hallway? And how hard to sit them on the hotel chair and tie them to it? Hotel chairs weren't made for it.

But when he woke up, blinking rapidly, I had indeed tied him hand and foot. And he looked surprised. What kind of opinion did they have of me? I'd survived countless missions. I was offended, honestly.

"Why? What?"

"Um...because I don't choose to be shot, Mr. Hair."

He blinked at me. "You expect me to talk!"

I actually knew that reference from a movie in this timeline. But in fact, I did not expect him to die. "Like a parrot!" I said.

"Why should I?"

I shrugged. "Who knows? I might talk if my brain were being manipulated, and I wanted to escape."

He laughed at me. "I'm not being manipulated. I am fully in on this."

"And this is?"

He gave a maniacal grin, then bit down hard.

Ten seconds later he was dead. World's oldest poison-tooth trick. Damn it. I hate corpses to dispose of on a mission. Sure, you can open a mini–time portal and send them to the main timeline. But I didn't want to do that. I didn't want to alert anyone to his death.

On the other hand, his link was full of interesting features. One of them was the ability to open portals to any timeline and any time. Um...

I used his finger for the gunlock before he turned cold. Then I locked the device to stop transmitting, and give only the impression of being off line, not changed. Then I changed the gunlock to my genes.

I cut him from the chair, opened a portal to Pompeii as the

volcano erupted, and shoved him through. Yes, he might very well be one of those corpse-impressions in plaster done around the negative space where lava encased a body. I've never looked. One more body. Who cared?

On second thought, I sent the phone that the Corps had provided for me after him. Don't know if any part of it was ever found. If it was, it wouldn't be the first. You see, there are all sorts of...uh...well, the best way to put this is that all those books and websites who talk about someone in an old picture using a modern device, or someone finding a can of drink or a screwdriver at a level where there were no humans?

All of those are real. They're just not the proof of ancient civilizations that the people sharing them believe they are. Look, no one is ever perfect, and Time Corps agents aren't an exception.

I stared at the link. I only needed an answer to my question. The question I couldn't ask anyone.

See, there are problems with being a secret agent. One of the things I'd found among Uncle Timmy's writings that I thought was fascinating was his saying that "being an operative in a secret organization is a problem. If you're out in the open, the rest of society acts as a check on you. But if you're secret, and the organization goes off the rails, no one knows."

He was right. One way or another the organization, or some number of agents, had gone off the rails. But when you deal with a cabal—to call it by its proper name—formed to manipulate time, how can you tell which part of it is staying true to the principles of the organization? And how can you tell which has gone astray?

I looked through Brian's link to find out. And I found out. Ooh, boy, did I find out.

To begin with, he was probably telling the truth that he wasn't implanted. He was a true believer. His link had the basic principles of the Corps, the document given to each of us on joining, of course. But his was annotated and written over. Apparently the point was not to preserve the lines for the greatest human happiness and freedom of choice possible, but to organize and order things in such a way that would eventually lead to the extinction of mankind.

Something about mankind being a cancer on the multiverse, one that, by being sentient, caused the multiverse to keep multiplying and would eventually lead everyone to madness. If humans were gone then the Universe would stop splitting so much.

Okay then. This was madness of a high order, when there were several Earths where life had never developed, and others where nothing beyond plant life developed. Maybe he thought time travelers were responsible for all those splits?

I read. It made my head hurt. I still couldn't tell what this was all about, except I had a feeling that there was something with the party. I wondered who had suggested the party.

So I did what someone who had had it up to here with the Corps—and had reason to think that perhaps every instruction I'd been given, including whom to contact, was wrong—would do.

I went to talk to Brandy Spraker.

She was in the middle of a crowd, laughing and cajoling, and—it looked like—organizing things. Some of the people around her were the people I'd been referred to, which made sense. They were volunteers in the con.

She looked over at me as I stood politely at the fringes. She looked at my name tag and her eyebrows went up. Then at my shirt, and she almost imperceptibly focused harder.

"Hi," she said, addressing me. "It's your first time here?" Since I had a ribbon saying "first timer" hanging behind my badge, of course it was.

I smiled. "Yes."

"Next year I will have you volunteer."

"I can volunteer now," I said, giving her an opening to find a way to talk to me in private.

She smiled. "Why, that's so sweet. Now that you mention it, there's something you can do."

She gave a few more instructions to people, and then we walked away down a hallway.

Her camera-proof space wasn't the same as Christine's.

"How many of them are there?" I asked as the door closed.

"Many of...?"

"These spaces."

"Oh, a few per floor. It's a long story, but it's why we're at this hotel for as long as we can. These are hard to build, particularly without help from the Corps."

I hesitated a moment at that, but then remembered Brian Hair's link. And no, that info hadn't been meant for me to find. I just happen to be good at making those things cough up their secrets.

So I told her everything, from the interview with Florus.

"I think," I said, wishing she'd show what she thought more clearly, "that I was set up to fail, possibly to be killed, maybe to kill the people whose names I was given. But I wasn't acting according to plan so they sent Brian after me."

Brandy nodded. "Maybe. May I see the link?"

I gave it to her. She spent a while examining it. "It's possible. But I think there's something else going on. I think they were observing you via your phone, and your interview with Christine alarmed them because you might deviate from script. But what's the script?"

So I asked the question that was bedeviling me: "Who set up the party for Time Corps operatives?"

She looked confused, which I'd guess was a rare thing. Then she thought about it. "Uh. I don't know. It just was everywhere at once, all of a sudden. Here, let me check." She sent a text from a phone I guessed was far more than a phone.

There was a long wait. "Interesting. No one set it up. But Lissa said she found a stack of cards with the time in the middle of the other preparations for the con, and thought I'd had them made."

"We can't not have it," I said.

"No. It would give us away. But we can't have it either. I'm going to guess that this was the plan: to gather all of us who are resistant to the implant corruption, and have become aware of what's going on into a room, and then...do something."

"Can we put dummies in the room?"

"What?"

"There was this thing Hannibal did, tying lanterns to the horns of cows and sending them into a valley. The Romans went after them and were destroyed."

"Um...The problem is making them fit thermally and read 'right' if they use scanning..." Brandy laughed. "Or we could be proper paranoid Corps agents and take some of the shielding and put it all over the walls of the room."

"Wouldn't that be a lot of work?"

"No, it comes in panels. We can prop them up."

And that's what we did, with the help of her circle, who, yes, were the same people I had been recommended to contact. And then we moved dummies in. They didn't have to be incredibly convincing, but as it happened there was a shop in town selling clothes display mannequins. Dressed in clothes that looked like those we'd wear, and sitting in a circle, on chairs, they looked convincing. For further verisimilitude, we put some snacks on a table in the middle.

Then we hid in the room above, having arranged to look through the ceiling. We had been supplemented by a young woman that Brandy called only Seville and by a burly young man wearing a T-shirt that said MINTY FRESH BEAST under a half-open button down.

For a long time nothing happened.

Then we realized that there was something coming through the vents down there. It was the slightest vapor. I almost went through right then, but Brandy said, "It's lethal. Wait."

"Why wait? They don't need to come in. They just rigged this to poison us all."

"They'll have to get rid of the corpses."

"Oh."

She was right. After enough time passed for the gas to dissipate, they went in. By that time the Minty Fresh Beast had gone downstairs, and came up behind and locked them in the room.

Where we found them yelling at each other over what had gone wrong.

Disruptor beams put them all to sleep. Later, we found that a lot of them had indeed received a slave implant. By the way, that was what was in those cartridges they'd given me. If I'd shot any member of Brandy's team, they'd have become Florus's slaves. As it was, most of the secret cell was salvageable. Except Bonaparte, it turned out. He was a knowing conspirator. I guess Napoleon complex.

I wasn't in on the team that took Florus out. Brandy arranged that. Cleaning the rot was harder and took longer.

I was involved in some of that, as some of the tainted operatives had gone very far in time and were, of course, causing trouble.

Two months later, when back at Time Corps Central, I found a message on my link: "The Director would like to see you."

I went, with some trepidation. It hadn't gone so well, last time.

It was Brandy Spraker, of course. And the room looked different. Most of the shelves were still there, but they were now white, and it seemed to me there was a lot more science fiction on them.

She had large, comfortable sofas brought in. There wasn't a

desk, which made sense, since most of the work we do is on links and computers, and no big, heavy desk is required.

She was standing by the window when I went in. As she turned around I realized the panorama from the window was a lot of... well, celebration. Fireworks. All around the Statue of Liberty, and probably more than one year, from the look of things.

She smiled when she saw me looking. "I have changed the view to Fourth of July over the Statue of Liberty, over the years. It reminds me of what we're here for. To maximize humanity's ability to explore, expand and be free. It's what the game is all about, isn't it?"

And I realized she'd make an excellent successor for her father.

Our missions have been interesting since. She's a minimalist, believing in the least possible intervention. But when she intervenes it is to either restore or create an opportunity for human liberty and happiness. And she's doing a fine job.

I've started reading that science fiction stuff, here and there, between assignments. It's not bad at all.

Oh, and she was right. This year, I volunteered at LibertyCon.

## Sarah A. Hoyt

**Sarah A. Hoyt** won the Prometheus Award for her novel *Darkship Thieves*, published by Baen, and has also authored *Darkship Renegades* (nominated for the following year's Prometheus Award) and *A Few Good Men*, as well as *Through Fire* and *Darkship Revenge*, novels set in the same universe. Her alternate history novel with Kevin Anderson, *Uncharted*, won the Dragon Award. She has written numerous short stories and novels in science fiction, fantasy, and mystery, as well as historical novels and genre-straddling historical mysteries, many under pseudonyms, and has been published—among other places—in *Analog, Asimov's* and *Amazing Stories*. Her According to Hoyt is one of the most outspoken and fascinating blogs on the internet, as is her Facebook group, Sarah's Diner. Originally from Portugal, she lives in Colorado with her husband, two sons, and "the surfeit of cats necessary to a die-hard Heinlein fan."

# HEART OF STONE

I met David Weber at the same 2016 convention that I met Chris Kennedy, HonorCon. Which made sense given that the "Honor" in the name is Honor Harrington from David's books. I saw him and spoke with him a couple of times but the one thing that stood out above all else happened after the convention was over. My wife and I had kept the room for another night so we could leave out toward Tennessee on Monday. Sunday night, Jonny Minion, who I had also met at this convention for the first time, sent me a text to come to the con suite. I entered the suite to find David sitting with the folks who ran the convention. The people who run the conventions do it out of a serious love of the author's work because they don't get to participate in the panels or much of anything else, since they are the ones running the convention. What I found in the con suite was David Weber sitting and telling stories for those that didn't get to participate throughout the weekend. I quietly sat and listened for several hours. When I returned to our room, I told my wife, "That is who I aspire to be. That guy who will stay an extra night just to sit and talk with the ones who didn't get to participate." I have the utmost respect for David and have learned from many more interactions with him that he is probably the nicest guy I have ever met since beginning this journey.

—CW

# Heart of Stone

*An Honorverse Story*

## David Weber

*<You must go, Stone Shaper.>*
*<No.>*
*<You must!>*
*<I am here. I am* staying *here.>*
*<Please, beloved.* Please *leave me.>*
*<No.>* Stone Shaper ran his true-hand gently down Golden Eye's muzzle, his eyes dark. *<You are my life. I will not leave you. I will* never *leave you, so you* must not leave *me.>*

*<But I have no choice.>* His mate's mind-voice was weaker, her mind-glow darker, and he lay down beside her, wrapping her limp body in all six of his limbs, burying his muzzle against the side of her neck. *<I have no choice,>* Golden Eye repeated, *<but you do. Our children, the clan. They need you, and you* must *stay.>*

*<I am in the only place I "must" stay,>* he told her. *<You are my life. I will never leave you.>*

*<I do not want you to die, too.>*

*<I know that.>* He tasted the pain in her mind-glow, her desperate wish for him to live, but he could not give her what she wanted. Not after so many hands of hands of seasons when she had been the center of his entire world. He could not save her, and he knew that, but this much he could give her, that she did not die alone.

*<I know that,>* he repeated gently, *<but we are one. We have been since first I tasted your mind-glow, and we have always been there for one another. I will not be less than we have been here,*

291

at the very end. So rest, beloved.> His arms tightened about her. <Rest, and I will be here, holding you safe.>

<I love you.> He could scarcely hear her mind-voice now, and he pressed his muzzle closer against her neck. <I love you.>

<I know.>

"Have either of you seen Mack or Zack this morning?" Lady Danette Schardt-Cordova, Baroness Schardt-Cordova, asked, poking her head into the farmhouse breakfast nook.

"Mom, it's not even nine o'clock and it's a *Saturday*," Dana, the oldest of her three daughters replied, looking up from her book reader. "You really think we're going to see either of them before noon?" She cocked her head. "You haven't been sampling the hard cider again, have you?"

"I have not," Danette retorted with admirable calm. "I never sample it before *ten* a.m., and you know it, young lady!"

"Just wondering what makes you think either of them are going to show before afternoon on a weekend. I honestly don't think Zack got back much before dawn. Is there something you need that Natalie and I "—she twitched her head in her youngest sister's direction—"could take care of?"

"Oh, gee, thanks," Natalie said, looking up from her corn flakes. At fourteen T-years, she was ten T-years younger than Dana. She was also ten centimeters taller, which Dana considered a gross miscarriage of genetic justice. "It's not like *I* had anything planned this morning, either."

She rolled her eyes, and her mother chuckled.

"Actually, I need to talk to the boys about the logging pattern for the firebreak. Do either of you know if Mack got the software upgrade on the saws loaded?"

"No," Dana said in a more serious tone. "I know he copied it, but he said something about needing to tweak it." She snorted suddenly. "I think what he *actually* said was 'Those saws are so ancient they wouldn't even recognize this app if they—you should pardon the expression—saw it.'"

It was Danette's turn to roll her eyes. She could just hear Mack Kemper saying *exactly* that in the full expectation that Dana would repeat it to her. Zack was the more flamboyant brother, but Mack had a quietly mischievous streak which had served him well over the years.

The temptation to smile faded. The Schardt-Cordova and the Kemper families had been friends since before the colony ship *Jason* ever departed the Solar System. They'd invested in the colony early and settled adjacent claims, and Danette and Bart Kemper had both been first-generation Sphinxians.

But the Plague Years had been hard on both families. Danette had lost three siblings and her mother in the first wave, and the Kempers had suffered an equally severe death rate. She was one of the people (there were quite a few of them, especially on Sphinx) who'd thought the new Constitution's provision ennobling the survivors of the original shareholders was silly, and it certainly couldn't compensate for all the loss and grief they'd suffered, but it had been ratified only after the worst was over. She'd thought of the title as the bookend for the long, bitter battle against the Plague. After all, they'd finally perfected an effective vaccine in 1496, hadn't they? Which had only made the final outbreak on Sphinx in 1510—the one that had hit fourteen years *after* the vaccine, when everyone thought it was over, the monster had been slain; the one the vaccine *hadn't* stopped dead in its tracks—hurt even worse.

Stringent quarantine and a medical system built and honed in the face of the Plague's original onslaught had kept it tightly confined, restricted to an isolated geographic area on a single one of the Star Kingdom's inhabited worlds, and prevented the sort of pandemic which had made the original plague so horrific. The death rate had been only a hiccup, compared to the staggering death tolls of the Plague Years, but it had hit hard before the medics managed to tweak the vaccine...and Danette had found herself a single mother at the same time Zack and Mack had found themselves orphans.

It had seemed so bitterly unfair, so *cruel*, of the universe to deal them such a blow once they'd finally begun to trust life once more. To be confident there would be a tomorrow, and another tomorrow after that, for the people they loved. Yet Danette had survived that blow as she had so many others, and she'd done it by refusing to give in. By refusing to break and fail the people she still had to love.

That had been twelve T-years ago, when Mack had been only six and Zack had been only four. There'd never been any question who was going to take the boys, and not just because they were on adjacent claims, and "Aunt Danette" had never regretted her decision.

Like many of the Plague's survivors, they had their own share of psychic wounds. Mack was very much the quieter of the two, but even Zack—who delighted in his exuberant, artistic (or "artsy-fartsy," to use Mack's occasionally repressive term) personality—had people to mourn, and not just his own parents. Neither of them allowed that to get them down, however, and they had injected a welcome dose of mischief into the Schardt-Cordova household.

Oh, they *could* be a handful, and she would never admit to them how big a place they had in her heart. They *knew*; she'd just never admit it! And they'd more than earned their keep as she struggled to keep both claims up and running. She was going to miss them—a lot—when they moved back onto their own claim again in another T-year or so. The Kemper homestead was located on the East Ridge River in the now-Barony of Kemper's southeastern quadrant, only about ninety kilometers (barely ten or eleven minutes by air) from this very breakfast nook, and she knew they'd still be around, if only because neither of them was a particularly good cook. But it wouldn't be the same, somehow.

"You say Zack didn't get back until dawn?" she asked after a moment, and Dana nodded. "And you know this because —?"

"Because she got back about the same time the boys did," Natalie offered.

"You did?" Danette looked at her older daughter speculatively, and Dana flushed slightly.

"Mom, I'm twenty-three!"

"I didn't say you weren't," Danette said mildly. "I was only... expressing a parental interest. Do you plan on introducing him—whoever he is—to us sometime soon? I only ask so that I can plan the number of place settings for dinner tomorrow, you understand. No rush."

"*Mom!*"

"Okay. Okay! Just teasing." Danette smiled broadly, but the truth was that she had a pretty fair idea where—and with whom—Dana had been, and she approved wholeheartedly. Not that she had any intention of giving up such excellent ammunition!

"And do either of you know where Cordelia might be this fair morning?"

"She's out on that survey you asked for. She grabbed some

cold cereal and left about thirty minutes ago. She took a couple of sandwiches with her, too. Said she probably won't be back until after lunch."

"She went alone?" Danette frowned, and Dana shrugged.

"I offered to go with her, but she said she's fine. She took her rifle and Barnaby."

Danette nodded, although not in complete satisfaction. They really needed that survey along the Red Bank Bottoms completed before the loggers moved in, but it was a long way from the house—or help—if something went wrong. On the other hand, all three of her girls were excellent shots—people in the Sphinxian bush tended to take marksmanship seriously— and Barnaby was a Meyerdahl Rottweiler. The huge dog stood almost eighty centimeters at the shoulder and, at seventy-three kilos, outweighed Natalie by a considerable margin. He was also both smart and fiercely protective. Between him and her rifle, Cordelia should be fine, but that didn't mean she wasn't going to experience a rather firm mother-to-daughter counseling session when she got home.

*Or maybe not,* Danette thought. *She is eighteen now, and you know darned well she's awfully mature for her age. All the girls are. That's what happens when you grow up on a planet where forty percent or so of the people died in a plague before you were even born.*

*And aren't I a cheerful soul this early in the morning?*

"Okay," she said out loud. "What are you two planning for the day?"

"I told Nat I'd run her into Twin Forks after lunch," Dana replied. "That swim club they've been trying to set up is having an actual organizational meeting at the Y this afternoon."

"Great!" Danette nodded enthusiastically. The planetary data net, coms, uni-links, and computerized classrooms let kids from all over Sphinx "meet" one another, but the Schardt-Cordova claim—only it was now the "Barony of Schardt-Cordova," of course—was a hundred kilometers on a side, and it was still smaller than a dozen other claims she could think of right off hand. Distances like that meant young folks stuck out in the bush got less physical "face time" with their age cohorts than she wished they could. VR was better than nothing, but it just wasn't the same. She'd experienced the same sort of isolation, growing up, and she was in favor of anything that might involve actual group activities for *her* kids, although swimming wasn't the very first one that would have sprung to mind.

Sphinx's enormous orbit imposed lengthy seasons, and its average temperature was significantly lower than that of either Manticore or Gryphon, the Manticore Binary System's other two habitable worlds, to begin with. Gryphon experienced a far more extreme seasonal swing each year, but Sphinx was the dictionary definition of "really, really, *really* cold" over the course of its sixteen-T-month-long winter. Even at the height of summer, Sphinx's natural bodies were scarcely what anyone would call warm, but at the moment, they were halfway through *autumn*. True, this summer had been exceptionally hot (for Sphinx) and dry, with far too many forest fires. The fall weather was continuing the same drought pattern, but at least it was cooling toward something a native-born Sphinxian considered comfortable...and anyone else would call "brisk." Which meant that even though Twin Forks was almost four hundred kilometers away from Schardt-Cordova—a good forty-five-minute flight, one way—the Y's indoor heated pool had much to recommend it.

*And so does the ice cream at the Red Letter Café*, she reflected. *Well, they work hard, my girls. They deserve an afternoon or two off, especially on the weekend.*

"All right, that works for me. But let me know before you leave. I need a few things from town. I'll put a list together."

"Gotcha," Dana agreed.

"And now to go beard the hexapuma. We've got to get those saws up and running by Monday, so wish me luck!"


"Dang, I wish you hadn't kept us out so late," Mack Kemper groused as he landed the air car in the clearing. The original Kempers and Schardt-Cordovas had chosen their claim sites in no small part because of how well watered they were, and despite the drought, enough moisture hovered in the air to produce a cool mist, and sunlight slanting through the towering crown oak canopy created gilded bars of gold.

"*I* kept us out so late?" Zack looked at him. "Who was that guy you were sitting with, again?"

"I don't know what you're talking about." Mack pressed the button and his nostrils flared appreciatively as the canopy slid back and the earthy scent of the forest reached them. "And his name, as you know perfectly well, was Brad. Jealous?"

"Not my type, man," Zack replied. "Way too nerdy."

"*Nerdy?*" Mack looked at him in disbelief as he climbed out of the air car and took his rifle from the rack. "This from the guy who came in second in the planetary 'Call of Earth' competition? You seriously want to call someone else '*nerdy*'?"

"Asks the guy who came in *first* in the planetary competition," Zack observed to no one in particular as he collected his own weapon—he preferred a shotgun to a rifle—and checked the chamber. "I, unlike certain other people, game because my sensitive and artistic nature craves expression. *Some* people, on the other hand, game because they don't have much of a life outside VR. I mention no names, of course. That would be tacky."

"I am *so* gonna smack you upside the head the next time we square off in 'Death Match,' buddy!" Mack warned him with a chuckle.

"Yeah, yeah, yeah. Heard it all before."

Mack tapped the remote and the canopy slid shut. Most dangerous Sphinxian wildlife tended to be on the large side, like hexapumas and peak bears. There were a few smaller critters who could be decidedly unpleasant, however, and finding one of them perched in the air car when they got back to it was not high on his Good Things list. Besides, they weren't far from several of the bigger near-beaver ponds. The sleek, six-limbed beasties had a pronounced fondness for chewing air car upholstery into shreds, and the near-possums were even worse.

"So, let's go kick some saws in the ass," he said, and Zack shrugged.

"I'm just here because someone dragged me out of my hard-earned sleep to make sure nothing ate him," he replied. "But that's okay! Don't mind my sleep-deprived state. Nothing I'd rather do than keep an eye on my brother's back!"

"I sure wish Cordelia hadn't grabbed Barnaby this morning," Mack said thoughtfully, leading the way through the misty sun shafts toward the hulking mass of the nearest robotic logger. "He's a *lot* quieter than you are!"

Stone, who had once been called Stone Shaper, lay stretched along the net-wood branch in the sunlight. He would have to change position soon if he wanted to stay in its warmth. Especially for him, and he did. The world had moved into leaf-turning hands of hands of days ago. The cold days would not be upon him tomorrow, but soon enough. Soon enough.

*So I have seen yet another green season*, he thought, looking out through the forest. *I suppose that is an achievement.*

He rolled onto his back, presenting his belly fur to the sun, and closed his eyes as he remembered. There were memory songs about others like him. Not many, but a few. He had always wondered why those other People had so stubbornly survived. Now it was his turn, and he could no more answer the question now than he could have then.

*I should have ended and gone with her*, he thought yet again. It was not a helpful thought. He knew that . . . and he could no more stop thinking it than he could have flown.

The truth was that he had expected to do exactly that, even if the gray death had not taken him, as well. People seldom survived the loss of their mates, especially when they were as deeply bonded as he and Golden Eye. Indeed, he had not *wanted* to survive when he realized he must lose her.

The gray death struck only rarely, but the People knew its signs well . . . and that almost all of those touched by it died. None of the memory songs told what caused it. It wasn't like eating death weed or any of the other poisonous plants. It didn't come from bad water, or from death sting venom. It just . . . happened, and it spread like wildfire in fire season. The only defense against it was to stay away from those afflicted by it. That was why the rest of Bright Water Clan had moved its nests from the golden-leaf in which he and Golden Eye had built their own nest. Neither he nor Golden Eye had blamed them for that decision. The clan's hunters and scouts had brought food and left it for them at a safe distance, and their friends and the mind-healers had stayed close enough to mind-speak them every day. Bright Water had not *abandoned* them. In fact, it had *refused* to, and it had done only what it must to save the rest of the clan.

Stone Shaper understood that. It was what had happened later that had driven him from the clan and its central nesting place forever.

And that was not Bright Water's fault, either. It was his own, because he had not died.

The gray death was not the only sickness that could kill. True, it killed far more of those it struck than most of those other sicknesses. Yet what made it especially terrifying to the People was what happened to so many of the tiny number of People it did *not* kill.

He remembered the day he had finally reemerged from the darkness he had thought was death. He remembered awakening, remembered the aching, awful silence where his beloved mate's mind-glow had been. Remembered the terrible grief, the need to follow her back into the darkness, never to emerge.

Yet he had not. Something had stopped him. Perhaps it was Golden Eye's forever-silent mind-voice whispering to him out of the stillness, telling him to live. Perhaps it was simple obstinacy on his own part. Golden Eye had always told him he was the most stubborn Person she had ever known, so perhaps that was the reason.

*Or perhaps I just needed to make my life a curse upon the world. Proof that it cannot kill everything I love only because it could kill the Person I loved more than all the rest of it combined.*

He had borne Golden Eye's still, stiff body up from their nesting place to the fork at the very top of the golden-leaf and placed her where the cleansing wind, the bright sunshine, could bear her spirit to that other place where he hoped she awaited him. And then he had returned to their empty nest, waited the double-hand of days that proved the gray death had left him, mourning her in silence, before he went out once more to meet the clan.

And discovered that the gray death had taken something far crueler than his life. It had stolen his mind-voice. And not just the ability to mind-*speak*, as was most common among those who survived the gray death. No. It had taken his ability to mind-*hear*, as well. The constant flow of mind-voices, the presence of all those other mind-voices around him, among him, *part* of him . . .

Gone. Simply . . . gone. Gone into a great, dark emptiness. Into a silence he had never known. And, perhaps worse even than that, he could still taste mind-glows. He knew exactly what the People around him felt, but for the first time in his life, he did not know what they *thought*. They could not speak to him, tell him, and he could not ask.

They had been horrified by how the gray death had maimed him, and his very presence had only added to their horror. There was no hatred, there was no resentment, no one *wanted* him away from them . . . yet his mere presence had frightened them, however hard they strove against their fear. Or against sharing it with him. He was the reminder of what might happen to any of *them*, as well. Almost worse, he had tasted their compassion—their pity. Their need to somehow comfort him . . . and the knowledge that they could not. They could no more avoid sharing their mind-glows than he could avoid tasting them, and the guilt they felt—the guilt about which neither he nor they could mind-speak—had only made it worse.

And so he had left.

Those same mind-glows had implored him not to go. The People well knew how unlikely a single Person was to survive. There were so many perils in the world, so many of them bigger and far stronger than any Person. Without the rest of the clan to watch and ward and aid, death almost always came quickly, and despite his silence, he was a part of their lives and their hearts. They had already lost Golden Eye, and their hearts had cried out against losing him, as well.

Yet he could not stay. Not tasting their mind-glows so deeply from his world of silence. Besides, without his mind-voice, he could no longer serve as the leader of Bright Water's flint shapers, anyway. How could he, when he could no longer hear what was needed or explain the other flint shapers' tasks to them? And so his place as one of Bright Water's elders had passed to Stone Biter. That was good. Stone Biter was his and Golden Eye's eldest surviving kitten, with a good heart, a strong mind-glow. He would do well by the clan.

And so he had changed his own name, in the silence of his own mind. It was not the name by which the rest of the clan might know him, but he no longer knew what they might call him now. So he had become simply Stone. A stone wrapped in stony silence, cast out not by the clan, but by his own heart and will as he set out on to find the death awaiting him.

But it had refused to find him, and he had discovered that he could not simply wait passively for it. He had nothing left except the stony determination that the world would not slay him as easily as it had slain his beloved. He would *fight* death, every step of the way, with bared fangs and claws, because it was the only purpose left to him.

He knew that. He accepted it. And yet that empty, bleeding silence within him longed for the day when he lost that fight at last.

*And is that not a pleasant way to begin your day?* he asked himself. *Perhaps you should be thinking about your next visit to the two-legs, instead.*

Stone doubted the rest of Bright Water would have approved of his raids upon the two-legs, but he was far away from Bright Water's range. Nothing that happened with these two-legs was likely to impact the rest of the People. Besides, the People had been raiding the two-legs plant places for cluster stalk long before Golden Eye left him. True, Stone had been a flint shaper, without the stealthiness of a scout or hunter, but there was also only one of him, and he had been careful in his forays.

And the two-legs were the only reason he had survived so long, actually. Their plant places provided many plants, some of them pleasant tasting and some not so pleasant, even at the height of the cold days. And there were other... interesting possibilities.

He had been very tempted to sample one of the long-eared creatures who reminded him of grass runners. They were somewhat smaller than a Person, yet large enough that one of them might have fed him for quite some time, and they smelled delicious. Unfortunately, he was sure the two-legs would notice if any of them disappeared, and while they might blame it on bark-chewers or sharp-snouts, it was unlikely. Neither of them would have been able to open the simple but effective closures the two-legs had constructed to keep them out. And so, regretfully, he had left them un-sampled.

On the other hand, there were the flutter-wings. It wasn't a very good name for them, but it was the only one he had. They were ridiculous creatures—fat, excitable, and for something with wings, unbelievably clumsy. Certainly they were nothing at all like a death-wing or wind-glider! They smelled even more delicious than the long-ears, though. And unlike the long-ears, they also laid eggs. Whatever the flutter-wings might *smell* like, their eggs truly *were* delicious, and they produced a lot of them. A short visit to the flutter-wing nest place with his carry net could feed him for a full hand of days without taking more than an egg here or an egg there.

He had also availed himself of other treasures courtesy of the two-legs. There was a place behind the main nesting place where they seemed to discard things they no longer wanted. They had some sort of made-thing that crunched up their discards, for some reason. Perhaps it was simply to make them take up less space, but a flying thing collected the eaten pieces every double-hand of days.

The important point was that they only used their made-thing the day before the flying thing came, and he had found any number of useful things prowling through the discard place. He had used them to build a nest that was both larger and warmer than anything a single Person truly needed—enough to shelter him easily even through the coldest of cold days—and he had gathered up other tools he needed to survive inside it, like the marvelous blade he used now instead of the stone tools of the People.

There were actually days when he was almost content.

Almost.

He suspected that he had learned more about two-legs than any other Person. It was a pity he would never be able to share what he had learned with the memory singers. But —

His thoughts broke off and he rolled over onto his hand-feet and true-feet as he felt the approach of a mind-glow. That was one of the things he could never share with a memory singer—the discovery that two-legs had mind-glows. Well, of course they did! Every creature that lived had a mind-glow, of sorts, at least. But two-leg mind-glows were much stronger than those of any other creature Stone had ever encountered. In fact, they were at least as strong as those of the People, although they were very different. Of course, he had no mind-voice, nor any ability to listen for *their* mind-voices, so he had no idea how similar to or different from the People the two-legs might truly be, but it *was* interesting.

Now he watched as one of what he'd come to think of as "his" two-legs made its way along the streambank with a thunder-barker slung over its shoulder. The big, black barker Stone took great pains to avoid in his excursions into the flutter-wing's nesting place scampered in and out of the low growing brush, ranging ahead of the two-leg but always circling back to it.

*Now what are you doing out here today, two-leg?* he thought.

No doubt the answer was some other incomprehensible two-leg thing, but at least following it would give him something to do.

"There!" Mack said.

"Oh? Are you finally *done*?" Zack inquired.

"I didn't notice you breaking a sweat to help," Mack observed.

"Not my job! You're the software guy. I'm the bring-my-shotgun-and-watch-your-back-with-steely-eyed-concentration guy. Remember?"

Since at that very moment Zack was sprawled comfortably in the shade of one of the logging robots with his hands clasped behind his head while he chewed a near-sage stem, his older brother might have been excused for the eye roll he gave him.

"Yeah, sure. But, as it happens, we *are* done here. So why don't we head back? It's almost lunchtime. Besides, I need to talk to Aunt Danette."

"And you broke your uni-link!" Zack said sorrowfully, spitting out his near-sage stem and climbing to his feet. "I didn't even notice!"

"You really are full of yourself today, aren't you?" Mack shook his head. "In this instance, however, I need to show her some diagrams on my pad while we talk. You know how visually oriented she is. There are a couple of trim patterns in this software I didn't realize were included. I think we're going to have more flexibility than we thought we were, but I really need her input to decide which ones we want to prioritize."

"Makes sense," Zack said a bit more seriously. "But you know she's really going to want to hear from Cordelia before she makes any decisions about that."

"Yeah, she is." Mack nodded.

Unlike some Sphinxians, Aunt Danette took her responsibilities as a custodian of the planetary wilderness dead seriously. That was why she wanted an eyes-on report from the ground to back up the drones' aerial scans. She wanted to know exactly what needed to be cut and what didn't, rather than resorting to the "cut it all down and let God sort it out" approach some of her fellow "nobles" would have adopted.

"There's enough daylight left we can still get back out here this afternoon to make any tweaks she wants," he pointed out, and Zack nodded. Sphinx's day was the next best thing to twenty-six hours long and, despite their late start, it was barely midday. "We need to start cutting Monday," Mack continued, "and I have plans for tomorrow."

"Plans that include what's-his-name? Brad?" Zack asked mischievously.

"*Plans*," Mack said repressively, and his younger brother relented.

"All right. Then why don't you and I head on over and give Cordelia a hand? I know she really prefers wandering around the woods alone, but she'd probably forgive us for horning in on her this afternoon. As long as we don't get into the habit!"

"You know, that's not a half-bad idea," Mack agreed. "C'mon."

Cordelia Schardt-Cordova made her way cautiously along the game trail. The Sphinxian not-so-near-deer, which she understood didn't look a great deal like the terrestrial species it had been named for, preferred flight to fight in the face of any threat. It also ran to around ninety kilos, however, and upon occasion its version of "flight" might be more accurately described as "run-right-over-the-threat-and-trample-it-on-my-way-out."

She figured the odds of any such encounter today were slim, partly because the trail didn't seem to have seen much recent use but even more because Barnaby would spot any near-deer—or anything else large enough to pose a threat—well before Cordelia did. The Meyerdahl Rotties had been genetically modified for a heavy-gravity environment and, although it hadn't been part of the modification's original objectives, the breed's already considerable intelligence had been tweaked in the process. The result was the almost perfect settler's dog for Sphinx, in Cordelia's opinion.

Now Barnaby came bounding back down the trail toward her like a furry, black-and-tan thunderbolt. He slid to a halt, and she braced herself as he rose on his back feet and planted his front paws on her shoulders, tail wagging and ears pricked.

"Don't even *think* it!" she warned him as he cocked his massive head, clearly contemplating whether or not to give her a lick. She scratched him behind his right ear and he decided to close his eyes and luxuriate in the caress, instead.

"Smart move," she told him.

He chuffled happily, then dropped back to all four feet and nosed her rucksack. She glanced down at him—it wasn't that far; he stood well above waist-high on her—and he waggled his head, flapping his ears at her.

"Well," she checked the time on her uni-link and discovered it was later than she'd thought, "I guess it *is* about lunchtime. Let's find a place with a view."

Barnaby sneezed explosively in agreement and went trotting along the trail ahead of her once more, and she shook her head as she followed him.

She kept her eyes open as she went, and not just to make sure nothing untoward pounced upon her. The drone dodging through the canopy overhead was actually as responsible for collecting the survey data she was out here to get as she was, but the impressions of a human observer were bound to play a role in its interpretation. Besides, humans had been on Sphinx for less than a T-century, even now. There were still plenty of things they hadn't figured out about their new planet. The Sphinx Forestry Service was constantly identifying new species of flora and fauna, many of which only reemphasized the need to treat the planetary biosphere with wary respect. And one reason Cordelia loved running surveys for her mom was the possibility of spotting new species herself. There was a bounty for identifying useful plants or animals, although it didn't amount to a whole heap of money. But Cordelia wasn't interested in the money. She wanted the naming rights that accompanied the bounty. A species' discoverer was allowed to propose the official name for her discovery, and Cordelia was appalled by how little imagination some of those discoverers displayed.

*Tell the truth*, she told herself now. *What you're really hoping is to turn up something like the Harringtons did, aren't you?*

Well, maybe she was. She wasn't sure she accepted the theory that these "treecats" were tool *makers*. Tool *users*, maybe. There were plenty of species on planet's humanity had settled who displayed that behavior, using sticks to dig, for instance. But if young Harrington was to be believed, her "treecats" went well beyond that, and that level of sophistication was far rarer. The Forestry Service seemed to agree with her, though. She was actually a Ranger now herself, despite being a couple of years younger than Cordelia, and she and her friends were fierce "treecat" advocates. Cordelia was willing to admit the possibility that they were right about the critters actually *making* tools; she just wanted firsthand confirmation of it before she signed off on the theory.

The woods began to thin ahead of her as the game trail angled back toward the streambank. More near-beaver work, she thought. For beasties that never exceeded a body length of fifty centimeters or so, they could be incredibly destructive. But the ponds they impounded could be enormous—the one she was approaching was well over two kilometers in its longest dimension—and they nurtured the wetlands that were key to much of the forests' lifecycle. That was one reason she was out here. The last summer had been decidedly too dry, and there'd *been* a lot of fires, especially over on the far side of Twin Forks. So far, the autumn had been just as dry, with precious little of the rains they normally expected. The parched undergrowth the summer had turned into kindling was in the process of turning into tinder, and the Forestry Service was warning everyone they were far from out of the danger zone. The higher elevations had seen some relief—snow was already falling up there, although there was less of it than usual and it was still mostly melting each morning—but the lower claims were in just as much danger as ever. In fact, in many ways it was worse than it had been at the height of the summer.

Feather-bramble was a critical component of the Sphinxian plant cycle. The resinous, low growing shrub provided a dense ground cover and the combination of its shade and deep root system played a major role in capturing and conserving rainwater. When there *was* any rain, at least. But it also died back every fall, leaving a skeletal lacework of highly combustible dead leaves and twigs. It was well into that annual die-back cycle now, and it was moving east as the season deepened, which meant it was all too likely to lead a fresh spate of fires in the same direction.

The Red Bank Bottoms lay directly athwart that threat axis. They followed the north-south course of the river for which they had been named, and while the Red Bank was only a modest stream (by Sphinxian standards), tribes of near-beavers had strung their ponds along it like beads on a necklace to produce the Bottoms. The water in those ponds was always critical for wildlife during dry summers, and the band of wetlands also provided a potential firebreak that guarded over a third of her mom's barony's western perimeter.

The problem was the feather-bramble along the *bottoms'* western perimeter and number of crown oaks growing alongside the river. Actually, the problem was the crown oak *branches* which extended clear across the river. Coupled with the picketwood thickets which exploded into the clearings the near-beavers' logging efforts produced, they created altogether too many bridges by which flames could leap the water barrier if the feather-bramble caught fire. A crown oak took decades—more probably centuries—to reach full maturity, so the decision to harvest one usually required careful consideration. Picketwood, on the other hand, grew so fast it could become a serious nuisance, and the long, dry summer had turned the blankets of fallen vegetation under the thickets into yet another pile of tinder waiting for a spark. Once Mack and Zack had the logging robots' new software loaded and certified, they'd move into the area to cut back the picketwood and clear out that tinder as a fire precaution. At least some of the crown oaks would be going, as well, though. Cordelia regretted that. As on most recently colonized planets, timber was a primary building material on Sphinx, but a typical crown oak was at least eighty meters in height and eight meters in diameter. Just one of them could provide thousands of board-meters of lumber, and they might be going to drop as many as a half dozen of them. That was an awful lot more timber than anyone was going to need.

In fact, that was really what she was looking for: places where the majestic trees could be topped or pruned to get rid of the fire bridges without taking them down completely. That would be far better for the forest in general, and Cordelia would feel less as if they were desecrating their planet.

Barnaby emerged from the picketwood thicket into a near-beaver-provided clearing, and Cordelia followed him gratefully. She loved the dim-majestic aisles of the crown oaks, but the temperature was decidedly on the cool side, even for her Sphinx-born sensibilities, this early in Sphinx's long day, and a little direct sunlight would be welcome.

She stepped out of the shade and found herself on the brink of the beaver pond she'd been working her way toward for the last forty-five minutes. It was even more impressive down here at ground level than from the aerial shots. In fact, its northern limb ran farther back into the crown oaks than she'd realized. It might well be the biggest single pond she'd ever heard of, she thought, making her way through the knee-high scrub that had taken advantage of the supply of sunlight. Near-beavers tended to take down the trees they intended to use and then let them season. They stripped off branches and leaves for immediate use, but the trunks often lay where they'd fallen for as much as a planetary year before they were hauled off for the current construction project. From the overhead drone's imagery, these beavers had been kind enough to leave several suitable benches from which to choose her luncheon perch.

Stone flowed along the net-wood, watching the two-leg and tasting its mind-glow. This was the closest he'd actually come to one of them, although he had seen them moving through the forests on more than one occasion. It was also the closest he'd been to one of their mind-glows, and it was even stronger than he had thought it was. Indeed, it seemed to be stronger than one of the People's mind-glows!

*And perhaps it only seems that way because it has been so long since you tasted another Person's mind-glow,* he reminded himself. Still, it was astonishing that he could taste it so clearly from this distance.

It tasted . . . nice. That was the only way he could describe it to himself. He suspected that this must be a young two-leg, judging by the bright edges of its mind-glow. This two-leg was still seeing things that were new to it, and he tasted its anticipation of seeing still more of them.

*Strange that I can tell that is what it wants so clearly. Even another Person's mind-glow would reveal less about his actual thoughts.*

On the other hand, he was close enough now to be confident that the two-legs had no mind-voices. In fact, they must be totally mind-blind, poor things. If not, the two-leg would had to have tasted his own mind-glow by now.

He eased a little closer, confident from their mind-glows that neither the two-leg nor the barker had detected his presence, and his ears pricked as the comforting warmth of the two-leg flowed over him. And that was what it was, he realized—comforting. It was as if he warmed his true-hands over a welcoming fire. Like the fire, the two-leg's mind-glow was not even aware of him, yet its brightness—its warmth—reached into the inner chill where Golden Eye had left him. And if it was not aware of him, neither did it feel pity for him. It simply was, and he followed even more closely through the dappled sunlight and shade, gazing down upon the crown of its head from almost directly above.

He was so lost, so enwrapped in his study of its mind-glow, that he did not realize where it was headed until the trees began to thin ahead of them.

He froze when he did realize, and shock and alarm rolled through him. Was the two-leg *crazed*? How could it —?

And then he realized something else.

*It does not know,* he thought. *It does not know! And neither does the barker!*

Their mind-glows made that obvious. And even if they had possessed mind-voices, *he* had none. He could not even warn them! Unless —

"*Bleek!*"

Cordelia paused in mid-step. She'd never heard an animal's cry quite like that one, and she turned, trying to find its source.

"*Bleek! Bleek!*"

Where in the world —?

Movement flickered in the corner of her vision and her eyes widened in disbelief as she saw the source of the cries.

*It's a . . . a treecat!*

That was all it could be, she thought. She'd seen enough imagery of them to know that! But what had it so upset?

"*Bleek! Bleek, bleek, bleek!*"

She didn't know why she was so certain its agitation had something to do with *her*, yet she was. Maybe it was just that she couldn't think of any other reason for it to be making so much racket—or to have revealed its presence to her in the first place! And now it was flowing back and forth along the branches of the picketwood. It raced toward her for a couple of meters, then turned around and ran in the opposite direction, looking over its shoulder at her.

What in the world —?

She turned and took a step toward it.

Yes!

Relief boiled through Stone as the two-leg paused, looked up, and saw him. He bleeked at it again, running back along the net-wood, and tasted the surprise and curiosity that erupted through its mind-glow. There was delight mixed with the surprise, and a sense of wonder that went beyond simple curiosity, and he tasted it turning to follow him.

Good! If he could only get it —

Cordelia Schardt-Cordova felt herself smiling hugely as she realized the treecat *wanted* her to follow it!

*My God, they really are intelligent!* she thought. *And this one wants to show me something? Is that what it wants? But why —?*

She took one more step, and that was when Barnaby's warcry

snarled through the clearing. For an instant, she thought it was aimed at the treecat. She whipped around in the Rottweiler's direction, eyes wide, and then froze as the entire shoreline of the near-beaver pond exploded with movement.

No! He had come so close to saving it!

Horror erupted through Stone as the needle-fangs swarmed out of the undergrowth.

Needle-fangs were among the world's most deadly hunters. Not because of their size—they were no more than half a Person's size—but because of their numbers...and their hunger. They would attack anything that lived, hands of hands of them swarming over it, pulling it down, literally devouring it alive, especially in mating season.

They were the reason there were no longer any lake builders here.

"Barnaby! Come!" Cordelia shouted, un-slinging her rifle and suddenly wishing she'd brought a shotgun instead. *"Come!"*

*Near-weasels!* She should have realized! That was why she'd seen no sign of near-beavers, why nothing was using the game trail! Normally, near-weasels were seen only in relatively small numbers, but in mid-autumn, the peak of their breeding season, they could run in packs of dozens or even more.

Barnaby's hackles had gone up the instant he scented the near-weasels, but he responded quickly to her call, bounding toward her as she backed toward the open ground where the crown oaks' canopy choked out the undergrowth. Near-weasels were territorial—that was why their packs grew during breeding season as they staked out territory and hunting grounds in which to bear their young—and if she and Barnaby could just get beyond the limit of the territory they'd claimed here —

Barnaby stayed between her and the oncoming near-weasels, flowing back and forth, rumbling his warcry, and it looked as if the creatures were slowing. Or maybe she just wanted to believe that. Maybe —

She was watching the threat. She didn't notice the root growing across the game trail until the heel of her right boot caught on it.

✧       ✧       ✧

No!

The two-leg stumbled, then sprawled backward, dropping its thunder-barker, and Stone tasted the bolt of pain that shot through its mind-glow. Not from the fall; from its ankle.

It fought to climb back to its feet while the needle-fangs surged closer, and he heard it cry out in pain. It managed to scramble back upright, but it swayed, fighting to stay there while anguish ripped through it.

Cordelia sobbed in pain as she crawled back to her feet and knew that she and Barnaby were about to die because of a simple stupid, *stupid* fall.

She didn't know if the ankle was broken or just horribly sprained, and it didn't matter. What *mattered* was that she could barely stand, far less run. She'd managed to recover her rifle on her way back up, and her hand found the pistol grip while her thumb snapped off the safety, but that was more a reflex act of defiance than anything else. Near-weasels were fast, and they were small targets. And —

Barnaby's rumbling snarl rolled up like thunder as the outliers of the near-weasel tide reached them. His massive jaws snapped shut with an audible crunch. His victim's squeal died abruptly, and he tossed his head, flipping it back into the pack. His jaws closed again, and then the near-weasels were upon him. They were small foes, but their teeth were needle-sharp. His thick coat and hide offered some protection, but not enough, and Cordelia raised her rifle.

*CRAAACK!*

The two-leg's thunder-barker bellowed, and Stone felt a flicker of hope. But the needle-fangs came on, undeterred. They had no idea what a thunder-barker was...and if they had understood, they wouldn't have cared. Their mind-glows were minimal at the best of times; now they were filled with nothing but rage and hunger.

"What the hell?!"

Zack Kemper bolted upright in his seat as the alarm pinged. He jerked up his wrist and tapped the face of his uni-link.

"What?" Mack asked tautly.

"It's Cordelia."

"What's wrong?"

"She doesn't say. In fact —" Zack tapped again, and his face tightened. "It's her fall alert on auto, Mack."

"*Shit.*"

The brothers looked at each other. Aunt Danette's rules were inflexible. No one ever went into the bush alone without activating the fall-alert function on his uni-link. The younger members of her household might occasionally roll their eyes over the precaution, but they didn't really feel like arguing. Falls were one of the most common accidents that could overtake someone in the bush, and in Sphinx's 1.35 gravities, that sort of "accident" often meant broken bones—sometimes a *lot* of them—for humans who hadn't been genetically enhanced for heavy-grav worlds. So if the uni-link detected a fall and its wearer didn't tap the "Are you okay?" prompt within ten seconds, it automatically broadcast a homing signal.

"Where?" Mack demanded. "I don't see —" He broke off as an icon flashed on his navigation display. "Got it! Ping Aunt Danette and tell her we're on it!"

Blood stained Barnaby's coat in a dozen places, but he was a Rottweiler. Not just a Rottweiler—a *Meyerdahl* Rottweiler whose person was in danger. He was far stronger, far tougher than any terrestrial Rottweiler, yet he possessed every iota of his ancestors' fearless, go-for-broke nature, and he ignored his own wounds, whipping around Cordelia, snatching away the near-weasels that tried to swarm up her boots and the tough, no-rip fabric of her trousers.

They moved too fast, were too elusive, for her to target them with her rifle, so she used it as a club, instead, sobbing with terror but refusing to panic. She smashed one near-weasel after another, trying to keep them off of Barnaby, but there were always two more in place of each one that she clubbed.

Stone snarled in fury as he tasted the mind-glows below him.

The two-leg's terror surged over him like a tide, but for all its fear, it was that mind-glow's focus that caught Stone by the throat. He recognized the despair in it. He had known that same despair as Golden Eye sank into her final sleep in his arms. Had felt it himself when he longed to never awaken and find her gone. But there was no surrender in the two-leg. It would fight against the needle-fangs until it could fight no more, and not just for itself. Stone tasted its desperate determination to protect the barker even as he tasted the barker's bloodred, furious determination to protect the *two-leg*.

They were mind-blind. Neither could taste the other, know that the other would die rather than abandon them. And it didn't matter. Not to them. They would fight, and they would die, together, as surely as any of the People would fight and die together.

And as he realized that, he realized something else, as well.

He could not let them fight and die alone. He knew too much of what that meant.

Even through Barnaby's howling fury and her own panic, Cordelia heard another sound. It was like tearing canvas. She'd never heard it before, yet a corner of her brain recognized what it had to be and she wanted to cry out. To reject what she knew was about to happen.

The treecat followed its battle cry down out of the picketwood.

It hit her shoulder, but only a glancing blow, a carom shot that landed it perfectly poised on all six limbs right at her feet.

And then it exploded into action.

Stone had no idea if the barker would realize that he wasn't simply one more needle-fang, but he had no choice but to take that chance. He flung himself into the mad swirl of needle-fangs around the two-leg's feet, slashing with razor-sharp claws and fangs as sharp as any needle-fang's.

Cordelia clubbed another near-weasel, sobbing for breath. The creatures had gotten through her trousers in several places, and she felt blood flowing down her legs, but her wounds were nothing beside Barnaby's. The Rottweiler was coated in blood, now, and the savagely fighting treecat was already bloodied, as well.

They were going to die. She knew they were. But if they were, then by God, they would go kicking and clawing to the end! Barnaby would never abandon her, she would never abandon him, and neither of them would abandon the treecat who had made their hopeless fight his own.

✧     ✧     ✧

Stone squealed in pain as the needle-sharp fangs sank into his right leg.

It wasn't the first time he'd been bitten, but this time those fangs had reached the big tendon in the back of his leg. The leg went out from under him, and he went down, rolling and lashing out with five sets of claws. The big, black barker's jaws ripped away one of his attackers even as two more of them swarmed over the barker, and Stone managed to lunge upright. Two of the needle-fangs took advantage of the opening, breaking past him and the barker, swarming up the two-leg's legs until they could reach its arms. It cried out, dropping its thunder-barker, beating at them to keep them away from its throat, and Stone flung himself upward, swarming up the two-leg in pursuit of the near-fangs.

He reached the closest and sank his right true-hand's curved claws into its haunch, jerking it back, severing its throat with his left true-hand while he clung to the two-leg's body covering with both hand-feet and the one true-foot that still worked. But he couldn't reach the second needle-fang as it eluded the two-leg's grip and lunged for its throat.

Stone leapt. It was not the strongest leap he had ever made—not with only one leg that worked—but it was enough. He hit the needle-fang, gripping it with both true-hands, ripping the life from it as he arced outward. Then he landed, too far from the two-leg or the barker for either of them to reach him.

The needle-fangs were waiting.

*"No!"* Cordelia screamed as the treecat disappeared into the sea of near-weasels. *"No!"*

She knew exactly what the treecat had done...and why. It hadn't had to join the fight at all, and now it had died to buy her a few more seconds.

More fangs chewed through her trousers, and three of the little monsters clung to Barnaby's back, biting and tearing. The Rottweiler was slowing as his blood loss mounted. It was only —

*BLAM!*

Her head jerked up and her incredulous eyes flared wide.

BLAM! BLAM!

It was *Zack!* Where —? How —?

✧      ✧      ✧

Zack Kemper killed his counter-grav unit and hit the ground outside the perimeter of the near-weasel pack surrounding Cordelia, and unlike Cordelia, *he* favored a shotgun. In principle, it was identical to the shotguns which had been used on Terra for thousands of years, but the design was rather more advanced, and he had dialed in what one of his Terran ancestors would have called an "improved cylinder choke." The weapon's cartridges were slimmer than those of an old-fashioned shotgun, as well. There were fifteen of them in his magazine, each loaded with razor-sharp, aerodynamically stabilized flechettes, and because Zack, for all his levity, was dead serious about watching his brother's back in the woods, it was also selective fire.

He went to one knee and a burst of fully automatic flechettes ripped a swath of shredded near-weasels across the pack attacking Cordelia.

Recoil hammered his shoulder, and he emptied the magazine, hit the release button with his right index finger without ever letting go of the pistol grip, and slammed in a fresh magazine with his left hand.

Cordelia sobbed in disbelief. She'd been so focused on the near-weasels that she'd never even heard the air car! Now it hovered above her, canopy open, and she saw Mack standing in it. He leaned over the side, shooting downward, and if he didn't have a shotgun like Zack's, his rifle was firing on full auto, and he'd attached the hundred-round drum magazine Cordelia had always teased him about. His fire sawed into the other side of the pack, and that torrent of death and destruction was enough to get through even to near-weasels.

The survivors began to break away, shock and terror finally penetrating their ferocity and hunger, and Cordelia stumbled. She went to her right knee, ripping at the near-weasels still clinging to her legs, feeling them chewing at her hands as she tore them free and hurled them away. But then she saw Zack changing his aim point toward the biggest remaining cluster of the creatures.

"*No!*" she screamed. "*No, Zack!*"

He didn't hear her. Or realize what she was saying, anyway.

And he didn't know about the treecat... or that it was what the near-weasels were attacking.

✦ ✦ ✦

Fury roared through Zack Kemper as the blood soaking Cordelia's trousers, arms, and hands registered. He dropped his holo sight onto the cluster of near-weasels. His finger tightened, and —

"*Barnaby!*"

He managed—somehow—not to squeeze the trigger as the bleeding, wounded Rottweiler leapt squarely into the near-weasels he'd been about to shoot. Zack jerked his muzzle up and surged to his feet. He didn't know what had possessed Barnaby to hurl himself right into the middle of his sight picture. Maybe he'd figure that out later. For now, though —

He charged across the swath of carnage his fire had left and brought the shotgun's butt down, clubbing the near-weasels still ripping at Barnaby.

At Barnaby and something *else*, he realized. The Rottweiler's blood-dripping jaws ripped a near-weasel away, tearing it almost in two, and Zack's eyes widened as he saw the mauled, blood-soaked creature—the *treecat*—at the bottom of the pile.

"Zack! *Zack!*" Cordelia sobbed, hobbling toward him as quickly as her ankle allowed. "Oh, Zack!"

"It's okay, Cordy," he said, shotgun in his right hand as he threw his left arm around her. "It's okay."

"Oh, Zack," she said again, burying her face against his shoulder.

"Bet *you* don't complain about setting the fall alert again!" he said, but his voice was gentle, and she shook her head hard.

"*Never!*" she gasped.

"We've got to get you to Doc MacDallan," he said, but she surprised him. She pulled back, shaking her head again, and went to her knees.

"*No,*" she said so fiercely he blinked.

She was digging through the dead near-weasels. Barnaby was beside her, pawing at the bodies, and Zack realized what they were after as Cordelia scooped up the treecat in torn, bleeding hands and cradled it against her chest.

"Cordy," he started to say gently, "I'm afraid he's —"

"No he *isn't!*" She glared up at him. "He's *not!* He's still alive! I *know* he is!"

"But —"

"He's alive! And we have to get him to Dr. Harrington, Zack! He saved my life!"

"But —" Zack began, then cut himself off as the bleeding treecat stirred feebly in Cordelia's arms.

"*Now*, Zack!" she said fiercely. "Him and Barnaby both! We can worry about me later!"

Stone floated unwillingly up toward the surface of his dreams and stirred in protest.

He should not be alive. The darkness for which a part of him had longed so hard since Golden Eye left him should have taken him, and he would have been glad. He would have perished doing something worth the doing, and he wished he had. He knew how badly he had been hurt, and that meant death would find him soon enough. There was no other possibility for a single Person alone in the world. And if he must die anyway, why could he not have died in his dreams? Died and been restored to his bond with Golden Eye, if only in a dream?

He could have died so happily in a dream.

But that had been denied him, and something touched his muzzle.

He opened his unwilling eyes and blinked, trying to focus. And as he tried, he tasted a familiar mind-glow.

His eyes popped fully open, and he stared in astonishment at Climbs Quickly!

What was the Bright Water scout doing this far from the clan's range? And —

Stone's thought broke off as he realized they were in one of the two-leg nesting places. It was night outside a transparent part of the wall, but the overhead light was daylight-bright. He lay on his side, strange scents surrounded him, many of them sharp enough to hurt his nose, and the surface under him was soft and warm.

Climbs Quickly stroked his muzzle again, and Stone blinked. He had not seen the scout in almost a hand of turnings, and it was obvious Climbs Quickly had been as badly injured as he since last they'd seen one another. One of his forelimbs was missing, and his pelt was swirled with the telltale traces of scars beneath it.

*It is too bad I cannot hear his mind-voice*, Stone reflected. His thoughts were oddly unfocused, and he wondered why the pain he felt seemed so distant, almost unimportant. *It would be nice if he could explain what is happening!*

From the taste of Climbs Quickly's mind-glow, he was thinking much the same thing, and Stone tasted a flicker of amusement—of *shared* amusement, he realized—at their predicament.

And then he recognized what he had just felt. Amusement. In the face of this fresh proof of how the gray death had maimed him, he had felt *amused*! What was *wrong* with him?!

The question burned through him, but then he realized something else. He had awakened from his dream of Golden Eye, yet the warmth, the love, the focus of her mind-glow remained with him. It was back...and that was not possible.

He twitched as Climbs Quickly touched him again, this time on the shoulder, and he tasted the scout's compassion. And something very like...joy?

This was all wrong. Not possible! Golden Eye had been taken from him, so how could he taste her mind-glow again? *He could not!* He —

But, no. It wasn't Golden Eye's mind-glow. And yet —

Climbs Quickly looked down at him, then pointed, and Stone turned his head, eyes following the gesture, and froze.

No, it wasn't Golden Eye's mind-glow.

It was the two-leg's.

*This is not possible*, he thought. *Surely it is not! It is a* two-leg!

Yes, it was a two-leg, not a Person, and the People could not bond with any other creatures who walked the world.

*But the two-legs are not of our world.* The thought trickled through his mind. *They are not like any other creatures who walk it. We have known that for turning upon turning.*

He stared at the two-leg—*his* two-leg, he realized, tasting the joyous strength of the bond between them. She—he knew now that his two-leg was female—was asleep on some sort of sitting thing beside the flat, soft surface upon which he lay and Climbs Quickly sat. She had wounds of her own, wounds which had been treated as his own had, he realized, and he tasted her exhaustion. Yet even as she slept, her mind-glow sought his. It was not the conscious, knowing seeking of another Person, and yet it was actually stronger in so many ways. Her mind-glow was so bright, so intense, even in her sleep, and it was *his*. It reached out, enfolded him, welcomed him. It was focused upon him, deeply concerned about his wounds and yet totally devoid of the pity which had driven him from Bright Water so long ago. Because the two-leg had no mind-voice of her own, he realized. She did not know what he had lost, and so she did not mourn it for him... and she never would. Her mind-glow was not Golden Eye's, and it never would be, and that was a good thing. This, whatever it was and however it had happened, was too bright, too special and precious, to be compared to anything else.

He opened to it, felt it flooding through the dark places deep within him, washing away the fear and the grief and the anguish, and knew he had come home again at last.

Cordelia twitched, then snorted, as a feather touched her face.

Her mom and her sisters had teased her about her snoring for years, and from the feel of things, she'd been snoring again, she thought drowsily. Now why had she been doing that? And why was she sleeping sitting up? It was —

The feather touched her again, her eyes popped open, and it all came flooding back. The terror, the pain, the —

The feather brushed her cheek yet again, and she felt... *something* else. She didn't know what that "something" was, but it was there. She knew that much. And it was coming from —

She turned her head, and her eyes widened. It wasn't a feather brushing her cheek. It was a long, wiry finger. One armed with a sheathed, razor-sharp claw. A claw she'd seen rending and tearing near-weasels in her defense.

She straightened in the chair and reached out very carefully, wondering how he had gotten into her lap. Dr. Harrington said he'd put twice as many stitches into this treecat as into Lionheart on the day he'd saved Stephanie from the hexapuma, and his right rear leg was immobilized where the tendon had been repaired. He had to be in a lot of pain, despite the anesthetics, but somehow he'd gotten from the table beside her into her lap, and she heard a soft, buzzing sound—a purr, she realized—as her arms went cautiously around him.

She held him close, cradling him like the most precious thing in her world. Because, she realized, that was what he had just become. She and Stephanie and Karl Zivonik had talked while Dr. Harrington worked on both the treecat and Barnaby. Stephanie had tried to explain her bond with Lionheart, but Cordelia had known she didn't really understand what the younger girl was trying to say.

Now she did, she realized with a sense of awe. She understood *exactly* what Stephanie had been saying...and knew *she* would never be able to explain it to someone else, either.

And that didn't matter at all.

"Hello," she told the treecat—*her* treecat—softly, eyes burning. "My name is Cordelia." She kissed him gently between the ears. "Thank you for the rest of my life."

Stone pressed his nose against her, listening to her mouth sounds, wondering if that was how the mind-blind communicated with one another. It was an interesting thought, and perhaps one day he would know.

But that didn't matter at all.

*<Hello,>* he thought in the silence of his broken mind-voice. *<My name is Heart Stone. Thank you for the rest of my life.>*

ॐ

# David Weber

I first met Tim Bolgeo at Magnum Opus Con in Greenville in 1992, I think. I had a couple of books out, and *On Basilisk Station* and *Honor of the Queen* were scheduled to print the following spring. He'd read *Insurrection* and *Mutineers Moon*, and somehow he'd gotten hold of an ARC for the first two Honor Harrington novels, and he'd actually liked them. So I heard someone say "Mister Weber!" and I turned around, and there was this round-faced, jovial, Italian Catholic boy from Tennessee inviting me to come play at his house the following year. That was my first LibertyCon, and I haven't been able to make it to as many as I wish I could have, but I have enjoyed every single one I have been able to make, and most of all because of Uncle Timmy, Linda, Brandy, and the entire Bolgeo Clan. Because Timmy was special. Timmy took so much joy in life, and he was, above anything else, my friend. I Tuckerized him at least twice, and he survived the second time, but the entire crew of HMS *Cutthroat* perished gloriously in the service of the Queen, due to a statistically highly improbable event, entirely because Timmy had set my nil bid by catching me with the three of clubs in my hand. It wasn't so much the set I minded, as it was the jubilant victory dance around the room chanting "I set Weber on the three of clubs!"

That was Timmy. That was *so* completely Timmy, and when I close my eyes and summon him up, *that's* the moment I remember best.

Sharon and I were so incredibly lucky to know him—all of them, and the entire LibertyCon family, really, not just the Bolgeos—for going on thirty years. Thirty marvelous, love-and-laughter-filled years. Years of conventions, of books, of spades tournaments, and years of the simple joy of living. He will never set another of my nils, never deliver another of those absolutely deadpan jokes, never share another pun, never cackle over someone else's joke, never drive Sharon over another curb at the Choo Choo in a golf cart. He will never do any of those things again, because we don't have him anymore. But Tim Bolgeo will never die as long as a single one of the people whose lives he touched still remembers him, and anyone who ever met him will remember him as long as they live.

Goodbye, Timmy. We love you, we miss you, and we look forward to seeing you again.

God bless.

—David Weber

With over eight million copies of his books in print and thirty titles on *The New York Times* bestseller list, **David Weber** is a science fiction powerhouse. In the vastly popular Honor Harrington series, the spirit of C. S. Forester's Horatio Hornblower and Patrick O'Brian's Master and Commander lives on—into the galactic future. Books in the Honor Harrington and Honorverse series have appeared on twenty-one bestseller lists, including *The Wall Street Journal*, *Publishers Weekly*, and *USA Today*. Additional Honorverse collaborations include a spin-off mini-series Manticore Ascendant with *New York Times* bestselling author Timothy Zahn; and with Eric Flint, *Crown of Slaves* and *Cauldron of Ghosts*. Best known for his spirited, modern-minded space operas, Weber is also the creator of the Oath of Swords fantasy series and the Dahak saga. Weber has also engaged in a steady stream of bestselling collaborations, the Starfire Series with Steve White; The Empire of Man Series with John Ringo; the Multiverse Series with Linda Evans and Joelle Presby; and has contributed to the Ring of Fire Series with Eric Flint. His most recent titles for Baen are time travel/far future adventures *The Gordian Protocol* and *The Valkyrie Protocol*, both written with Jacob Holo. David Weber makes his home in South Carolina with his wife and children.

# BUILDING THE *BOLGEO*

In his day job, Timmy was an engineer for TVA for decades. As a fan, Uncle Timmy had a long and storied career, and his works touched many people. Les Johnson is one of them. Les is a fantastic speaker and popularizer of very difficult scientific concepts. And Timmy recruited him early on for his program. Klon Newell and Kerry Gilley were directors of programming at LibertyCon for many years (Rich Groller is the current guru of program juggling), but I'm pretty sure Timmy had a big hand in deciding what would go on in the initially quite limited space. And one that has consistently outgrown its confines is the late-night Mad Scientists panel—which for many years Les Johnson was not only a participant in, but the moderator for—no easy job. Presented here, a piece of speculative nonfiction, imagining and explaining what it would take to build humanity's first nuclear-powered human-bearing spaceship.

—TW

# Building the *Bolgeo*

*Nuclear Power and Propulsion for Exploration of the Solar System*

## Les Johnson

Somewhere in deep space, at a time not too distant from today, a command will be given to begin pumping 300,000 pounds of liquid hydrogen through the fuel rods in the core of the nuclear reactor on the *Bolgeo*—a spaceship bound for Mars. The fissioning uranium atoms will heat the hydrogen fuel to a temperature greater than 4600 degrees Fahrenheit, accelerating it through a cluster of three rocket engines 25 feet long, each weighing approximately 12,000 pounds and out the business end of an expansion nozzle 7 feet in diameter. The hydrogen will be given so much energy that it will start cleaving the normally coupled $H_2$ into monatomic hydrogen (single-proton hydrogen, not the typical diatomic version, $H_2$, that we experience every day in a sip of $H_2O$), providing an extra "kick" of thrust to the engine.

The engines will operate for about sixty minutes—long enough to burn all 300,000 pounds of super-cold liquid hydrogen stored in the huge tank attached just above it. Liquid hydrogen is stored at minus 423 degrees Fahrenheit, lest it become a gas and leak away. The engines will then stop and the reactor powered down to approximately 5 kilowatts. After the propellant is expended, the spacecraft will be on its way to Mars. And the *Bolgeo* will do so using less than half the propellant that would be required using a conventional, state-of-the-art chemical rocket, while simultaneously shortening travel time and allowing the spaceship to carry much more payload.

In short, a nuclear thermal rocket engine like the one described

325

above is the next logical step in our exploration, utilization, and settlement of space. The technology is within our grasp and will be built from some of the same technologies that nuclear engineers use every day when operating the USA's approximately one hundred nuclear power reactors. The technologies that will be flown are based on the same fundamental processes and principles that were used by engineer Richard T. Bolgeo nearly every day of his career at the Tennessee Valley Authority.

These same fundamental principles and technologies will also soon be adapted to provide reliable, long-duration power for robotic missions to the outer solar system and for human settlements on the Moon and Mars.

Before we conceptually design these systems, we should first discuss the physics of nuclear power and propulsion and cover a bit of history. *Deep history.*

A little over 13 billion years ago, the universe began with the Big Bang. In the first 20 minutes (or so) after the event, the material from the Bang cooled to the point where hydrogen, helium, and a trace of lithium could be found. None of the remaining elements in the periodic table were yet formed. As the universe expanded, small variations in the universe's initial mass distribution allowed some regions of space to have more hydrogen and helium than others. Thanks to gravity, these hydrogen clouds soon began to coalesce into denser and denser clouds, getting smaller and smaller as their mutual gravitational attraction increased, until they were so dense that the hydrogen atoms bumped strongly enough into each other to fuse into helium, releasing energy in the process— and stars were formed. Stars shine because of the fine balance between the inextricable force of gravity pulling the mass into a dense core and the thereby-initiated nuclear fusion, simultaneously synthesizing helium and releasing energy. This energy release creates an outward pressure which, for a time, creates a balance, allowing the star to not continue collapsing into a smaller and smaller volume. The inward pressure of gravitational attraction is balanced by the outward pressure created by the fusion.

In stars with masses between 40 percent to 80 percent of the mass of our sun, more and more hydrogen is converted into helium until there is not enough hydrogen to continue fueling the hydrogen-to-helium fusion cycle (which produces the outward radiation pressure and has kept the star from collapsing); the core collapses yet further, forcing the helium and hydrogen atoms close enough together to form yet new elements, like lithium, carbon, and nitrogen. When this process begins, the gases that make up the star redistribute themselves due to this new fusion process (which produces a different amount of energy), and the star expands in size (making it a "giant" star), burping massive amounts of its initial mass into the space surrounding it. In the life cycle of these stars, up to 80 percent of their initial mass can be lost to space. Once the fusion products are mostly carbon and oxygen, the fusion process lags, gravity then causes them to decrease in size, and they become white dwarf stars.

If the initial mass of the star is less than 40 percent of the mass of our own sun, then helium will be the primary fusion product. These small, less massive stars, known as red dwarfs, burn through their supply of hydrogen less rapidly than their more massive cousins. While other stars burn through only the hydrogen *at their core* before coming to the end of their lifetimes, red dwarfs consume *all of their hydrogen*, inside and outside their core. This theoretically will enable them to live for trillions of years—unlike the few billion years lifetime predicted for our star, the sun. Red dwarf stars are the most common type of star in our galaxy.

Although space is very large, the initial lumpiness of the universe after the Big Bang left enough residual hydrogen and helium for stars to form relatively close to one another. If one of these white dwarf stars happens to be near another star that is in its giant phase, the dwarf star's gravity will begin pulling in some of the hydrogen gas burped by the giant star, igniting a massive explosion called a Type Ia supernova. The explosion is caused by the added mass forcing the carbon in the star's core to rapidly fuse. (Note: A rapid release of energy in everyday life is what we call a bomb. It's no different in a star, except for the massive scale of the explosion.) This explosion of energy at the star's core sends a blast wave outward, causing a myriad of other fusion reactions that would not ordinarily occur—and some of these reactions produce uranium.

Uranium is also produced under similar circumstances, quite spectacularly, in stars that have masses many times the mass of our sun (8 to 25 times larger than the sun), in explosions called Type II supernovae and, it is now theorized, by the merger of neutron stars.

These processes created the Earth's uranium and most of the elements of the periodic table heavier than helium. In other words, the universe's early stars were factories that spewed elements into the interstellar medium from which our sun and the planets that circle it were created. We are, as Carl Sagan said, truly "star stuff."

The bottom line? The uranium used in our near-future spacecraft was created billions of years ago and has been patiently waiting on humans to discover how to use it.

What makes uranium so special that we can use it to produce energy and propulsion?

To understand this, we need to discuss what makes up an element and how elements differ. Elements consist of protons, neutrons, and electrons. Protons and neutrons are bound together at the center of the atom and are surrounded by the electrons. The number of protons in the core of an atom determines its designation as an element. For example, an atom with only one proton is always hydrogen. If it has two protons, then it is always helium. Ditto for lithium (3 protons), beryllium (4 protons), and uranium (92 protons). The number of neutrons in a nucleus can change and the elemental status remain the same. For example, hydrogen with one neutron is simply "hydrogen," but if it has two neutrons, then it is called deuterium—but it is still hydrogen. An atom's various forms, determined by the number of neutrons in the nucleus, are its isotopes. Most uranium on Earth (>99%) has 146 neutrons and is what physicists call uranium-238 (uranium with 92 protons + 146 neutrons = 238). It is the other <1% that makes uranium extremely interesting and useful.

Mixed within Earth's natural stockpile of uranium-238 ($^{238}U$) are isotopes of uranium-235 ($^{235}U$) and 234 ($^{234}U$). If the $^{235}U$ can be extracted from the $^{238}U$ and bombarded by a beam of neutrons, then the $^{235}U$ will split, or fission, producing, among other things, more neutrons. If configured in the right geometry, once the initial neutron bombardment begins, enough secondary neutrons produced in the fission reaction will then collide with and induce fission within other $^{235}U$ atoms, creating yet more neutrons in a self-sustaining chain reaction. If you can control the rate of neutron production, you can then control the reaction rate and use the energy produced for your own purposes. It could be used to heat water, making steam to turn turbines and create electrical power in a terrestrial nuclear power plant, or to

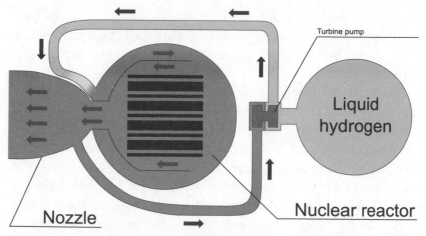

FIGURE 1. A nuclear thermal rocket generates thrust by pumping liquid hydrogen through the core of the nuclear reactor, where the hydrogen is superheated and then expelled through a rocket nozzle.

*(Image courtesy of Tokino under the Attribution-ShareAlike 3.0 Unprotected license from Creative Commons.)*

or to superheat hydrogen for use in a spaceship's rocket propulsion system (Figure 1).

We are now back to our spaceship and its nuclear thermal propulsion system. Conventional chemical rockets derive thrust through chemistry—taking a propellant, mixing it with oxygen, and burning it. The heat of the combustion of the rocket's fuel produces a very hot exhaust gas that thermally expands out one end of the combustion chamber through a rocket nozzle. The superhot gas moves in one direction and, thanks to the conservation of momentum, our rocket then moves in the other direction. (If you add up the momentum contained in all the exhaust gas and subtract the spacecraft's resultant velocity, you get zero. Voilà! Momentum is conserved and Sir Newton is happy.) Typically, the hotter the propellant, the faster the exhaust gas is moving, providing larger velocity changes to carry our robots and human explorers into the far reaches of the solar system.

Nuclear reactions can be hot. Very hot—from over 500 degrees Fahrenheit in a commercial nuclear reactor to nearly 4600 degrees in our spaceship's nuclear reactor. (Depending upon the reactor design, how it is moderated, coolant used, etc.) The hot reaction is why a nuclear reactor is an attractive option for rocket propulsion—we can heat the propellant to extremely high temperatures and get a lot more thrust per pound of propellant than is physically possible in a conventional chemical rocket. Chemical reactions just don't release as much energy as nuclear reactions.

The increased efficiency of nuclear thermal propulsion enables more rapid travel between the planets and a dramatic reduction in the amount of propellant required. And it gets better.

If you can increase the temperature of the reactor and have the materials that can sustain these temperatures from which to build your rocket, then you can increase your thrust and efficiency yet further, making crewed travel to destinations beyond Mars a very real possibility. These "next generation" nuclear thermal rockets will enable people to reach the moons of Jupiter and return to Earth in only a little more time than a worst-case round trip to Mars would take in nuclear rockets we are capable of building today—two to three years. Europa, here we come!

And while we are generating all that heat...

Future spaceships will have a way to tap the heat of the nuclear reactor to generate electrical power in a fashion analogous to, but not the same as, those used in their earthly cousins. This is important because solar power, which is extremely useful in the inner solar system where the Sun is visible and bright, is next to useless in the outer part of the solar system (at Saturn's orbit and beyond) where the sunlight is extremely dim. Current missions to the outer solar system are powered by the radioactive decay of the element plutonium—but these systems are limited to producing only very small amounts of power. These plutonium power packs are called Radioisotope Thermoelectric Generators (RTGs) and have been used on several spacecraft, including *Voyager* and *New Horizons*. While they produce enough power to keep small robotic spacecraft warm, alive, and functional, they only produce tens to hundreds of watts—an output woefully insufficient for more complex robotic spacecraft, let alone ships carrying humans which may need many thousands or millions of watts. Ships with nuclear fission reactors, powered by $^{235}U$, can provide hundreds of kilowatts to megawatts—more than enough to support a human crew in deep space.

And it gets even better.

With all this power available, a future spaceship designer can increase the propulsion performance by replacing the nuclear thermal rocket engines with highly efficient electric propulsion systems powered by the electricity produced with our space nuclear reactor.

Electric propulsion systems derive thrust by accelerating their exhaust using electric and magnetic fields instead of chemical combustion. You may recall that, in electrical systems, "like repels like and opposites attract." If your spacecraft propellant is an ionized gas, meaning that it has a net electrical charge, then you can use electric fields to accelerate the ionized propellant and produce thrust. In an electric propulsion system like the one shown in Figure 2, the propellant, in this case ionized xenon, is accelerated by electric and/or magnetic fields to extremely high speeds and expelled from the right side, producing thrust.

These thrusters are real, with more than 500 electric propulsion systems having flown in space. Current electric propulsion systems operate on limited electrical power, making their thrust much less than is possible with state-of-the-art chemical propulsion.

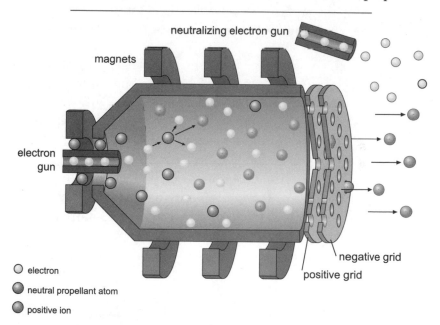

FIGURE 2. One incarnation of an electric propulsion system is the electrostatic thrust as shown here. In an electrostatic thruster, all the propellant acceleration is achieved using an electric field. The magnets are provided to keep the charged ion exhaust focused.

*(Image courtesy of Oona Räisänen without modification,*
*https://creativecommons.org/licenses/by-sa/3.0/deed.en.)*

However, they can provide a small thrust for an extremely long time, making a much more efficient use of the available propellant and, in many cases, provide more net thrust than a comparable chemical propulsion system. They are, pound for pound, much more efficient than their chemical (or even nuclear thermal) counterparts. Consider your late-model, energy-efficient, small gasoline-powered car and compare it to a semi-trailer truck. The car probably has low acceleration and could never move the mass of a big-rig trailer containing consumer goods bound for your local big box retailer—but it can perhaps achieve more than forty miles per gallon of gas operating on its own. The semi, on the other hand, can hook up to the big-rig trailer and simply start pulling it—achieving only about six miles per gallon in the process. Today's electric propulsion systems are like the small car, due primarily to the current limits of producing power in space from sunlight. This can all change with a nuclear reactor creating electrical power.

So how real, in terms of engineering, are all these nuclear systems? As you might expect, some are more near-term than others.

First of all, in 1965 the US built and flew the Systems for Nuclear Auxiliary Power (SNAP-10A) reactor, the world's first fission power reactor in orbit. The mission was partially successful and demonstrated the ability of a space-borne nuclear reactor to generate over half a kilowatt of electrical power in space. Though the USA has not flown a nuclear reactor in space since SNAP-10A, the Soviets/Russians flew over forty, some generating up to 10 kilowatts of power. There is no intrinsic reason that would prevent us from flying a newer, lighter-weight, and more efficient one in space today.

Though they never flew in space, the USA built and tested multiple prototype nuclear thermal rocket engines in the 1960s and '70s as part of the Nuclear Engine for Rocket Vehicle Application (NERVA) program. Several nuclear rocket engines were tested, including one that operated at over a gigawatt (thermal—no electrical power was generated) for over 3600 seconds—demonstrating most of the attributes that will be required for human exploration missions to Mars (Figure 3). The NERVA project was canceled in 1973 when it became clear that NASA would not need the capability offered by NERVA, due to there

FIGURE 3. A nuclear thermal rocket engine during a test conducted at Jackass Flats located on the Nevada Test Site on July 1, 1959. The hydrogen exhaust plume that blurs out the mountains in the background is mostly invisible and dwarfs the visible central column.

*(Image courtesy of NASA.)*

program for sending people beyond low-earth orbit anywhere in (budgetary) sight. As an aside: One of the NERVA engines built for live-fire testing, but never tested, is on display at the NASA Marshall Space Flight Center in Huntsville, AL. In 2013, I had the pleasure of taking Richard "Uncle Timmy" Bolgeo on a tour of NASA MSFC, during which he was able to see and touch the engine. The smile on Timmy's face was large and memorable!

Technically, there are no significant technical barriers preventing the flight of either a nuclear power or propulsion reactor in space. The barriers today are most likely fiscal- and policy-related—alas.

The key to fully exploring, developing, settling, and utilizing the solar system lies with ships powered and propelled by the energy of atoms created in stars billions of years before the Earth formed.

Star stuff indeed.

*Richard T. Bolgeo was an electrical engineer who devoted his thirty-plus-year career working on, in, or around nuclear power plants, mostly those overseen by the Tennessee Valley Authority. He earned his B. S. in electrical engineering from Christian Brothers University, served in the United States Air Force, and for many years helped keep the Sequoyah Nuclear Power plant operational and providing power to its customers. He was an in-demand consultant whose expertise was extensively utilized across the TVA network. Timmy knew the benefits and risks inherent to nuclear power and had the vision to advocate for its use in the exploration of space. His vision may soon be realized.*

ᢒᩣ

## Les Johnson

I met Timmy at a con (not LibertyCon) in early 1988 and we immediately struck up a friendship, engaging in conversation about space travel, nuclear power, and great science fiction—no surprises there for anyone who knew Richard Bolgeo. During the last night of the con, local teenagers decided to invade in search of beer—resulting in multiple fire alarms, rowdiness to the point where sleep was impossible, and intervention by the local police. The next morning as my wife, Carol, and I were checking out, I mentioned to Timmy that I felt I had outgrown fandom and conventions—and that this one would be my last.

Timmy would have none of it. He informed me that he and others had started a "literary, family-oriented con" and he wouldn't let me leave fandom (or the hotel!) until we promised him we would come to this new convention and give it a fair shake. That July, we participated in LibertyCon #2 and were hooked. Timmy, Klon Newell, and the rest of the crew became our new extended LibertyCon family to the point that we plan our summers to allow our pilgrimage to Chattanooga for what has become our favorite weekend of the year.

There are too many wonderful LibertyCon/Timmy moments to detail here so I will limit it to one: At LibertyCon #8, I was honored to become LibertyCon's official rocket scientist—with a twist. At the banquet, Timmy called me forward to bestow upon me one of the coveted LibertyCon Black Shirts. He proudly unfurled the shirt with my name on the front and "Our Real Rocket Sceintist" on the back. Noticing the prominent misspelling of "scientist" for the first time as he displayed the shirt, Timmy attempted to pull it back with a promise to have the shirt redone with the spelling corrected. I quickly replied, "Not on your life!" I proudly wear my "Rocket Sceintist" shirt only one day each year—on Saturday night at LibertyCon. Thank you, Uncle Timmy!

—Les Johnson

**Les Johnson** is a husband, father, physicist, author, and NASA technologist. He works at the NASA Marshall Space Flight Center where he serves as the lead for NASA's two interplanetary solar sail missions: Near Earth Asteroid Scout and Solar Cruiser. His books include *Mission to Methone, Rescue Mode* (with Ben Bova), and *Graphene: The Superstrong, Superthin, and Superversatile Material That Will Revolutionize the World*. Les has been attending science fiction conventions since he was in high school and credits the genre for being one of the inspirations that led him to pursue a career in physics.

# "BRANDY (SPRAKER, THAT IS)"

Brandy—she-who-must-be-obeyed—welcomed me as the 2016 LibertyCon Master of Ceremonies and made me feel like part of the family even though it was my first time there. Her energy and enthusiasm were palpable, and it was impossible to be around her very long without smiling even when it was obvious that she was working on a hundred different details at once. So it didn't take long for me to start thinking about doing a version of the Looking Glass song, "Brandy," that would be expressly about LibertyCon and its committee chairwoman. But I didn't do it right away....

At my second LibertyCon, in 2017, they asked me to reprise "LibertyCon Oddity" during the Opening Ceremonies. That was okay with me, even though I was already thinking about my version of "Brandy," because I didn't want to set up the expectation that I would show up there every year with a new song. Plus, part of me wasn't sure how well the song I had in mind was going to go over. For one thing, I didn't know if Brandy even liked the song, "Brandy"—it seemed possible that she could have grown up hating it, because she would've been reminded of it all the time—and I wasn't about to ask her in advance because the idea for each of these songs was that it would be a surprise.

So I took the risk in 2018, a little nervous about how she would respond to it. Thankfully, the Opening Ceremonies audience took up the chorus with enthusiasm—a great boon, because it covered my slipshod guitar playing—and seemed happy to show their appreciation for Brandy along with me. And I was delighted to find out that she actually really liked that song and was named Brandy after it. I was very pleased that she received my version with good grace.

—Gray Rinehart

# "Brandy (Spraker, That Is)"

## Lyrics by Gray Rinehart

*To the tune of "Brandy," by Looking Glass*

There's a con in Chattanooga town
Where the fans and pros can let their hair hang down
And forget, 'til Monday rolls around
The troubles of this world

And there's an army of dedicated volunteers
Who put the con together year after year
Out of love, respect, and a little fear
Of a very special girl

*Chorus*
> *And all the fans here say Brandy, you're a fine girl*
> *What a good con this will be*
> *There's no other con anywhere else like Liberty*

There are crepes that Todd McCaffrey cooks
And lots of authors ready to sign their books
And there are well-armed friends everywhere you look
'Cause that's a part of being free

And it all started thirty-something years ago
When Uncle Timmy decided to put on a show
But at that time he could not know
His little girl would take the reins

*Chorus*

### Bridge

Now Brandy, she's a longtime fan
  of movies, games, and stories
She grew up with tales of con SNAFUs,
  and Southern Fandom glory
She may greet you with a friendly hug,
  but she rules with an iron hand
'Cause she wants everything to be
  perfect for the fans

I hope you'll take the chance, before the con is through
(Though she has a thousand different things to do)
To let her know, how much it means to you
To be at LibertyCon again

### Chorus x2

# AFTERWORD:
# ON PAYING IT FORWARD

## Toni Weisskopf

Several of the authors here have related their first meetings with Uncle Timmy Bolgeo. I confess I don't remember mine. To me, a teenager starting to go to conventions in the early 1980s, Timmy had always been there, a giant, exuberant presence. He was just part of the complex and colorful fabric of fandom that had always been and always would be. But, of course, he was not. He had a beginning and, sadly, he had an end. But he was part of a greater work, and the patterns that he wove will happily continue after him.

To understand the enduring popularity of LibertyCon, the convention he founded in Chattanooga, Tennessee, with a dedicated group of volunteers, you have to understand some earlier fan history. Especially, you have to understand Wilson "Bob" Tucker.

Bob was one of the first to make our world what it is today, and he passed much of what he loved about fandom on to Timmy—and, indeed, many, many others, including me. The first and most obvious influence on this volume is "Tuckerization," simply the act of naming characters in your stories after people you know. They may or may not share characteristics with these real people. If I recall correctly, the names Tucker originally used, in mystery novels, were just names, and shared nothing in particular with the people whose names he used. Another term for this practice, especially when used to name spear carriers who then go on to die, is "redshirting," from the belief that Star Fleet security and engineers who wore red died more frequently in *Star Trek*.

A new variation on this practice has been to auction off these opportunities, the money going to charity. Thousands of dollars have been raised when authors donate opportunities for naming, and then even more to decide if the honoree dies a glorious death or a terrible one. One of the many things Uncle Timmy was known for was his skill as an auctioneer....

I don't know that we have broken the record for Tuckerizations in one volume—surely *Fallen Angels*, the SF novel by Larry Niven,

Jerry Pournelle, and Michael Flynn, comes close. But let it be known that Chris Woods does not think small.... All of those Tuckerized here, all volunteers at the convention, are listed in the back of this volume. Chris personally contacted each one and got their permission to do this.

Of course, Uncle Timmy and Tucker were friends. Timmy was one of a small group of Southern fans who made a point of leaving the region, attending Worldcons and other conventions outside their home area, and in the course of his travels he met Tucker. Tucker, at the time—the late 1970s to '80s—was in much demand as a convention master of ceremonies or toastmaster. He was perennial toastmaster at Chattacon, the original convention— and still ongoing as of 2020!—in Chattanooga, including during Timmy's tenure as convention chair. So when Timmy started his own summer convention, complementing the winter Chattacon, Tucker was his choice for toastmaster, too. And so Tucker remained, enjoying the hospitality of Tim and his wife, Linda, before and after the cons, until health concerns forced him away from the travel that he so much enjoyed.

Tucker helped set the tone for this convention, and at the time it began it was one of many that were local, literary, party-oriented, and in general the very definition of fannish fun. Today, in 2020, it is one of only a handful that have the feeling. Subcultures grow, and change, and science fiction fandom is a different beast than it was when it started in the 1930s. While LibertyCon has grown—the capped limit on attendance was raised for the twenty-fifth anniversary convention and never lowered, if I recall correctly—it has retained its earlier feeling. This is a tribute to not only Timmy's force of personality, but the structures and practices he put in place to make it so.

One of the reasons LibertyCon lives on after its founder has left is because he made it a point to welcome new people to the fold, to give them a place to thrive. This was always his way—and Tucker's—but it should be noted here that Timmy made conventions for people of all races, sexes, creeds, and persuasions. His conventions were open, inclusive, and happy places to be. Let this volume be the testament his legacy deserves.

Proceeds from this volume will go to fund two charitable efforts. The first is LibertyCon itself, a 501(c)(3) organization that every year donates tens of thousands of dollars to local Chattanooga charities, each year a different charity.

The second is a competitive scholarship administered by the Tennessee Valley Interstellar Workshop that is open to a full-time college student majoring in engineering, math, or sciences on the basis of an essay about space science. Going forward, one of those scholarships will be named for Richard "Uncle Timmy" Bolgeo.

The Tennessee Valley Interstellar Workshop is also a 501(c)(3) organization, created to "facilitate interstellar research and exploration by hosting regular summit meetings ... in the service of enhancing public understanding and dialogue toward interstellar exploration." In other words, it's like a LibertyCon panel, all grown up! Since 2011 it has hosted six Interstellar symposia, and sponsored one special symposium on the Power of Energy. All have involved not only scientists and engineers, but writers and educators as well. I highly recommend participation for anyone interested in the field. Go to tviw.us for more information about the next meeting and how to get involved.

# ABOUT LIBERTYCON

## Brandy Spraker, Ann V. Robards, and T.K.F. Weisskopf

Below you will find a chart of basic information about the science fiction convention LibertyCon. It includes venues, guests of honor, each year's selected charity for donations, and so on. Such charts usually include the convention chairman for each year. This one doesn't need to because there have only been two in over thirty years: Richard T. "Uncle Timmy" Bolgeo for the first twenty-five, then his daughter, Brandy Bolgeo Spraker. She probably would have taken over earlier, but she was only fourteen when the convention first started.

Attendance was reckoned at 450 for the first year, and statistics weren't kept religiously after that but appear to stay at about that number until the convention moved to the East Ridge location (because of hotel kerfuffles with the downtown hotels), when it became capped at that number. For several years, hotel capacity was a limiting factor. The convention-crowded Memorial Day weekend also kept numbers low, but attendance started exploding after the twenty-fifth anniversary convention. LibertyCon 28 was the first to hit the new limit of 750 paid guests in 2015, and the convention has sold out every year since then.

For a more complete picture of the convention, you can head to the LibertyCon.org (not dot com, that's another group entirely) website. There you will find scans of every single program book, lists of volunteers and Board of Directors for each convention, as well as many, many pictures taken by attendees and the official photographers.

From the beginning, the convention was intended to be a charitable organization run by a volunteer board of directors. The convention has paid for itself after the initial influx of seed money, and has made significant donations to local charities every year, many of them with ties to the members. One of the most significant was the J.J. Johnson Memorial Scholarship fund, which became fully funded after several years. We should note that there are no free rides at the convention: everyone not either a current or past headlining guest pays the membership fee, from the board to all of the volunteers who run the convention.

From the beginning it was important to Timmy and the board of directors that the philosophy guiding the choice of guests was to showcase some of the elder statesmen (and women) of the field, to keep the history of the field alive by introducing them to their younger fans. To complement that, they would also try to pick a new, up and coming, author or artist to give them a boost. And the strategy for both types of picks was to keep the generations together. From the beginning there was an artist guest; the science guest was added in 2010, because the science track was so popular. But the idea was always to include those people who would enjoy interacting with the fans, and keep attendance at such a size, so you could meet your favorite author or artist organically, at a party or at the bar—to form a community. This feeling of "family" so many of the contributors have alluded to—it is by design. As it's evolved, everybody—attendees, program participants, guests, volunteers—all bring something to the party.

The con suite in particular has been a locus for such giving. In the beginning Brandy's grandfather, John Vanucci, was famous for his spaghetti and "gravy." You could count on big pots of noodles boiling away Saturday night in the consuite. Brandy's then-mother-in-law, Sandy McDade, would make piles of pimento cheese and egg salad sandwiches. Especially in the first few years Sandy would also hustle donations from local businesses—like Little Debbie! And who can forget author Todd McCaffrey flipping crepes in the breakfast line over at the Choo Choo?

The con suite was also usually the site of the "dead dog" party—held Sunday night for the staff and those guests staying over until Monday. For a while there were not only themed banquets for the con, but also themed dead dogs. Dead dogs are a way of saying thank you to the volunteers—the sole perk of volunteerhood is to go first through the food line at the dead dog! This was usually pizza provided by the con, but also supplemented potluck style by the members.

From the beginning LibertyCon has been a family affair. It started with a small group of fans gathered around Tim and Linda Bolgeo's kitchen table; now it's Brandy's dining room table. The more things change, the more they stay the same. People brought their kids to the convention—David Robards's first convention was when he was about a year old. His mother has filled many roles at the convention, starting out in programming and now running the art show. His dad printed the program book for the first few years. They are not the only family to so contribute; in several cases we are on our third generation of fans working the con.

There have been weddings, vow renewals, and even baptisms at the con. And of course there are the parties. We could tell stories about these, and the heroic efforts around them (the epic drive to find booze the one year the con was held in a dry county, for instance. That was after The Year There Was No Con—because the hotel burned down—not our fault; it happened six weeks before the con). But then we'd have to black out the names to save the reputation of the innocents unwittingly involved. So we will refrain. But suffice it to say the atmosphere at the con is stimulating in many ways.

Long may it wave!

| LIBERTYCON | HOTEL | CHARITY | IN MEMORIAM |
|---|---|---|---|
| 1<br>July 10–12, 1987 | Sheraton City Center, Chattanooga, TN | MDA | N/A |
| 2<br>July 8–10, 1988 | Sheraton City Center, Chattanooga, TN | MDA | Kirk Thompson |
| 3<br>July 7–9, 1989 | Sheraton City Center, Chattanooga, TN | MDA /<br>Robert Adams Hospital Fund | N/A |
| 4<br>July 13–15, 1990 | Sheraton City Center, Chattanooga, TN | Robert Adams Memorial Fund | Robert Adams &<br>JJ Johnson |
| 5<br>July 19–21, 1991 | Sheraton City Center, Chattanooga, TN | JJ Johnson Memorial Scholarship Fund | N/A |
| 6<br>July 10–12, 1992 | Sheraton City Center, Chattanooga, TN | Chattanooga Jaycees /<br>JJ Johnson Memorial | N/A |
| 7<br>July 9–11, 1993 | Sheraton City Center, Chattanooga, TN | Chattanooga Jaycees /<br>JJ Johnson Memorial | N/A |
| 8<br>July 8–10, 1994 | Days Inn & Convention Center,<br>East Ridge, TN | JJ Johnson Memorial Scholarship Fund | N/A |
| 9<br>July 7–9, 1995 | Days Inn & Convention Center,<br>East Ridge, TN | Chattanooga Jaycees /<br>JJ Johnson Memorial | N/A |
| 10<br>July 12–14, 1996 | Days Inn & Convention Center,<br>East Ridge, TN | Chattanooga Jaycees /<br>JJ Johnson Memorial | N/A |
| 11<br>July 25–27, 1997 | Radisson Read House, Chattanooga, TN | Suzie Skelton Memorial Fund /<br>Chattanooga Jaycees | Suzie Skelton /<br>Dixie Walker |

# LIBERTYCON

| SPECIAL GUEST | LITERARY GOH | ARTIST GOH | SCIENCE GOH | MASTER OF CEREMONIES |
|---|---|---|---|---|
| N/A | L. Sprague & Catherine de Camp | Vincent Di Fate | N/A | Wilson "Bob" Tucker |
| N/A | Gordon R. Dickson | Ron & Val Lakey Lindahn | N/A | Wilson "Bob" Tucker |
| Tom Dietz | Robert & Pamela Adams | Bob Maurus | N/A | Wilson "Bob" Tucker |
| Timothy Zahn | A.E. Van Vogt | Debbie Hughes & Mark Maxwell | N/A | Wilson "Bob" Tucker |
| Sharon Green | James P. Hogan | David Cherry | N/A | Wilson "Bob" Tucker |
| Will Bradley | Katherine Kurtz | Kevin Ward | N/A | Wilson "Bob" Tucker |
| John Maddox Roberts | Michael McCollum | Mark Fults | N/A | Wilson "Bob" Tucker |
| Kelly & Laura Freas | F.M. Busby | Doug Chaffee | N/A | Brad Strickland |
| Andy Offutt | Jack Williamson | Dixie Walker | N/A | Wilson "Bob" Tucker |
| Les Johnson / 10th Anniversary L. Sprague & Catherine de Camp | Timothy Zahn | David & Lori Dietrick | N/A | Wilson "Bob" Tucker |
| David Weber | Fred Saberhagen | Vincent Di Fate | N/A | Charles Fontenay |

| LIBERTYCON | HOTEL | CHARITY | IN MEMORIAM |
|---|---|---|---|
| 12<br>May 22–24,<br>1998 | Ramada Inn,<br>East Ridge, TN | Chattanooga Jaycees /<br>JJ Johnson Memorial | N/A |
| 13<br>May 28–30,<br>1999 | Ramada Inn,<br>East Ridge, TN | Chattanooga Jaycees /<br>JJ Johnson Memorial | N/A |
| 14<br>May 26–28,<br>2000 | Ramada Inn,<br>East Ridge, TN | Chattanooga Jaycees /<br>JJ Johnson Memorial | Catherine Crook<br>de Camp |
| 15<br>May 25–27,<br>2001 | Ramada Inn,<br>East Ridge, TN | AIM Center | L. Sprague<br>de Camp /<br>Gordon R.<br>Dickson /<br>Rick Shelley |
| 16<br>July 25–27,<br>2003<br>(DSC 41) | Econolodge,<br>East Ridge, TN | Special Olympics<br>Tennessee | N/A |
| 17<br>July 23–25,<br>2004 | The Holiday Inn<br>on the Hill,<br>Cleveland, TN | Chattanooga Food Bank | N/A |
| 18<br>July 29–31,<br>2005 | Comfort Inn & Suites,<br>East Ridge, TN | Special Olympics<br>Tennessee | N/A |
| 19<br>July 28–30,<br>2006 | Comfort Inn & Suites,<br>East Ridge, TN | Chattanooga Food Bank | Jim Baen /<br>Irvin Koch |
| 20<br>July 27–29,<br>2007 | Comfort Inn & Suites,<br>East Ridge, TN | Special Olympics<br>Tennessee | Wilson "Bob"<br>Tucker |
| 21<br>July 11–13,<br>2008 | Comfort Inn & Suites,<br>East Ridge, TN | Orange Grove Center | Sandy McDade /<br>Hank Reinhardt |
| 22<br>July 10–12,<br>2009 | Comfort Inn & Suites,<br>East Ridge, TN | Chattanooga Area<br>Food Bank | Thomas Franklin<br>Deitz |
| 23<br>July 9–11,<br>2010 | Comfort Inn & Suites,<br>East Ridge, TN | Special Olympics<br>Tennessee | Sharon & Bryan<br>Webb |

| SPECIAL GUEST | LITERARY GOH | ARTIST GOH | SCIENCE GOH | MASTER OF CEREMONIES |
|---|---|---|---|---|
| Wendy Webb | Lois McMaster Bujold | Lubov | N/A | Wilson "Bob" Tucker |
| Cheryl Mandus | Chelsea Quinn Yarbro | David Mattingly | N/A | James P. Hogan |
| Kenneth Waters | C.J. Cherryh | Jon Stadter | N/A | Timothy Zahn |
| Debbie Hughes | David Drake | Gary Ruddell | N/A | Eric Flint |
| John Ringo | Steve Stirling | Darrell K. Sweet | N/A | Darryl Elliott |
| N/A | Larry Niven / Jerry Pournelle | Steve Hickman | N/A | David Weber |
| Timothy Zahn | Frederik Pohl | Beth Willinger | N/A | Robert Lynn Asprin |
| Dr. Travis Taylor | Ron Goulart | Pete Abrams | N/A | John Steakley |
| Dr. Greg Matloff / David Weber 20th Ann GOH | Jack McDevitt | Vincent Di Fate+G2 | N/A | Timothy Zahn |
| David B. Coe | Harry Turtledove | David Mattingly | N/A | Eric Flint |
| Toni Weisskopf | Ben Bova | Darrell K. Sweet (Unable to show) | N/A | Tom Smith |
| Dan & Sarah Hoyt | Terry Brooks | Darrell K. Sweet | Les Johnson | Eric Flint |

| LIBERTYCON | HOTEL | CHARITY | IN MEMORIAM |
|---|---|---|---|
| 24 July 15–17, 2011 | Comfort Inn & Suites, East Ridge, TN | The Ronald McDonald House | N/A |
| 25 July 20–22, 2012 | Chattanooga Choo Choo, Chattanooga, TN | Challenger STEM Learning Center / Chattanooga Food Bank (in memory of Sandy McDade) | John Steakley et al.* |
| 26 June 28–30, 2013 | Chattanooga Choo Choo, Chattanooga, TN | Chattanooga Area Food Bank | N/A |
| 27 June 27–29, 2014 | Chattanooga Choo Choo, Chattanooga, TN | AIM Center | Roseanne A. Di Fate |
| 28 June 26–28, 2015 (1632 MiniCon) | Chattanooga Choo Choo, Chattanooga, TN | Bethel Bible Village | N/A |
| 29 July 8–10, 2016 | Chattanooga Choo Choo, Chattanooga, TN | Lana's Love Foundation | N/A |
| 30 June 30– July 2, 2017 | Chattanooga Choo Choo, Chattanooga, TN | Austin Hatcher Foundation | Klon Newell / Kerry Gilley |
| 31 June 29– July 1, 2018 | Marriott Downtown, Chattanooga, TN | Chattanooga Room In The Inn | N/A |
| 32 June 28–30, 2019 | Marriott Downtown, Chattanooga, TN | A Smile For Troops | Uncle Timmy Bolgeo |

*The full 25th Anniversary Libertycon In Memoriam list included:

ARTISTS: Doug Chaffee, Kelly Freas, Darrell K. Sweet, Dixie Walker.

AUTHORS: Robert Adams, Robert Lynn Asprin, Jim Baen, F.M. Busby, Catherine Crook de Camp, L. Sprague de Camp, Perry Chapdelaine, Gordon R. Dickson, Tom Dietz, Charles Fontenay, James P. Hogan, Andre Norton, Fred Saberhagen, John Steakley,

| SPECIAL GUEST | LITERARY GOH | ARTIST GOH | SCIENCE GOH | MASTER OF CEREMONIES |
|---|---|---|---|---|
| Julie Cochrane | S.M. Stirling | Theresa Mather | Stephanie Osborn | Allen Steele |
| Larry Niven / Jerry Pournelle | Brandon Sanderson / Timothy Zahn 25th Ann GOH | Don Maitz & Janny Wurts / Vincent Di Fate 25th Ann GOH | Les Johnson | Eric Flint |
| Michael & Paul Bielaczyc | Kevin J. Anderson | Vincent Di Fate | Catherine Asaro | Larry Correia |
| David Cherry | Jody Lynn Nye | Kurt Miller | Travis Taylor | Jim Minz |
| Steve Jackson | David Weber | Sam Flegal | Dr. Robert Hampson | Howard Taylor |
| Melissa Gay | Jonathan Mayberry | Todd Lockwood | Dr. Ben Davis | Gray Rinehart |
| Todd McCaffrey / Faith Hunter 30th Ann GOH | Kevin Hearne / John Ringo 30th Ann GOH | Dan dos Santos | Dr. Eliza Quintana | Toni Weisskopf |
| DB Jackson / David B. Coe | Mike Resnik | John Picacio | Dr. Kevin Grazier | Charles E. Gannon |
| Uncle Timmy Bolgeo | Sarah A. Hoyt | Mitch Foust | Arlan Andrews | John G. Hartness |

Wilson "Bob" Tucker, A.E. van Vogt, Sharon & Bryan Webb, Jack Williamson.
STAFF & FRIENDS: Ken Cobb, Rusty Hevelin, J.J. Johnson, Irvin Koch, Sandy McDade, Bert McDowell, Ken Moore, Mandy Pack, Bill Payne, Hank Reinhardt, David Shockley, Suzie Skelton, Kirk Thompson, "The Real" Bob Tucker.

# CAST OF CHARACTERS

*(The Awesome Staff of LibertyCon)*

### The Bastion

Peggey Rowland
Brandy Bolgeo
Tim Bolgeo
Linda Bolgeo
Jonny Minion
Scott Tackett
Joe Green
Karen Boyd
Ken Roy
Connie Triebor
Charmalee Bulinski
Lori Martin

### The Final Mission of Specialist Astroga

Philip Booker
Douglas Goodall
Sarah Shikenjanski
Steve Jackson
William Alan Ritch
Byron Fike
Kathy Wormsley
Terri Harry

### The Liberty Con

Richard Cartwright
Sue Phillips
Ginger Cochrane
Bill Zielke
Regina Kirby
Conlin Baggott
Martha Knowles
David Rowland

### An Arizona Weremyste in Chattanooga

Colonol Fritz Fotovich
Randall Walker
Elayna Little Cook
Nora Pieper
Matthew Fanny
Ann Davis
Mark Paulk
Leigh Smith

### LibertyCon 100

Phillip Schultz
Randall Pass
Agatha Jean
Debbie Gants
Jason Bolgeo
Debi Chowdhury
Ann Darwin
Karin Harris

### Hidden, a Fairy Tale

"Vonn" Gants
John "Trieber"
Doug "Burbey"
"Cisca" Small
Lu Ann "Curlee"
Clint "Hendren"
"Gerry" Martin
"Cathe" Smith

### Liberty for All

Heather Booker
Scott Richardson
Melissa Sleeman
Crystal Ritchie
Doris Manning
Mike Bast
Bobby Bolgeo
Robert Gants
Cisca Small

### Or Give Me Death

Taylor S. Hoch
Zach Waller
Teresa Fike
Andy Green
Jeremy Cook
Inga Johannesen
Greg Eden
Jeff "Worm" Wormsley
Christine Chapin

### The Tuckerizing

Rich Groller
Tish Groller
Shannon Souvinette
Michelle Farenci
Alex Spraker
David Robards
Max Poddubny
Cecil Curlee
Brandy Spraker

### Partners

Katie Cochrane
Annastasia Webster
Linda Zielke
Michael Gants
Sande Ankenbrandt
Liz "the Lizard" Rowland
Beth Spraker
Alana Gants
Carol Hoch
Peg Smarekar
KC Charland
Monika Beeman

### Open Season

Matthew Fanny
Don Puckett
Gerry Martin
Regina Kirby
Joe Buckley
Fritz Fotovich
Vonn Gants

### In the Details

Ann Robards
Randall Hartwig
Gary Shelton
Emma Bosker
Dave Watson
Angus Smith
Tammie Darden
Alyssia Nixon
Sarah Martin

### For Liberty

Richard Hailey
Lissa Hailey
Tara Urbanek
John Pieper
Christine Dorsett
Tyler Gants
John Stewart
Melisa Todd
Janet Baggott

### Heart of Stone

Zacharia "Zack" Nesmith Kemper
Clarence "Mack" Barton Kemper IV
Danette Schardt-Cordova
Dana Schardt-Cordova
Cordelia Schardt-Cordova
Natalie Schardt-Cordova